The Apocalypse Origin
The Undead World
Novel 11
Peter Meredith

Chapter 1
The Courage to Survive

A note from the author— Ezekiel Cross:

The following four stories involve a most peculiar girl named Jillybean. If the name sounds familiar it's doubtless because you've heard of her. Everyone has, although most people know her as Jillian Martin. It may be hard to believe that the woman who is savior to some, queen to others, and a murdering tyrant to those who oppose her, was once a little girl, and a perfectly innocent little girl, at that.

Now, when I say stories, I should note that these are *true* stories. This is a distinction that is necessary to make since so much fictional nonsense has already been written about her, and spoken about her, too for that matter. As I'm sure you know, Jillian is the focus of almost endless gossip, ranging from fanciful misrepresentation to straight-up lies. Sometimes, it seems as though people talk about little else.

Having interviewed her at length, I can tell you that she finds the lies about her rather amusing and if one is particularly flattering she will be sure to enhance it in some way. As the world's first post-apocalyptic biographer, they are an eternal thorn in my side, especially the ridiculous lies of the eye-rolling sort.

No, she is not part demon, or possessed by one for that matter. She doesn't drink the blood of her vanquished enemies or use their flayed skin to upholster drums or any musical instrument. Nor does she sit on a throne built out of their skulls, which sounds both appalling and very uncomfortable if you ask me. And let me put to rest the silliest lie of them all: she did not start the apocalypse. She was six years old and only a few weeks into the first grade when the plague of zombies swept the earth, destroying the old world.

At the time, she had recess to attend and soccer balls to bat about and best friends to collude with, that is to say, she was much too busy to destroy the world.

I suppose it is *somewhat* understandable that people believe so many outlandish lies about her when it is considered how frequently she has been able to accomplish the seemingly impossible. Most people attribute her improbably fantastic exploits to her native genius, and, as most people usually are, they are all perfectly wrong.

Any objective observer, and there are very few of us around these days, would be the first to describe Jillian's intellectual accomplishments as being largely derivative. Although she has flashes of intuitive brilliance and a memory that borders on amazing, the scientific accomplishments she is most known for, the medicines, vaccinations, explosives and all that, had been thought of or invented long before she was born.

I'm not belittling her intelligence, I'm only trying to put it in perspective.

If the time before the apocalypse were properly dissected instead of glorified as is generally the case these days, it would show that intelligence played little part in shaping great events throughout history. More often than not, the world has plunged through waves of unmitigated stupidity and, perhaps because of this, it is rare that geniuses dive into adventures such as the ones Jillian has been a part of.

As an example, back in the *Before*, there lived a man named Albert Einstein. He was supposedly very smart and knew all the math there was to know, but intelligent as he was, he was not remembered for his heroism or bravery. He lived through a great war, or maybe even two of them and yet didn't fight a lick. I'm not suggesting he was shy or a complete chicken, I'm just saying he was a genius, not an adventurer.

I'm sure you're thinking that if it wasn't Jillian's intellect that made her who she is, then it had to be her infamous insanity! She has not been called the "Mad

Queen" for nothing and assuredly it was madness to try to wield armies of the dead as she did against the Azael, to blow up dozens of bridges and boats controlled by the River King, and to stand up to the might of the Black Captain backed only by a handful of peasants, was the definition of lunacy itself.

It is tempting to attribute Jillian's greatness to her insanity, but it would be intellectually lazy to do so. The fact is, she is great despite what she calls her "mental aberration."

I believe the fairest reading of the past reveals that Jillian became equal parts famous and feared not through her intelligence or insanity but because of one exceedingly rare attribute: courage.

The audacity she has so often demonstrated, which can easily be confused with, and attributed to, stark raving madness, was in truth, tenacious valor that has few equals in all of history. Time and again she risked her life, not just for her friends and family, but also for utter strangers and sometimes even enemies.

Yet there was a time when Jillian was a tiny girl named Jillybean and feared the world and everything in it. She was so afraid that she couldn't bring herself to even step out of her own front door.

As you might have guessed I had to dig deep into the past, and dare the dangerous continental crossing, to uncover the truth about Jillybean.

It took me a month to get to Philadelphia, a city now deserted. In what had once been a pretty suburban neighborhood, I discovered Jillian Martin's childhood home. In the attic was a pillow fort, grey with dust, and pinned to a rusting kitchen refrigerator I found faded, curling preschool artwork. On the door-jamb leading to the basement were a series of small, vertically spaced lines, each with a date written in the dimming grey of old pencil lead.

And this is where the story of a child's first tiny steps out of a life of paralyzing fear begins…

Ezekiel Cross

March 23rd 2047

***

"Well, that can't be right," Jillybean groused, her hands planted on her non-hips exactly where her purple sweater met her pink jeans. She was staring, with distinct displeasure, at a line she had drawn using all the care and precision her artistic ability would allow. She knew this ability wasn't what it should have been and blamed it on the fact that her first-grade career had been cut so tragically short.

Whatever the excuse, the line was an embarrassment. Impossibly, it sat right on top of the last line which had a date written next to it in her mother's perfect hand of October 1, 2013.

She tried again. This time she stood against the jam just as straight as she could with her neck stiff, and her shoulders, her chin, even her eyelids lifted in an attempt to give herself that much more height. All for nothing. The second line she drew had only thickened the first.

She made an angry noise in her throat as once more she stared at the line. "What do you think, Ipes? Is it the pencil? You think it's busted?"

Sitting on the kitchen counter was a stuffed zebra of about seven inches in height. Over a bulging, cookie-fed belly he wore a little blue t-shirt that read: *Too Cute.* His name was Ipes and although he had the beadiest eyes of all her stuffed animals, he had very good vision. Sometimes his vision was too good. He could spot any error Jillybean ever made in a snap. She held the pencil out and he eyed it from all angles.

Busted? If you mean curved or warped, then no, the pencil looks good. You know what your daddy would've said. He would've called it operator error.

She didn't know anything about what an operator might be, but an error was sorta like a mistake. "Oh hush," she snapped. Jillybean never liked to be told she was wrong, and certainly not by some silly stuffed animal, and she wasn't at all ready to admit to a mistake just yet. "If it's not the pencil…" She went to within inches of the disappointing line and studied it closer.

"Then maybe…maybe I had bigger hair back then." Her face was angelic and heart-shaped, seemingly carved out of the whitest, smoothest porcelain. She had huge blue eyes, high cheek bones, baby soft lips and a small, pointed chin.

Above that perfection was a jungle of bushy, overgrown and neglected hair.

Bigger hair back then? Ha-ha! Ipes laughed so hard he fell off the counter and laid sprawled on the floor, shaking in mirth. Self-consciously, she touched her wild mane of brown hair. Jillybean's hair had not been brushed in a month and even that had been an aborted fiasco. Every pass with the brush had resulted in the discovery of new and more painful knots. At one point the brush had become so stuck in a particularly dense snarl that, rather than risk having it become a permanent part of her head, she had cut it out with scissors.

Ipes had laughed hard then as well, resulting in an extended period in timeout.

She was just thinking he was due for another spell in the corner when a thought struck her: If she had more hair now than she did seven months before *and* she hadn't grown a lick, then… "That's what means I'm shrinking!"

This had come out in something close to a shriek and Ipes sighed, *I don't see why this is such a calamity for you. It's not like you were ever big.*

"That makes it even worser. What if I shrink away to nothing?"

How Ipes managed to roll his plastic eyes she didn't know; she didn't like to think about things like that, nor did she like to consider how he talked without a mouth. Those thoughts made her stomach feel greasy, like she was about to vomit.

Shrinking that far will never happen...probably...but let's say it does. How cool would it be if you were my size? Or maybe even smaller! If you got small enough you could ride me like a real...hmmm, horse. The statement had ended on a sour note. Being ridden like a real horse sounded a lot like work and if there was one thing Ipes hated was actual work—and vegetables. He hated vegetables with a passion.

"Small enough to ride you? I can't shrink that far, can I?" The idea did have merits and it sounded fun. Still, logic suggested that if she shrunk that far, what was to stop her from shrinking even more? What if she itty-bittied down to ant size? Or even smaller to crumb size? After that there was only speck size, then dust size and then probably death.

"I need a mirror!" she cried, touching herself all over, feeling her rail thin body start to cave in on itself. Unfortunately, there was only one full length mirror in the house and that was all the way up in her mommy's room. As always when she thought about her, Jillybean's stomach knotted itself.

She hated going in there and yet she was drawn to the room. On most days she would sit outside the door for hours, reading aloud because of the awful silence. Sometimes she would go in and stare and it was always horrible.

Her mommy had died in bed. On the day Jillybean's daddy had gone away and never came back, her mommy had gone up to her bedroom, shut the door in Jillybean's face, climbed in bed and waited to die, doing nothing but staring at the ceiling. It had taken a long time for her to die. In poor Jillybean's mind it was days and days, and very probably months, as she slowly went from being her mommy to being a human scarecrow.

Then one day her mommy breathed out and never breathed back in. She was alive one second, her skin no more than white paint over the bones of her face and her eyes like wet blue gems that sat deep in her head, and then she was dead.

Things had been horrifying before that: monsters eating people and guns going off and screams day and night, but when her mom died everything became a zillion-billion times worse.

Six-year-old Jillybean was utterly, terrifyingly alone. Her world became a nightmare within a nightmare. She grew so frightened that her heart began to skip beats and bounce around in her chest, and the inside of her head became black and there were dreadful sounds coming from deep in that darkness like there was something huge and alien and evil living in her mind that was trying to eat its way out.

That was when Ipes had started talking to her like a real person and everything was better—not the best of course, but so much better that she never questioned her friend and how he could talk and move about with only fluff for his insides.

Still, she didn't like going into her mommy's room because what if her mommy started talking just like Ipes?

Just stop being silly. Your mommy isn't going to talk and about all this shrinking business, it's a common fact that no one shrinks that far. I think. You're probably just not getting all your nutritionals. Remember your mommy used to always say stuff about eating all your dinner so you can grow big and strong. You just need to eat more.

Thinking about eating, hurt her stomach even worse than thinking about her mommy sitting up in her bed and staring at her even though she didn't have any eyeballs left.

"We don't have no food. How am I oposed to eat without food?"

It's ANY food and there's always food. You just have to find it. That meant leaving the house and going out into the world where all the monsters lived. She glanced once at the window and then hung her head.

"I don't wanna. I'm ascared."

Ascared? Of what? A few monsters? Oh please, they're nothing. And you know what? I'll be with you. I'll teach you all about the really important things. Everyone knows zebras are the smartest animals in the world. It's in the stripes. Not only are they slimming they also add extra super stripe-power to our brains. You see it's all in the...

His endless prattle wasn't working this time. If she'd had the guts to leave, she would have run straight out of her house and never looked back the first time her mommy had moved. A few hours after she had stopped breathing and had grown cold and stiff, her mommy had sat up in bed.

But she hadn't sat up like a normal person would. She had sat up with dreadful slowness as if invisible hands were bending her in half an inch at a time. Then Jillybean watched in horror as one of her mommy's arms curled up and around her back with a sickening stretching sound. Then the other arm pulled all the way over in front of her as if she were trying to choke herself with it. And her eyes! One had been cocked wide and the other sagged low, protruding like an over-easy egg, looking as if at any moment it might fall plop out onto the stained...

That was all Jillybean remembered. The next thing she knew she was waking up in her bed with Ipes in the crook of her arm.

Your mommy was like that because she wouldn't eat, Ipes said, there in the kitchen where everything was light and pretend cheerful. *You don't want to be like that, do you? That's why you have to go outside and search for food, but don't worry, I'll be with you every step of the way.* When he wanted to, Ipes could change his voice, making it go deeper so that Jillybean could swear he sounded a lot like her daddy.

"Okay," she said in a whisper. She didn't head right away for the front door, however. That would've been silly. After all, this was her first *expedition*—a word she mistook for adventure—and it wouldn't be smart to go out unprepared.

She went to her room, skirting the hopscotch grid in the hall which had originally been drawn in chalk, but as that had faded from use and her stick of white chalk had worn down to a nubby little thing, she had dared to use a magic marker on the floor. Her mommy would have been furious, if she weren't dead that is.

Once in her musty and rarely used bedroom she went to her closet where her backpack sat in all its fading glory. It was brilliant pink and had, once upon a time, been the envy of the first grade since it was a *Power-Puff* backpack. Back then having a backpack such as that was a lot like having a million dollars and a sparkly tiara.

Ipes went in one of the mesh pockets on the side of it, where he had a good view and could act as look-out.

Next, she glanced around her room, wishing she had a sword of some sort or at the very least a carven walking stick as tall as she was, one that could shoot flames or lightning, like she had seen in a cartoon movie once. She missed cartoon movies. The TV hadn't worked in a very long time.

"I think some string would be smart to take. And some extra socks, and a few rubber-bands, and this green marker…"

A green marker? For what? Ipes demanded. *We're going out for food, not for school.*

"Well, Mister Smartypants, I might have to take notes on where we gone to. We don't wanna go to the same place twice." Reluctantly Ipes agreed this was a good idea. She reached for her notebook from the first grade and flipped passed what suddenly seemed like childish work until she reached a blank page.

It had dawned on her that no expedition was complete without a map. "We need a map," she told Ipes before he could ask. She wrote the word "Map" on the top of the paper, then curled her lip at the way the three-letter word gave the impression that it was sliding towards the bottom of the page. She was the first to acknowledge that her penmanship had degraded since she had missed so much school, which she assumed had been going on for everyone else this entire time. Now her blocky letters would sometimes come out backwards and they had an annoying habit of "slipping away" just like this one annoying word.

With much more care, she drew a map of her neighborhood as seen from her window. She even drew little blocks to represent houses, marking those she knew: Bily, Becca, Paw-la, Mister... "S-m-i-t-h? Is that right?"

Yes, except Paula is spelled with a U. Remember she gave you that note, and her name had a U right in the middle. It's probably like a foreign name.

"Oh sure," she replied, without wondering how he knew about the note. He never went to her school except once for Show-n-Tell.

She made a mess of things as she fixed the mistake and had no room to write Miss Colter's name in the next box. The box after that was Mrs. Bennett's house and Jillybean only put an X through it.

Mrs. Bennett used to be this mean ole lady before she turned into a mean ole monster. Ipes said it was because there wasn't all that much to change with her. For months now she had wandered back and forth in front of her old house, stopping every once in a while to glare for no reason at all, or to eat leaves from a tree.

"Now what?" Jillybean asked, after slipping the marker and notebook into the backpack. "A knife?" By this she meant something more than a butter knife.

Bringing along a real knife, one with a sharp edge and pokey point would break a very significant rule that her parents had set down *in stone* back when Jillybean was a baby.

It was significant that Ipes, who was always such a 'fraidy cat' that Jillybean wondered if he was part chicken, said, *I think so.*

From the "forbidden" kitchen drawer, she chose a carving knife that was as long as her forearm. She wanted to pull it from its cardboard sleeve and brandish it, but Ipes reminded her just how easily eyes could be popped and made her put it in her pack.

"I guess that's it," she said, feeling the fear swirl around in her stomach which was otherwise empty. She hadn't eaten in two days and it would have been much longer if her mommy hadn't stopped eating all those weeks before.

Go slow, Ipes warned as Jillybean went to the front door. *Be Jilly-rabbit. Eyes up, ears alert, muscles ready to run.* He coached her in that deeper, daddy-like voice until she reached out a shaking hand and opened a door that hadn't been cracked in two months.

What struck her first was the silence. There were no kid noises or car noises or plane noises. There were no barking dogs or radios blaring from two blocks over. It was a heavy, heavy silence, almost as if the air had thickened up and that in time it would gradually solidify until it couldn't be walked through at all.

A stray breeze ruined that mental image and yet the tiny breath of wind only made the silence feel that much greater. It knocked an old curled-in leaf from a tree and its whispering impact as it struck the street seemed to be magnified. Jillybean hunched at the *click*, ready to dart back inside, certain it would bring the monsters running from all over.

But there were no monsters as far as she could see. After a few seconds, when she hadn't yet got eaten, she edged further out the door, going all the way to the sidewalk in front of her house—and it was okay.

There on the sidewalk was the remains of her bike. A long winter had speckled it with rust and the tires sagged so badly they were about to drip off the rims; otherwise it was fine…or perhaps "normal" was the better word. Rust was to be expected she was sure, and the tires always had been a bit *holey,* bleeding air over time.

The bike wasn't the only wonderfully normal thing she saw. There in the edge of the brown grass was her beanbag!

Hurrying to it, she brushed away the dirt. It was the marker she used when she and her bestest friend ever, Becca Risbon, played hopscotch. Jillybean used to draw hopscotch courts halfway down the block, designing them with such convoluted trickery that she would twist Becca's skinny legs into pretzels.

You know you can't eat that, Ipes said, as she slipped the beanbag into her backpack. *This is a foraging expedition, not a walk down memory lane.*

"I know this isn't Memory Lane, duh. This is Peakview Drive. I lived here longer than you, you know. I lived here since I was a kid. And you know what else, Mister Smartypants? It's a *bean* bag. A person can eat beans." Not that she liked beans. Oh no. They were all sorts of grotey, but the point had to be made.

I suppose. This was Ipes way of admitting he was completely wrong and was secretly dying of embarrassment.

Having gained a great win over the insufferable zebra, Jillybean had been grinning, however the grin died away when she heard a branch snap behind her. In this newly silent world, it sounded as if the branch had snapped only paces away when in truth it was most of the way down the block.

Jillybean spun, her heart caught up in her throat, her hands blaring in a strange electric numbness as adrenaline shot through her system. Seventy yards away was a monster, the first one she had ever seen without at least a pane of glass between her and it. Seventy yards of sidewalk and empty air—her vulnerability was so great that she felt less than naked, almost as if she didn't have skin.

She froze in terror, her muscles locked and rigid, her huge eyes stretched and unblinking, as the beast lurched right at her. Five seconds went by—an eternity in a situation like that—and still Jillybean could not move. She didn't even think to move. Her brain, awash in terror, was as stricken as her body as she stared and stared at the grey-skinned creature with its oozing sores, its long, outstretched clawed hands, and its many, many teeth.

Run!!! someone, her daddy maybe, screamed from behind.

She spun, expecting to blunder into whoever had screamed, only the sidewalk was impossibly empty. Her head wobbled in confusion for a few more wasted seconds until her fear, which was both tremendous and powerful, swallowed the confusion whole, blotted out rational thought and overrode her new insanity.

With her stick-like legs turning in big circles, she fled down the block and straight across the next street, for once in her life not looking in any direction except straight ahead. Everything around became a blur of sad, abandoned porches, dusty, dead cars, and endless sidewalk cracks.

These breaks in the sidewalk, like little hurdles, came one after another at perfect intervals, passing under her flying feet with every other step. If it were possible those cracks only added to her fear and she began making a little leap over each. Obviously, if she tripped over one, the monster would be on her in a flash and eat her. There was a second reason for her panicked little leaps—Step on a crack, you'll break your mommy's back—began to run through her head in a jarring loop.

Even as her lungs began to burn, and a stitch lanced into her side, and even as the monster drew steadily closer, its harsh, ragged panting growing in her ears, that awful chant kept playing over and over. It grew louder in her head, eclipsing things that were best not thought about, such as how the fetid, disgusting smell of the beast was growing in her nostrils, and how its shadow had already caught up to her and was beginning to merge with her own.

A new sound, the blubbering whine of a terrified child, was the chant's only competition.

Somehow Jillybean's legs felt like they were both rubbery and weighted with anchors. She threw everything, every last drop of energy she had into running, but she ran in vain. The monster's scabby, diseased hand reached out and caught her hair, yanking her head back, turning the blubbering whine into a soul-tearing shriek.

Turn! Turn! Ipes or her daddy, she couldn't tell which, screamed into her head with such force it finally obliterated the chant.

She turned sharply, feeling a vague searing pain along her scalp as behind her, the monster, with a handful of her hair in one of its hands, went stumbling face first across the sidewalk. It left a smear of black blood and what looked like a sheaf of grey snakeskin on the cement as it scrambled to its feet.

Jillybean was already out of sight.

Her abrupt turn had led to a driveway. On her right was an immense leafless, overgrown shrubbery which formed a veritable wall. In front of her was a run of open concrete that led to a detached garage; its wide door dangled from a single metal spring and hung cockeyed.

To her left were the remains of a picket fence, drunkenly guarding the front yard of a two-story brick house. The yard had not been cared for even before the monsters had come. It had gone to jungle and would never again be the civilized close-cropped square of perfection it had once been. The old summer weeds were likely the only thing keeping the fence upright and although they were a dead shade of brown, they were still so tall they could easily hide a girl if she were small enough.

Jillybean threw herself over the low fence and lay as still as she could, trying to breathe as quietly as humanly possible. She failed at both. Her exhausted body was wracked by tremors and her breath ran in and out as if she were still running madly for her life.

It was her good luck that the beast was even louder. With Jillybean's apparent disappearance, it screamed in rage and began tearing at the wall of shrubbery, sending sticks and old leaves flying in all directions.

Don't just sit there, Ipes hissed from his pouch. *Find a better place to hide than this.*

There really was only one choice, and that was the brick house looming above her. As the front door might be locked and she couldn't chance being caught out on the stoop in plain sight of the monster, she crept and crawled through the weeds towards the back of the house where a porch sat, looking like a hunched and unhappy addition.

It had once been screened in. Now, the screen hung in ghostly tatters that swayed in the light wind, and it certainly didn't help Jillybean's fragile state of mind that the edge of the porch wore a thin beard of hoary ivy, or that beyond the screen was a door that opened onto what appeared to be a pit of pure blackness. If ever there was a haunted house this was it.

Supposedly there was no such thing. Her mommy had always said ghosts and haunted houses weren't real; then again, she had said the same thing about monsters and she had been wrong about that in a big way.

If Jillybean had any other choice she would have taken it. Without one, she crept up the porch and went cowering inside, certain she would feel the cold breath of a spook on her neck at any moment. She shook and trembled, looking and feeling smaller as she crumbled in on herself.

It was Jilly-mouse who crouched against a wall, afraid to move any further than was needed into the haunted house. For twenty minutes, she crouched as her body gradually ceased shaking and she finally got her breathing under control.

The ghost must be asleep, Ipes opined. *It probably sleeps in the day and only comes out to haunt people at night.*

This made such perfect sense that she recovered almost immediately and was able to raise herself up until her eyes crested the plane of the windowsill. "Ugh, it's that's mean old Mrs. Bennett," she whispered, glaring at the monster that had chased her. "I shoulda knowed it was her. She hates me. Boy howdy, if I was a grode-up…"

You'd do exactly this, nothing, Ipes tsked. *You know there are more of them around. There always are. That's why we have to be smart and patient. Do you know the meaning of the word patience?*

"I can read, can't I? I probably know all sortsa words more than you." This wasn't really an answer and Ipes only cocked a nonexistent eyebrow. "Fine. It's what means waiting without fidgeting or fussing. Everyone knows that." She wanted to stick her tongue out at him, only she was sure that such an action would fall under either the fidgeting or fussing categories and she didn't want to hear a lecture just then.

To kill time, she watched Mrs. Bennett who was no longer filled with that awful rage. She stood, swaying and blank eyed, surrounded by broken sticks. All the hate seemed to have seeped out of her and Jillybean grew bored.

You could always look for food here, Ipes suggested. *Maybe the ghost has kept any other people from scavenging this place. Maybe there's like real food here. Maybe they have cookies.* Ipes was mad for cookies and Jillybean liked them enough that she was able to throw off most of what remained of her fear—not all of it of course, the house was most certainly haunted, after all.

She crept down a long, dark hall, shrinking back from the darker shadows and twitching away from doorways. She found the kitchen, easily enough. The place was a complete mess: scattered pots and pans, broken dishes, cupboards flung wide. Underfoot was a crunchy spray of what she at first mistook for dried maggots.

It's white rice, silly, Ipes explained. It was the only food in the place and amounted to just a bit more than a handful. By the time she had scraped it up and had poked about as much as her constant fear of ghosts would allow, Mrs. Bennett was gone, lurching back to her home. Jillybean went the opposite way, deciding to put a few more blocks between her and the neighborhood monster.

After ten minutes of slinking from car to tree, to bush, to another car, and so on, she came to her fifth or sixth cross street and saw an amazing sight down one of the side streets—her elementary school!

Above, the sky was uniformly lead in color and the breeze, barely strong enough to budge the stagnant air and yet the vision of her old school lifted the weight of what had been a dreary and frightening day. She was so excited that Ipes had to scold her twice for going too fast.

Once she got to the school her enthusiasm disappeared in a blink. The building was no longer bright and airy, filled with the laughter of children. It was very dark, very empty, and somehow even more frightening than the haunted house she had left behind. Still she didn't leave

19

right away. She slunk around the edges of the grounds hoping against hope that she would see her old teacher Miss April, or any of her old friends. She would've even settled for seeing 'ol Donny Serov who had stuck gum in her bushy hair and who had laughed at her because she hadn't noticed for three days.

The dark, still, and eerily quiet building did not just frighten her, it disappointed her as well. Unless there were ghosts in there, too, something she hadn't ruled out, the place was deserted. The outer grounds were not, however. Halfway around the building and just after the designated parent pickup spot, she came to the playground and there, standing against the backstop of the baseball diamond was Becca Risbon!

Jillybean knew that long brilliantly red hair from a mile away.

Stop! Stop! wailed Ipes, but she would not listen. She had been dreadfully alone for months and she craved human contact, especially with the dearest bestest friend she'd ever had in her whole life. Jillybean leapt from the bushes and raced across the field that was used for both soccer and baseball.

She was quite out of her head with joy, and wanted to yell Becca's name but, although she was ignoring most of Ipes' survival rules, she did remember that she was supposed to be quiet so as not to attract the attention of any monsters who might be lurking nearby. She didn't utter a word as she came up to her best friend. Becca was turned away and didn't see her friend coming until, "Becca!" Jillybean finally gushed when she was close enough.

Now her friend turned. Jillybean was fully expecting the same green eyes and freckles, the same beaming smile, but instead she found herself looking into a face that looked like month-old porridge. Set in that ugly churned up mush of a face, Becca's eyes were sadly grey in color and devoid of that beautiful spark that made Becca, Becca.

"No," Jillybean whispered, her heart torn in two and her muscles no more than loose string hanging from her bones. With Ipes screaming in her mind, Jillybean tried to back away only she tripped, falling on her tiny, bony bottom. She was sure Becca would attack her, however Becca's right arm was stuck through the fence and trapped somehow.

Although the little Becca-monster had the will, she lacked the strength to tear her own arm off to get at Jillybean. All she could do was growl and moan in hungry agony.

"No, Becca, please," Jillybean said, tears dripping down her face. "You don't have to be a monster if you don't wanna. Just try to be good, okay. Just don't eat people and…"

Jillybean, Ipes said

"Maybe if you had a bath. I could take you home with me and…"

Jillybean! Now he sounded like her daddy and she quieted except for the occasional sniffle and the hitch in her unhappy chest. *That's no longer Becca Risbon. Becca is in heaven, now. That's just a monster that looks like her. We should leave her alone and get going.*

"No. Becca was my friend and I know that's her. And I can't leave her." Jillybean picked herself up and went closer to the snarling creature. "Whoa, Becca. I just wanna see where you're caught." The problem was not only that Becca's jean jacket sleeve was caught on a spur of metal, it was also her own famously long hair that had somehow snaked within the links forming a tangle that even Jillybean couldn't have reproduced.

"I'll just cut you free. Just, just be good, okay? Don't try to get me." She wasn't so deluded that she cut Becca free without climbing over the fence. Once on the other side she drew the big knife. "Now, try to hold still. No, Becca! Be good!"

Becca was not good. She wailed and snarled and did everything she could to get at Jillybean and kill her. Even when she was finally free, she didn't revert to being good, which was disappointing to a girl who had read a story once about a mouse and a lion with a thorn in its paw.

"That's how you're oposed to be. You know, grateful." Becca was not grateful at all. She threw herself at the fence and tried to tear it to pieces. She even tried to bite the links, breaking her front teeth. It was so awful Jillybean began to cry again and allowed Ipes to lead her away.

"I wanna…go…home," she said, her pitiful voice breaking with each hitch in her chest. "Let's forget…all this and…and…go home."

Ipes would not hear of it. A handful of rice would last them only a single meal and a disappointing one at that. He made her stop in the next pleasant-looking house they came to. They passed a few little ranch-style houses with Ipes saying, *Shoddy*, to the first and *Trashy,* at the second, while with the third he gave it a *hmph*, though what he meant by that Jillybean didn't know.

The fourth was more to both of their likings. It had a welcome mat sitting precisely on the little square of a stoop, flowered curtains hung in the front window and there were four different bird houses set about. None held birds or nests but that was beside the point. The house was nice and Jillybean needed a touch of nice just then.

Judging by the mess, many others had come through looking for nice. *Why do they always tear everything apart?* Ipes griped. *Why throw the dishes on the floor? Why?*

Jillybean shrugged, already too tired both emotionally and physically to care about dishes. Listlessly, she went through the motions of searching what the rampaging mobs coming out of Trenton and Camden had already searched. She was in the master bedroom on the second floor, looking with glazed-over eyes at the mess someone had made of a nightstand when something caught her attention outside.

It was a person!

A *real* one! This was no zombie. This was a real man. He was bearded but looked clean. His jeans were vibrantly blue and his flannel jacket was black and red checkered perfection. And the way he moved: like a cat, from cover to cover wasn't at all comparable to the way the monsters shambled or shuffled or lurched.

"Ipes!"

I see him. We should be careful because you never know what sort of...Jillybean! Stop! He could be mean or a bad guy.

She wasn't listening. Even more than before her run in with Becca Risbon, she *needed* people, very, very badly. It's what drove her in a frantic sprint down the stairs, along the hall where the pictures were only a blur and out the front door. She only stopped when the man spun and pointed a rifle at her, and even then, it was only because he was way across the street and she wasn't really supposed to cross the big street.

"Hi," she said with a wave of her tiny hand, as she was struck with an acute case of shyness.

"Who you with?"

The simple question brought on a sharp panic. *Do I tell him about Ipes? Would he understand that Ipes wasn't a normal zebra?* She began to make a hesitant hand motion, gesturing behind her when something else caught her eye—a flash of red-orange racing at the man.

Right away she knew what, or rather who it was. "Becca, no!"

Becca seemed to have forgotten her name. She didn't even blink those wickedly greedy eyes as she came on. The man, turning from one child to the next, faltered, his trigger-finger stiffening as sharp confusion froze him for just a second too long.

He blinked once in an overly large and somewhat comic way, then almost too late, he fired at Becca.

Jillybean had heard guns, big and small for months now. This was the first time one had been fired with her so close and with nothing between her and the gun. It sounded like a giant explosion. The sound was so immense and frightening to the six-year-old that she felt the urge to run, and she even took a step back, tripping over the final stair leading into the house and falling inside the doorway.

Though she fell, with Ipes squawking in fear as well as indignation about being "mushed," she couldn't take her eyes off the scene in front of her.

As there was all sorts of dark blood pouring down from the top of her head and into her red hair, Jillybean was absolutely sure poor Becca had been shot. Only it hadn't slowed her down for a second. She came shooting in under the long rifle and attacked the man's tummy with such unholy ferocity that they both went down in a heap.

"Son of a bitch!" the man yelled, grabbing a handful of that bloody red hair. Becca was like a rat terrier. She tore through the man's heavy coat with frenzied determination and already there was fluff or feathers plastered in her blood. But she was small and he was large.

"Get the…" He thudded the side of the rifle into her head. "Hell…" Again, the rifle smashed her. "Off me!" A final strike, one delivered with all the force he could muster in such close quarters, crushed the side of her head and she went limp. Still snarling curses, he threw her aside and stood staring as he turned his hands this way and that.

Seemingly satisfied, he muttered, "Alright," and wrestled his heavy pack off his back, then pulled off his coat. Even with the beard, Jillybean saw his lips twist in disgust before he took to more muttering, this time so low that all she heard was: "…perfectly good coat. Stupid little…"

It was then that he appeared to remember there had been a second girl. He tossed aside the coat and looked in her direction, not seeing her at first, because she had fallen or so she supposed. He didn't have time for a proper search; at that moment, a rasping moan came from up the street. It was followed by more.

There were monsters coming and they were close. Stark terror shot through Jillybean, and Ipes began calling for an immediate panic and yet the man appeared more perturbed than frightened. As if he had all the time in the world, he shouldered his pack, reached for his rifle and then yelled, leaping suddenly and struggling back.

Becca wasn't dead after all. The blows that would have killed Jillybean had only stunned Becca and now her jagged teeth were half an inch deep in the man's right ankle. He yanked his leg out of her mouth, backed up with a hopping step and aimed his gun at the girl monster. But he didn't fire. His face took on a look of shocked bewilderment as if never in a million years he would've guessed the preceding moments could have transpired.

He looked down at his leg and then at Becca who was crawling towards him, and then he looked down the street where the real monsters were coming. He still didn't shoot, he only stumbled off, that bewildered look worse now as he couldn't seem to close his drooping mouth.

We can't just sit here! Ipes said in a frightened whisper. *We have to get inside. Hurry!*

Jillybean wanted to race after the man. In fact, she *needed* to for survivals sake. Her great fear wouldn't let her, and she slunk into the house, feeling her chickenness pervade her innards as if she had swallowed something greasy. As she went upstairs, Ipes tried to tell her she was doing the right thing or the smart thing, but it only felt like the chickeny thing.

She was certain she had lost her one chance at having a friend and went to the master bedroom to watch the man leave forever. To her great happiness, he hadn't left! He had only ducked around an SUV and slipped up into a house cattycorner from the one she was in.

"I bet he's nice," she stated with complete confidence. "He coulda shot Becca and he didn't. Yeah, he sure bonked her pretty hard, but she had bitted him which everyone knows is wrong. If her mommy or Miss April had seen that, boy howdy, she woulda got in trouble."

Jillybean went up on her tippy toes to look for her friend and saw instead that the street was flooded with monsters. Quick as a wink, she ducked back down. After a two-minute wait in which she sat tapping one sneakered foot, she took another peek. "They're still down there," she griped.

You have to be patient, jeeze. Maybe you should consider taking a nap.

"A nap? Jimney crickets, Ipes. Do I look like a two-year-old to you? Now hush, unless you have a better idea than a stinkin' nap. Sheesh." Ipes was properly chastised and sat in a stony silence which loomed largely as Jillybean tried to practice her patience. Sitting still wasn't her best thing, however and she only lasted four minutes before she took another look.

"I thought I heard something," she said, by way of an excuse.

Sure, you did.

"What's that oposed to mean? If I say I heard something, then I heard something for all darn it. I think it's time you went to the corner for sure this time." He crossed his flappy hooves and brooded in the corner as she went back to the window and poked her big blues eyes over the sill. Becca was gone or was hidden by the dozens of other monsters shambling about in the street. They were disgusting. Some didn't have hands or faces, and all of them seemed to have gone to the bathroom right in their pants.

"See. I told you I heard something. It's like a parade down there. 'Cept they don't have no giant balloon animals or any walking around bands or nothing. And Becca's gone, too. Ooh, I see the guy."

Just as she was, he was standing at a second-floor window, staring down at the zombies. Jillybean thought he seemed unhappy. "Prolly lonely or maybe that bite hurted worser than it looked. That reminds me, I forgotted band-aides when I packed for our expedition! Maybe they have some here."

She left the window in a tearing hurry and went scrounging in all the places a person would keep band-aides. There were none to be had, however she did find a half a bag of cherry cough-drops under a bathroom sink and when she came back, she had one bulging out each cheek.

Ahem, Ipes said, pointedly.

"Ahem yourself, Mister Smartypants Zebra. Are you gonna be good?"

He said he would, so she released him from the corner. She even went so far as to offer him a couch-drop which he turned down as it wasn't chocolate chip flavored.

She then went back to the window. The man was still there, looking as unhappy as he had before, and the monsters were still there and they never looked anything but unhappy.

Four hours later, when Jillybean woke from a long and accidental nap, the scene was the very same. "Wha? What's happening?" She was fuzzy-headed, still wrapped in a fraying curtain of sleep. "Did he leave?"

No, but you did. You took a trip on the nappy-time express. Ipes laughed so hard at this that his blue shirt rode high up on his belly. *I thought you were a big girl?*

"You better zip it, for all darn it." She threatened him with a fist little bigger than an egg. Despite its lack of real menace, he pantomimed drawing an imaginary zipper across an equally imaginary mouth. "That's better. It was your fault anyways. No one wants to hear about the great zebras of an-quick-ity."

Antiquity.

"Where-ever, and it's not the point. Zebras aren't the best at every single thing in the whole world, and I really don't think they invented any lights or nothing. In fact..."

A sudden, shrieked curse, one of the real bad ones Jillybean wasn't even supposed to guess the meaning of, blared out from across the street, making her jump. She poked her bit of a nose over the sill, expecting to see something other than the monsters going in circles. Other than the top of his head, little could be seen of the man in the house. He was still at the window, however he had his head down and looked to be laughing.

Or crying, Ipes noted.

There was no need for Jillybean to wonder exactly what he might be crying over. There was always something. She felt like crying ten times a day. Luckily, she had Ipes who always told her a funny story or played games with her or told her about the *Zebra Kings of Siam,* of which there had been many, each prone to bravery and klutziness in equal measure.

Jillybean watched the man for a long time and he was indeed crying. She started crying as well and no amount of Ipes' silliness helped since she wasn't crying for herself.

The man cried for an hour and then paced around the room for another hour. His growing aggravation was not just felt across the street but in the street as well. Another curse, a crash, and breaking glass had monsters heading toward the house. Gunshots roared out one after another.

Then nothing.

"We should go home," Jillybean said, in a stunned whisper.

We can't chance it. All that racket will bring more of them. Ipes could be annoyingly correct most of the time. Now, he was frightfully correct. Jillybean lost count of the number of monsters that came lurching and moaning from all directions. They brought with them a rotting stench that had the dozen or so cough-drops in Jillybean's belly threatening to come up.

She found it wacky that the man did nothing but shoot the monsters one after another. Since he had so many guns and bullets he could have tried running away, but he never did. "What's wrong with him?"

The moment the question was out of her mouth, she wanted to take it back. Her bellyful of cherry cough-drops began to slosh and heave as if there was a great red sea inside of her being brewed up by a storm of nerves.

He's dying. She swung her head violently toward the zebra who was sitting on the bed with his flappy hooves resting on the pudge of his belly. *He's becoming one of them. You know, a monster. Becca bit him. You saw that.*

She realized that she didn't just see it, she had caused it. First, she had freed Becca and then she had managed to distract the man just as she had attacked him. "I did this," she said, hearing the words in her ears in an echoey sort of way as if she were outside of her head and yelling through a tunnel at herself.

No, you didn't! You didn't make Becca a monster and you didn't make that guy come here. You were just trying to do the right thing. You should always try to do the right thing. Are you listening to me, Jillybean?

It was her daddy's voice coming to her in that same echoey way. She stared around as the room spun and spun and the gun shots roared out and the zombies wailed and moaned…before she knew it, she had fallen, bouncing off the bed and landing on the plum-colored carpet where she immediately puked up a great gout of red fluid.

The sun was setting by then and the cough-drop/ stomach acid concoction looked exactly like blood.

"Ipes, help me, I'm dying." She crawled away, moving towards the door thinking she would crawl home and die in her bed, just like her mommy had died in hers.

We can't go yet, Ipes told her. *Remember, I'm supposed to be helping you. Listen.*

Obediently, she paused, her head cocked. There wasn't much to hear. The gunshots had stopped and so had the moans. The only thing she heard was the crying. Jillybean had always been sensitive to the pain of others and she found the strength to stand once more and make her way to the window.

The man was in the street, surrounded by twenty or thirty dead monsters. "I-I did my part," he said, just loud enough for Jillybean to hear. "You're welcome world. And now it's time. It's time. Jesus, it's time…but not here."

He staggered inside. There was a thirty second pause, followed by a flash and a last gunshot. Jillybean waited and waited for him to appear either in the window or the street or anywhere. He never showed. "Where'd he go?" she asked Ipes. "Should we go try to find him?" Ipes only sighed and she suddenly understood, at least as much as she could understand. "He shotted himself?"

Yes.

"Can we please go home now?" she begged.

No. He had a bag. He must've had food.

"Hold on," she said, blinking, her head still tilting. "You want me to steal? First I made him suicide himself and now you want me to be a stealer person?"

What I want is for you to live. You have to have food, or you'll die. Besides, I bet that man had filched all sorts of stuff from here and there. It probably wasn't his in the first place. It's the same as those cough-drops you ate. They weren't anyone's anymore so it's okay.

This made more sense and it was with a minutely clearer conscience that she shouldered her *Power Puff* backpack and went out into the evening. Jilly-mouse was in charge and she scampered with all the care in the world across the broad street. She was a taut spring, ready to run at the first sign of trouble, however when trouble came, she did not run. She paused on the stoop to look into the living room window and there was the bearded man, sitting on a heavy, leather reclining chair, his feet up, his jaw, once again slack, his eyes closed as if he were asleep and a hole in the side of his head.

The sight flipped a switch in the girl's much abused mind and she froze, unable to either step in or leave. To step in was to confront her guilt. To leave was to die. It was too much for a six-year-old and she was still standing there when a monster lumbered up the road, drawn by the gunshots. It was a big one, wide both side to side as well as front to back, and it was tall, over six foot. It would be able to eat most of Jillybean in one bite.

It spotted her and came charging around a vague lump of a minivan that took up the entire driveway.

She wanted to run but her fear was too powerful. She had been afraid every moment of every day for months now, however just at that second, her fear had grown beyond her ability to cope. It rooted her in place. Ipes screamed and screamed, but his shrill little voice was nothing compared to the colossus of panic inside of her. And it was nothing compared to the monster. It was too big, too strong and too fast.

On top of all of that, there was nowhere to run. The yard was enclosed by a black iron fence too high for her to climb over. She was trapped; the best she could do was slip from the stoop and cower in some scant bushes next to the house.

I'm going to die. Of all the voices she heard in her head and there were more than just Ipes' and her daddy's, this one was a first. It was her own. Once again, she had that strange out of body experience when the beast, a truly wicked creature that looked ten-feet tall to the tiny girl, got around the minivan. There was nothing between her and it. She felt her heart stop dead in her chest.

She had hit the very pinnacle of fear. Even if a million more monsters came, she couldn't absorb one more iota of dread. The thought, *I'm going to die*, came again and it was spoken inside of her with the utmost truth. There was no hero hiding in the shadows waiting to dart out and save her at the last moment. She had no secret weapon that she could whip out and blast the creature apart. There was no meteor plummeting right toward it at that very moment.

It was just the two of them, alone.

The monster had only one play in its playbook: it charged with a bloodcurdling roar—and tripped over a crack in the cement, falling on its face in such a cartoonish manner that Jillybean heard a distant chuckle; Ipes she assumed.

Then the thing stood up—directly into the sideview mirror, breaking it right off and causing it to let out a new kind of roar, one of frustration. The chuckle grew to a laugh and yet the monster was even closer, and she was still scared out of her wits. Only now the beast noticed movement in the van's window. It was seeing its own reflection but without a working brain it couldn't tell the difference and attacked the glass, and the door, and the entire side of the van. No monster had ever looked so frustrated and this, at last, broke the spell of fear that had gripped her.

Jillybean was over the side of the stoop's railing and in the bushes just as the beast turned back to the door. In a mountainous rage, it went stumbling up the stairs and blasted through the front door as if it were made from nothing but popsicle sticks.

Now's our chance, Jillybean! Run! screamed Ipes.

She couldn't. She was too weak to stand and still too afraid to try the driveway and so she scurried, bunny-like along the side of the house, hoping to see a gate in the fence. When she reached the edge of the house, she saw there wasn't a gate, but there was a small rabbit run that went under the fence which she could shimmy under if she took off her pack.

As the monster rampaged inside the house, sometimes just on the other side of the wall from her, Jillybean rested, letting her pounding heart calm and her nerves and muscles cease their trembling. It was only when she felt she could stand that she remembered the food in the man's pack. The pack had appeared to be very immense, so big that she could've curled up inside of it, and all she could think about was the great mass of food that was undoubtedly stored within it. Perhaps enough to feed her for a year.

It'll still be there tomorrow or the next day and besides, you have that rice and those beans. And you can't eat anything if you're dead, so come on, let's go.

"What if it's not there tomorrow?" she replied, hesitating. "What if someone else heard all the shooting and such?" The answer was simple: someone would come by, see all the dead monsters and take the food, and Jillybean would starve in her bed like her mother did. She didn't want that. Ever.

Then we should go wait across the street. Quickly. Quickly. Ipes was practically wetting himself to get away. *You know it can be hours before the monster leaves and more might come in the meantime and we can't be stuck out here without any cover. Remember, the lessons? Become Jilly-mouse and escape.*

"And die," she muttered, to herself, torn by indecision. Having not eaten well in weeks and not at all in the last few days, her situation was getting desperate. Her body felt as though it were becoming unglued, as if her stringy muscles were pulling away from her bones and her teeth were starting to wobble in her gums.

She *had* to get food somehow…only she didn't know how. Her parents had shielded her from the horrors of the monsters, and then, when they were both gone, her own fear took over, keeping her safe, but completely ignorant of them. Ipes was just as bad and his only suggestions were to either run or hide.

"We need to get that thing outa there. Hmmm."

For the next few minutes, that "hmmm," was the closest thing she had to a thought. No experience, in all her six years of life, prepared her for the challenge in front of her. There was no bad guy or silly "monster" in her books back home that were anything like the terrible creature in the house, and the tv cartoon movies she used to watch only advocated "understanding" the villains, none of which ever ate people for real. In school she had been taught about bullies, though she wasn't about to "Say No!" to these monsters.

"What do we knowd about monsters?"

A lot. We know they're mean and that they eat people —and probably zebras. They're stinky and ugly and stupid.

"Yes, good. What else?" Ipes added more descriptors, all of which were synonymous with either stinky, ugly or stupid. It wasn't very helpful. "That's not very helpful. We gotta think of a way to get it outa there. What about using fire?"

Ipes raised an eyebrow. *You know you aren't supposed to play with fire. And how would a fire help? You'd just burn up our food.*

She looked down her nose at the zebra. "I did go to school, you know. We learnded more than just our A, B, Cs. We also done fire-drills and that's what means you pretend there's a real fire. Too bad there ain't no more 'lectricity in the walls. We coulda lit a *small* fire and when the alarm went off, out he'd come."

Don't say 'ain't' and don't even think about playing with fire. It's far too dangerous, just like it's too dangerous to sit here out in the open plotting. You're being too loud.

33

If it comes out and sees you that'll be it for both of us.
You've heard how delicious grass-fed cows are. Let me tell
you that cookie-fed zebras are doubly delicious.

Jillybean, who thought cows ate hay, dismissed the
zebra's ranting except for one small fragment: *If it comes*
out and sees you. "We need a worm, like catching fish.
You know something that'll..." Her vocabulary wasn't
extensive enough to finish the sentence.

Lure it out? Ipes asked, reading their shared mind.
Like what? The only thing they like to eat are...wait! he
cried. She had started to nod, realizing that the only thing
she had for bait was herself. Ipes wouldn't hear of it. *This*
is a terrible idea. You can't. What would your daddy say?

"I think he wouldn't want me to be hungry to death.
It'll be okay. You can stay with the backpack." He didn't
want to stay with the backpack, but she didn't listen to his
protests. They undermined the first bit of real courage she
had ever shown in her entire life.

It was only a very small portion of courage and
couldn't overcome the shivers that wracked her
malnourished body as she crept to the front door. There
she left her pack and the still bleating Ipes and went up the
three steps of the stoop as if she were heading towards the
gallows. With each faltering step, the weak and sputtering
flame of her courage grew smaller and smaller until it was
snuffed out entirely as she saw the horrific monster.

And that was okay. She didn't need actual courage for
the next part of her rudimentary plan which was simply to
run for her life. At the sight of the pale little girl and her
huge, wet blue eyes, the monster let out a terrific bellow
and charged at her.

Run! screamed Ipes. She ran as fast as she could, her
eyes locked on the narrow trough beneath the black iron
fence. Too late, she remembered the hood of her pink coat
which had once been frilled with fake white fur. The fur
was now grey and shabby and would catch on the
underside of the fence, choking her and pinning her in
place long enough for the monster to grab her up by the

ankles and dangle her momentarily over its immense gaping mouth before it bit her head clean off.

The thought brought on a mad fear that nearly equaled what she'd felt earlier. Her legs went spastic and she stumbled, a shriek lodged squarely in her throat as she fell. Now she was scrambling, crawling like a panicked, frantic baby right to the fence. Just before she went under, she yanked her hood over her head, and dove so low her face went into the dirt.

She came through the other side wearing a beard of dirt just as the beast struck the fence full force, sending up a dull clang. At first it tried to tear the bars apart, but when it discovered it couldn't, the huge monster attempted to follow her under. There wasn't enough room between the bottom of the bars and the hard-packed dirt for its thick body.

It didn't care. Jillybean watched in sickened horror as it almost tore itself into pieces as the metal bars cut grooves, three-inches deep through its grey flesh. Black blood gushed up, turning the dirt to mud. She could see bones snapping and muscle pulling like taffy and still it came on. It would never stop.

Run, Ipes said, speaking into her ear as if he were right next to her. She ran, blindly at first, tripping over a sprinkler and bouncing off a tree. She fell twice more and each time she was up again in a flash. It was only after a block and a half that she began to regain her senses. She looked back and with the pervasive dark she couldn't see any sign of the monster.

Time to be Jilly-mouse.

"Yeah," she replied, in a breathy whisper. Crouching down, she crossed the wide street and made her way back to the "nice" house. The giant monster wasn't far away. It had freed itself but at a terrible cost. It bled buckets of black juice and dragged along a ragged grey skein like a shadow built of horror.

When it passed, she counted to a hundred, slipped to the bush next to the house and fetched Ipes. "I did it," she said, flushed with pride.

35

I always knew you could. Now, let's go see if the man had any cookies. I call dibs on any Double-stuffed Oreos!

"No way. I did all the work, and asides, you didn't want me to do this in the first place and that's what means I can have Oreos, too."

Dibs is dibs. That's called logic. Sorry.

Jillybean ground her teeth together. She didn't know what logic was, but she was bound and determined to find out and when she did, the world had better watch out, especially if it planned on getting between her and a package of *Double-stuffed Oreos*.

***

Author's End Note:

From a biographer's perspective there were many interesting aspects of this story, not the least of which was Jillian's absolute reluctance in telling it. She found the outright fear she demonstrated to be degrading and unfit to be told given the rest of her many heroic deeds.

I was able to persuade her only by stroking, what I have described in other works as: "an infinite ego, justified solely by the history of her time, the shape of which was molded almost exclusively by her own hand." When I explained that, although her initial all-consuming fear was utterly normal, her ability to overcome it was in fact, singular. This has been proved painfully true. Only a handful of other children her age lived through the early stages of the apocalypse, yet none were ever on their own so completely or accomplished so much as such a young age.

There was another aspect of this story that was fascinating from both a writer's point of view as well as a psychoanalytical one, and that is the juxtaposition of

Jillian's first display of raw courage and the first stirrings of her utter ruthlessness.

I'm sure you're asking yourself, "What utter ruthlessness?" The answer came out of what I thought was more or less a throw-away question at the end of my third interview with her.

"Did you ever see Becca Risbon again?" I didn't expect much more than a simple yes or no. Instead, Jillian froze, her blue eyes went completely blank and then her head began to go side to side, very slowly. "No," she said.

It was as bald a lie as I had ever heard, but I didn't take offense since Jillian herself wasn't even aware of it.

"Are you sure?" I asked, skating across ice that was both thin and dangerous. Doubting the Queen has led to more than one death and who knew how many disappearances. Despite this, I persevered. The job of biographer is not for the faint of heart, after all. "Perhaps you saw Becca and might have forgotten."

Instead of growing angry at my temerity, Jillian grew still and unsettlingly cold. "Who are you again?"

At this seemingly simple question, I could feel my face grow stiff and my pulse begin to race. Jillian had a towering intellect that had lost nothing in forty-one years. She was as razor sharp as ever and she definitely knew who I was. The woman in front of me was not Jillian. I was in the presence of Eve and though she was small and thin, and I was a robust six-feet, young and strong, a wave of goosebumps rashed out across my flesh.

Eve was the stuff nightmares.

"I'm Ezekiel Cross. I'm your b-biographer." I was abruptly aware that Jillian invariably carried weapons and that Eve would know exactly where they were.

"Ah, *she's* looking to polish her image," Eve said, sitting back, one hand sliding out of sight. I tried not to notice. She went on, "Good for her. *She* needs it, but I don't. I want you to capture me in all my wicked glory. Promise me." It was an order and one with an unspoken "or else" hanging over it.

"Of course."

She smiled with all the affection of a Mako shark. The smile then curdled. "*She* wants to come back, so I have to hurry. You asked about Becca Risbon? Becca was as dull in her undeath as she was in her short life. She was a lurker. They never stray too far, and it was easy for Jillybean to find her the next day. Did you note I said 'was' when I mentioned her?"

"I did." And I had.

"Yes, she became a *was* very quickly after Jillybean and that stupid zebra filled their bellies. *She* went looking for her bestest friend in the whole wide world and found her at that same fence and you know what she did?"

I wanted to say something along the lines of *Put her out of her misery?* only Eve still had that hand hidden along the side of her leg, and that godawful smile had never left.

"Murdered her?"

Eve scoffed, making me feel small and stupid. "You can't murder a zombie, moron." I could tell she wanted to go on, digging the knife deeper into me, but Jillian was coming back and would not be stopped. "From one side of the fence, she called over her bestest friend who obediently reached through the chain links. Then this six-year-old girl tied her outstretched hands together, calmly walked around to the other side of the fence and beat what was left of Becca Risbon's brains in with a brick. What a beautiful child, huh? And people wanted to adopt *her,* instead of me? So, what do you think of her now?"

"I guess I think she did what she had to do," I said, slightly embarrassed to be defending my subject. "She was making amends, I suppose."

"Then why'd she bury it so deep? If it was the right thing and all, why did she hide it even from herself? Ask her that when she comes back. I'd love to hear her excuse for killing her bestest friend ever."

Eve was gone seconds later and in her place was Jillian. It had been a very strange but subtle transformation —it almost looked as though one soul had ousted another. After a final shiver, Jillian pierced me with such a long look that it felt as though she were looking straight through my flesh and at the wall behind me.

"I take it you got everything you needed?" she asked, replacing the hard look with a wintery smile. "Or do you have more questions."

Had she heard? Did she know what Eve had asked? Did it matter? I hesitated, deciding the answer was, no. It didn't matter. Jillybean had done what was right. In killing her best friend, she had shown maturity and strength far beyond her age, even if it had widened the already deep fissures of her young mind.

"No. I have my story," I told her, "and it's a good one for a first adventure."

Chapter 2
The Witch: *Jillybean in the Undead World*
Rippling, Missouri

***

A quick note from the author— Ezekiel Cross:

I am sitting on a hillside above a pond where a thirteen-footer has its hideous face in the water. Every half a minute or so it lifts its head and sucks down air. It'll drink seven or eight gallons this way before it moves on to feed or sleep, unless it sees me. If it does, I'll drop my pack and run.

Only a fool would consider fighting the monsters now. Most of them weigh close to two-thousand pounds and have the strength of a bull elephant. I'm nervous, of course, but it's a fear that's understandable. The cause of my fear is a tangible beast fully capable of tearing me into little bite-sized pieces.

As anxious as I am, it's not the most frightened I've been on this journey. Not even close. There is something far worse in the wilds of southern Missouri: the Witch of Rippling. Tales of her sadistic cruelty have stretched across the country and there are few campfire story sessions that don't involve at least one mention of the torturous "experiments" that her victims were forced to endure.

Since I was in the area, tracking down the missing pieces of the Queen's life, I decided to look into the rumors to discover what was true and what was fable. Shockingly, all the terrible rumors were true. What wasn't shocking to me was that Queen Jillian and the Witch of Rippling had crossed paths.

The Queen is a magnet for evil. She draws it to her and, many say, she absorbs far too much of it. After all, it's common knowledge that the Queen has been involved with her own, extremely questionable experiments. Was it from the Witch that she learned that humans make the best guinea pigs? It's what I wanted to find out—

Ezekiel Cross

1

The little girl stood in familiar surroundings. The bedroom was pink, gilt with white trim. In the center of the room was a cream colored carpet and in the center of that sat a canopy bed fit for a princess, and sitting square in the center of that were stuffed animals: three teddy bears, a koala, a pair of penguins and a turtle.

They appraised the girl with glass eyes, each sitting up straight, hoping to be noticed, each trying to set themselves apart from the rest.

It was a little girl's room, but not hers. Despite that she was hungry and her stomach was an empty bag, the little girl had ignored the kitchen and had passed through the dim house leaving footprints in the dust, heading directly for the upstairs bedrooms. She had peeked in each room, hoping to find exactly this. For her it was a treasure trove.

She stood for a minute waiting, listening to the unending silence that blanketed the world. When no one spoke, she said: "Is anyone here?" She held her breath in the usual hope; however the stuffed animals remained silent. None so much as twitched.

A sigh escaped her as she went to the bed, her hand running over the soft comforter. There was a layer of dust on it that swirled up and tickled her nose. The stuffed animals were dusty as well, then again, the entire world was dusty with age. Dust was normal now that all the mommies were dead.

She picked up each of the animals. She squeezed them gently, taking their measure.

They had to be just the right height, and just the right weight to fit her needs. "Nope...nope...maybe." The penguins were close, very close, close enough to be dropped into the green trash bag with the others. The bag

41

was a *Hefty* that she had spun from a roll in the first house she had entered that day and it was already half-filled with stuffed animals.

"Sorry," she said to the twin penguins. They'd be going into the river, which was sad if she thought too much on it; sad but necessary.

The little girl then tortured herself by going to the closet. It was, as expected, filled with outfits that would've been perfect for her. There were purple and blue skirts that she could've gone to school in—if there was school anymore—and a lime green one with sequins that would've be perfect for Saint Patty's Day—only she was pretty sure that Saint Patrick was dead—and there were cute blouses and fun tank tops she could've gone to the mall in—except the malls were all filled with rotting corpses and she didn't like to go there anymore.

Worst of all, there was a First Communion dress that was snowy silk and so beautiful it made her insides ache.

She stood there for ten minutes running her hands over the material, wishing to try on the dress. She even thought about throwing it on over her "normal" clothes. Her clothes were hardly what anyone would consider normal: she was dressed in the sown together shreds of three different outfits. She was a bizarre, amorphous shamble of green. It was almost impossible to tell that she was an actual girl beneath the clothes…and that was purposeful.

Thus the reason she longed to put on the dress. She licked her lips feeling like an addict, feeling like a starving bum staring in the front window of a bakery.

Her name was Jillybean and she hadn't worn a dress in more than a month and even that dress had been worn as a means to an end. She was only seven years old, but despite that she always considered both the ends and the means in every decision she made. Her survival depended on it.

A noise outside the window had her turning from the closet and the beautiful silk dress—no sigh this time. The sigh which had escaped her earlier had been a luxury she couldn't afford. Extraneous noise, superfluous motion, garish colors like pink and purple, attracted attention. She was seven and alone in an apocalypse; she couldn't afford attention of any sort.

The noise outside the window was, as she expected, a monster. As far as monsters went, it wasn't a big one. It stood with its one remaining eye staring at something on the ground, its diseased mouth hanging open, a few shards of teeth showing in its grey gums.

Some people called them stiffs, or Zekes or Zs, or grey meat, or the walking dead, but to Jillybean they were nothing more than monsters. They ate people. That was the very definition of a monster in her book.

She could still remember the first monster she had seen the year before: it had been partially dressed in a police officer's uniform; its shirt was ripped open just as its chest had been, just as its face had been. Sure, it had been very much disgusting and horrible; however, she hadn't been all that afraid—back then she still had her mommy and daddy, and her greatest feeling at seeing the monster was of curiosity. The fear didn't come until later when everyone had died or had become a monster and she was all alone in the world.

Jillybean grabbed her green garbage bag and slipped into the next room over—it was the parents' room, she knew because of the double dressers and the giant bed, and also simply because she knew these sort of things on an instinctual level. She knew a great many things on a level that bracketed understanding, meaning she understood a great many things that she should have as well as an unnerving amount that she shouldn't.

Jillybean was seven and alone in an apocalypse. Her parents were long dead; nine months dead: one from a zombie bite that had turned him into one of *them*, the other by suicide. By all laws of nature, she should've been long dead, too. She should've died of dehydration in the depths of that first endless winter, but she hadn't. She should've frozen when the heat went out, but she hadn't. She should've starved, she should've been eaten, she should've succumbed in one way or the other.

But she was still alive and kicking.

Others had lived because of their strength or their wits, their training, their speed, their looks, or by their God-given luck. Jillybean had survived because she was a genius.

No one who knew her before the monsters swept the earth would have called her a genius. For the most part, people back then had labeled her as "cute." In school, she had been "chatty." To her parents she had been "sweet" because of how loving she had been, but she hadn't come across as brighter than the average kid in their eyes.

Genius was strange like that.

Her particular form of genius was exceedingly subtle. She knew nothing of physics or neurobiology or anthropology or any other ology for that matter; she couldn't tell the difference between Euclidian Geometry and Plato's *Allegory of the Cave*; she knew only one language and that was little kid English. She had not even finished the second grade.

Still she knew things that she shouldn't.

She saw patterns where everyone else saw chaos; her mind clung to insignificant facts and was able to arrange them into masterpieces; she had a kinetic understanding of nature that amazed lesser minds: given four coat hangers and a pair of shoelaces, she could build a rabbit trap or snowshoes or a pulley system strong enough to lift her weight. Given a cut of wood and a length of rope she'd give you a plow, a battering ram, or a fulcrum that could jack up a car. Given some C4 and a good enough reason and she could destroy a kingdom.

She wasn't particularly happy as a genius.

Before seven billion people had died, for the most part eaten alive and screaming until their vocal cords tore and the only sound they could make was a keening noise that was nothing more than the saddest wind, Jillybean had used her genius to enjoy life. Back then, before the monsters came, her life had been perfect: she had just about a bajillion friends, a family who lived for her, a perfect attendance record in school, and, what she considered the primo role in the Christmas play: she had been the angel who had appeared before the shepherds. While on stage, she walked everywhere with a curious twitch so that her wings would shake in imitation of flight.

Now her life was, *less than*. Now she was forced to creep around, hiding from the monsters. Now she rarely smiled and never laughed. Now she killed when she had to...and sometimes when she didn't have to.

She was somewhat tired of being a genius. It made her different from the other survivors. It made her a commodity, something to be used. It also made everyone around her dumb. When people found out how bright she was they stopped using their brains. They reminded her of the monster out front which eventually stopped its dull staring and went down on its hands and knees to feed.

It was eating crab grass like a goat or a sheep would. The monsters could eat anything: bark, squirrels, maggot-covered roadkill, even leather. Yeah, she'd seen one monster eating a belt once. They liked to eat people the most of all. If she walked out the front door, it would go crazy.

But she would never do that. That would be suicide. She knew all about suicide. Her mommy had killed herself and so did a woman named Melanie who had slit her own throat so that all her blood came out of her and made a mess of her shirt. It hadn't been much of a loss; Melanie had been dumb even before she had met Jillybean.

Jillybean glanced around at the bedroom, noting so many details that had been overlooked by the others who'd come into the house. Just like every house in America, the three-bedroom bi-level with the spacious kitchen and the updated bathrooms and the 42-inch flat screen had been ransacked months before by starving survivors. However, they hadn't bothered to search the bedroom except for the nightstands and beneath the bed; looking for guns, Jillybean thought.

They weren't looking for food in the master bedroom because they missed the details: the plus-sized dress hanging on the closet door, the "new" gym bag in the corner with the long-expired fitness club membership card attached to the handle. The card was two years old, the clothes inside worn once or twice. On the bathroom counter were bottles of pills boasting of their fat burning abilities.

Jillybean went to one of the dressers and pulled open the second drawer, knowing there would be panties and bras within it—and there were. She also guessed that there would be chocolate hidden beneath the panties—and she was right about that as well.

Three Snickers and an Almond Joy, a good haul.

The Snickers went into the backpack which sat under her shredded outer garment. She ate the Almond Joy over the course of the next hour, savoring every bite and watching the monster outside fill up on grass. When it had a full belly and green teeth, it moseyed on in the vague way monsters did and only then did Jillybean throw the hood over her head and slip out the front door.

2

The shambling mound paused at the bridge. The little girl in the homemade gilly-suit turned a slow circle, her sharp blue eyes peering out from the hanging shreds of cloth. Her eyes were sharp but her ears were sharper, only they didn't pick up a thing; the world was silent as a tomb.

The world is a tomb, she thought. *One giant tomb.*

Nothing moved in the world except the river flowing gently by. Satisfied that she was as safe as could be, Jillybean cast back the hood and wiped away the sweat that had been collecting on her forehead as she crept down out of the forest. She was in Missouri and it was late August or maybe early September, either way, the air was still and muggy; barely breathable in her opinion.

She was at that particular bridge and at that specific time for a purpose. She'd lost her best friend there seven weeks ago.

"So who goes first?" she asked in a whisper, opening the garbage bag. Thirty-four sets of empty eyes looked up at her and none answered. A brilliantly colored Toucan sat on top. With its rainbow beak and its purple body, it was a good first choice. "Sorry, Mister Toucan," she said and then lobbed it into the river where it splashed and then bobbed on its way down stream.

Her eyes followed it until it was out of sight. She then reached for one of the teddies, thought better of it and pulled out a flamingo—the pink would be nicely obvious. Three minutes after the Toucan went in, she threw the flamingo. It began sinking very quickly, eliciting a: "Hmm," from her.

Over the next two hours all thirty-four stuffed animals went into the river, not as part of some tribute to her friend, but as part of an experiment. Her friend had been thrown off this very bridge at exactly this time of day and she had to replicate the disaster as close as possible if she had any hope of finding him. You see, her friend, her very best friend in the whole wide world wasn't human.

He was a zebra, a foot tall, with a spiky mane, a big nose, and a belly full of stuffing. Despite this, he could speak. In fact, his English was better than Jillybean's and he was constantly correcting her or he used to, that is.

Jillybean was, in a word, crazy. It was a sad fact, but a fact, nonetheless.

She had been six when the monsters came. They killed everyone. They killed every single person Jillybean ever knew and almost all the rest of the people she didn't know. The police and the army had tried to stop them but couldn't. Her daddy had tried to stop them but had come home one day bleeding from a bite. He was all sweaty and bug-eyed and he kept licking his lips.

"Take care of your mother," he had said before leaving to turn into one of *them*. He had died with his blue jeans full of pee and poop and his blood sweating out of his forehead, and that had hurt Jillybean on a level she couldn't understand.

Jillybean's mother had also been crazy, though no one knew it. Nadine Shaw went catatonic the day her husband had been bitten. When he left to die, Jillybean sat at the living room window crying and begging in a whisper for her daddy to come back home and while she did, her mommy climbed in bed and stared at the ceiling. Nadine stared at the ceiling day and night, not saying a word, not eating or drinking, not even thinking as far as Jillybean knew. She was like one of the dummies with the fancy clothes and the empty plasticine eyes down at the mall, in the Macys or the JC Pennys.

Jillybean had tried her best to keep her mother alive but her mother did not want to live. She only wanted to stare at the ceiling as her skin slowly pulled tight across her skeleton. When she died, so had part of Jillybean. Or rather a part of her snapped like a twig.

Once, a year before on a camping trip to Niagara Falls, Jillybean had helped her daddy make a fire. In order to make kindling, she had bent a stick over her knee until it had bowed in an ever deepening arc and then...*Crack!*

That had been Jillybean's mind when she came into her mother's room one day and found her staring up at the ceiling with dead eyes: *Crack!*

One moment she had been fine and coping with a world filled with monsters, and the next she was broken. She didn't go catatonic as her mother had, and she didn't sit in the corner of her bedroom drooling onto the floor until she froze to death, but there was a definite rift in her mind, a fault, a seam, a fissure that marked the difference between healthy and sick.

One clear sign of this rift was when her stuffed zebra had begun speaking to her.

At the time she had taken it in stride as if a talking zebra was the most normal thing in the world. In truth, the crazy in her head had been helpful...at first. The talking zebra was a coping mechanism to help her deal with the tremendous stresses she was living under.

But then the stress she was under began to escalate and escalate and escalate, until it began to grind her under, and the danger she faced grew exponentially, until every waking breath came with the poison of fear corrupting her, and then...and then her best friend had been thrown right off this bridge.

The fissure in her mind, the little seam between sane and not so sane had broken wide open and all the hell pent up in her spilled out into the world.

After that, she had killed...no, she had murdered. Innocent people had died at her hand and she had laughed and laughed. Her crazy was full on deadly, in fact she was so deadly that eventually she came to the realization that she no longer needed to be afraid of the evil things skulking in the dark.

They needed to be afraid of her.

Oddly enough, from that moment she began to heal and she was able to repair the great fissure in her mind so that she was no longer the vile thing she had been. Still the wound had not closed completely and never would. The closest she could come to normalcy was to put a band aid over the fracture and hope it wouldn't come undone.

She knew that it would, some day. It was why she was on the bridge. She needed Ipes the zebra. She hadn't laughed once in all the time he was gone.

3

The bone-skinny girl with the fly away brown hair and the blue eyes that belonged more in the head of battle-scarred soldier than a second grader sat up in the forest above the river for the remainder of the day, exhibiting patience well beyond her years.

She needed time for the floating parade of stuffed animals to sink or snag or drift their way down stream. A day was a good enough head start. To pass the time, she slid a book from her backpack: *Middle School Mathematician*. She had looked at a book called *Modern Day Math for Dummies*, but had been somewhat insulted by the title.

Until the rain came, she lazily slapped at mosquitoes and nibbled, mouse-like on one of the Snickers as she lost herself in basic geometry, absorbing the formulas as if they were as simple as: trees are green and pigs say *oink*. But the rain ruined her fun.

Throwing her hood over her bedraggled hair, she crossed through the forest, cutting north to a blacktop. From there she made her way east, walking through the woods, keeping the road always a hundred yards on her right. She went slowly, head on a swivel, her sharp eyes trying to see in every direction at once.

There was no hurry in her. She was patient and prudent, allowing herself to be soaked to the bone, not trusting simply to her disguise to fool the monsters.

That led to being eaten.

The rain made it difficult to hear; it clouded things on her periphery; it blended the grey beasts in with their background. It ran into her eyes and one time too many she brought up a very human hand to wipe her face. This little human act was all it took to give her away.

Jillybean froze. Movement on her right. A splash and a muffled moan. It was a monster, six foot in height, its dank mouth showing snaggy teeth, its fingers ending in notched claws with old blood under them. It was naked save for a single work boot and what might have been a pair of blue jeans caught up around its ankle.

Slowly, Jillybean sunk into a knee-popping crouch as the monster swung its ugly mug her way and tried to peer through the rain with its yellowed eyes. From twenty feet, she might have been a bush or a shrub or even a pile of dirty laundry, but that didn't stop the thing from coming to investigate.

It was infinitely hungry, hungry enough to eat a pair of panties if it was still human-flavored. It came on, squishing through the mud. It must have seen her hand or just a splash of her face and, although the rest of her outfit was a confusing mish-mash, her clear skin might as well have been a neon sign over an all you can eat buffet.

With her heart picking up in tempo, Jillybean slid her hands under the ghillie suit; her left hand gripped the hilt of a bowie knife, the exact same sort of knife she had used to kill a man not more than a month before—that knife she had left in her victim's back. She'd been lucky that time. The blade hadn't got caught up on a bone the way they sometimes did. Its previous owner, a tribal duke, had kept it wickedly sharp and it had passed through muscle like it was butter, in way that Jillybean had found horribly agreeable.

She liked to think she wasn't a killer anymore and yet she had found a new knife so much like the old that it should have set off warning bells. Lovingly, she had honed the blade until there was nothing sharper. Yet, she didn't rely on the weapon. Monsters were frequently unfazed by knives even when they were getting their guts ripped out by one.

The bowie was secondary; it was there just in case things didn't go well with the marble.

The fat, walnut-sized marble in her right hand was her first line of defense. When Ipes the zebra had been with her, the marbles held power, or so she believed. They were magic and always worked in the stickiest of situations, and this was a sticky one indeed.

The monster wasn't just big; he was fully formed, not missing any large body parts that would hamper his ability to chase Jillybean down. Some monsters had been so mangled and eaten during their creation that they were more of a nuisance than a danger; however, some, like this one, and probably her daddy as well, were fast and strong. It would be able to run for an hour without tiring. It would be able to smash through any window or door. And it absolutely would not stop coming until Jillybean was good and eaten.

And yet, Jillybean was not afraid. Or rather she was afraid, only she was controlling her fear with a strength of mind far beyond her age. She had discovered that her *crazy* had stemmed, in part, from her fear. She hated being crazy with such an untamed passion that she was able to throw aside her fear and look death in the eye with a mild expression on her face.

This was how she was able to crouch there, ready to throw her magic marble the moment the monster looked away. They usually did. They usually had bad eyesight and wagged their heads side to side, but this one seemed extraordinarily focused and bore down on Jillybean as if she was the only thing in the forest.

It dawned on her that the magic marble wasn't going to work this time. She switched to her back up plan—this still did not focus on the knife. Her hand went to her LED flashlight. She had never tried this in the daytime before, but with the heavy clouds and the rain, she figured it was worth a try.

It wasn't as if she had a lot of choices, in fact it was either the light or the nearly useless knife at her side; she lacked both the strength and skill to use the knife against an automaton like the monster was, which could take the blade in its eye and not feel a thing.

It was the flashlight then. The monster came up, dragging the blue jeans it had died in, making a moaning noise in the back of its throat. It appraised the lump that was Jillybean with half-hooded, dull eyes, before it reached out with its diseased claws. A single scrape from those claws and Jillybean would be done for. She'd be feverish in two hours and turned into one of *them* in four more.

The second the hand started for her she burst up and sprayed the light into the monster's eyes. LEDs gave off an ugly, harsh light that could take over the mind of a lesser creature such as the monster. The light dazzled it and paralyzed it, at least for the time it took for Jillybean to leap up and run.

For five seconds, the monster stood blinking, its brain taken up with the change in its environment. Everything around it had to be re-ordered into those things that could be eaten and those that could not.

The little girl sprinting away fell into the former category and on instinct it chased after in its lumbering manner.

Monsters were completely without grace or dexterity. If there was a branch in their way it was axiomatic that they would trip. Jillybean picked her path through the forest with exactly that in mind. She could outrun a monster, even a complete one such as this, in a short sprint; however any run over a hundred yards would go to the beast. Her scrawny legs with their stringy malnourished muscles just couldn't go for long.

Like a rabbit, she had to get to a point of safety very quickly.

Unfortunately, the forest was wide open and the nearest town was a little blip of a thing on the map a mile further on. Three times the monster tripped over the obstacles on the course that Jillybean chose and yet, after a few minutes, it was beginning to catch up; Jillybean's wheels were losing steam.

With the instinct of a wounded animal, she darted to her right where the land sloped gently. Her run was now into its two hundredth yard and her breath was harsh in her throat. The beast was a good fifty yards back; way too close in this sort of forest. She kept running, going slower and slower. There was a thick stand of trees ahead. It was the only thing that would keep her alive, but only if it was deep enough for her to get lost in.

It was not. The trees clumped around a small spring-fed stream and on the other side of it the land was even more open than before.

Jillybean was a little girl. She wasn't a track star or an Army Ranger. Her heart was going a mile a minute and her lungs couldn't keep up with the demands of her body. The only thing she could rely on was her brain. Seeing the open forest and realizing that if she continued on as she had, she'd be dead in minutes, Jillybean slid off her ghillie suit, threw it over a branch and then practically fell down a little slope next to the stream where years of leaves had collected in a hollow in the earth.

She burrowed beneath them, imitating the groundhog, the weasel and the mouse. A second later, the monster was through the trees. With a ferocious growl, it tore down the ghillie suit, rending it into shreds even worse than the shreds it had started as. When there was nothing left to it but strips of cloth, the monster stood there staring around with a look of disappointment...angry disappointment.

Jillybean didn't dare move. She barely breathed despite the fact that she was seeing black blobs growing and shrinking in her vision. The monster would go away, she told herself. It would wander away like they always did and then she'd be able to get up and dust herself off, if she was dusty that is. She was more muddy than dusty. The leaves were cold, damp and moldy. They smelled of old earth like the kind of earth thrown over a grave on a winter's day.

The only problem was that the monster didn't leave.

It stood there with rain cascading off of it for what felt like ages to Jillybean. Eventually, she was able to get her breath back and the strength returned to her legs and her skinny bottom was able to go numb from lying in the same position for what she was sure was an hour, judging by the fading light.

Eventually, she made a discovery: she had to pee.

The next hour was even longer than the first. Her bladder swelled and grew and expanded and hurt. It kept hurting and still the monster stood there as though guarding the remains of her ghillie suit. It stood there even after Jillybean shrugged beneath the leaves and let her bladder go in a hot rush. At least she was warm…for the moment.

The moment didn't last and she was soon shaking. She was starting to lose core body temperature; from her reading she knew what came next: hypothermia, shock, and then death. The nighttime temperature, on the front end of a late summer cold front could drop into the low fifties. Soaking wet as she was and shedding body temperature by the minute, death was a real possibility for a seven-year-old girl with two-percent body fat.

She had to do something that didn't involve sitting in her own pee until the elements killed her. Gradually, she shifted position. She had to make a run for the town. It couldn't be more than a mile distant. If so, there'd be outlying houses or farms closer than that, if not, she'd smell the decaying breath of the monster on her neck seconds before she was dragged down from behind and eaten alive.

Jillybean watched the monster from beneath the leaves; it swayed in place, its head moving gently from side to side as if it was in some sort of a trance. At the furthest arc, Jillybean jumped into a squat reminiscent of a major league catcher making a throw to second base. The magic marble arced across the forest snapping against a tree, centering the monster's yellow eyes away from the little girl breaking from cover.

Seconds passed before it realized that its quarry was pelting away through the forest. Her pack thumped against her back. Her legs churned out the yards, this time in a study of efficiency. It was going to be a longer run than before; a half mile would be her death; a quarter mile and she *might* live.

She ran with determined efficiency, sacrificing speed for endurance and again she ran in such a way as to put every obstacle in the monster's way that she could. It obliged, tripping over each. Still, her death was imminent when after five minutes of running, she saw the house: two stories of slat with a corroded shingle roof that leaked rainwater into its innards. Its porch leaned away from its foundation like a drunk at a urinal. Outside, on a pair of dirt ruts that marked a redneck driveway, an old Camaro rusted out the remainder of its life canted back at an angle on a pair of jacks as though it was about to blast off into the sky.

Jillybean ran for the car, her head spinning and her gait wobbling as though she had an unseen pendulum swinging her from side to side. She was nearly done in from the run, and the monster was within a stretch of its long arms of getting her when she got to the Camaro. She dropped and rolled as she had been taught to do if she was ever on fire. She rolled to the center of the car as the monster threw itself down into the mud.

While her heart thundered in her ears, the two of them locked eyes. The beast's breath was as foul as she guessed it would be. It made her head swim and her stomach turn, but did she bat an eye? No. Why should she? This was life in an apocalypse. This was the way things were whether she whined or cried, whether she lived or died. She was no longer at the top of the food chain. She was someone's dinner.

Jillybean waited until the monster committed to coming after her before she rolled to the other side of the car. Then she ran to the far side of the house, hoping that simply being out of sight would make her out of mind as well. She didn't count on it; so far, the monster had been extraordinary in its persistence and she guessed that it would be coming around the corner any second.

She waited at the far corner of the house, letting her breath catch up with her heart as she rested her legs. Though she waited, she wasn't idle. In one of the pockets of her backpack was twenty feet of nylon rope; in two seconds it was out and by the time the monster came around the far corner of the house, she had fashioned a slip knot with a loop the size of a basketball hoop.

The creature stood there for only a few seconds before it started for the end of the house where Jillybean had her eye at the corner. This was more than a touch disconcerting. The monster should have wandered off or at least simply stood there unthinkingly until some outside stimuli caused it to move on. That it would head in the most logical direction that its quarry would flee meant that it had at least two functioning brain cells and that they were firing on all cylinders.

So much for a fire, Jillybean thought to herself. She'd been hoping that the beast would wander away and that she'd be able to slip into the ramshackle house, build a fire and warm herself up. But she wasn't still alive because she used hope as a survival tool; the rope and the practiced noose could attest to that. The Boy Scout handbook had demonstrated how to make a snare to catch bunnies to eat during emergency situations. The noose was simply a bigger snare.

She ran down the length of the house to the backyard where she saw a clothesline; given the rustic state of the house, Jillybean had fully expected it and the peeling paint and the rust on the metal T shaped poles wasn't a surprise either. Again, the Boy Scout handbook proved its worth as she tied the rope fast to the closer T, using a modified bowline knot.

Next, she picked up two discarded clothespins and, going up on her highest tiptoes, fastened the noose so that it hung open at head height.

The snare was set with about three seconds to spare. The monster was charging and Jillybean used herself to bait it on, making sure to position herself in such a way that the monster would catch the trap just right. Her first attempt failed. A sudden lurch sent the thing's head just to the left and Jillybean had to sprint away.

Again, she was much faster than the monster, at first. She ran in a wide loop before going back to the trap. Panting like a dog, she stood on the other side of it, knowing that she didn't have much energy left. She was cold, wet, hungry and her panties were squishy with pee.

"Right here, dummy-head. No, a little to the left...there you go, keep coming. And...die."

The monster had the noose full around the neck and was practically strangling itself trying to get at the little girl. Practically strangling itself wasn't good enough. "That's a job half done," she said, quoting her father from, like a million years ago. Now that she had it in a noose, killing the monster was easy: she simply walked in large circles.

Even though the monster was a genius for its kind, it followed her eagerly, and with each rotation, the leash around its neck grew that much shorter. After forty turns around the pole, there was so little excess rope that the beast couldn't turn any longer, though that didn't stop it from trying. It strained against the choking noose until the nylon was an inch deep into its skin and it bled black blood all over itself.

Then it died. Quite simple.

Monsters were scary and *much* harder to kill than people, but they weren't magical. Their brains still needed proper blood flow to keep their involuntary systems operating and when the brain shuts down, the heart does as well.

The monster's legs gave out and it sagged against the pole, its neck slowly stretching. "Hmmm," the little girl said with a frown. She was hardly satisfied with the kill, despite the fact that this might have been the single toughest monster she had ever faced. She'd lost her rope. It had been a good rope.

The world was filled with rope, she told herself and then turned away from the creature and went into the house.

4

The inside was as dilapidated and dirty as the outside and, what was worse, it smelled of ancient cigarettes. The kitchen linoleum curled up at the corners, there were patches of rust in the sinks and bathtub, there were cobwebs so large that she feared she'd find spiders the size of dinner plates, and the living room carpet was so threadbare that she could see the plywood that made up the subflooring right through it.

The best thing about the place was the barn owl that lived in a second-floor bedroom. Before the sun went down behind the heavy clouds, she saw it twice, gliding away from the house in perfect silence.

With the setting sun, she hung old blankets across the living room window so that the light of her fire couldn't be seen. She then rigged traps at each entrance, sprinkled the floor with glass, washed her clothes in a steel pot, made one of her remaining cans of soup and read until she was sleepy.

The loneliness of the world was oppressive. It shaped actions, frequently to a dangerous extent. In the deepest part of the night, Jillybean sat up from the musty smelling blankets and looked around. The fireplace held nothing but smoldering embers that resembled a dozen glowing demon eyes. The rest of the house was formed out of shadows, irregular and foreign.

For reasons she could not explain, she crept outside and stood holding a cardboard box above her head; the patter of the rain was light and merry, the dark form slumped against the pole under the clothesline was not.

"Hey," she said to the corpse. When it didn't stir, she picked up a stick and gave it a prod. It was dead. With the rain washing away the filth it had been covered in and plastering down its wild hair, the monster wasn't so monstrous. It sort of looked human, except for its neck which was stretching out like an extended slinky.

"I'm sorry," she added and then stood there until the box began to wilt.

In the morning the rain had turned to drizzle. Jillybean went to the coat closet by the front door armed with a pair of scissors. Inside were a few jackets and more cobwebs, but no spiders. She pulled down the smallest jacket—tan with a soft fleece interior—and commenced to cut it open in a number of spots.

She wasn't making another ghillie suit, that took too much time and she was in a hurry to get back to the river. Instead, she was remaking herself into a monster. First the tattered clothes, then the mussed hair, then the make-up applied with increasing artfulness on the face and hands. Next came the stumbling gait and the low moan.

That's all it took to blend in with the monsters.

The monsters were stupid and their eyesight varied from poor to terrible depending on the number of eyeballs they still had, and their sense of smell was even worse than a human's and that was really saying something. Of course, it was only logical as each distinct odor had to be interpreted by the brain and everyone knew monsters were basically brainless.

Jillybean went stumping toward the river, looking and acting like a monster. This was a safer way to travel, but it was achingly slow and it made too much noise for her taste. The ghillie suit was better, except in the rain as she had found out the day before.

Just because her monster disguise was nearly perfect, it paid not to get too close to real monsters if it could be helped. Jillybean found her route blocked by an entire herd of the creatures, moaning and schlepping along right across her path. There were hundreds wandering in a line a mile long. This sort of inexplicable weirdness happened from time to time.

She turned south, hoping to skirt the herd and get around it, but after detouring far out of her way, she was shocked out of her role as a monster as the smell of cooking meat came to her.

Jillybean was no longer the emaciated waif she had been after her parents died. She could fish and trap better than most adults and so the smell didn't cause her to rush off and beg for food. It did, however, stop her in her tracks. Only real live people cooked meat and it was the power of loneliness that had her creeping toward the source of the smell.

Caught up in the moment and the need to be around people, she had forgotten to remain in character. Instead of looking like a little monster, she looked like a little orphan child from Victorian England or maybe something out of a play...or both.

Movement in the corner of her eye reminded her and she sobered quickly, switching with surprising speed back to a monster. The drizzle was coming down in sheets now obscuring whatever it was she had caught a glimpse of and, fearing that it was a real monster, she angled away, heading toward the little town, the "blip" on the map.

It was tiny indeed. Eight buildings big sort of tiny.

The town's name was Rippling but the small river that bubbled alongside of it was of such little consequence that it went unnamed and unnoted on the map. Everything, and there wasn't much to the everything that was Rippling, centered on the gas station. In the *before,* the gas station was the only reason anyone would stop in Rippling.

It was the gas station that kept the twelve-seat diner across the street still in the business of selling pies and it kept the three-aisle supermarket from becoming a one aisle convenience store, and it kept Sally's Antique Shoppe from being renamed Sally's Secondhand Junk Shoppe as it should've been.

And without all that there would've been no reason for Missouri Power & Light to build a substation in Rippling and even less of a reason for the Catholics to stick a red brick church right between the substation and the second most popular destination in Rippling: the liquor store.

There was smoke coming from a strange collection of pipes running from one of the church's stained-glass windows. It was from there that the smell of meat emanated.

The misting rain made the world sullen and affected Jillybean in the same way. She needed people, but frequently she hated being around them as well. They were generally petty and greedy. Frequently they were evil and deadly. Rarely were they brave and noble. It was a gamble for her to see them and to interact. Her *crazy* would come out if they were evil and her *crazy* was a bad sort.

She had a genius for numbers and spatial reasoning but she also had a genius for destruction and she excelled at explosions and fire and killing in general.

"I'll just give them a quick peek," she said. This wasn't just the idle talk of an addict; she really could satisfy her loneliness by watching others. With her binoculars she'd be able to study them and get a feeling for them. She couldn't read lips but she'd know what sorts of people they were by their body language, how they treated those smaller than themselves, and by their generosity or lack there of.

It couldn't be a big group. The church was small, shaped like a Lego block with a steeple. It was neat as well. There wasn't a lot of trash around the building; it meant they were disciplined. Usually a good sign. Slobbish groups tended to be lazy and mean.

Jillybean slid back into the forest so that she could move without being seen by anyone in the church. Here was where she missed her ghillie suit. It would have made her completely invisible from almost every direction and she could have moved silently.

In the monster outfit her steps were as quiet as ever and yet she felt compelled to moan even though she was sure there wasn't a monster anywhere around her; she had quick ears and surely would have heard one. Her ears were quick enough to hear the sharp intake of breath from somewhere just ahead.

The little girl slowed, her pointy chin came up an inch and her blue eyes stared out from beneath her bedraggled hair. With the rain turning everything grey, it was hard to see who or what it was, but there was definitely a someone thirteen feet away standing in a half-crouch.

At first Jillybean thought it was a little old lady. It was a she and a skinny one. Her hair was so pale blonde that it looked almost white. She wore a strange quilted coat and carried a matching handbag. And finally, to add to the illusion that the person was old, she had on granny glasses that were fogged-over giving her a buggy appearance.

The she and Jillybean froze as the rain picked up. It drummed between them adding tension and an element of danger. Jillybean reacted first, sliding her bowie knife out; it seemed the only thing with any definition. The blade looked hard and sharp and deadly.

Even with the rain and the moisture fogging up her glasses, the girl saw the knife just fine. She let out a yelp and took off running to her right. This was such a shock that Jillybean only stood there with her mouth open—who would run from a tiny little girl like her? She was the smallest person left in America as far as she knew.

Not wanting to scare the girl, and she guessed by her wild sprint that it was a girl and not an old woman, Jillybean followed at a distance. They crossed the river, the strange girl first, slipping on rocks and half dunking herself. Jillybean, going with more caution, leapt from rock to rock as nimble as a goat and, once across, she followed the terrified girl to the church.

Jillybean slowed, keeping out of sight, afraid that a dozen armed men would come rushing out to shoot her or otherwise kill her in some unpleasant manner. She slunk down in the electrical substation, hiding behind a steel box that had heavy wires running into it. Even though there was almost no electricity left in the country, Jillybean kept her hands to herself.

She was so unnerved by the possibility of electricity in the air that she slipped the bowie into its sheath and, even though she was only thirty yards away, she brought out her binoculars just as the windows of the church started to creak open. The faces showing were all surprisingly young.

"I don't see her," someone in the church said in a hissing voice that carried.

"I swear it was the witch," yelled a girl's voice; she was practically in hysterics.

A boy of about fifteen stuck his head out of one of the windows and stared all around. His lips were tight in a grimace. "She's disappeared again. I say we lock up tight."

"So, they think I'm a witch," Jillybean whispered to herself. "Huh? That's funny." She was pretty sure that there wasn't any such thing as a witch. They were only in stories. Still, she glanced behind her at the tired remains of the town with a shudder.

What if she was wrong? What if there was really something out there? The children in the church sure thought so...but what about the adults? Why weren't they charging out to confront this witch? Why weren't they showing their faces?

"What if there are no grode-ups here?" Jillybean asked aloud. That was more unsettling than any silly idea that a witch was running around the tiny blip of a town. "Unless the witch killed all the adults." With that even more unsettling thought, she turned her binoculars on the forest and the rest of the town, scanning as best she could through the rain.

If there was a witch, she was invisible—this thought triggered yet another shudder.

Suddenly she wanted to get as far away from Rippling as possible. The only problem: she'd have to go through a witch-infested forest in order to do so. That made things very dicey and she decided to take her chances with the kids in the church. She was sure she would be able to convince them that she wasn't a witch at all...and a monster, too.

She figured once they got a closer look at her, they'd be able to see through her disguise. After one final look around, she stood and hurried to the front doors of the church. Up close, the church was even less impressive. The doors were simple metal, devoid of any artistic flair or religious symbolism. They were solid, however. Her first attempt at knocking was a barely audible thump.

With too little thought, as it turned out, she slid her bowie from its sheath and gave the door a whack with the butt of it.

"It's the witch!" someone cried from inside.

Jillybean was just wondering if it would do any good to deny the charge when another voice, this one male and angry, said: "We have to kill her! Now!"

The door burst open just as Jillybean had decided it was high time to get out of there. The boy she had seen earlier in the window charged out waving an aluminum bat. Behind him were two more boys, both just old enough to have begun sprouting a few hairs on their chins. One had a bat as well and the other a homemade spear.

"Get her!" cried the older boy with the bat.

This was happening far too fast for Jillybean. Couldn't they see she was just a little girl? Certainly, they couldn't be afraid of her. That was preposterous. Ridiculous. Moronic, really. And yet, they were afraid. She was as well; she was nearly petrified by their violence. All she could do was brandish her bowie knife, though what that would logically accomplish she didn't know.

The children of the church were not operating logically and so, as the firelight caught the blade of the knife just right, it blazed with light and the first boy with the aluminum bat shied back from it. This gave them a second to recognize that Jillybean was not a witch at all.

"It's a zombie!" a tall girl behind the three boys yelled, pointing at Jillybean. "It's a zombie with a knife!" Again, logic dictated that a witch had to be more of a danger than a tiny monster such as Jillybean appeared, knife or no knife, and yet the three boys shied back.

The barely teen boy with the spear pointed it at Jillybean and stammered: "I-It's l-like zzzombie-Joe."

"Who's zombie Joe?" Jillybean asked. The very question shocked the children and they all stepped back another step, holding their weapons out in front of them, not to strike, but as if to ward Jillybean off.

"It can talk," breathed out the girl with the horn-rimmed granny glasses whom Jillybean had first come across in the forest.

"Of course, I can talk. I'm not a zombie at all. I'm a just a girl. I'm wearing a costume, you see?" Jillybean smoothed her bushy mass of hair and turned her face this way and that so that it could be seen that her monster make-up only extended so far.

Everyone relaxed, some going so far as to breathe exaggerated sighs of relief; all except the boy with the metal bat. He stared past Jillybean out into the rain. "And where's the witch?" The children's over the top fear had convinced Jillybean that there wasn't a witch around at all. They were being paranoid. They had probably seen a funny tree or the shadow of badger or had scared themselves into the idea by telling stories around the campfire at night.

There were thirteen children in the church, ranging in age from ten to seventeen. They didn't have any grownups with them which was all sorts of bad and, what might have been worse, they didn't have any guns either. They were a frightened bunch, skinny as alley cats and dirty. In spite of the fact that that there were entire department stores filled with clothes, the children were dressed as urchins in clothes giving over to rags.

Over all they looked like the cast of Oliver Twist.

Jillybean shrugged. "I haven't seen a witch. And really who would be afraid of a witch who was my size?" When no one answered her question, she followed it up with: "And who's Zombie Joe? Is that a person?"

Her guess was that Zombie Joe was a zombie wrangler —a man who understood the monsters well enough to control them, at least to the degree one was able to control a monster.

She was wrong. "No," said the boy with the bat. "He's a zombie, duh. Now, stop asking questions. We should be asking you questions, not the other way around."

Logic didn't necessarily suggest that, however, the boy seemed to have been made cranky by being frightened by a seven-year-old and so Jillybean submitted to questioning.

Where are your parents? "Dead. Well really my daddy gots turned into a monster, but my mommy is dead."

Why did you scare Renee? "I didn't mean to. She ran before I could say hi or anything."

Are you in league with the witch? "League?" She only knew the word in conjunction with a bowling league or little league. "We're not on the same team if that's what you mean."

Where are your people? For the first time, Jillybean hesitated before answering. She had run away from her people. Her crazy had gotten out of control and she had murdered. They said she was forgiven but she had not gone back. "Colorado," she answered without adding anything damning.

The boy with the bat had narrow, disbelieving eyes. "No, your people are here, somewhere. Where are they? How many of them are there?"

"I don't have people. I'm alone."

"That's a lie," the boy asserted. He looked around at the others. "She'd be dead if she was all alone. So that means she's lying. They're probably out there watching us."

The eldest child, the tall girl, stared down at Jillybean. She looked to be about seventeen and had very strange hair. It was angular hair: a straight hundred and eighty degrees across the bangs, a perfect line segment to the newly geometrically minded Jillybean. From there her hair was shorn at forty-five degree diagonals back to her ears where upon it dropped straight down a foot. Whoever had cut it understood precision but not beauty; she looked like she was wearing a brown helmet.

The tall girl eventually said: "I doubt anyone is watching us. Why would they send her here all alone? That doesn't make no kind of sense to me. My only question is, does this work? Dressing like a zombie I mean."

"Yeah, but you have to be careful. You have to look and act like them for reals or they'll eat you." This had the children re-appraising Jillybean's outfit. The tall girl even picked a leaf out of Jillybean's hair that she had carefully entwined there. The staring and the silence became a little uncomfortable. Jillybean blurted out: "So who's Zombie Joe?"

"He-he's j-j-just a zzzombie," the boy with the spear stuttered. "B-b-but a b-bad one." Jillybean had never heard a stutterer before and she didn't know what to make of it. She figured that he was cold for some reason, though he looked dry enough to her and the church was quite snug.

"He's not just a bad one, Ryan," the boy with the metal bat said. "He's evil. Way eviler than the rest. And he can think, at least a little. He can work a doorknob."

This pronouncement, accompanied by a great deal of nodding by the others, was unnerving. Jillybean had never heard of a smart...or rather a smart-ish monster before. The repercussions were awful. "He can work a doorknob; that's really dangerous. Wait, he isn't a naked monster is he?" The thirteen nodded in unison, a few of the younger girls making faces of disgust as they did. Jillybean sighed dramatically in relief. "Well then, that's good. He can't hurt you now. I…"

The boy with the bat glared. "Good? How can you say that? He is the single most dangerous zombie anyone has ever seen."

That wasn't true for Jillybean. Zombie Joe had been a scary one alright; scarier than most, however she had encountered a giant monster once, locked in a school gym. The thing had been nearly seven feet in height and was over three hundred pounds with a head the size of a pumpkin. It hadn't needed to know how to work a doorknob to get through any door ever made.

She was just about to tell the story of the giant monster when the boy went on: "Zombie Joe killed my dad and it killed Monica's dad, too, and he had a gun."

This brought up a dozen more questions in Jillybean mind but she bit them back. "I'm sorry to hear about all your daddies but I only meant that it's ok because I killed Mister Zombie Joe. He was a tough one and all but he's dead now so you don't have to worry about him none."

The boy with the metal bat cracked a half-smile that didn't have any joy or laughter in it. Jillybean hated those kinds of smiles; they weren't smiles in her eyes; they were looks of hate. "You killed Zombie Joe? You killed…"

Lynette, the tall girl with the sharp-edged haircut interrupted him. "Johnny stop. She's just a little girl."

Johnny's hateful smile dipped for a moment before it came back greater than before. He tapped the bat on the thinly carpeted church floor and asked: "Are you saying that because she's small she's allowed to lie? She's… what's your name?"

Jillybean was loath to answer. She knew Johnny would make fun of her name; he had the bullying sort of look in his eyes. Resolutely, she said: "My name is Jillybean. Jilly-bean, and yes, I killed Zombie Joe. He's east of here at this house I slept at last night. He was a tough one, but not so tough as all that. He might could use a doorknob but that didn't make him a genius. A genius is what means someone who's real smart."

"I know what a genius is," Johnny answered. "And there's no way that you killed him."

"Come see," she answered right back. "I killed him with my rope."

This declaration didn't do a thing to change Johnny's mind. The other children looked ready to believe Jillybean, but she saw it as mostly just a wild hope. She found their fear and Johnny's disbelief annoying.

The little girl turned on her heel and headed for the door. She was no longer afraid of the "witch." The children were clearly jumping at shadows; understandable since there weren't any grownups around; understandable but still annoying.

"Ya-ya-you're g-going out there?" Ryan asked. Before Jillybean knew it, the boy had hold of her torn up monster coat, easily holding her back. In spite of the nervous-sounding stutter and his skinny frame, he was resolute and had an air of toughness to him. "Ya-ya-you ha-have n-n-nothing to prove."

That was the opposite of truth. She had something very important to prove; the children needed to see the body of Zombie Joe. They needed to see it in order to get beyond their fear.

"It's ok," she said, pulling his hand off of her. She walked straight out the door. Behind her, the children glanced around, giving each other silent looks of warning that read: *We shouldn't go out there*. Johnny didn't heed the looks and marched after Jillybean. Ryan followed right behind. The rest came on in a clump.

Jillybean's internal compass was unerring and she cut straight east. Her only fear was that the monster she had killed the evening before had got up and walked away—a phenomenon that was perfectly possible in a land where monsters and perhaps even witches roamed the streets.

Zombie Joe was still there, slumped against the clothesline pole, naked save for the one boot, his face slowly going black. "Is that him?" She certainly hoped so. She didn't like the idea of facing a tougher monster than this one had been.

"Ya-ya-yes," Ryan said after a few tries.

Johnny agreed: "Yeah, but you didn't kill him. You found him like this, didn't you? That's a professional knot. Like a sailor would make."

A sigh escaped Jillybean. With a roll of her eyes, she whipped out her bowie. There was a worn length of twine that sagged between the twin T-shaped poles; she had given the twine a quick look the day before when she realized that there was no way she was going to get back her twenty feet of nylon rope. After only a glance, she hadn't bothered with the twine. It was half-rotted through and wasn't good for anything besides a demonstration.

She had to leap to cut it off the Ts, but once it was down, she tied a slip knot from memory; the noose was done in three seconds. She then fastened the free end of the twine to one of the poles, scouted around on the ground for the pins that Zombie Joe had dislodged when he had been snagged and clipped the new noose in place.

Johnny stood across from her. "Come at me like a monster would," she said. What would happen if he did was patently obvious. His smile now looked a little sick and he didn't budge.

"Sh-sh-shhhee did it," Ryan said. "Zzzz—ombie J-Joe is dead!" He'd been loud with enthusiasm but the others cheered in a very muted manner. *The witch*, Jillybean guessed. They were still afraid of it.

"I was wrong," Johnny admitted. "That was really impressive. You...you really don't have any people with you? No grownups?"

Should she tell the truth, that even grownups weren't safe around her? Or should she lie? If she lied, they'd want her to stay. Hell, they needed her to stay. "No...I don't have any people with me. I can be insane sometimes. That's what means crazy. They say its past-chromatic stress in order but it's just craziness, I know."

"That's post-traumatic stress disorder," Lynette said, "and I think we all have it at least a little bit."

Again, the gaggle of children nodded, looking even more like the cast of *Oliver Twist*. It was obvious they needed help, perhaps even her help but she didn't think she was in the position to help anyone. There was no telling how many of them would die if she did. Hoping that she was reading the situation wrong, she asked: "So where are all of your grode-ups?"

5

The answer wasn't surprising.

"Dead," Lynette replied, dropping her chin, letting her linear locks fall before her eyes. All of the children followed suit and stared at the puddles leaping with sky-tears and more than one ran a soggy sleeve across their noses.

The oldest child went on to tell a tale that could be sadly repeated by almost all the children left alive in the world: parents who gave up their lives to save them, slavers always on their heels, their dwindling group constantly on the move, constantly in danger as they fled from place to place. Bandits taking everything they had, and rapists taking their virtue when there was nothing else.

And of course, monsters.

One thing was different: the witch. Jillybean was suddenly nervous again. She glanced around at the forest; it hung with Halloween mists. "Does she do magic?" she asked. Most of the children nodded emphatically. They seemed eager for the tale to be over with so that they could get back inside where it was safe and dry. Channeling an old friend, Jillybean added: "Talk and walk," as she headed back toward town.

"She does magic," Johnny stated, striding next to Jillybean. "She can turn invisible. Dale saw her just, poof, disappear two weeks ago. Tell her Dale." Dale was the boy with the wood bat who had accosted her along with Ryan and Johnny at the front of the church. He answered only in a nod.

Johnny frowned at the lack of an answer and told the story: "She put out her hand and Mrs. Williams was floating there right in the middle of the forest, her legs kicking like a foot off the ground. It was just like Darth Vader, you know what I mean? Like she was using the freaking force. But then she saw Dale and *poof* she was gone."

Poof? Was that possible? And what was Darth Vader? Jillybean had no frame of reference for something called Darth Vader, though it was an ominous sounding name.

Jillybean was quiet, considering all of this though mostly she dwelt on the concept of invisibility. Her train of thought was more like a line of toppling dominoes that leapt gaps. First there were monsters when her daddy had told her there were none. Then there was the destruction of the world when everyone knew that could never happen. Then the monsters could think? Zombie Joe hadn't done much thinking that was true but it had done more than any other monster had ever done, possibly it had done more thinking than all of them combined.

And now a witch. Jillybean's mind lacked the maturity and the scientific base necessary to discount the idea of a witch out of hand; for her it was a possibility, though a remote one. They had marched back into town and were up the steps of the church when Jillybean asked: "Where did this happen?"

Thirteen hands shot up to point to the southwest where the woods were particularly heavy. "I was going to go fishing in the river," Dale explained, "and the witch and Mrs. Williams were on the other bank."

The idea of fishing and the river in general were facts that weren't facts to the girl. They weren't important. What was important was the distance between Dale and the witch, the depth of the woods as an obscuring factor to an eyewitness and lastly this force business. What sort of force was it? What...

One of the smaller girls, one that was only several inches taller than Jillybean slipped past with her head down and her hands close to her chest. She was afraid to touch Jillybean which was very odd.

Jillybean watched her walk into the church and go to one of the pews where the girl picked up a stuffed animal —a penguin. "Where did you get that?" Jillybean asked, sharply, forgetting for the moment the witch and the train of thought she'd been on.

The girl clutched the toy as though afraid that tiny Jillybean would bully it away from her. "The river," she said defensively. "It just floated by."

"That river?" Jillybean asked, pointing to the south side of town. The girl nodded and Jillybean's eyes went huge as she dug out her map and studied it. There was no river anywhere near Rippling, at least on her map. "There's a bridge on Spring Hollow Road about four miles east of here. Is that the same river as this one?"

Everyone looked to Lynette, who shrugged and answered: "I think so."

"It has to be," Jillybean said, striding forward to look at the penguin. She thought it very *likely* that this was one of the penguins she had thrown in the river the afternoon before. Likely, but not definitive. Toy penguins, much like their real life counterparts, looked very similar to each other.

Jillybean was just thinking that she should have put her initials on the stuffed animals she had thrown into the river when a new thought entered her mind: Maybe Ipes had been fished out of the water as well.

"How long have you been here?" she asked. "In this town?" She could feel the *crazy* inside of her bubbling up good and hot, and it must have shown on her face.

Lynette looked wary as she answered: "About two months. Why?"

Two months! That meant they were here when Ipes was thrown into the river. "And have there been any other stuffed animals in the river? A zebra? A little one with a fat belly and a big nose. His name is Ipes and he had on dark blue shorts and a lighter blue shirt that said *So Cute* across the front."

The crazy had her advancing on the much bigger Lynette, who stepped back despite the difference in their size. "No," Lynette said.

LIAR! A voice screamed in Jillybean's head. *She's lying. They're hiding him. You need to search the church.*

The voice wasn't familiar. It was a new one and a loud one. Nothing much frightened Jillybean anymore but right

73

then she was white as a ghost. The voice scared her something bad. She did her best to ignore the voice, but all the same her eyes swept around the church. Sleeping bags on the floor. Backpacks littered about. Clothes in heaps. Cardboard boxes near the fireplace. The place smelled of feet, except for one of the sleeping bags which smelled of urine. No zebra.

They've hidden him! Ipes is here!

The other children were staring at her; they hadn't heard the voice even though it spoke in a hurricane scream. The voice scared her mainly because she didn't know who it belonged to. It could be anyone...or anything. There were demons inside of her, after all.

Jillybean forced a smile onto her face. "Ok, good. I—I was just asking. Anyways, this woman who died from the Darth force, where is her body? I should look at it." There would be facts associated with the body, facts that would let Jillybean know whether this was a real witch. Just then she needed hard facts to take her mind off the voice.

"The witch took her," Johnny said. "She always takes her victims. She eats them. Sometimes we can smell burnt hair."

This pronouncement took the focus off of Jillybean; the children were all looking at the floor. "How...how many have there been?" Jilly asked.

Reluctantly, Johnny answered: "Eight. First, she got the last of the grownups and now she's after us kids. I think we should run away but Ryan and Lynette won't let us." Lynette just glared but Ryan started to say something however he was so upset that he could only make a continuous Bu-bu-bu sound. Finally, Johnny explained: "Lynette's mother and Ryan's dad left to scrounge guns and gas a few weeks ago."

Again, Ryan started to say something. Lynette interpreted for him: "They'll be back. I know it. I'm not going to run away and have them searching all over the state for me."

Jillybean thought that they were crazier than she was. Eight people killed in eight weeks? The number seemed high except when she considered the mortality rate of her own group over the last couple of months or if she thought about the mass death over the past year. Still, she would've left and she planned on leaving, just as soon as she found Ipes.

He would help get rid of the voice in her head.

"Well," she said. "That's brave of you guys to stay." She started for the doors, stopping only to pick up the leaf that Lynette had pull from her hair.

Lynette hurried after her and pulled Jillybean around. "Where do you think you're going?" Lynette asked.

"To find a friend. I really shouldn't kill this witch of yours. I...I...it's not good for me. Sorry."

"Who said anything about you killing the witch?" Lynette asked. "I'm worried about the witch killing you. There's no way you should go out there, especially all alone."

Jillybean shrugged off the hand. Her need to be around people was diminishing with every passing second. "Why not? She was out there." With a jut of her chin, Jillybean indicated Renee, the girl in the granny glasses. Renee ducked her head in embarrassment.

"She has a shy bladder," Lynette explained. "She can't go to the bathroom with people around. It's a medical issue."

It sounded like a mental issue, just like Ryan's stutter and whoever was wetting their bed. It also sounded like someone else's problem. Jillybean couldn't get involved and she knew she would if she stayed. She would want to help them and she would end up killing again; it would only make the voice in her head worse than it was.

"Either way, I'm not ascared of your witch and I do have to get going. If I see anyone's mom or dad, I'll tell them that you're all here waiting for them." No one stopped her as she headed to the door this time. If they had known what she was capable of, they would have begged her to stay; they would have begged her to kill the witch. Instead, all they saw was a weird little girl who was going to get herself killed.

75

"Good luck," Lynette said.

Jillybean put her hands in her hair and muffed it so that it went everywhere. She then tied the leaf back into it once more and answered: "You, too."

6

With the rain washing away the mud from her face, Jillybean had to walk with her hair in front of her eyes, making it difficult to see. The sound of the rain pelting down made it difficult to hear. The water scrubbing the air made it difficult to smell.

She was in a dangerous spot and she knew it.

In all likelihood the witch was safe and warm in her witch hovel, wherever that was, and so it was monsters that she had most to fear—and she really didn't fear them all that much. The day before, she would have said she didn't fear them at all; however her experience with Zombie Joe had made her a little gun shy.

She moaned with greater gusto and she lurched through the sucking mud in a perfect imitation of a little monster, of which there were plenty in the world. Catering to her safety first mindset, she went slowly and it was two hours before she reached the bridge that she had cast the stuffed animals from.

Swaying gently in the downpour, she gazed out over the river. Somewhere along its path, the river took a hard right and went due west; she would find out where, unless by some miracle she found Ipes first.

Crossing the bridge, she meandered, zombie-like down to the banks and started making her way downstream, following the rushing water. From a scientific point of view, the rain was screwing up her test results. If Ipes had filled with water and sunk to the bottom, she might never know where. Or if he had snagged on an overhanging branch, he might have been pushed free and be halfway to the Mississippi by now.

Still she had to try.

It was terribly slow going. Even if she hadn't been in monster-mode, the swampy banks would have made things a challenge. As it was, it took her four hours just to pull even with the town of Rippling once more and in all that time she found only one stuffed animal.

One of the penguin twins was face first in the reeds— none of its white belly was visible. She thought it was only a cloud-shadowed rock at first, but then she saw it bobbing slightly and, as everyone knew, rocks didn't bob, they sank.

It was depressing, worrisome and very confusing. Even with the rain, the river really wasn't much more than a stream and in some places, it was almost a brook. There should have been more evidence of the stuffed animals. It wasn't until Jillybean was a mile further on from where she had surprised Renee that she came across another stuffed animal.

And it wasn't even in the river.

A game trail ran up to the river and, hoping to see a baby deer or a baby wolf, Jillybean peered through her bedraggled hair and saw a splash of color in all the dreary grayness of the day. It was the toucan!

She did not react. If the trees had eyes, they would have seen only a little zombie standing in the rain. Jillybean did not go down the trail; that would have been suicide. No animal and no monster had moved the toucan. Only a human could have and only the witch had any reason to. According to Disney, witches ate little girls.

Jillybean might have looked like a dull monster standing in the rain but she was thinking furiously, her entire body a taut spring, ready to race out of there at top Jilly-rabbit speed. No witch ever made would be able to catch her. But Jillybean did not want to run for two reasons. To start with, she was eaten up with curiosity about the witch. Was there really such thing as a witch? Was magic possible? Could she use this Darth Force to lift people in the air...or was it all a sham? She had to know.

The second reason that she didn't run was because she still wasn't afraid. She was nervous, that was true, but afraid? No. In her time, she had pitted her wits against a mad scientist, an even madder cult leader, a River King, an entire family of royal evilness, two different bounty hunters, and her most challenging opponent: her own diabolical mind.

She did not think that someone stooping to trickery, which she suspected was what the witchcraft business was really all about, could match up to her level of genius.

This was why she continued slowly down the river for another sixty yards until the deer trail was well out of sight. Only then did she slip away from the bank and move with surprising stealth back toward the game trail. Every step was calculated to keep her in the shadows and to keep her away from any ambush points.

It took thirty minutes to traverse a hundred yards and the day was growing darker, but she was able to move right up to the trap without being seen. The game trail opened up into a small glade and right in the middle of the glade was a wooden chair that had once sat in someone's kitchen and on the wooden chair sat Ipes the Zebra, looking altogether miserable.

The trap had been set with amazing specificity. She was its only target. Seeing Ipes sitting there was like magic, white magic and the blackest of black magic. She wanted to run to him and at the same time she wanted to run away, knowing that she had made the biggest mistake of her life.

Don't Jillybean, it's a trap! Ipes cried. She had been about to run away, however the voice in her head stopped her feet. It was such a welcome voice that she faltered; it was like a mother hearing her baby's heartbeat after it had been declared stillborn. It turned her insides to jelly and it took another cry from Ipes to get her moving: *Run before it's too late!*

Jillybean ran, and it was almost too late. A hulking figure was crashing through the forest heading in from the very direction she had come from. Another was seen through the rain fifty yards to her right and a third, fifty yards to her left—she was being hemmed in, leaving her with the one choice of dashing into the clearing where she feared the hidden dangers just as much as these brutes closing in.

She ran into the clearing, but not toward Ipes and nor did she run for the game trail; she sped straight across the clearing where the edge was bordered by a clump of rhododendron. She was down in the mud in a flash, zipping beneath the broad, slightly waxy leaves like a squirrel with a fox on her tail.

It wasn't a deep bush and she was almost to the other side when she saw a print. Not a shoe print, or a footprint...it was a knee print. Someone of great weight had hollowed out an irregular bowl-shaped print there recently. There was only one reason for someone to have knelt on the other side of the bush like that: another trap had been laid.

Now that she was looking for it, Jillybean saw the trap: a tension snare. There was the wire hoop, almost invisible among the foliage, and there was the anchor, holding the trap down until she had her head right in the noose, and there, bent well over was a birch sapling capable of hauling Jillybean into the air by her neck.

The trap was impossible. Whoever had set it must have known that Jillybean would bypass the game trail and ignore Ipes sitting on the chair. Whoever set this trap must have known Jillybean would come right through this exact spot. That sort of foreknowledge spoke of a keen intellect, perhaps one even keener than her own.

"Oh jeeze," Jillybean whispered, real fear squirming in her belly.

Her first instinct was to crawl to the right away from the trap; however, Jillybean was not an instinct kind of girl. Whoever set the trap, the witch probably, would guess that she would go either left or right, but not straight ahead. Going straight through the trap was counterintuitive.

Jillybean reached out a bold paw and swiped at the trap, knocking the precariously balanced anchor and releasing the birch. There was a sound like a whip snapping and then came a rain of leaves on Jillybean's head as she crawled through the last of the bush. Then she was in the open and running...for three steps and then the leaf-covered forest floor just disappeared beneath her feet and she was falling.

7

She landed in mud covered over with several inches of rainwater. It wasn't a deep pit she found herself in; probably just a hair over seven feet. Seven feet or twenty, there was no she could get out of it, not without her rope that was still wrapped around the neck of ole Zombie Joe.

"Think!" she hissed to herself. In her pack were three books, her flashlight, a few cans of soup, a few feet of string that would never support her and a number of other odds and ends, none of which were weapons or a miniature ladder that she could extend to get out of the pit.

Still, she was not beaten yet. She dropped down and felt the floor of the pit. Besides the mud, she pulled up the leaves and sticks and long grasses that had been used to build the fake covering of the trap. She'd been hoping for some sort of center beam but there wasn't one.

"Well, well, well," a woman's voice floated down. "What has the spider caught in its web?"

Quickly, Jillybean scooped up a heaping double handful of mud and threw it into her own face. She then began to growl and moan as any self-respecting hungry little monster should. She even clawed at the dirt and stared upward as if eager to get at what had to be the witch.

A tremendous beast of a woman came to stand at the edge of the pit. She was wrapped in shawls with a tent-like poncho thrown over them. It was the witch; nothing else could be so cruel and ugly. She sneered down at Jillybean showing wide gapped teeth and a tiny nose on a heavily jowled face.

"You can stop the act, Jillybean," she said.

Jillybean ceased her growling immediately. She had been caught dead to rights and there was no use trying to fool this person. "How do you know my name and how come you have Ipes?"

The witch smiled, likely in the same manner an alligator would, if one could. "Oh, I know you, Jillybean. I know what you did to that fool the River King. I was even there when you killed his bounty hunter." The witch laughed at Jillybean's shocked expression. "Yes. You weren't subtle. The radio was alight with all sorts of interesting conversations that day, so I crept up out of my woods to see the fun and who should show up but you and that stupid man. I got to watch you kill him."

A shudder ran up Jillybean's back. It hadn't been her that had killed the bounty hunter, it had been one the voices living in her head. That *other girl* had really enjoyed killing the hunter and she had laughed when she had killed two of the River King's men, shooting them right in the back a few minutes later.

"And Ipes? Why do you have him?"

"Don't pretend to be stupid. You know I kept him as bait. I was hoping you would come back for him. The real question is why did I want you to come back?" Jillybean knew the ugly old witch would tell whether she asked or not and so she remained quiet. The witch already knew too much for Jillybean to be giving away any more free information.

Her silence did not anger the witch. Far from it, she beamed. "You are everything I hoped you'd be. You should have seen yourself run my maze. I built this maze just for you. Really just to test you. I needed to see if you were as smart as the rumors suggested."

Jillybean looked around at the pit and said: "I guess not."

"You guess..." The witch broke down, almost crying with laughter. "You guessed wrong! There are thirty traps all up in these woods and you got caught in the very last one. I was beginning to think I wasn't going to get you. Trust me, anyone with even average intelligence would have been caught nine ways from Sunday. You blasted through my maze, making every right decision there was to make. Except for this one."

"You still haven't told me why you wanted me," Jillybean said.

"I was getting there...hold on." The witch stepped back from the lip of the pit. There was a wet cracking sound of something heading toward the pit. "Stay! Stay, Gary. Good boy." The witch reappeared, still wearing the ugly, gloating smile. "You're here because I need you. I need to make the perfect zombie and you will be her."

This didn't scare Jillybean as much as it perplexed her. There was no way she would make a good monster; she was simply too small. She'd have trouble killing anything larger than an armadillo.

"Yes, you," the witch said, seeing the skepticism. "Remember Zombie Joe? Guess who made him? I did. He was my first experiment at making a newer, better kind of zombie."

Jillybean was almost too stunned to speak but she was just able to spit out: "W-Why would you want to make any kind of zombie?"

"Don't be daft. The zombies are a resource and anyone who can control them can control the world."

Jillybean shook her head. "It's been tried by the Azael and they failed."

"They failed because of you, Jillybean. I know the entire story. But where they tried just to herd the zombies, I'm trying to shape their minds."

"They don't have minds," Jillybean said, but then remembered Zombie Joe. He understood more than he should have and his sight and sense of hearing was greater than any other monster she had come across.

"They *could* have minds," the witch explained. "The virus doesn't destroy their minds. It changes them, it turns them hyper-aggressive, but it doesn't destroy their minds, at least not completely. In my experiments I've found that it's the zombie fever that destroys ninety percent of a person's brain tissue. If you can control a person's fever as they turn, then the subsequent zombie retains a greater than average intellect...greater than the average zombie, I should say."

Jillybean pictured the witch working in a lab with a thousand beakers and test tubes and hissing smoke-filled pipes. She could guess how she would make her monsters: innocent people strapped to gurneys covered in ice before they were injected with the virus. "You use ice?"

"Yes and fever reducing medicines. And it works. Watch. Gary! Come!" There was a shuffling of feet in the leaves and then a monster came to stand at the lip of the pit. Any normal monster would've fallen right in, however Gary kept his toes well back. He was naked from the waist down and wearing a stained Christmas sweater up top.

On his neck was a bulky collar.

"Gary, sit," the witch ordered. Gary had the yellow eyes of a monster but they were sharper and focused—he was looking at a little box in the witch's hand. He sat down, awkwardly, yes, but he still sat. "Up, Gary." He stood.

"Like a dog," Jillybean said, dismissively.

The sneer swept across the witch's cruel features again before she could hide it behind her smile. "Yes and no. He'll attack and kill on command. He was the one who dug this pit. He's a servant and a guard dog, but just think if I had an army just like him? Those idiots in that little town are providing me with all the cannon fodder I need to get started. I have six of their parents chained up in my basement and it's only a matter of time before I get the rest. But just think if I had someone even smarter?"

She gazed pointedly at Jillybean. "That's why I want you. The smarter someone is going into the process, the smarter they are coming out."

Jillybean stomach began to hurt. She shook her head as if she had a choice and the witch laughed. "There's only one way out of that pit and that's if you agree to be my pet. If you don't, I'll send Gary in there to eat you alive. He's so well trained that he'll start on your toes and eat upward. You'll be alive a long, long, long, painful time, little miss.

Think about that. The alternative is significantly better. The way I turn you, it'll barely hurt. It's much more humane."

The little girl's head began to spin and she was afraid that she was going to swoon. "So, what's it going to be?" the witch asked. Somehow Jillybean found it in her to shake her head a second time.

"Maybe I should give you some time to think about what a great opportunity this is. An hour or two in this pit will change your mind and, as an added bonus, it'll get your body temperature down. Now, throw your bag up here and no funny business or I'll send Gary in. Come on, let's have the bag. Who knows what you have in there?"

Without a choice, Jillybean tossed up the bag. The witch rifled through it, grinning at the choice of books and then tossed it aside. "And your knife. Yes, I saw you pull it on that ridiculous girl, earlier." The witch stepped out of sight. Jillybean sighed and then chucked the knife out of the pit. She didn't throw it to hurt the witch, she threw in a high arc in the direction of the town of Rippling on the off chance that if she could escape she could pick it up as she ran...or that someone might come along and find it and figure out that she was in need of rescuing.

"That was stupid," the witch said, rolling her eyes. "I'm going in where it's warm but I won't leave you all alone. Gary will guard you. Gary, come."

The witch had her own bag and from it she took a length of rope. "Turn around, Gary. Good boy. Guard and no feed! Guard and no feed!" She tied Gary to a tree, leaving plenty of slack in the rope for him to walk all around the pit. "We've done this before. He'll only eat you if you try to escape, which I don't imagine that you could, but just in case, right? I'll see you in one hour."

The simple words: *No feed* did not instill much confidence in Jillybean. In fact none at all when the witch left and Gary came to stand at the edge of the pit with a murderous hungry look in his yellow eyes. Summoning her courage, Jillybean ordered in her fiercest voice: "Go away, Gary! Go to the trees, Gary!"

Gary the monster wasn't very bright. He looked confused and then took a few steps away. Jillybean craned her neck well back and couldn't see him. "Yeah," she whispered. It was the smallest of victories and didn't seem to amount to much, especially since she was still stuck in the pit with no way out.

She took stock of her possessions: her ripped-up monster coat, her Keds, her jeans, her sweater, her two-foot long belt, a razor blade stitched into the belt just at the small of her back, and a paper clip tied up in her hair.

All useless for escaping a pit.

"I could..." Nothing came to her, except the idea of using the razor blade on her own wrists, unfortunately that would only attract Gary who would be overcome with bloodlust and eat her before she could die an easier death.

"Great, I've figured out how to attract a monster. Now that's genius. If only I had my bowie, I'd be able to dig a staircase." She could envision a rude set of stairs carved in the dirt...and she could also envision the rain turning those stairs to mush.

Depression swept her as did fear and the cold realization that she couldn't think her way out of the pit. Her legs went jelly and she sunk into the cold mud. One of the sticks jabbed her in the butt and in anger she threw it at the wall of the pit where it bounced back and nearly bonked her on the head. She began to cry, her tears mixing so well with the rainwater that no one would have known. No one but the voice she had heard earlier. It began to grow in her mind, stirring up echoes.

It was an awful, voice, whispering hate and revenge. She hated all the voices inside of her, all of them except Ipes.

"Ipes!" she screamed at the top of her lungs. "Ipes!" There was no answer, except from Gary, who came back to the edge of the pit to look down on her and moan in hunger. "Go away, Gary." Gary looked indecisive as though its hunger was winning out over its training. Jillybean leapt to her feet and brandished the stick, crying: "Get out of here, Gary!"

It ambled away and Jillybean in her grief and anger stabbed the wall with the stick. The tip sank in three inches and just like that, something clicked in her mind. An idea began to form and her brain began to process information faster and faster. She stood there in the deepest concentration, forgetting the cold and the setting sun. Her mind seemed to open up and expand. It grew so much that the hated voice was nothing in comparison, blotted out as the rudimentary idea became a bold plan.

8

In a flash, she dropped to her knees and began scouting around in the mud, pulling up the sticks that had been woven together to make the false cover of the pit. Sticks alone wouldn't cut it. Alone they were too weak. And they were blunt. They'd have to be driven deep into the dirt and she was not strong enough using just her skinny arms.

When she had a dozen sticks, she then looked for a rock. There had to be at least one. No one dug a pit in this part of Missouri without running into a bajillion rocks, but for some reason she could only find one and it barely fit into her palm. It was almost too small to fit her need and that meant she had to get creative.

The razor blade came out and she began to whittle the ends of the sticks into points, dulling the blade, making her more and more nervous with each pass. She needed the razor as sharp as possible.

When the twelve sticks were spiky, she began wrapping them, two per bundle with the long grasses that had acted as the weave of the pit cover. These were her stairs. She then hammered them with the rock into the dirt at a forty five degree angle, uncaring that Gary might hear; even if he came to investigate, he wasn't smart enough to figure out what she was doing and besides, she was running out of time. She had to get out of the pit and back to Rippling before her hour was up and before the dark came. Already there wasn't much light in the pit.

Once the stakes were hammered into the corner of the pit: two on the left and two on the right, Jillybean brought out the razor blade once more. Blood attracted monsters, everyone knew that. She pulled off her monster coat, tied it in a bundle with its own sleeves, and hunched over it so that she was blocking it from the rain. She then sliced her own forearm open in one quick motion.

The pain was a shriek that went up her arm and she wanted to cry and wail like any seven-year-old would when there was a three-inch long gash in their flesh. She only allowed herself a whimper as she bled freely into the coat. When it was soaked red, she started climbing: seven feet was not high when one had a ladder, even a makeshift one and in seconds she was just below the lip of the grass.

There was no way she could risk peeking her head up to see where Gary was; she had to pop up and throw in one motion and hope to God he was near enough to smell the blood on the coat, but not so near that he smelled it on her.

With her freezing hands turning to blunt clubs on the stubbed ends of the stakes, she pushed herself up the final four inches so that her head was just above the lip. There was no hesitation on her part. Gary was eight feet away, hunched against the rain and turned slightly away. The bundled coat went flying to land almost at his feet and she was back down a quarter second later, praying that Gary would go for the coat and not wonder where it had come from.

If he didn't go for the coat that would mean a chase, one that she didn't think she could win, especially since it would begin with Jillybean having to clamber the rest of the way out of the pit.

There was a snarl and a growl and the sound of cloth being torn—Gary had gone for the coat. This was Jillybean's only chance and it really wasn't much of one. Gary was so close and if he was anything like Zombie Joe, he would be fast.

I just have to be faster, Jillybean thought to herself. In a rush of adrenaline, she pushed off the stick ladder only to hear something snap beneath her right foot. The sticks had broken beneath her! Stifling a cry, she flung out her hands and grabbed the edge of the pit, holding on to the grass with all of her puny strength.

Gary was right there, so close, so very close. He had his head dug down deep in the bloody coat and, for the moment, he was too distracted to see the girl clinging to the edge of the pit. Her feet began scrambling at the wall, desperate for purchase, however the earth had turned to slick mud; leaving her practically running in place.

Panic wanted to set in. It wanted to cloud her thinking and take over her mind. If it did, Jillybean would soon be dead; already her breathing had picked up and was loud in her own ears. She knew one thing that would stop her fear and, oddly enough, that one thing was math. More than once in her life she had used math to occupy her mind in order to battle soul-crushing fear.

What's the area of a square, five feet on a side? she asked herself. *Too easy: twenty-five square feet. What about the pit? What was its area?* Again, it was a snap. *Six feet by eight gave an area of forty-eight.*

It wasn't working. The math was too simple and she didn't have the time to explore more difficult equations. Her brain started to splutter and useless math facts crowded together: *volume of the pit-three hundred and thirty-six, A squared plus B squared equals C squared, the angles of the rectangular pit are ninety degrees and together their sum equals...*

Angles!

Her mind clicked on the word and immediately she stopped uselessly flailing at the flat, muddy wall. Her fear was gone and in its place was cool deliberation: the only way to get up was to use the angles created by the junction of the two walls. First, she pushed up and to the left with her right foot and then up and to the right with her left. She repeated this twice more and in a second she was able to throw her right foot over the lip of the pit and scramble to her feet.

Somewhere in there she had grunted. It hadn't been much of a sound, but Gary had heard it. His head swung up, showing lips smeared with Jillybean's blood. Time seemed to jump forward by a second or two. Jillybean found herself up and dashing away in a sprint that would have left any other monster far behind, but Gary was different.

His coordination was almost as good as a human's and his strength twice that. He was so close to catching her that she could smell his hot putrid breath on her neck and in her periphery, she could see his clawed hand reach out...but then there came a *twang!* and a grunt and a thump.

Gary had been brought up short by his collar. He was straining at it like a dog on a leash, snapping and growling.

"Yes," Jillybean said, standing just out of reach, her fear calming by degrees. "Just like a dog. A mean one." She liked animals very much, however she didn't like mean ones. No not at all.

She had to get going to warn the children that they were in much more danger than they realized, but first, she had to take care of this mean dog. Looking around, she saw the glint of her bowie knife. It wasn't a weapon to use against a creature as terrible as Gary was, however it could be used to create one.

In a minute she had found the largest stick she could carry. It was long and when she had hacked the end into a point, it was basically a spear. She took it to where Gary was still growling and going crazy at the end of his leash. She then ran to her right and Gary ran parallel just as she knew he would; his yellowed eyes never leaving her face.

She then started racing back the other way as fast as she could, only to stop suddenly. Gary recovered slower and charged back, only to be brought up short by the spear. Jillybean had planted its butt against the jutting root of a nearby maple and held the shaft at an angle so that Gary impaled himself. The spear went deeper than Jillybean could ever have stabbed with her skinny arms; it ruptured his diaphragm and punctured a two-inch wide hole in the lower ventricles of the heart.

People misunderstood monsters and thought that the only way to kill them was to cut off their heads or shoot them in the brain, however Jillybean knew they could die in other ways as well. There wasn't anything magical about their cellular structure and their brain cells died just as easily as that of a human's when deprived of oxygen.

With Gary's heart torn open, it ceased to beat and blood ceased to flow to what was left of its brain and, gradually, Gary died.

Jillybean was long gone by the time Gary pitched over on his side and breathed his last. The little girl threw away all pretense. She could not waste a minute pretending to be a monster, or worrying about being stealthy. She had to warn the others; she had to get them away from Rippling as fast as she could.

Since she was already soaking wet and practically freezing, she didn't bother trying to cross the river where it was shallow and the stones had their backs humped up out of the water; she simply splashed through taking the most direct path to the church.

It was the beginning of an early twilight by the time she arrived, panting and shaking from cold and hunger. The doors were locked. "Open up!" she said in a hissing whisper as she thumped them with her tiny fist. She was afraid to be any louder for fear that her voice would carry into the woods. "Please, open up."

The witch wasn't a witch, the little girl was certain of that, and yet the old hag seemed to know too much about Jillybean. It was almost as if the witch could read her mind. Did she know that Jillybean had killed her guard-monster? Did she know that Jillybean had escaped? Was she coming to get her right then?

Jillybean turned as she thumped the door, her eyes scanning the shadows behind her and trying to pierce the rain. She was still turned away when the door opened suddenly, nearly spilling her onto the carpet.

"Well, well, well," a cruel voice spoke as a sharp-nailed hand closed on her arm. The witch wasn't coming to get her, she was already there.

9

There was no time for math to help her fight her fear. Seeing the witch and the giant shotgun she had pitched up on her shoulder, and the two monsters that had herded the other children into a corner was enough to freeze Jillybean's heart. It literally felt like a lump of solid ice in her chest.

The witch grinned at Jillybean's stricken face. "It's always a surprise with you, little miss," she said before taking Jillybean by the arm and spinning her around. Her pack was yanked off and her bowie snatched from its sheath. "I was going to surprise you," the witch hissed in her ear. "I figured you would be all about cooperation when I was skinning your friends alive." She spun Jillybean back around and was about to say something nasty when her eyes went big, staring down at Jillybean's arm. "Did Gary do that?"

Jillybean had forgotten about the cut she had given herself. Glancing down, she saw the line in her flesh; it was far too perfect to have been made by a monster. It took a moment for her to find her tongue: "No. How would he have done that?"

"So, you slipped and cut yourself?" the witch asked and for some reason she wore a grin that suggested superiority, as though this minor "mistake" made up for the fact that Jillybean had escaped her neat little trap. Jillybean didn't correct her.

"Gary is dead, by the way," Jillybean said as if going tit for tat, when she was actually trying to undermine the witch's confidence. Ipes would have approved. He preferred psychological attacks rather than physical ones —they were a lot safer. Jillybean wanted desperately to ask about Ipes. She hadn't looked in the clearing for him after killing Gary. There had been no time and no light to see all the traps by.

And then there was the fact that he hadn't answered when she had called. It could only mean that the witch had taken him.

Or it means he's nothing but a stuffed animal and you are crazy as a loon. It was that unknown voice again, the one that she feared. It was as cruel as the witch who was staring at Jillybean with a curl to her lip. She couldn't seem to come to grips with the idea that a tiny little girl had killed as ferocious a monster as Gary had been.

Finally, she spun Jillybean roughly around and shoved her hard against the wall. "Hank, come!" Hank, one of the monsters, came up to the witch and stood eyeing Jillybean as if she were a steak. Around his neck were a number of four-foot long lengths of chain. They were heavy looking and even heavier feeling when the witch wrapped one around Jillybean's neck and snapped a Master Lock on it.

The witch then went to each of the thirteen children and hung chains around their necks as well. She then began chaining them together with more of the locks. Jillybean watched all of this with a secret hope. The locks were keyed locks, meaning she'd be able to pick them with the paperclip hidden in her fly-away brown hair.

When all fourteen children were chained in a row, the witch prodded them out into the rain with the barrel of her shotgun. Many of the kids cried and sniffled as they were marched across the river and through the forest.

"Stop your damned whining," the witch snapped. "There are still zombies in these woods who'll eat your faces off if you don't shut up." This quieted the children, though half of them still cried silent tears.

Just ahead of Jillybean in the line, Johnny only glared, grinding his teeth and opening and closing his fists. In front of him, Ryan walked with a more deliberate manner about him. Jillybean could see him noting landmarks and the direction in which they traveled. He also eyed the strange monsters that were under the thrall of the witch.

Their names were Hank and Erik. Erik wore a strange leather mask and had oven mitts taped to his hands. Jillybean guessed he wasn't as trained as Hank or Gary had been. The witch was constantly snapping at him and pointing her little black box at him. It had to be a remote control for the shock collar he wore.

Two miles in the cold rain was a long walk especially as Jillybean was already tired and cold. What made it worse were the kids chained in front and behind her; they each took turns tripping over every other log or rock, or so it seemed and each time they tripped they dragged Jillybean down by the neck.

It was a miserable trek and it was somewhat of a relief to see the rather impressive two-story home of the witch. It was tall and wide and very sturdily built. And although it was also dark and scary, it was dry. The children sagged in their chains and Jillybean could read their expressions: whatever torture lay ahead of them, at least they figured that it would be warmer than this.

She knew better; she knew about the icy deaths that they were being led to.

The witch threw open a cellar door and pointed into the dark beneath the house. Lynette, who was at the head of the chain, went first, slowly taking each step as if she expected to be attacked.

"Get your ass down there," snapped the witch. "Go!"

Jillybean was near the back and she took the time to study the house, the property around it, the consistency of the mud that formed the yard, the windows of the house, what sorts of rooms they likely belonged to, and the number and type of footprints around the house. Her mind began forming plans. Escaping such a place was not going to be easy.

They were forced into the cellar where the only light was the last of the twilight filtering in through little rectangles of dirty glass. The windows were all barred same as the cellar door, barred and locked. There was nothing inviting about the cellar. The ceiling was very low and the floor was cement with twenty years' worth of dust covering it.

There were pipes running along the ceiling, making the place seem even more crowded down and oppressive.

The older children had to walk stooped over as did the witch. With the two monsters staring at the children as though famished, the witch unlocked them one at a time and then dragged each away into the dark where there were little recessed areas like alcoves along the walls.

When it was Jillybean's turn she was led past a number of shadowy people chained in the dark. They stank of pee and poop and overwhelming fear. None said a word. They cowered despite the fact that they were grownups. Before Jillybean got to her little spot, she passed a staircase that led to the main floor. It was guarded by a monster who, like Erik, wore a mask and oven mitts. He too had a stiff leather collar from which he had his own length of chain that kept him held in place at the bottom of the stairs.

"This is Cain," the witch told Jillybean. "I wouldn't even think about trying to escape, he gets very excited and will maul you, mitts or no mitts." Cain was a real beast. His arms were bigger around than Jillybean's legs and he was crisscrossed with scars. He was also an annoying beast, growling constantly, hungrily.

"I want you to make yourself at home, Jillybean," the witch said as she chained the little girl to a ring bolt nailed into the wall. "I really want to make you perfect and there are still a few kinks to work out, so if you promise not to try to escape, I'll give you a few perks."

Jillybean couldn't imagine what sort of perk a witch could offer in a dungeon such as this. Thicker gruel, perhaps? "Like what?"

The witch smiled, her cruel toad smile as she said: "There are things I can do for you, but I'll let you live down in this squalor for a few days first so you'll appreciate the fact that you're special."

"I think I can appreciate it now," Jillybean answered in a meek and properly fearful voice, hoping to get the preferential treatment right off the bat. Despite the paperclip hidden in her hair and the dulled razor at the back of the belt, escape was beginning to feel like a far-fetched prospect.

Another of the awful grins crossed the witch's face. "You aren't fooling me. I know you're braver than you let on. I know you've been in the River King's dungeon and I know you escaped. Would you like to tell me how?"

She answered right away as if eager to please. "The bars were too far apart. I just slipped right through. It was really nothing." That was how the initial part of the escape occurred, the rest was far more complicated but what the witch didn't know...

"The bars were too far apart?" The witch seemed skeptical.

Jillybean nodded vigorously. "Yessum. They were made for grode ups, not for little kids." She put all of her innocence and sweetness into her explanation, however the witch wasn't moved. She started to turn away and in desperation, Jillybean cried out: "Where's Ipes?"

The evil toad smile crept back as if she had been waiting on exactly this question. "Give it a day or two. Be good and maybe we can talk about your zebra friend."

The witch left Jillybean to think about what it meant to be good. The little girl had a guess: sit quietly in the dark and hope that maybe, perhaps, possibly, IF she was "good" then she might catch a glimpse of her best friend.

"Ok!" Jillybean answered excitedly. "I'll be good. I promise."

The toad grin widened and then the witch disappeared into the murky dark. She thought that she had Jillybean over a barrel...and she was right.

Then give up, the nasty voice in her head hissed. *You should slit your wrists. It'll be easy and fun. Or you can hang yourself like Zombie Joe. How far will your neck stretch? A foot? Or will your head just pop off and roll around on...*

"Shut up," Jillybean said under her breath. "Go away."

No. You go away. Or better yet take out that razor blade and swallow it. Let it slide down your throat on a slick flow of blood and...

The little girl stuck her fingers in her ears and began to rock. It was important for her to keep calm...to keep sane.

She forced her mind to the matter of escaping. First, what did she know?

Jillybean had learned more about the witch than she had learned about Jillybean. All the witch had gleaned was that Jillybean had climbed out of a simple dirt pit and had killed her pet which had been chained by the neck, and she had escaped the River King by slipping through some widely spaced bars. In other words, nothing special. It probably seemed as though anyone could have done those things.

On the other hand, Jillybean had learned that the witch had seriously underestimated a seven-year-old. She had been shocked to the core when Jillybean had shown up at the church—the shock had been stamped on her face as if a weighted press had been smushed there. She had also believed Jillybean's story about how she had broken out of the River King's prisons as if wide bars had been the only obstacle she had faced. And she had also been clearly hooked by Jillybean's pleading about being good.

As well, Jillybean knew the exact number of the witch's minions. Even though she had counted five different footprints outside, there were only four sets of moanings within the house, and that included Cain. The fifth set of prints had been Gary's and he was dead.

She also knew that the witch had no witchy powers at all. She was just an ugly evil thing of a person; nothing Jillybean hadn't seen before.

But what did all of this knowledge get Jillybean? Not much compared to the obstacles before her. If Jillybean wanted to escape, all she had to do to was pick a very complicated and sturdy lock, kill another of the monsters, this one with the strength of a bull, slip up the stairs where three more monsters awaited her and then kill the witch, something that was going to be infinitely more difficult than just throwing water on her like how Dorothy killed the Wicked Witch of the East.

It was a very depressing list and hanging on the edge of it was the voice. It was still there.

Once the other children were chained in place, Jillybean stood and looked around, squinting in the dim light. Her chain was four feet in length, held in place by a Master Lock linking the chain to the ringbolt. A second lock held a loop of chain in place around her neck. She gave the chain as hardy a pull as her skinny arms could apply—it was like trying to pull down a mountain.

The chain was just long enough to allow her to lie down or stand. She could swing wide to visit her neighbors; on one side, was one of the littler girls. She was pale and blonde and three years older than Jillybean and half a foot taller. Despite all of this, she seemed like an infant compared to Jillybean. On her other side was Ryan.

He only stared around him into the shadows. He seemed shell-shocked by how quickly they had gone from a semi freedom to what could only be called a dungeon. When he looked Jillybean's way, it was with accusing eyes.

"Don't blame me," Jillybean said, giving her chain another pull. "The witch has been watching you guys all this time. She could have taken you guys whenever she wanted. And she has some of your parents."

Ryan perked up. "Who? Wh-who d-does shhhhe have?"

"I don't..."

What sounded like a lawn mower engine turning on filtered down from above, and immediately a feeble forty-watt bulb flickered on. It hung from the ceiling on a wire and showed the children just how terrible their predicament was. The other prisoners were filthy, their hair was a mass of wild tangles, and their clothes were rags that hung off their pitifully skinny frames.

They squinted at the children and when they saw one of their own, they smiled, showing grey teeth.

"D-Dad?" Ryan asked, staring at one of the miserable creatures. "I th-thought..."

"Sshush," one of the adults hissed. He put his finger to his lips and pointed to the ceiling. He then mouthed: *She can hear you.*

97

Everyone looked up as if expecting the witch to come bustling down right that second carrying a whip...and she did indeed come down, though she didn't carry a whip. She had dried herself and had changed into what looked like her pajamas with an enormous housecoat thrown over the top. The stairs creaked as each slippered foot stepped down.

Her smile widened as she saw the terror she was causing. "Oh, don't be like that," she chided, gently. "Every one of you was going to be eaten at one time or another. You were all destined to zombies but now you get a chance at a much better undead life. You should be thanking me."

"We should be slitting your throat," Johnny growled. The adults tried to hiss him into silence; however he ignored them. "No, I won't be quiet. She's already going to turn us into grey meat. What else could be worse?"

"Oh, there's plenty I can do," the witch said. She came to stand in front of Johnny and in her hand was another black box; only Jillybean noted that this one was different. She held it out toward Johnny, pressed a button and two little darts shot out to strike the teen in the chest.

He jerked in a strange spasm and then fell on the ground, where he began to writhe in pain. Jillybean had heard about tasers and guessed she was seeing one of them in action. It was terrifying. No one said a word in Johnny's defense, not even Jillybean. Just like the others, she timidly backed to the wall and hoped that the witch wouldn't turn to her next.

Eventually, the electricity ran out and Johnny lay on the ground crying. No one tried to comfort him.

"That was excellent, Johnny," the witch said, walking slowly among her prisoners, inspecting each. "That was a fine demonstration of what you can expect if you're bad. Anyone else thinking of being bad?" The room was dead quiet and no one had the guts to look up from the floor. "Good," the witch went on. "Now, what I came down to inform you was that I will be starting some new treatments. There are too many of you and I'm afraid things might become unsanitary." Pretty much the only thing in the basement other than the prisoners was a large mop bucket that was a quarter of the way filled with a brown liquid which stank worse than anything Jillybean had ever smelled. The witch gave it a little kick setting the contents swaying. "Can't be unsanitary. That's bad. We can't have any of you getting sick before you become a zombie."

She chuckled like a man might, deep and throaty, coming to stand before Jillybean, who was sitting in a ball, her bony knees drawn up to her chin, as docile as the others. "So, who's it going to be? Jillybean?"

Jillybean thought that she was being chosen and her mind gave over to panic. A hot coppery taste of fear flooded her mouth and her limbs froze, her joints turning to rust in an instant.

10

"Who should I pick, Jillybean?" the witch asked. "I want to start with the stupidest one of them. We're going to be doing some radical stuff tomorrow and I don't want to chance screwing up someone good."

"Radical?" Jillybean asked, uncertain of the word.

The witch had fever bright eyes as she explained: "I'm going to bleed them first, almost to the point of death. Then I'm going to freeze them, again, almost to death, and only then will I introduce the zombie virus. I'm hoping that this will retard the spread of the disease so that the brain will be the least affected. But, since I have no idea if this will work, we'll try it on someone expendable."

"I—I really don't know any of them," Jillybean said. "I don't know who's stupid." Despite her denial and against her will, her eyes swiveled to the right and she found herself looking directly at Renee, who was staring right back. More than ever she appeared fifty years past her real age. The granny glasses were flecked with dirt, giving her eyes a rheumy cast and her hands were bony and hooked right in front of her chest.

"Her?" the witch asked giving Renee a once over.

Jillybean was quick to deny it. "No...no, not her. I don't know any of them, really. They're all pretty smart and..."

"Shut up," the witch snapped, her eyes never leaving Renee's stricken face. "Yes, I see it: the vacant eyes, the bland expression. Good job, Jillybean. Stand up, girl." Renee began swinging her head back and forth in wide arcs. "People don't say no to me," the witch hissed. "Stand up or I'll taze you and have Cain drag you up the stairs by your hair."

Renee stood, though it was a struggle for the poor thing. She shook like a leaf and the tears on her face splashed down into the dust. No one said a word as she was led up the stairs. When they were gone, everyone stared angrily at Jillybean. She ignored them. Her entire mind was focused on the sound waves coming to her— Jillybean was mapping out the layout of the house based on the footsteps, the creaking stairs, doors opening, the fall of ice cubes and the flush of toilets.

She had already figured out the dimensions of the house; now she knew there was a centrally located hallway, a kitchen twenty feet to the left of the basement door, another set of stairs down the hall that led to the second floor, a bathroom above the kitchen and slightly to the right. She also knew where the monsters were.

Eric was stationed just outside the basement door. "Back, Eric!" the witch had said as she brought Renee into the hall. A monster named Icky was stationed in the upstairs hall, outside whatever room that Renee was being bled practically to death in. "Stay Icky! No feed! Guard."

The last monster, Hank was on the second floor, somewhere. Jillybean heard its heavy footsteps on the stairs and then nothing. The sound of the generator kicked up a notch and then there was another loud humming in the kitchen. When a familiar sound came to her, she guessed it was an ice machine. Every few minutes a cube would tink off metal and bounce across the floor.

When she was satisfied that she could navigate the house, Jillybean looked around the basement and was taken back that everyone was staring at her. "Who is this?" Ryan's father asked, not bothering to hide the note of suspicion in his voice.

"Her n-name is Ju-Ju-Ju..."

"My name is Jillybean," she said when Ryan couldn't spit it out. "Have any of you been upstairs? We came in through the woods and I couldn't see if there was a garage attached to the house at all."

"Why would you care if there's a garage?" Ryan's father demanded, sounding as though he was on the verge of yelling for the witch.

Lynette, who was at the other end of basement, pulled to the end of her chain so she could see Jillybean better. "Are you going to try to escape? Take me with you, please."

"Me too," someone else whispered.

"And me," said the girl next to Jillybean said. She had her legs stuck out in front of her and they were at least a foot longer than Jillybean's.

Why don't you guys find your own way out of here? Jillybean wanted to ask. She didn't like how any of them were looking at her—the suspicious ones or the needy ones. She had been down this road before and she hated it. She hated the stress that piled on her shoulders and the burden of responsibility that forced her into life and death situations. She hated the guilt that always left her feeling wasted and diseased whenever anyone in her care died or was hurt.

And she hated the *crazy* that came to occupy her mind, the voices, the strange anger, the ugly desire to kill not just the bad guys but everyone. The children didn't realize it, but they were hurting her, breaking her mind and staining her soul.

Jillybean turned away, the heel of her hand pressing against her forehead where a familiar ache began just behind the bone.

The begging continued as did the mean looks. And then a hand touched her on the shoulder. "I-It's ok-k-kay," Ryan said. "W-we c-can figure s-something out, ours-s-selves."

A laugh escaped her. It wasn't a mean laugh or a bullying one making fun of his stutter. It was really just a noise of surrender. They couldn't save themselves. Jillybean would have to do it and there would be more killing and murder, but what else could she do?

"That's alright," she said to him. "I have a plan." She spoke quietly so only Ryan and the girl next to Jillybean heard. "We just need to be patient." Over the next two hours, she examined everything she knew about the house, the witch, her horrid, new-fangled monsters and the cramped basement. It was a long two hours in which the others gradually crept in close to each other for warmth, leaving only Jillybean by herself.

And that was ok. She had to think: step one: pick the lock. She untied the paperclip that had been bound up in her bushy hair and held it up at eye level. It gleamed under the weak light. She had used paperclips to pick handcuff locks before, so she was relatively confident.

The Master Lock turned out to be a whole other animal.

When the witch stopped moving around upstairs and Jillybean figured she had gone to bed, she went to work on the lock holding her chain to the ringbolt, but no matter what she did or how she bent the clip or how she sawed it back and forth and up and down, she couldn't, for the life of her, find a way to unlock it. An hour went by with everyone watching quietly and still nothing. A few of the children said things like: "Here, let me try," or "Lemme see that," but she didn't trust them.

Just about when the second hour rolled around the paperclip broke, jamming up her lock forever. "Oh no," she whispered, holding up a bent and abbreviated half of a paperclip.

"I knew you should have let me do it," someone hissed angrily. It was Dale and he was looking as evil as the witch.

"There's still a bit left," Jillybean answered hotly. "Show us all how to do it." She threw the half a clip at him angrily and then watched in smug satisfaction as he failed to unlock his chains.

You won't get us free with that attitude, a voice said in her head.

"Ipes?" she whispered, turning to the wall. She held her head cocked to the side hoping to hear more from her friend the zebra, but there was nothing. Still, the one sentence warning focused her. He was right, she couldn't just sit there sneering self-righteously and expect to escape. She had to think. She had to use the materials she had at her disposal: a belt, a dull razor, her clothes, her Keds and a mop bucket with a quart of excrement floating inside.

The bucket was disgusting and yet her eyes were drawn to it over and over. "May I please have the bucket, Mister Ryan's Dad, sir?"

Just like everyone else, he had been watching Dale struggle with the paperclip. He shoved the bucket with his foot, as did the lady next to him, and, gradually, the bucket was passed around the room until it got to Jillybean. Why, she didn't know, but for some reason, she looked inside— and immediately wanted to puke. She began breathing through her mouth as she pulled the bucket closer and when she dumped its contents onto the floor, she did so with her head turned away and her face twisted into a grimace.

The expected outcry came but she ignored it, she was too busy trying to hold in the contents of her stomach. She kept retching, which did not stop her from turning the bucket on its side and sitting on it so that it bent inwards.

The handle of the bucket was metal and she had an idea.

Once she fought one side of the handle out, the other slid out with ease. People whispered question after question at her, but still she ignored them; she stood facing the wall where her ringbolt was nailed securely in place. Nailed, but not screwed. There was a world of difference between the two.

Without hesitation, she stuck the metal handle into the ringbolt and then pulled down with all of her might; the only problem was that she didn't have much might. In fact, she was rather mightless. She then hung on the handle but she didn't have much weight either.

She still had a brain and so she hooked part of her confining chain over the top of the handle, braced her legs and pistoned out with the strongest muscles in her body—still nothing.

"Let m-m-me help," Ryan said, taking Jillybean's chain a foot from where it looped around her neck. He also braced his legs and pulled until his arms shook and veins began to throb in his neck.

"Stop," hissed the girl next to Jillybean. "It's bending."

The handle was indeed twisting. "Keep going," Jillybean ordered.

Ryan hesitated. "But it'll b-b-bend al the w-w-way."

"Just do it."

He blew out noisily and then began pulling just as hard as he could and sure enough the handle bent neatly in half like a capital U, while the ringbolt hadn't budged. "That's good," Jillybean said and then worked the bucket handle out of the ringbolt. She then flipped it over and wedged the bottom of the U back into the ringbolt and slid her chain over the top. "Now it's twice as strong."

Grinning, Ryan began pulling. In seconds, there was a groan of metal and the bolt bent back a quarter of an inch. Ryan looked at his hands where the metal had bit deep into his flesh. "Give me your shirt," Jillybean said to the girl. When she started to protest, Jillybean snapped: "Now!"

The girl turned away and slid her shirt off, making sure to cover her flat chest with her arms. Ryan wrapped his hands with the shirt and then he and Jillybean began to pull again. Slowly the nails holding the ringbolt in place pulled out of the wall until suddenly there was *thunk* and they fell back. "Yes!" Jillybean cried, jumping up. She still had a collar of heavy metal and a four-foot leash of thick chain but at least she could move around.

Unfortunately, she was the only one who could. The bent handle was permanently stuck in the ring bolt that hung at the end of her chain. They tried everything to get it out, but it wouldn't budge.

"Now what are you going to do?" Ryan's father asked. "There are bars on the windows, two zombies to get past, and all the doors going to the outside need keys to open and there are also rigged with alarms. All you're doing is getting yourself in even hotter water and we're going to suffer along with you."

"Then when I open the doors, don't come with us," Jillybean shot back. She turned from him as he began to go red in the face. The obstacles in front of her were high hurdles, but ones she felt she could handle with the right tools. Going around the cellar, she found she was extremely limited on what anyone would call tools.

"Excuse me?" She was stopped in front of the girl who had given up her shirt. She had it back on again and was looking up at Jillybean nervously. "I need to borrow your shoes; I'll give them back, I swear." With the prodding of the others, she reluctantly gave them up.

Jillybean unstrung the shoelaces, saw that they weren't going to be long enough and then commandeered two more pairs of tennis shoes. After making two "ropes" out of the shoelaces, each about four feet long, she tied slipknots at one end of each and then, after eyeballing a couple of measurements, she approached Cain.

The beast of a monster strained at his leash like a dog. Jillybean was perfectly safe as long as she kept out of range of its mitted hands; although he couldn't grab her, he could club her into a very long sleep. Moving to her right, she tied one of the ropes around a support beam and then, as Cain stretched out his arms to "get" her, she tossed the slipknot end over his left hand.

He was just smart enough to know that wasn't right and he pulled his hand back, tightening the noose in the process. "Uhhhuh!" he howled, yanking on the shoe-lace rope.

"No Cain!" Jillybean snapped. "Look at me. I'm right here." The monster obliged and forgot his hand as Jillybean moved now to her left and tied off the other rope, making sure to keep just out of range. There was sweat on her brow this time; if the first rope gave way, she would be one dead little girl. Cain was being held back by one wrist and three laces spliced together.

It didn't break and after two tries, she corralled Cain's other hand. Now, his arms were spread and Jillybean again placed her life in jeopardy by stepping in toward the beast who was straining at his bindings. They wouldn't hold, not against his great strength. Not for long.

She had to rob him of that strength.

The razor blade, even dulled by whittling the sticks was still sharp enough to do the trick. She slashed Cain's throat and had to step back to keep from becoming covered in his black blood. A normal man would have been dead in one minute. It took Cain five minutes to die; he was still struggling when there was only a trickle seeping down his neck.

This was somewhat ominous seeing as the next monster she would have to face wouldn't be tied at all.

"Ya-Ya-Ya k-killed it!" Ryan almost shouted and when he jumped up in excitement, his chain almost choked him and he bumped his head making his eyes tear up.

"Yes, now hush," Jillybean chided. "That's what means we have to be quiet." She cut Cain down and used one of the lengths of her homemade rope as a trip wire. She tied it across the stairs, three steps from the top. Everyone watched her in silence as she put her ear to the door.

Eric the monster was just on the other side moaning as they all did, though his moan was somewhat muffled by the mask he wore; mask and mitts were the only thing going to keep Jillybean alive and that was if she was nimble and fast...and deadly. She psyched herself up with a couple of deep breaths and then before she could chicken out, she threw open the basement door and leapt back down the stairs like a gazelle.

She was fast but the monster seemed to have been shot out of a cannon. It acted as though it had been expecting the door to open at that exact moment and in three strides it was within an inch of Jillybean's flying hair. And then it hit the trip rope Jillybean had slung across its path and down it came in a rumbling tumble. It crashed face first into the cement floor.

This did not slow it down for a second. It gathered itself to spring up but Jillybean beat him to it. She jumped full on his back, gripping with her thighs around his middle and with one hand in his hair. With the other, she drew a red line across his throat with the razor...

...And then she was flying as the monster flung her off. When she hit she wasn't quick to get to her feet; she was dazed, her knees shaking, her heart thumping in spastic useless *ka-bangs* that were powerful but somehow couldn't send blood to her hands which were numb with fear.

Eric was peering at her through his mask, blood flowing heedlessly from the wound at his neck. He didn't care that he would be soon dead, all he cared about was killing the girl; she'd never in her life seen something so evil. She wanted to scream. Her razor, her one pitiful weapon against this monster, had flickered off into the dim cellar when she had landed and now, she had nothing to defend herself with.

With a roar, he jumped to his feet to charge the little girl and, simultaneously, there came an almighty *THUMP!* It shook the house. Eric had leapt straight up, driving his own head into the low ceiling with all the force of someone getting their cranium cracked open with a baseball bat.

This still didn't stop the beast. It charged Jillybean, however it charged at an odd angle as if its legs were confused. What's worse, blood was not only gushing out of his throat but also out of his head. He couldn't see through the red wave covering his face.

Jillybean jumped to her right, putting a support beam between her and Eric. He hit it a good one making a cartoon sound: *Brrruung!* The force knocked his body one way and his mask the other. He was blind now and when he charged next, Ryan stuck out a leg and tripped the monster sending him again to the cement.

The little girl saw her chance and used a weapon that she just realized she had: she had a four-foot long length of chain with a heavy padlock at the end. Before Eric could get up, she was cracking his head like an egg with repeated thumps until he finally went face first in a pool of his own blood.

She had done it! She had slain two monsters almost single handedly...almost empty handedly.

But she wasn't out of danger. Eric's crash down the stairs had woken the witch and when he had hit the ceiling, she had heaved her tremendous carcass out of bed and was running for the stairs in a fearsome wrath.

Before Jillybean could escape, the witch was at the top of the stairs, a giant shotgun in her hands.

11

From where she stood with a spill of sharp light behind her, the witch could see Cain sprawled and unmoving. She could see blood and bloody footprints everywhere. She could also see Eric's feet; they weren't moving, either. But she couldn't see Jillybean.

The little girl had ducked under the stairs and was in the shadows, her mind working furiously and coming up with nothing. She hadn't planned on the witch being out of bed.

Above her, the stair let out a sad moan as the witch came down another step. Jillybean's only hope was for the witch to trip on the shoelaces that were still strung across the stairs. She didn't. The witch saw it, made an angry noise in her throat and thumbed the string so it made a sound like an out of tune guitar.

With a grunt and another squeal of protesting wood, the witch stepped over the string. Now she was almost directly over Jillybean's head and the little girl prayed a silent prayer that she would take one more step. If she did, Jillybean would reach out and grab her foot. If the witch went down the stairs, she would likely break her neck.

But the witch did not go any further. She crouched and looked around the basement. "Where is she?"

"I told her not to try to escape," Ryan's father said in a begging sort of voice.

"Where is she?" the witch screamed.

Before the man could say anything, Ryan pointed, not at Jillybean but at the doorway behind the witch. The witch turned as though expecting an attack and when one didn't occur, she crept up the stairs. The second she was out of the room, Jillybean breathed out a sigh of relief and at the same time she felt her stomach twirl as if she was about to throw up.

You're not done, yet, a voice said in her ear. It was Ipes the zebra.

"Where are you?" she whispered.

Upstairs. You have to rescue me and them. Please. For a moment, Jillybean hesitated. Ipes was never this calm and he was usually much more concerned about saving his and Jillybean's skin rather than anyone else's. *I've changed,* came the voice again. *I've changed and so have you.*

There almost seemed to be a hint of accusation in the words. He was right to accuse. She had changed since she had lost her friend. She had become mercurial, deadly cold and evil in her own way. Even right then, she felt the fury of revenge begin to burn inside and with it came the ageless need to let it out in a great fiery explosion.

She had begun to really get a hankering for explosions.

You may need one, Ipes said.

Need was fine especially when it matched the *want* so closely. Jillybean slid out of the shadows beneath the stairs. Putting a finger to her lips, she started up them but paused when Ryan blew out a short whistle. In his hand was her razor, red as a valentine. On whispering feet, she went to retrieve it and it was then she heard the witch yell: "Hank come!"

Jillybean oriented on the voice and knew it was coming from the far end of the central hall. This gave her a free shot at the kitchen and she was up the stairs and in it in two seconds as Hank came lumbering down to the main floor. She put him out of her mind as her eyes flicked about, resting on every single item in the kitchen for a millisecond each. She saw everything and categorized each depending on their immediate usefulness.

Although she wished there was a gun or a bomb sitting around, she did see something almost as useful. Her backpack was reclining on the kitchen table with half of her possessions strewn on the scarred wood. She went right for it; there were necessities inside: wire, lighter, magic marbles, an extra shirt. Most of the items went into her pockets, the shirt she flung over one shoulder.

Jillybean then began to open and close cabinets, again scanning; however she didn't have time to complete a search. "Hank! Kitchen. Hank kill!"

Her little heart stopped as Hank's pounding steps came rushing down the corridor—Hank hadn't been wearing a mask or oven mitts before and he sure as hell wasn't wearing them now.

What might have been worse was the fact that the witch didn't follow her monster to the kitchen. The witch stood at one end of the house with her shotgun ready and was sending Hank to flush Jillybean out. The little girl was smarter than this and so cool under pressure it was unnerving for anyone to experience it firsthand. With the beast roaring down the hall to the kitchen, Jillybean slipped into one of the cupboards that she had previously opened: it held only a few odds and ends of Tupperware.

There was plenty of room for a tiny child.

She was hidden away just as Hank came in. He shook the floor as he walked, and silverware rattled in their drawers. Jillybean expected that Hank would walk around a bit and then leave—but Hank was advanced for a monster, perhaps smarter even than Gary.

He opened one of the cupboards!

Just then the witch's voice began playing and replaying the same words: *Hank kill, Hank kill, Hank kill*...Jillybean was stuck in a loop until Ipes called out from somewhere in the house: *Throw a magic marble before it's too late!*

Jillybean fished one out of her pocket, cracked her cupboard, saw that Hank, all grey-skinned and gnarly, was right there within reach. He was a mass of old scars and long pus-dripping lesions that ran up and down his body. His toenails were sharp and curved like a vulture's talons and his fingernails were as hard and long as a bear's claws.

He was bent over, looking into the cupboard next to hers and would straighten up any moment—she let the marble fly, aiming for the hall. She missed. The marble clacked off one of the kitchen walls, blinked off another and rolled nearly to the hall.

Hank had his head out of the cupboard before Jillybean could pull her arm back. He didn't notice the skinny arm; he was too intent on the sound of the marble. Jillybean thought it had a desperate note to its bouncing as if it too wanted to get away from the monster and the witch as fast as it could. The monster chased after it and Jillybean chased after the monster.

Sitting in the cupboard and throwing magic marbles wouldn't keep her safe; she had to take fantastic chances in order to live. She slid out of the cupboard and ran up to the wall where the kitchen met the hallway, only five feet from Hank, who was staring all around his feet as the marble continued to hop. When he went to pick it up, she flicked down the kitchen lights and then reached into the hall to flick down the hall lights as well.

"Hank!" the witch screamed. "She's right there. Kill!"

Hank had his back to Jillybean, and it was obvious that he didn't know where "right there" was exactly, especially since the only light coming to them was a weak glow from the basement. But he would find out quick enough when he turned—Jillybean was creeping up on the creature with only the shirt she had taken from her backpack as a weapon.

She threw it over Hank's head and down into the basement. In full attack mode, Hank followed it, charging down the stairs, hitting the trip line that was strung across the third stair and then falling with what sounded like a hundred crashes.

Jillybean slammed the basement door after him and then dove into the dining room just as the witch pulled the trigger of her shotgun. There was a deafening roar, a blast of light and a rain of splinters.

The little girl was on her hands and knees crawling as fast as she could into the darkened dining room. She was not crawling to safety; there was no safety in the house as long as the witch lived. The dining room was connected to the living room through an archway and the same sort of archway opened up from the living room to the hallway.

She hurried just to the edge of the archway, straining to hear the sound of the witch with ears that rung from the gun blast. It was impossible. Her ears were no good; however the soft skin of her palms picked up the vibration in the wood—the witch, an obese woman, was hurrying up the hall.

Jillybean ducked through the arch and paused just on the other side with her back to the wall.

"Come out, Jillybean," the witch hissed from the archway where the dining room met the hall. "You're trapped. All you can do is run around in circles and we both know I'll catch you. And if I don't, Hank will. He'll be up here pretty quick and he's awfully hungry..."

The witch went on and on. She had a mesmerizing way of speaking. It was the same sort of mesmerizing hiss that a snake used on a bird with a broken wing. With a force of will Jillybean tuned her out. She had to concentrate; she had to take in every aspect of her surroundings. She had to pick out those mundane items that a seven-year-old could turn into a weapon powerful enough to slay a witch and her pet monster.

And she had thirty seconds to do it: Hank was already coming up the stairs in a hurricane of fury.

There wasn't much in the living room that would help her: a lime-green couch with cushions that were covered in plastic, a coffee table with nicked edges and crocheted coasters sitting on it, a wet bar with a half-drunk bottle of whiskey on its counter, a shag carpet the same ugly color as the couch, a fireplace with no fire, a few pictures on the mantle.

In other words, there was nothing. Her heart quailed.

Hank momentarily forgot that he could think and was pounding on the basement door with fists that sounded like they were made of granite. Jillybean peeked around the corner and saw the witch backing to the basement door; she was about to let the beast out to hunt down Jillybean.

The little girl had eight seconds left, perhaps enough time to throw herself through one of the windows. They looked thick and she calculated that there was an eighty percent chance that she would only bounce off. It was worth a try...

No, Ipse said forcefully, loudly. It was as if he was right there in the room with her. *The answer is in front of you. All you have to do is think: what kills a wicked witch?*

"Water *doesn't* kill a witch," she whispered just as the witch had her hand on the basement door. Water was a silly way to kill a witch unless they were drowned, but if it wasn't water that Ipes wanted her to use, what was it? Then her eyes fell on the bottle of whiskey and she breathed out the word: "Fire."

The basement door came open just as Jillybean darted behind the wet bar where more bottles of alcohol greeted her. They were lined up like trophies. There were also cleaning rags, cans of soda, and other items that were useless to her.

"Last chance, Jillybean," the witch called. "Come out now or I will set Hank on you."

Jillybean ignored this lie; she snatched up a bottle of *Bacardi 151*, unscrewed the cap, doused one of the rags and shoved it into the mouth of the bottle.

"Fine!" screamed the witch. "You could have lived forever, but now you're going to be eaten alive. Hank, kill!"

Now the lighter was in Jillybean's left hand. The hand was steady as a rock. What she was doing was child's play compared to the fires she had set in the past. Hank charged through the dining room and into the living room. He had seen the light of the burning rag and it drew him straight to the bar.

The little girl leapt to her feet, the flaming bottle in her hand cocked back ready to be thrown with all her strength. She feared that she lacked the power to break the bottle when she threw it so she gave it everything she had, not realizing that the heat was already weakening the glass.

The improvised Molotov cocktail struck Hank full in the chest. There was a flash of white light, a blast of super-heated air and then he was burning like a torch. This stopped him in his tracks. He lifted his arms and stared as the flames ate him alive.

Don't watch, Jillybean, Ipes cried. *The witch is coming!*

Ipes was right. The witch had entered the dining room and was now twenty feet away, staring with her mouth hanging open as Hank's hair danced with flames and his skin blackened and charred. Then she saw Jillybean through the flames and raised the gun.

Quick as a wink, Jillybean was back down behind the bar as the gun fired. Chips of wood exploded off the bar and rained down on the little girl. The bar was no protection especially since the witch could just skirt it to her right and shoot Jillybean like a rat in its nest.

Jillybean had to keep the witch from coming closer and she had to do it in two seconds. Another Molotov cocktail would take too long and nothing else was deadly enough. Jillybean resorted to trickery. She grabbed one of the cans of soda and whipped it as hard as she could at the arched wall that separated the living room from the dining room. It hit with a bang and then spun like a crazed top, hissing out a foam of carbonated soda.

The witch, not knowing what it was at first, let out a yelp and backed away, but only for a moment. Jillybean had bought herself four or five seconds, again not enough time for a proper Molotov cocktail and so she improvised a third time. She smashed the neck off a bottle of vodka and hurled it over the bar where it splashed the living room, spreading the fire coming off of Hank.

"Stop!" yelled the witch. "You'll burn down the house!"

Jillybean was already throwing another broken bottle and then another; now the living room was bright and alive with death. The fire was spreading on its own now, taking up half the room. Hank, his eyes seared out of his skull and his lungs shriveled to ash, toppled over as the heat escalated. The plastic on the couch looked shiny wet as it melted just prior to the cushions erupting into flame.

When the curtains caught and the fire raced up them and began eating away at the ceiling, the witch screamed something and ran. She didn't run for a fire extinguisher, she ran for the kitchen door, looking to escape a runaway inferno.

With the fire taking up half the room and the heat a torture, Jillybean grabbed another bottle and crawled around the bar, hugging the wall like a mouse scampering from its hole. She had saved herself for the moment, however she knew she couldn't allow the witch to escape. The witch would lock the door behind her; she would trap her prisoners in the house as it burned down and shoot them one by one if any managed to escape.

The moment Jillybean made it into the hall, she almost fainted. The abrupt temperature change had her head spinning and she walked at a stagger toward the kitchen unscrewing the top off the bottle she carried; in her right hand was the last rag. In seconds it was soaking wet and stuffed into the bottle. The stink of the alcohol made

Jillybean's face crinkle, the idea she was about to trap herself in a burning house made her heart tremble.

Standing just in front of the kitchen door, the witch had her shotgun cradled in an awkward position, holding it pressed against her prodigious bosom with her elbows as she fumbled at a large set of keys. There were keys to practically every door in the house on the ring. She found the right one just as Jillybean flicked on her lighter. The rag caught fire as if it was eager to kill.

The witch jerked around when she saw it. "No! Jillybean don't do..."

Jillybean didn't have time for pleading. The fire in the living room was spreading by the second and there were people still to save. She threw the bottle.

12

The bottle hit the wall next to the witch, shattering into a thousand pieces and spraying her with liquid fire. Her hair went up in flames like it was kindling. The fire, two or three feet in height, danced on the witch's head as she screamed in a high, terrified voice and ran to the sink with her eyes closed. She missed, hitting the counter.

The scream went on and on. The witch couldn't find the sink. The flames were eating her face, blinding her so she searched with her hands wide but she kept going over the same few feet of counter; back and forth. In seconds, she was bald save for a black crackling of charred skin. The fire then took her nose and her lips and so she screamed out of a red hole. For a brief moment, Jillybean considered killing the witch to put her out of her misery, only the shotgun had fallen in a pool of gin; it and the front door were burning now as well.

Only when the witch finally fell to the floor and writhed there like an earthworm on a skillet, did Jillybean turn away. She had no time to watch the witch's final minute of life. The house was choked with a hellish black smoke and the flames from the living room were sliding into the dining room. The heat was outrageous.

Jillybean ran for the garage door—the knob was hot and only when it turned did she realize it might have been locked. She was curious as to why it wasn't until she flicked on the light: a door led to the backyard; it was solid metal, and the garage door was steel and not aluminum.

There was no getting out from this direction. But Jillybean wasn't in the garage to escape; she was there to get proper tools. Her mind buzzed a mile a minute as her eyes scanned the room. "That's what I need," she said, running to the tool bench. She started with a drop cloth which she threw on the floor. She then grabbed an axe that looked like it could only wielded by a burly lumberjack; she needed two hands to lift it. She plunked it down onto the drop cloth and then she grabbed a hammer, pry bar, two screwdrivers and a remote control for the garage.

She gave the door opener a "click" but nothing happened. It went into her pocket anyway. This was all the time she had to gather supplies. Grabbing one end of the drop cloth she hauled it into the kitchen where the smoke immediately had her coughing and the heat had her squinting to keep her eyes from shriveling.

Although she was still on fire, somehow the witch was alive, crawling across the kitchen floor.

Jillybean zipped around her and tried not to look; it was too horrible. She went to the basement and was so intent on getting the tools to the other prisoners that she forgot about her tripwire. Luckily, she was so short that it hit her across the knees and she only lurched instead of pitching down the stairs.

"Jillybean!" Ryan cried when he saw her skinny blue-jeaned legs.

His father seemed astounded that she was still alive. "What happened up there? Where's the witch?"

"Dead," Jillybean said even though it wasn't exactly true. The little girl thumped and jangled the drop cloth down the stairs and pulled them to Ryan's father. She handed him the pry bar and his son one of the screwdrivers. "Here. Free everyone. I'm sorry but you're going to have to chop your way through the cellar door."

She then gave out the remaining tools and turned to head upstairs where the roar and crackle of the fires was growing in intensity. "Where are you going?" Lynette asked.

"I gotta get Renee and Ipes," Jillybean said over her shoulder as she mounted the steps.

The heat in the kitchen was blinding and she had to move by feel alone, one hand on the wall, the other across her face. In the hall it was the tiniest bit cooler like going from an oven to a barbecue pit.

The smoke was worse, however. It was no longer a nuisance, causing a cough or two. Her lungs bucked in protest and threatened to seize up altogether. Breathing into her still very damp shirt helped and it allowed her to get to the top of the stairs, where the smoke was collecting like a black fog.

Through it, Jillybean could see the last monster that the witch had created. Its name was Icky and because of that she had expected it to be much more disgusting than the others, however it resembled most other monsters in other words, it was very scary.

Icky was hulking like the rest and wore a bulky collar. It moaned and coughed, and its hands opened and closed eagerly as it tried to peer through the dark haze, perhaps trying to make out who Jillybean was and if she was good to eat.

Jillybean was utterly defenseless against the monster. She didn't have a gun or a knife and she didn't dare use fire against it, afraid that one more out of control blaze would consume the house with her in it. All she had was her mind and the remote control she had found in the garage.

"Icky, back!" she yelled, doing her best to sound like the witch. The choking smoke helped, turning her voice hoarse, like an old barfly who kept a lit cigarette dangling from her mouth all night. Jillybean held out the remote in a threatening manner. "Back Icky, now!"

The monster hesitated and so Jillybean advanced, holding the remote with her thumb poised above the useless switch. "Back, Icky."

It may not have known Jillybean but the creature understood the tone in her voice and it thought it knew what the little black box did. Slowly it backed away and Jillybean eased to the door it had been guarding. When she put her hand on the knob, the monster's yellowed eyes widened and the moan turned to a growl.

"Stay, Icky!" Jillybean snapped and then opened the door and walked through. The room was blessedly cool and the air only faintly hazy. Renee was spread eagle on a bed, her hands and feet zip tied, a plastic line coming from the crook of one of her arms. It was filled with blood and dripped into a bucket that was four inches deep with a thin red gruel.

Renee looked at the little girl with sleepy eyes. "Wha-ja do?" she asked, slurring her words.

"Uh, I lit the house on fire," Jillybean answered as she pulled out the line from the girl's arm and then dug in her pocket for her trusty but dull razor blade. She began sawing at the plastic zip tie holding Renee's left foot. "Have you seen a zebra anywhere in the house?"

"A zebra?"

Her expression suggested she couldn't tell a zebra from a giraffe. Jillybean wanted to ask her if she had been given drugs by the witch, however she figured it was a waste of breath. "What about toy animals? Have you seen any?"

"Toy maminals?"

"Never mind," Jillybean said. She then picked up her voice and yelled: "Ipes!" The zebra was the only reason she had come back to Missouri and the only she reason she had stayed and the only reason she had dared the witch-infested woods. Jillybean needed Ipes. She wasn't whole without him. She wasn't sane without him...not that she was particularly sane with him either.

But it was much worse when he was gone.

The zip tie finally broke and she moved onto the second. "Iiiipes!" she screamed again as loud as she could. There was no sound from beyond the door other than the voice of the fire, which was a roar, now. Jillybean sawed at the zip tie and listened with her ear cocked, hoping to hear Ipes' cry.

Renee started to speak, but Jillybean shushed her.

The second tie broke and she went to work on the third which took a full five minutes to break. By the time it did, a nightmare smoke was roiling in from the bottom of the door. Jillybean grabbed the blanket from the bed and stuffed it into the crack, but not before yelling for Ipes a last time with a voice that broke. There was no answer and Jillybean cried as she sawed with the now dull blade at the last tie.

She had lost her best friend for good this time. He was somewhere in the house roasting to death and a large part of her wanted to roast as well. Life as a crazy person didn't seem worth living. She cut Renee's last hand free.

"Get up," Jillybean said and pulled the girl by the arm. When she was standing, blinking like an owl, Jillybean stripped the bed of the sheets, tied them together and then tied one end to a radiator that sat beneath one of the windows. She then opened the window and was blasted by cold air; the edge of the air was cut by the rain. It was a blessed feeling and perked Renee up.

"You're going to have to climb," Jillybean said and was expecting a bit of an argument from Renee, but the girl, though not the brightest, was a child of the apocalypse. Survival was a way of life.

She went down the sheets slowly, hand over hand with her legs wrapped tight. When she was safe on the ground, she went to stand a few feet back from the house where there was a belt of perfect temperature balanced between the cold night and the intense blaze.

Reluctantly, Jillybean threw a leg over the windowsill but just then caught sight of a door at the other end of the room. It could have been a closet or bathroom or a door to another world where Ipes was alive and happily sitting in a plate of cookies, smearing chocolate all over his fur because that was just the way he ate cookies as everyone knew.

Downstairs there was a booming crash that shook the house and the heat instantly ticked up twenty degrees. Still, Jillybean didn't climb out of the window. She was drawn to the door. Like a sleepwalker she went to it slowly, her eyes longing for the door, longing to see what was on the other side.

Her happiness was on the other side. It had to be. She had not felt a moment of joy in two months, and now she would be with her friend again and she would be able to laugh and sing and dance and...

The door opened onto a closet, one that was piled high with boxes. Some read: "Winter Clothes" others said: "Christmas." There was a fine layer of dust over everything. Ipes wasn't there. The house shuddered violently, and the floor lifted beneath her feet. And among all the noise she thought she heard a little voice cry: *Run! Run away!*

Blinded by tears, Jillybean ran.

Epilogue

Jillybean led thirteen children and six adults back to Rippling. Apocalypse survivors or not, none of them were functioning at a high level and she figured that they would get lost if she let them go on their own. They'd end up dying of exposure and she was sure she would blame herself if they did.

She slept at the church and barely spoke and barely anyone spoke to her. They looked at her not in awe, but with a nagging fear. Seemingly bare-handed, this scrawny girl had killed five of the toughest zombies in existence and then had killed a witch to boot.

They looked on her as more witchy than the witch.

Morning could not come quick enough for Jillybean. Feeling as though they owed her, she helped herself to the choicest cans of food, someone's backpack, and a number of items she felt she would need, including a jacket which she shredded up.

In no time she was back in monster-mode and heading for the door, a tiny sad-faced little girl.

"Ya-ya-ya-you w-won't st-stay?" Ryan asked.

One of the voices in her head sniggered at his stutter.

"No," Jillybean said. "I need to be alone. I told you about Colorado. It's a long way, but it's the only place I know of that's safe."

"I think we'll go," Lynette said. "We have to gather some supplies and rest up a bit, but we'll go."

"Good," Jillybean said and then opened the door to the church. The world was as white and cloudy as if heaven had crashed to the ground. The fog had rolled in just before sunrise—she wasn't a fan. It meant slow going.

Not that she knew where she was going.

She had an idea for the morning but after that she didn't have a clue. The witch had set up a number of traps for her in the forest and Jillybean was extremely curious to see if she could best them all. And if she couldn't? What did it matter if she was strung up by the neck?

If Ipes was there, he'd be dead set against her taking such risks. "But he's not here," Jillybean whispered. She gave a final wave to the people in the church and left them to whatever fate was in store for them.

Slowly, very slowly because of the fog, she went to the forest to find all the traps. First, she came upon the pit she had escaped from. It was just a hole and the corpse of Gary was just that, a lifeless corpse. Next, she went along the edge of the clearing with fog swirling around her ankles.

There was the toucan and beyond it another pit, artfully hidden. Beyond that was a snare and along a side trail was a deadly spear trap. It was so obvious that Jillybean cast her eyes about for the "real" trap. The witch was well learned in the art of illusion. With a person's eyes on the spear, they would fail to see...a weighted net strung up in the trees.

All in all, Jillybean counted twenty traps before she moved onto the clearing itself. She stopped just on the edge with her heart in her throat. The greatest illusion of all was sitting square in the middle of the clearing on a wooden chair.

It was Ipes.

Jillybean's heart started whamming in her thin chest as if someone was using her breastbone as a bass drum. Throom, throom, throom! Jillybean slunk down, turning into Jilly-rabbit, ready to dart out of there lightening quick. After all, she had never seen the witch actually die.

She could be out there in the fog, her head charred and cracked, her nose, nothing but two slits, her mouth a lipless and raw red hole.

She's not here, Ipes said.

"Right," Jillybean answered, not believing that for a moment. Her eyes went about quicker than humanly possible seeing everything and seeing nothing.

Couldn't it be possible that she left me here? Ipes suggested.

"No. You're here because she's here," Jillybean replied. Only just then she had a worse idea. "Or you're here because I'm seeing things." After all, she was hearing voices and wasn't it just a small leap away to seeing things? "It's either I'm seeing things, or the witch is here, because if you don't recall, I heard you in the house last night, Ipes."

Or that was your only crazy moment, Ipse said. *Perhaps you were hearing things then. There's an easy way to tell. If the witch is here, she'll spring her trap on you right about...now!*

Jillybean spun, waiting to see where the trap coming from, only no trap was sprung. Ipes started to laugh. *You should have seen yourself. What a maroon! What a gull-a bull! What a nim-cow-poop.* He was quoting Bugs Bunny at her. Only he would do that, the witch would never, ever.

"So, there's no witch," she said.

Nope. Not anymore at least.

"And you've been here all night?"

He was as bedraggled as she had ever seen him. *Yep.*

"So that means I was crazy yesterday, hearing your voice." It was either that or she was crazy now. But she didn't think so. It was so much easier on a damaged psyche to think one *was* crazy before but was all better now. She certainly felt better.

Yep, you were all sorts of loony, yesterday. But I'm glad you killed that witch. She was bad news. You know, I asked her which she preferred Nutter-butters or Tollhouse?

Did it matter that he knew she had killed the witch when he had been sitting on the chair all night? Not at all. Ipes knew all sorts of stuff. "She chose Nutter-butters, didn't she?" He nodded and Jillybean swore: "That fiend!" A giggle escaped her. It was a giggle that came from a spring deep inside of her where the water was pure and sang joyfully among her frail bones and the flimsy thing that had once been her soul.

She had progressed across the clearing where two sets of double traps were easily side-stepped. With a trembling finger, she touched Ipes' belly which should have been simply plump with cookies. "Your belly is soggy."

So is your head, Ipse said.

A grin spread across her face going from one dimple to the other. The seven-year-old picked up her stuffed toy and squeezed him until he cried out and rainwater dribbled from his fur. She had gone through hell and had found happiness.

The end

Chapter 3
The First Giants

A quick note from the author— Ezekiel Cross:

The role of biographer is far more expansive than most people believe. To the great majority, a biographer is just a fancy word for a well-paid stenographer. It's thought that they do little more than write down someone else's life story, with maybe a few minor splashes of poetic flourish thrown in to spice up the more mundane aspects of their subject's life.

Ah, if it was only so easy. The true biographer, of which I count myself among a very short list, has to be a great deal more multifaceted than a parrot with a typewriter. They have to play the role of confidant, archeologist, detective, world traveler, psychoanalyst, treasure hunter, confessor, and above all they must be a human lie detector.

The sad truth is that most people lie, and the number one subject of their lies is themselves. When it comes to the weather or sports or draperies, people almost never lie. They are veritable saints when it comes to these subjects. But ask a person about themselves and they become just shy of being pathological in their avoidance of the truth.

And that is your average person, whose lies are like glass: transparent and brittle.

Now picture the herculean task of trying to decipher the words of perhaps the greatest propagandist in history. Queen Jillian's talent for self-promotion invariably spills into self-aggrandizement on an unheard of scale. What's worse is that weeding fact from fiction is nearly impossible since so many of the people in her stories have a tendency to die, and those who are still with us are understandably reluctant to pit their memories of events against her completely unequaled ability to level revenge against those she perceives to have wronged her.

What may be more difficult than unravelling the truth from the lies wound throughout such subjects as the War with the Azael or the slaying of the Black Captain is the excavation of Jillian's hidden memories. These buried memories are not just of specific events, which can be understandable because of her violent nature, but also of entire blocks of time that, on occasion, encompass months.

The story that I will relate comes from one those hidden times in the Queen's life. I first noticed the blank in her memory after I had painstakingly researched and constructed a comprehensive timeline of her life and discovered that very little is known concerning her whereabouts during the months following the war with Azael.

After she escaped her imprisonment in Estes and killed Augustus, King of the Azael, we know she faced the Witch of Rippling and her infamous "thinking" zombies. From there, she seemed to disappear from history until she had her first encounter with Grannie Annie in the vast emptiness that is Oklahoma.

It was nearly four months of her life that seemed to have been erased from history.

To unearth those four months of missing time took me two years, in which I traveled over three thousand very dangerous miles to hunt down clues to what was easily the strangest secret from her past. Strange and infuriating. Had I known what I was getting into when I interviewed her during her second incarceration among the Catalonia Reavers, I wouldn't have climbed those many steps to the top of their prison tower.

Her cell had a single barred window that faced south. It was mid-afternoon and there was just a narrow rectangle of pure sunlight beaming brilliantly onto the floor. Like a cat, she sat directly in that rectangle of light, her eyes closed. I got the feeling that if she could purr, she'd be doing so.

"And after the Witch?" I prodded gently. "You were reunited with Ipes and…" I flipped through my notes. "You let yourself be a kid again. That's what you told me. So, this begs the question: why is it such a blank in your mind? You told me that you named a fish 'Shedrick' and that…"

She interrupted without opening her eyes. "Chedrick."

"Okay, Chedrick. That was one fish that you kept in a bucket for an hour, thirty-five years ago. How do remember that but not this great block of time?"

"Like some people, some fish are simply memorable, Emmanuel."

"It's Ezekiel, your Highness. Ezekiel Cross. But I think you know that." She smiled up into the light and then finally deigned to look my way. Since our first interview, she had undergone a dramatic change in both her looks and her accommodations. Then she had been queen for the third time and at the height of her powers; now she was locked away. Her signature wild locks had been shaven down to her scalp. Without hair, her eyes looked even larger than ever. They had even stripped her of her usual long black coat and knee-high leather boots. Her current attire was a pink, crushed velvet warm-up suit.

She looked small, soft and weak. This apparent change was a mistake on the part of the Dead men. She had always been small, soft and weak. Her power had never come from her physicality, and to think they had diminished her in some way with a haircut and a change of wardrobe was laughable.

The Queen ignored my name but not the question. "Ah, yes, the witch. The Witch of Rippling. Nice hook. I bet you sell a lot of books with that title."

"Some," I allowed. "But people know that story. What they are dying for is something new. Something no one's ever heard before. Like what happened during that summer."

"Hmmm," she answered, gently running her hand along the bars, sensuously. "That was a long, long time ago. You know, I think it's somewhat unsettling that you are constantly asking about my childhood. Do you like little girls, Zeke? Do you like to picture them? Maybe in their underwear?"

127

Yes, this is the sort of abuse I have to put up with on occasion…but not from Jillian. She would never stoop to such tactics. This was Eve. I had been talking with her for fifteen minutes and only just caught on. "Since this predates you, Eve, will you let me talk to the Queen, please."

Eve gave me a slow smile. "I am the Queen. You know that. You know I proclaimed myself Queen long before Jillybean ever considered it."

"That is still in dispute."

"By whom?" she seethed. "You? Pssh. Please. Look at you, brave now that there are bars between us. We'll see how insolent you are when I'm free."

"I'm not trying to be insolent. I was just stating a fact. May I please speak with Jillian?"

"Jillybean," she insisted.

Eve made me jump through many hoops before I was allowed to speak to Queen Jillian. As always, the transformation from one to the other was so subtle that even with me watching for it, I didn't see any betraying tic or even a different cadence in her breathing. The Queen stroked the bars and looked around the room as if she were still Eve.

This was how the Queen worked. She was always cautious. "Ezekiel," she eventually said and put her hand through the bars. For the first time I didn't kiss it. The guard was only a few cells down, watching me closely.

I asked her the same questions that I had asked Eve and Jillian was understandably reluctant to try to fill in the blanks in her memories. "There's usually a good reason why I don't remember everything that has happened to me. Conversely, there's rarely a good enough reason to uncover those things that my psyche wants to keep hidden. The risk to reward ratio suggests that we let sleeping dogs lie."

"Are you afraid?" I asked her, attempting to use the question of courage to goad her.

"No, I'm not afraid. It's very unlikely that we will excavate some nugget that'll be worse than anything else that is a matter of public record."

She was always so exact that when she strayed from her imprecision even a little, bells went off in my head. "Unlikely? I'm sorry, your Highness, but when someone says the word impossible in conjunction with your name, I have to laugh. To me 'unlikely' is almost a sure thing."

This made her grin. "I suppose I can take a break from my work." She gestured at the thirty or so uneven piles of papers littering her cell. "They allow me to do research but no pen to write with. I organize my thoughts better when I can condense them and write them down. As it is I have to memorize an overwhelming amount of what may be useless knowledge."

"What are you working on?" I asked, sitting down opposite from her and pulling out a single pen and one pad of paper, which was all I was allowed to bring into the cellblock.

"The only thing that will keep me alive."

I was sure that it was some sort of weapon or device which she could use to disintegrate the bars, and I leaned forward, eagerly. But not too far forward. Neither Eve nor Jillybean could be trusted and if she escaped because of me, I would be held liable.

"A vaccination for the zombie virus. People will pay out the nose for it. It'll make me indispensable. Right now, I'm familiarizing myself with Cyrllic script; which is what the Russian alphabet uses. Our good friend Yuri Petrovich not only wrote all his notes in Russian, he also encrypted them in it."

She wanted to change my focus. She wanted this to be what I took away that day. Like I said, she understood the value of propaganda better than anyone. "We'll talk about that when you've made progress. Right now..."

"And how does someone make progress without the simplest of tools? All I'm asking for is a pen. You'll send along my request?" It wasn't really a question, it was a threat. She would clamp her mouth shut and not say another word if I didn't agree. When I finally nodded, her smile returned. "So, you would like to delve into my mind and rummage around a little?"

This surprised me because it was exactly what I was hoping to do. "In a manner of speaking, yes. What I want you to do is lie down and assume a comfortable position. Yes, just like that. Now close your eyes and take a few deep breaths. Progressively relax all your muscles, from head to toe, or toe to head. Try not to smile. Try to relax the muscles of your face…"

She snorted laughter. "I'm sorry. I don't mean to be rude, but do you really think you can hypnotize *me?* Because of my issues, I have firewalls on top of firewalls. Nothing can get out and nothing can get in, especially not a stranger."

I was prepared for this. "What about you? Can you get in and out with the information? Sort of like an old-time bank heist?"

"A bank heist? I'm going to take that as a joke. Why don't you just say what you really want? You'd like me to attempt self-hypnosis." I shrugged and jerked out a brief nod; I'd been caught a second time trying to fool the Queen. Instead of being angry, she said: "It's not a farfetched idea. In truth, all hypnosis is self-hypnosis. Even the weakest-minded person has to *allow* the hypnosis to take place."

She stared up at the ceiling from her cot for a minute and I actually thought she was making the attempt, however she was only thinking, perhaps still going through the ramifications of what may come out of her mind. Finally, she agreed, saying: "You will not print anything unless I approve it first."

"I suppose."

Her eyes, still on the ceiling, went hard. "The answer is either yes or no. And if you cross me and try to print something that I have not given permission for, there will be repercussions. I hope you know that this cage will not hold me forever."

I agreed, knowing she was right; the cell was temporary. No one could hold the Queen captive for long and when she got out, there'd be hell to pay.

Ezekiel Cross

***

1-

The Queen remembered the witch of Rippling, Missouri with a shudder, and she remembered the children and the handful of adults she had rescued from her dungeon-like basement with just a touch of contempt, although they undoubtedly deserved more. The fuzzy filter of time shaded their cowardliness and the meek, craven manner in which they had accepted their horrible deaths in a somewhat nostalgic light.

She remembered freeing them before going out into the chilly wet night and searching for Ipes, and finding him sitting on a chair in a clearing. She remembered hugging him and crying. Then came an odd jump: the tail end of a fine summer with the two of them sitting in a strange house chatting over freshly brewed pine needle tea; the two of them at a playground, squealing with laughter, as they spun on a tire swing.

She saw them roasting marshmallows, playing tag, and hide and go seek. They put on a play about King Arthur and rode bikes. They explored cool forests and pulled up logs to find salamanders.

These wonderful memories played through her mind like a movie she had starred in, and it was fantastic right up until the last memory: her and Ipes having a "who can make the biggest splash" contest in a clear blue pool. The pleasant memories ended with a strange flash of brilliant but terrible light. It was an explosion, a massive one, and she saw herself lolling listlessly in a river of black water that was filled with dead bodies.

"The River King's barge," she said in a whisper as a cold tingle ran up her spine, causing her skin to tent with a million goosebumps. "But that was earlier. That happened before the Witch. Where was I after that?"

The splash again. She remembered the splash and laughing and falling, no, jumping. It was the late summer of Jillybean's seventh year. The world was full of monsters and death and evil, and the skinny little girl felt that the best way to deal with it all was to jump from a bridge. With a wild laugh, she tucked into ball and flew like a...

"Cannibal!" she screamed, in a high-piping voice. Below her was a rain-swollen steam where minnows shot away in mindless confusion. Above and behind her was a two-lane bridge set just high enough over the water to make the jump scary, but not too scary. She struck the clear water with a great *throom!* and sunk to the sandy bottom, where she kicked off and broke the surface a second later.

"How big was that one?" she asked her friend. He was still on the bridge and had no intention whatsoever of jumping in.

Ugh! First off, it's cannonball and second it was too big. Look at me. Look at my shirt! He furiously held out the edges of the blue shirt he always wore. There were a few drops of water on it. *Do I look like an otter to you? Ugh. I feel like one, all slimy and wet. Ugh.*

"I coulda put you up on the railing, you know. You wouldn't fall in and even if you did, it wouldn't be like the last time." The last time they'd been on a bridge like this, a horribly evil bounty hunter had thrown him into water. Although Ipes was just a stuffed animal, Jillybean had killed the man for it. She had shot him without blinking.

The bullet from her .38 had punched through his chest. It wasn't a neat little hole and there wasn't a long teary good-bye from the bounty hunter as he slowly slipped into death. No, it was violent and bloody. A huge chunk of flesh and bone had blasted out the back of his shirt. Rib-shrapnel punctured his heart in three places and burst his lungs like two balloons. He was down on his back before he could comprehend what was happening.

"I bet you didn't see that coming," she had said to the bounty hunter, just a hint of a smile turning up the corner of her mouth. He grunted and coughed up blood. And that was good. She appreciated the way his face turned red and how his throat worked up and down as he struggled to find his last breath...

"No," she hissed. She shook her head sharply, whipping her wet hair around, trying to strike the image from her mind. That hadn't even been her, not for reals, and she had promised herself that she was done thinking about it. She was starting a new life and a new life didn't come with old memories, at least as far as she understood things.

"Y-You won't fall," she said again.

Could you put me on the bike? Maybe in the basket? He asked this in the most innocent way he could, complete with giant eyes and hooves clasped together. *It is awful hot out. Half of me might get sunburned and red and black really isn't a good look for a zebra.* Before she could answer, he added a long *Pleeeeease* at the end.

"Fat chance of that," she said, frog-kicking to the reedy shore. "If you're worried about getting a sunburn, I can put you in the shade but you aren't going anywhere near those cookies, mister. Those are both of ours." Only that morning, while poking through a cabin in the Missouri woods, they had come across a find of monumental proportions. Not one, but two packages of Girl Scout cookies. Yes, one had been Samoas and that was unfortunate since neither Ipes or Jillybean really cared for coconut even when lightly mixed with chocolate, however the other package had been S'mores which made up for everything.

The cookies had been guarded over by a squadron of voraciously hungry mosquitos and a skeleton in a moldy green coat lying cuddled in on itself. It was really and truly dead, something that was never a certainty anymore, but Jillybean still hadn't been able to simply snatch its pack

133

away. She could see through its cave-like eye sockets and into its head where an ugly brown soup of unspeakable stuff had congealed.

When she had finally summoned the courage to grab the pack and run, they discovered water bottles, canned soup and even bullets. These were huge fat slugs as big as her thumb. She took it all, but the only things that the pair really cared about were the cookies. Until they had found the pool of water beneath the bridge, it was all either of them could think about.

Ipes went back to grousing, while Jillybean climbed out of the water for the third time. She wore only a pair of white panties and a green shirt with a cartoon kitten on the front. It really made no sense even to wear this much since she hadn't seen another human in the last six days. There were tons of monsters about, sure, but no people. Still, she had been raised—up until the ripe old age of six and a quarter-years old—to be a proper lady, and proper ladies did not cavort about in their "altogether."

That had been her mommy's way of saying naked.

Jillybean left tiny elf prints as she went back to the bridge where she hesitated for a few seconds. *Don't do it*, Ipes warned. The rail and all its dangers beckoned. *Your mommy wouldn't care for you doing that*, Ipes chastised, invoking her mom's name in the hope of keeping her sane.

She was well beyond sane and besides, she couldn't help it. Mountains were made to be climbed and kids were made to jump from the highest perch they could dare; she climbed up on the rail. *You should get down before you fall off there and break your neck, or worse: do a bellyflop.*

The idea of a bellyflop made her hesitate. There was little in life more terrible than a bellyflop. That was perhaps the most common of all knowledge. Everyone, even people living in deserts, knew that. On its own her right foot started searching for the lower wrung to climb back down. She stopped herself, hissing, "No. We gotsta face our fears, amember? That's how we beat them up."

Conquer them, Ipes suggested.

"Yeah, that too," Jillybean said, through lips that were pressed tight to her teeth. It was not logical or based in anything even remotely mathematical, but being up on the four-foot high railing made her feel as though she were suddenly six stories in the air, teetering on a tightrope with an invisible tornado doing a foxtrot of a wind dance all around her.

What was that about conquering your fears?

"Shut up," she whispered, afraid that even speaking normally would tip her one way or the other. She had been in higher spots than this, but that was always out of necessity and usually there was something to hold onto. Now, all she had to grip with were her toes, and they had as monkey-like of a grip as a human could manage.

Jump or climb down, Ipes said. *You're making yourself a target. What if there's a zombie way down in that copse of trees?*

Far down the intricate, headlong rushing brook, a small squadron of nodding, sleepy willows kept an uncertain watch over that section of the river. Their whip-like branches hung down, creating a screen, keeping from sight whatever might be within them.

"If there are monsters in there, they woulda came out by now. And you know there ain't no bad guys down in there."

Isn't any, he corrected. *And you don't know that.*

"Sure I do. It's all scrubby ol' farmland from here to eternities. If somebody took a truck or something in there, where are all the tire marks? Why isn't the bushes all knocked about or bent over? 'Sides that's a good place to hole up in at night, but why would anyone still be there now?"

It's not like people have jobs anymore. Maybe they're sleeping in.

"It's the middle of the day, for all gosh darn it." Jillybean rarely slept more than five hours and couldn't understand how people could lay about any longer than that. To her, minutes were precious. There was always so much to do, to learn, to discover!

All I'm saying is you can't stand up there forever.
Jump or get down.

"I'm gonna jump."

Then jump.

"I am. Don't rush me. Jeeze."

I'm not rushing anyone. I just don't think you got the guts.

"What? I got the guts."

Then jump.

"I will."

Okay. What are you waiting for?

She didn't have an answer to that. She stood on the railing with her arms out for balance, looking down past her newly painted toes—pink on the right foot and purple on the left. She was all ready to procrastinate even longer —the brook really did seem a long way down, and she was pretty sure that half of it had drained away while she had been conversing with Ipes—when she heard a rumble that was somewhere on the scale between thunder and the roar of an extremely large monster.

Looking around caused her to lose her balance slightly and she pinwheeled her arms until she was able to stand straight again. As she was without shoes, even the four-foot drop onto the rock-strewn cement wasn't exactly inviting. When she regained her balance, she looked around for the growing rumble and nearly lost her balance a second time when she saw an approaching cloud of dust coming up the road.

It was coming faster than any hurricane; faster than anything she could ever remember seeing in her life. "Jeeze!" she whispered. The thing was a black blur and the only reason she didn't think it was a rocket ship was that it was clearly following the road. It had been about a mile away when she first saw it and as her eyes turned to round blue circles, it flew at her so quickly that she could barely run the simple calculation for assessing an object's speed in her head.

It tore up half a mile in nine seconds which, if her mental math was correct, roughly equated to 225 feet per second or a jaw dropping 150 miles-per-hour!

The numbers were not just staggering, they were stunning as well. So stunning in fact that it took her three precious seconds to realize that she had left *Betty Lou* square in the middle of the low bridge.

Don't! Ipes screamed as Jillybean bent slightly to hop down. *You'll never make it!*

The decision to try to get *Betty Lou* out of the road in the eight seconds left to her was taken out of her hands as she over-balanced forward and then over-balanced backwards, way backwards, way, way backwards. A high, shrieking scream filled the air as she started falling, bottom first, towards the swollen brook.

It took her only a second to hit the water, another for her to sink so that her bare feet crunched softly into the sand at the bottom of the brook, and a third to shoot back up, just in time to hear the end of that scream and see *Betty Lou*, for that was what she had named her trusty her three-speed Schwinn, go flying.

Betty Lou had been a magnificent bike: a sparkly, purple body, white streamers jutting from either end of gleaming chrome handlebars, and a large white basket in front. Now, she sailed ass over teacups across the bridge, as an explosion of papers billowed and swirled in the air behind her. "My books," Jillybean whispered.

My cookies! Ipes cried as though mourning a death in the family.

2-

Even as the bike and the papers sailed through the sky, there were three secondary bangs one after the other, as the car bounced from rail to rail, went sideways off the road on the other side of the bridge and struck a faded yellow *Slow* sign and bent it at a forty-five degree angle.

The car's engine died with a rumbling choke. Jillybean's first impulse was to slip down low in the water.

She wasn't just unarmed; she was mostly undressed. With the world filled with monsters and perverts, she was in precarious position. The brook was not wide or deep, and as she had mentioned to Ipes, the land around it was wide open. She was in a worse position than a sitting duck; they at least could fly.

Maybe the driver died in the crash, Ipes said, trying to be helpful. He wasn't. If he had died, she would be mostly to blame for leaving her bike where she had, and her conscience couldn't afford too many more innocent deaths piling up on it. The ones that were there: Baby Eve, General Johnston, a hundred or so people on board the two ferryboats that she had set on fire in New York, and at least twice that many witless *Believers* in Georgia, were already straining the band-aids and duct-tape keeping her mind together.

It turned out that the driver was far from dead. Just as Jillybean swam under the bridge, there was a thud and a creaking sound. This was followed by a low curse, a light *thunk*—metal on metal—another curse and the distinctive *click* of an M16's safety being flicked off.

As distressing as the sound would have been to most people, it added little to the girl's fear. On her hierarchy of preferred deaths, being shot was number seven, behind: old age, any death while asleep or unconscious, catastrophic stroke, sudden massive heart attack brought on by years of overeating, suicide by lethal injection, strangulation and then being shot.

Ipes preferred "death by chocolate" though what that exactly entailed, beside massive amounts of chocolate, he could never articulate.

One of the reasons guns failed to throw that much fear into her was due to the fact that she was so small that using a gun on her made little sense. They were loud and would be a waste of ammo, when every grown man alive could crush her throat with just a squeeze of his hand.

And the man who came softly stalking up to the bridge, walking not on the sandy cement, but in the high grass so that his steps were barely audible, could have crushed her throat with just two of his fingers without any effort whatsoever. He was long and tall, wearing blue jeans, black biker boots and a sharp, white V-neck t-shirt that still had the creases in it.

He went into a wary crouch at the far edge of the bridge, holding an M16A4 up to his shoulder, but not quite to his eye. He was searching the reeds and the shallows.

Looking for an ambush, Ipes told her.

She wanted to say: *No duh,* only she had to remain perfectly still and absolutely quiet. Her green shirt was a match in color for the reeds and her dark brown hair could be mistaken for shadowed dirt. Her giant blue eyes, however could not be mistaken for anything else. The man stiffened as he saw them and the gun jerked up, quickly, but he didn't shoot—this was the other reason Jillybean didn't fear guns: since her true, inner villainy was hidden away, people had a tendency to see her "cute" exterior and dismiss her as just a kid.

This man was not so quick to dismiss anything. He gave her a nod and then scanned past her.

He's looking to see who you're with, Ipes noted, displaying a keen grasp for the blatantly obvious. Even if there hadn't been zombies making a mess of the world, children Jillybean's age never traveled alone.

The man stared into the reeds and along the banks of the brook and while he did, Jillybean stared at him. He was very tall and up on the embankment as he was, he seemed to tower over her like some primitive beast. His hair was deep and dark, almost black, and it was as wild as a lion's mane and just as long. His eyes were the color of the forest; a beguiling mixture of green and brown.

He said, "Hmmm," a lot, letting one slip when he had examined both sides of the bridge, and again as he spied up the brook as far as he could see, and a third as he turned and gazed far behind him across the fields. Oddly enough, he even said, "Hmmm," as he gazed up at the sky.

"Who you with?" he asked when his eyes came back to earth.

Don't bring me into this, Ipes whispered. The zebra was still right out on the bridge, doing his best to blend in with the background by acting the part of a tiny white and black shrub in a light blue shirt and darker blue shorts.

"No one," Jillybean lied. "It's just me and I don't have a gun or nothing." This was only technically the truth. Hung on the belt of her pants was a bowie knife, while sewn into the back of the belt itself was a razor blade—but those were up on the bridge and she was down in the water.

"It's just you." He didn't ask this, he said it, incredulously. He looked around a second time in visibly growing ire. "It's just you in this great big world and you choose to park your mother-fu…your stupid bike right in the middle of the road? What the hell is wrong with you? You could've killed me!"

Tell him he was driving too fast for the condition, Ipes whispered, out of the corner of his non-existent mouth. *We saw the speed limit sign. It said 40MPH. Not a bazillion miles a second.*

There was firm logic to this, however when one was a mostly naked girl and there was a big, angry man with a gun yelling at you, it's hard to deliver the most cogent arguments. "Sorry," she said, dropping her chin. "I-I didn't know anyone lived around here."

"Who said anything about living around here? And you're really all by yourself? Hmmm." Once more he glanced around, even squatting low to see if anyone was clinging like a spider to the underside of the bridge. His lips were puckered as if he were just about to kiss his grandmother. When he looked at Jillybean again, and said, "Hmmm," those puckered lips cut to one side of his face, giving his straight nose a slight bend. "You're really all alone?"

The idea seemed to disgust him.

She nodded and shrugged. "Yeah, can I get my pants on, please." He grunted but didn't turn around; she swam backwards to the far bank, and after tugging down her shirt to mid-thigh, she started edging up the bank. He rolled his eyes at her and turned to the side with a sigh.

"It's really too bad about being alone and all," he said, speaking loudly, as if he were speaking through an invisible bathroom door. "But that's the nature of fate, you know? Maybe you were just meant to be alone. Then again, maybe not. We never know what will be, so why worry about it. Right?"

He glanced over and caught her trying to get one wet leg into her jeans. "Sorry, sorry," he said, again staring out over the fields. "You just have to learn to let all of life's miseries go. That's what I do. I roll with the punches and there have been a lot of them in my past. You got any parents?" There was a note of hopefulness in his voice.

"They're both dead," Jillybean told him.

"Oh." Now he sounded disappointed. He rallied, however. "At least you had parents. I was given up ages ago even before the apocalypse. Can you believe that noise? Your own parents saying they don't want you? I used to say that if I ever found my father, I'd tune him up good, but now, I'd just laugh in his face and let it go."

A second glance caught her trying to hide the bowie knife behind her back. "Keep it," he said, all smiles. "A girl all alone should carry a knife or a gun. And if I had one, an extra I mean, I'd let you borrow it. Who's your friend?"

He had an easy smile to go along with his tanned, handsome face. Ipes didn't like him one bit. *Don't tell him my name! I'm a wanted zebra in seven states for crying out loud.*

"Just a, you know, a run-of-the-mill stuffed animal." Jillybean tried to slip the zebra behind her back along with the knife.

Run-of-the-mill? You make me sound like some dusty, old, left on the shelf, Walmart teddybear. Sheesh. You could have just said I was your friend, or maybe your confidant. That would have been better. And it probably wouldn't hurt to mention that I am something of a genius. It impresses the little people.

141

Jillybean cleared her throat to shut him up and stuck out a hand. "My name is Jilly…ah, I mean it's Jill. My name is Jill." At the last moment she had realized that she too was wanted in seven states.

His lips pursed again, and she could almost hear his mental *Hmmm* as he took in the extended hand. He scratched the underside of his chin before he decided it was safe to shake the seven-year-old's hand. "Mine's Christian Niederer."

"Need what?"

"Niederer."

Shouldn't it 'Niederest? Ipes asked with a little snort.

"Behave," she hissed, giving the hand a shake. "That sounds like a great name. So, do you live around here? Was your wife about to have a baby or something? You were driving awful fast and whoa! What kind of car is that?"

She had just got to the crest of the bridge and saw, resting against the canted *Slow* sign, a yellow and black racing car. It was beautiful and sleek. It hugged the ground with only inches to spare. Its body was like an arrow, swooping back to what looked like a sideways fin. She had never seen anything like it.

"That is a McLaren P1," Christian stated proudly. "It has a top speed of 217 mph, with a 0–60 miles acceleration time of 2.7 seconds. Under the hood is a 3.8-litre twin-turbo V8 engine that harnesses over *nine-hundred* horse power. Huh? That's not too shabby if you ask me. But what's even better…hey, hold on."

She had been drawn to it and was now close enough to touch the fancy car; he seemed to think her tiny fingers would do more damage than the sign had.

"Okay little girl, we are in what's called a looky-no-touchy situation here. Kids and cars don't mix. Sorry, but that's the law."

"Hold on, yourself, Mister Christian, sir that's not a real law. And I droveded before. It was a truck and I did just fine." She had ended up crashing the truck through the front doors of a PigglyWiggly, but as that had been her aim, she figured it shouldn't count against her driving ability.

Christian shook his head. "Sorry. This isn't just some truck. This is a perfectly designed piece of engineering art. Do you know how much this baby cost? 1.6 million dollars! It's bad enough you and your bike put some dings in it…but like I said, we take the good with the bad. Right? How about we go take a look at that bike of yours. That's more your speed." He put a hand on her back and, with a gentle push, started leading her away from the car.

A litter of paper ran from the car to the bike and Jillybean insisted on picking it all up. Wearing a worried look, she darted here and there after each piece. She had written copious notes on a variety of subjects and didn't want to have to re-write them all.

"Who's this for?" He had a hold of her biology book. There was a tragic gash on the cover and the spine was sadly broken. "I thought you said you were alone?"

He was about to snatch up another book: her 9th grade algebra book, which had, for reasons that were never explained within its pages, a cover photo depicting a person just about to snowboard off a cliff of ice. She got to the book first. "These are mine. I-I like the pictures." As the algebra book was thick and heavy and she was tiny and very young, this lie seemed like something that was more believable than the truth.

"The pictures? What the hell are you talking about?" Christian looked as though he wanted to grab the book out of her arms. Quickly, she stepped back, which earned her a suspicious eye. He thumbed through the biology book, saying, "Hmmm," to himself. When he had gone through it, fanning the last three-quarters in a blur, he gave her another sharp look. "The truth, now. Whose are these?"

"Mine."

"You know I really don't care one way or the other, but I just don't like being lied to. These aren't the kind of books kids read. And no kid your age is…well, is alive, but if they were, they wouldn't be alone. The reason I ask either way is that I need some gas and I'm looking to make some trades. That P1 is a beauty, but she's a thirsty machine."

Don't even think about trading any of my cookies, Ipes hissed.

Jillybean turned slightly away, muttering, "We could use a gun, you know. And you're already too fat anyways."

Christian had heard her. "I told you I just have the one gun and it's not for trade. I do have some extra bullets and some canned food. How about you tell me about who you're with. Let's start there. How many are with you?"

Counting Ipes, there were two of them, but since big people never counted Ipes as a real and true person, she said, "It's just me. I sorta kinda ran away. My people are really far away."

His lips pursed again. "Hmmm. You ran away. Hmmm. I take it they were mean?" That was a loaded question. They were angrier than me. It was a true fact that her people had sentenced her to death for assassinating their leader, which was understandable, she supposed. But on the plus side of things, she had given them the key to destroying a zombie army that had been besieging them, and she had practically killed the entire Azael ruling family by herself, thus ending a war her people had no chance of winning.

"I wouldn't call them mean. Really, only some of them. My family wasn't mean at all. They mostly love me, I think. You see, I can be sorta a problem child sometimes. That's what means bad things just sorta happen around me, but I don't mean it. I'm being good now."

"Do you call almost killing me, being good?"

"Almost? That's not fair. I wasn't even trying." If she had been trying, she could have killed him with ease. Traps were a specialty of hers. If she had known he was coming and she was in a killing mood, she could have turned that million-dollar racer into something that resembled a crushed beer can. Images of it came to her: the car tumbling end over end, tires flying, glass shattering, a body half in and half out being turned to bloody mulch with each revolution of the disintegrating car.

It would've been easy: a simple log dragged to the far side of the bridge and laid across the road would have done the trick. At the speeds Christian was traveling, he wouldn't have been able to see until he hit the crest—too late to stop and nowhere to turn.

She saw this in an instant. Killing came easily to her broken mind. And it was no wonder. She hadn't finished constructing herself the way everyone else had. Normal people got to practice being human before anyone ever expected to actually be one. It's what childhood is all about. Children teach themselves how to be human through play in which they mimic what they see around them.

Pretty much all Jillybean ever saw was killing and pain. She was baptized in a fountain of blood and her lullabies were the shrieks of her neighbors being eaten alive. Yes, it was no wonder that she had already devised three different ways to kill Christian, and that was without trying.

His brows came down and he seemed a slight bit unsettled by what she had said. Quickly she gave him a nervous smile. "I-I mean, all I did was park my bike on the bridge. I didn't do it on purpose. And asides, you were the one who was speeding."

"I guess I was. Karma, right? We both got a dish of it."

He gestured to where *Betty Lou* lay in a mangled heap in the high grass. The once magnificent purple frame was twisted, one of the tires was popped and the basket was hanging from a single strap like the last relentless tendon holding an executed man's head to his body.

But where are the cookies, Ipes whispered, his voice shaking with emotion.

"They're with the backpack," she told him. "We left it on the bridge, remember?"

"What's with the backpack?" Christian asked.

She shrugged indifferently, her eyes never leaving the bike. "Just some cookies for Ipes. Gosh, I don't think I can fix her." The tires could be replaced, and the straps of the basket could be melted together and then repainted, but the frame would be a job she couldn't handle.

"Lucky for you, bikes are pretty much everywhere," he said, dismissing her anguish. "I'd try that little town." The world on that beautiful was split into two halves: above, everything was the purest blue and below it was a mottled green as far as the eye could see, except for a grey smudge to the southwest.

Is he going to leave us here?

"I think so," Jillybean answered. "Hey, Mister Christian, sir, are you going to leave us here? That doesn't seem right."

"Us?" he asked, with an eyebrow raised. "I knew you weren't alone." He raised the gun and his voice. "Alright, come on out. I don't want to hurt you or take your stuff, okay? I just want to know who I'm dealing with."

Jillybean sighed and held up her stuffed zebra. "His name is Ipes and he doesn't like guns all that much, 'specially when they're pointed at him." Christian's pursed lips swung to the corner of his mouth again. He didn't look like he believed her. "It's true," she insisted. "It's just us two. I was having a splash contest when you came along and smashed poor *Betty Lou* there. And ain't she...*isn't* she proof that I'm alone? Wouldn't there be a second bike if I was with someone?"

"I guess." The gun lowered. He shrugged, looking a trifle confused. "It still doesn't change anything. You must follow your path and I must follow mine. There is a reason fate had you set your bike there and I have a feeling you'll find it in that town. Good luck."

He's really going to leave us, Ipes said in amazement. *I think we might be better off without him. He is not a good guy. Not that I ever wanted to go with him, but a good guy doesn't leave a little girl and a starving zebra out in the middle of nowhere, bikeless.*

"I think you're right, Ipes, he's not a good guy at all." Her hair was plastered to her head, her shirt was like a second skin, and she was shoeless—in other words, she looked the human version of a sewer rat, and yet she was able to muster a condescending look that had Christian's forest-colored eyes growing angry.

"Don't try to play the guilt game with me, little sister. When you park your bike in the middle of the fuc…the middle of the road, things are going to happen. Not bad things or good things, just things. It's the same with people. There are no bad people or good people, there are only people. Good and bad are a fiction."

Jillybean scratched her bottom. "Huh?" Fiction meant story books.

"It means we have made up the ideas of good and bad. There is no evil and no Satan and no God and no heaven either. The world is just this." He waved his arms around, gesturing broadly at Missouri. "So just enjoy it. If your joy is a splash contests and zebras and textbooks, that's all-good. My joy is experiencing everything that I couldn't before, and I can't do that with a tag-along."

She started to open her mouth to protest, but he held up a hand. "There's no use pleading or batting those big blue eyes. You had people and you ran away. That's on you. You parked your bike in the middle of the street and that's also on you. If it was cold or rainy, or if there were zombies about, I would consider giving you a ride, but this just might be the nicest day I've ever seen for a walk. I say you make the most of it."

With a wink and a look of immense self-assuredness, he turned and walked over to his 1.6 million-dollar McLaren P1. Just as he reached for the handle of the door he stopped with a jerk. "What. The. Hell?" he demanded with his chin raised, his voice raised, his whole physical being raised as if he could lift off from the ground by the ardor of his anger.

The two tires closest to the *Slow* sign were flat.

3-

"You don't have no spares?"

147

Any spares, Ipes corrected. She glared at Ipes with her lips pursed very much how Christian pursed his. She then hid the zebra behind her back.

Christian didn't answer right away. He continued to swell, seeming to expand and expand, looking as though he just might pop. Of course, he didn't and Jillybean knew he wouldn't, still she let out her own pent-up breath when he suddenly laughed.

"Just when you think you know what's what, fate give you a kick in the nards." He smiled down at Jillybean. "I guess I'm coming with you."

Ipes snorted and Jillybean said, "I know, right? Maybe you should be more politer about it Mister Christian, sir. That's what means you were just telling me that I couldn't come with you! Who says I want you to tag-along with me?"

"Well, I'm going to head on over to that town and hope to...hope to heck that they have a tire store. We can either go together or separately. Your choice."

"I'd like to think it over some," she said and turned away, whispering to Ipes, "What do you think?"

I don't know, Ipes answered. *There's something weird about him. His name is supposedly 'Christian' but he doesn't believe in God? That's whats called a big red flag. And look at his hair. How do you have perfect hair after crashing a race car? You know what I think? I think he could be a child molester. Sure, he doesn't look like one, but he could be in disguise. This could all be a set-up! He probably popped those tires when we weren't looking. Aghh! Run, Jillybean!*

Although she dismissed the talk of him being a child molester, she kept a close eye on him after she agreed to walk with him to the town.

"I'm not carrying any textbooks by the way," he told her as she eyed the remains of her gear. "Take only what you need to."

Should I tell him or are you going to? Ipes asked. He was talking about the full five-gallon fuel tank Christian was planning to haul all the way into town. He had heaved it out of the passenger seat of the P1 and had tested its weight on his broad shoulder.

"Adults don't like to be told when they're being stupid," Jillybean whispered.
"They get cranky. Still, if there's any monsters down there, and there always are, it would be better if he wasn't carrying so much." She cleared her throat. "I take it you're getting a car down there?"

He smiled showing off white teeth in a tan face. "Why else bring the gas? Cars aren't much use without it."

"Yeah, I know. It's just that really looks heavy and if there's any monsters about, well I was just thinking that maybe you didn't have to bring all of it. Gas weighs 6.3 pounds per gallon. That's 31.5 pounds and with…"

"Let me just stop you right there. Thanks for the concern and the math lesson, but I got this. Besides, this is my only container, so I'm stuck. Okay? I'm not going to pour it on the ground."

Here was where things got delicate with adults. "You actually have another container," she told him. He had a half-empty water bottle which he started to lift. She shook her head and pointed to the McLaren. "You can empty all but a gallon or so into the car and then pump it back out if you can't find the right tires."

He said, "Hmmm," to this as if Jillybean hadn't already thought through every other course of action. Normally when Jillybean thought of something, she covered all her bases. "I guess that might work," he said, eventually.

After emptying most of the gas into the car, the two set off cross country toward the town, each carrying very little. Jillybean had Ipes, her backpack, the algebra book, three cans of food, nine cookies—three for each of them, something that had Ipes giving her the silent treatment—a few odds and ends to guarantee her survival and her homemade ghillie suit. This last had Christian chuckling again.

She looked at the cloak-like outfit she had put on over her backpack. "What's so funny? It's called a ghillie suit

149

and all the best soldier men have them." Hers was made up of strips of green and brown cloth she had layered over each other so that she appeared like some sort of forest shag monster, except for when she remained perfectly still. Then she seemed to fade into most backgrounds. "I don't know why you're laughing. They really do come in handy. The monsters don't even notice you at all. They think you're just some sort of walking bush. You know, like a tumble weed, 'cept a walking weed would be more like it. I could make you one if you want."

"I'm good, don't worry about me. There isn't a zombie alive that can catch me. I hate to brag, but I'm awful fast."

He sighed and stared off into nothing as they tromped through high grass. Jillybean was feeling itchy as her shirt dried. She twitched, making her ghillie suit rustle. Christian looked at her and she smiled up at him. He found the smile disconcerting and looked quickly away.

I must have been batting my big blue eyes at him, she thought. A mile went by in silence and the entire time, she did her level best not to blink in his direction. When she grew bored, she began skipping which was cool because of the way the suit swished and because she needed to keep up with Christian who wouldn't slow. Normally, she would never skip in a ghillie suit, but he was striding along as big as a billboard. Besides, she liked to skip. It seemed to her the most natural form of ambulation and it was a wonder more people didn't do it.

She began to sing a song about a very small spider and a very tall spout. After the third time through, Christian gave her a look, which she interpreted as *please stop*. Shutting up was difficult for her after being alone for so long and she couldn't help asking the question that had been eating at her. "What's a nard? Is that what means your family jewels? I knew a boy named Ricky back in the before. He said he got kicked in his family jewels and said it was worserer than getting kicked in the shin. I don't know if I believe that at all. Especially when I asked to see those so-called jewels. I guess I was expecting something more, I don't know, something nicer since he did call them jewels. Jewels are supposed to be pretty, right?"

"Um," Christian answered.

"But what he showed me weren't pretty at all, no sir. Jewels are supposed to sparkle, you know? These were like skin-colored raisins. I asked Mister Neil about them; he's my adopted dad, and he…" She paused, noting that Christian was wearing the exact same expression that Neil had. "And he didn't know what to say," she finished up, lamely.

Christian was clearly uncomfortable with the nard talk. He changed the subject quickly. "You gonna do something about that hair of yours? It's starting to go crazy."

"Oh, it just does that."

As expected, he said, "Hmmm," and then was quiet for a few minutes. As he walked, he snatched glimpses of her. "Maybe you should try braiding it. You'd look a lot prettier."

For an hour, she thought to herself. She had braided her hair once before. It had taken the better part of an evening to grimace and wince her head into respectability. Sometime during the night, her hair had passed into open rebellion and by morning her hair resembled the Gordian Knot with the tips of a couple of red bows just visible, drowning in a brown sea.

Remember how after a week you had to cut them out with scissors? Ipes asked, laughing behind a flat hoof.

"I thought you were giving me the silent treatment," she reminded the zebra. Christian looked uncomfortable again. "He was saying mean things," she explained. "Never mind, okay? So, you were going to do stuff that you couldn't before? Like what? What did you do before?"

"I was a pro ball player. A little second base, a little shortstop, but mostly centerfield, you know. I bounced around the minors for the last ten years and ended up in Triple A with the Brave's farm team in Richmond." He paused perhaps to let her ask more questions, but all this was Greek to her. Mining and farming she understood and being brave was a good thing, but the rest was all babble

151

and what any of it had to do with a game she couldn't fathom. He went on, "I wonder sometimes if I made the right choice. I had a free ride to Florida State, and what did…"

"A free ride? Like on a bus or something?"

He laughed, relaxed now that he wasn't talking nards with a little girl. "No, it meant they would let me go to school for free if I played ball for them."

Now it was her turn to say, "Hmmm." Hadn't she played with balls back at her old school? Maybe that's why she hadn't had to pay for anything except for milk at lunch. It seemed like a very strange compensation system, but many things that happened in the before were strange to her.

"I played a little kickball and some tetherball. You know."

"I bet you were one of the best," he told her. It was nice, but untrue. She had never been particularly big, strong or fast, and, unlike the boys who reveled in dirt and enjoyed a good sweat, she preferred games where her innate talents could shine. Few could rival her in hide-and-seek, for instance.

She shrugged off the compliment. He didn't notice; his eyes were set faraway, dream-like. "It may sound terrible, but the apocalypse has been somewhat freeing for me. I got no more money issues, no more people telling me what to do, no more responsibility. For most people it's all about death and pain, but that's life anyway. We all die. We all get hurt. We all feel sadness."

"You don't look too sad," Jillybean noted. She didn't hear even a hint of sadness in his voice. "Because you really aren't. You said you didn't have parents, which means you didn't have to watch them die. You also didn't have brothers or sisters. And since you bounced around mining and farming and playing ball, you didn't have a wife or kids. You didn't really lose anyone, did you?"

He lifted one arm in a what-can-you-do half-shrug. "Nope. I've been lucky and smart. I don't stick with groups because they all get ripped apart one way or another. And I don't make any long-term attachments, you know, girlfriends, that sort of thing, because someone always ends up hurt. And I definitely don't take in strays." He shot her a look just in case she missed his meaning.

"I'm not a stray. I have a home." *Possibly*, she didn't add. All she had to do to fit in back in Estes was prove that she wasn't a crazy murdering sociopath.

I could be a character witness for you, Ipes said. *I could tell them that you haven't killed anyone for almost two weeks. That's practically a record for you.*

She was about to agree that her self-restraint had become nearly superhuman, but Christian had begun speaking again: "I keep to myself except for the occasional trade or the quick roll in the hay here or there when the opportunity presents itself. It's all for the best. I get to roam around doing my thing."

"And what's your thing?" Jillybean asked with a hint of nervousness. Her friend Ricky hadn't just shown her his family jewels, he had shown her his "thing" which had been just as weird.

"Living the high life," he said, with a grin. "You saw that McLaren. Back before the apocalypse, that baby was just a dream. Only mega-rich dudes could afford those babies. Same's true for this scope." He held out his rifle to show her the fancy scope attached to it. "State of the art thermal scope. Guess how much it was?"

She couldn't even begin to shrug before he answered his own question. "Almost eight *thousand* dollars. Look at it. It's a freaking thing of beauty."

It looks like a gizmo to me, Ipes said. *Like one of them video game toy thingies.*

Jillybean was equally unimpressed, and the more she thought about the race car of his, the more she thought it really wasn't a practical car. She didn't bother telling Christian this, partially because he seemed to love it so very much and partially because he hadn't stopped talking about this fancy type of whiskey that was a hundred dollars a sip or the priceless sword he had carried at the beginning of the apocalypse that had once belong to some famous revolutionary general.

"And look at these." He fished in his backpack for an eight-inch white tube. She was surprised when he let her touch it. "Go on, open it." Inside was what looked and smelled like a very large, brown cigarette. "That is a Gurkha Black Dragon. A thousand dollars a piece."

"It smells icky."

He chortled over this observation as he cut off one end of the cigar and lit the other with a gold lighter, puffing at it like an asthmatic dragon for a few seconds. The smell of smoke wasn't altogether bad, in fact she found it intriguing.

A sigh escaped him. "I know. It's captivating, isn't it?"

"Maybe a little. So, that's what you do? You go around in your fancy car picking up fancy stuff?"

"That's not all I do, but it's what I like to do. Just like jumping off bridges is what you like. To each their own is what I say." It seemed like a very shallow sort of existence in Jillybean's mind and she was about to say so, however just then Christian added, "As long as you're not hurting anyone, I say do what you want."

This shut Jillybean up. She had hurt thousands of people, which meant she was the last person to comment on someone's life choices. "I guess that's smart. Maybe I'll start doing that sort of thing, too." In a way, she already was. She had cast herself loose from her family to find her best friend and since then she really hadn't been in a rush to get back. To put it bluntly, she had dillydallied for the last two weeks, moving somewhat westward in fits and starts, without ever committing to actually traveling.

"Sure," Christian told her. "It's a great life. Just remember, don't start batting those baby blues my way. This is a one-man traveling show. Now if you have an older sister, maybe our paths might intertwine a bit longer."

"I do, but she's all the way in Colorado."

He paused with his cigar clamped between his lips. It kept them from puckering as he said, "Colorado, hmmm. There's a lot of rumors coming out of Colorado lately."

Jillybean felt a little tremor start on the edge of one shoulder and track across her back to the other. She remained perfectly still, except to raise her downy eyebrows. "Oh really? It's been months since I was there. Did something happen?" Like did the largest bandit kingdom in America drive ten-thousand zombies against a small outpost in the Rockies, only to be defeated by tremendous courage and the terrible genius of a seven-year-old? She didn't dare ask this.

"Just that there's been trouble," he answered. "Probably nothing to worry about. From what I hear, it ended well. I might even take a trip up there…in a few years." He added this last part quickly, even though Jillybean hadn't reacted. "Right now, I'm on a baseball stadium tour. It's pretty boring stuff; you wouldn't like it. St. Louis is next on my list. Busch Stadium is supposed to be pretty with the Gateway Arch visible over the centerfield wall."

He wore a peculiar dreamy look as his hands came together like he was holding an imaginary bat.

"Man, I would've given anything to play in the bigs. Fifty thousand people going crazy, cheering, screaming your name. Girls throwing their…" He stopped suddenly seeing Jillybean eye him curiously.

"Throwing their what? Did girls play baseball, too?"

He shook his head. "No. They'd just throw things to you if they liked you. But that was in the bigs. The girls in some of those little crap-hole towns I played in, eeesh! Ten years in the minors and I've seen my share of girls that make some of the zombies look good. And on dollar beer night, it would get downright ugly."

"I think I'd want to see other places than just empty baseball stadiums," Jillybean said. "I don't really know what, though. Everyone talks about seeing New York but it was really scary."

"Oh, I have a full list." He had it out in a second. "The Eiffel Tower. The Empire State Building. The Sahara Desert. Kodiak Bears on whatever river they fish at. The sunset from the Golden Gate Bridge. The Pyramids."

Other than bears, the only thing she had ever heard of were the pyramids. She'd had a geometry book that had a picture of them in it with an accompanying caption: *The Pyramids of Giza, Egypt.* Of all the mathematical sciences she had explored, she had found geometry, with its simple formulas, the easiest subject she had ever studied. Strangely, geography was one of the more difficult.

At a certain size, maps existed in the abstract. Borders were invisible lines that no one cared about anymore, oceans were vast, impassable barriers, and distance had regained a sixteenth century perspective. A trip to Egypt was something to dream about, not something a person would ever undertake.

"I know the way to St. Louis," she told him and pointed north. "I can take you there, if you want. It's kinda dangerous if you're not careful."

He threw his head back and laughed a great belly laugh. She understood perfectly that it must be a little weird to be given advice about danger from a little girl. She was used to it; she had to put up with it from a stuffed zebra who had never been to preschool. Still the advice was clearly needed. His bright shirt, his way of walking, tall and direct, and his booming laughter had already caught the attention of some of the monsters in the town.

She saw three of them lurching their way.

Without a word, she slunk down and to the left next to a row of strange, frantic plants growing in chaotic confusion. They were in a farmer's field where a twenty-acre crop of overgrown soybean plants had mingled with shoots of corn, high, thrusting sunflowers and cottonwood saplings. Added to all of this were old dead branches and viney weeds. The long orderly lines of plants were now unrecognizable. They had become ugly, melded, greenish walls that marched on further than she could see.

Christian and Jillybean were somewhere in the middle of these rows, but with the plants growing so high, it was hard to tell exactly where. "What are you doing? Do you have to go to the…" Christian started to ask. Then he saw the danger coming. He wasn't exactly overcome with fright. Casually, he lifted the rifle to his shoulder.

"We could hide you know," Jillybean said. "It's almost always the safest thing to do."

He flicked off the safety and said, "Here's a little something you should learn. Always kill them when you can."

She was just about to reply when he fired the gun and blasted a fist-sized chunk from the head of the first of them. It collapsed, its legs and one arm spazzing in a sickening manner. The two others were shaggy and disgusting female monsters which came on even faster, excited by the gunshot which echoed in the still air.

The air was not still for long. It was soon rumbly and growly. Jillybean lifted slightly so she could see beyond them and over a little swell in the field.

"I agree," Jillybean said. "You should, but only when it's safe. Look." She pointed past the two closer monsters at the mob of ragged undead coming behind them. Even more suddenly began to crash through the wall of shrubs across from them. They were filthy, more brown than grey as if they had just risen up out of the earth.

4-

"Ahh, son of a bitch!" Christian growled, giving a long look around. "This is why I don't pick up strays. If you weren't here, I'd just run away. No harm, no foul."

"Please run away," Jillybean urged as the two female monsters drew closer. Somehow, they had both retained their bras and no other stitch of clothing. "I'm not in any danger."

Unless he keeps shooting and you keep talking, Ipes reminded her.

Much to Jillybean's disappointment, Christian wouldn't leave her. "No. It wouldn't be right. I told you about karma. I'm pretty sure that if I let you die, it'll be bad ju-ju for me. Just sit there and try not to be a problem."

You heard the man, Ipes said.

"I did."

So why aren't you sitting there not being a problem? What you're doing looks a lot like a problem to me.

As Christian stood, firing his rifle and knocking down zombie after zombie in a wonderful display of marksmanship, Jillybean had grabbed the gas can and was dousing the wall of shrubs just behind them.

If you use up all his gas, he's gonna be pissed off, Jilly. Jilly? Jilly! She used up all the gas.

"I had to," she told him, pulling out her own lighter—a battered Zippo she had painted flat black. She lit the bushes. Christian turned to stare as twenty linear feet of shrubbery went up in a roar of flames. He choked when he saw the empty gas container tossed to the side. "I had to," she explained. "You don't have enough bullets." By doing a quick, five-second analysis using two random subsections of the attacking monsters, she had calculated that there were at least a hundred and six coming at them, and she knew Christian had only brought along three magazines. Even if he killed one with each shot, there would still be at least sixteen to deal with, though she figured it would be closer to double that number because no one was that good of a shot.

"And now I don't have enough gas!"

"I had to use it to save you."

"I don't need saving. I'm the grown-up!"

In her experience, grown-ups needed saving all the time. She ran and grabbed his hand, thinking she would pull him to a four-foot section within the flaming wall of fire where she had not poured any gas. There was a gap near the ground to crawl through. She yanked on his hand and he yanked back. She strained even harder; it was like trying to pull an oak tree through a door and she almost pulled her own arm out of its socket.

"We have to go!" she shouted. The summer had been a dry one and the plants might have gone up even without the gas. She could see his pursed lips and knew he was saying, *Hmmm* though she couldn't hear it. "What's there to think about?" she demanded. "The smoke will hide us. We can escape."

"I know, which is why I was thinking that this might be a good time to take off. Most of them would come after me and you could go do what you like to do on your own."

He wants to leave me in the middle of all this? Her eyes went to slits as her mind turned to a dark place where there was nothing but screams of rage and howls of pain. It was in this dark place where she kept the murderer. She tried to tell herself that she had expelled the beast, but that was just a lie that allowed her to sleep at night. The murderer was still there, eager to get out, eager to kill. In fact, she was eager to kill Christian. She would use the bowie knife, cutting the tendons behind his knee when he turned to run away. He would fall and the monsters would be on him in...

Jillybean! Ipes yelled. He was loud and his voice was very daddy-like. It brought her back, but it did so with a touch of reluctance.

Ashamed of herself, she couldn't look at Christian as she said, "You can still run. I won't hold it against you. But you better hurry." Every second drew the undead noose around them ever tighter.

Indecision gripped him until he finally groaned, "We'll talk about it later, but I wasn't going to 'run.' I was going to draw them away. There's a difference, you know."

He's talking now, Ipes hissed, frantically. *He said later, so why is he talking now of all times?*

"I don't know. Through there, Christian and shut up for all darn it!" She pushed him towards the gap. Instead of crawling through the gap, he charged through the whole shrub, more like a football player than a baseball player.

Jillybean leapt through behind him, and behind her came a raging wave of undead, howling and spitting.

On the other side of the flaming wall, the two of them found the exact same thing, more monsters crashing through the lines of shrubbery in a long wave. Jillybean and Christian were caught in the middle.

The smoke from the fire was like a low mist that cast the entire battlefield in a grey pall. It threw the undead beasts into such a state of confusion that the two waves collided, and monster attacked monster with such savagery that the two humans were almost lost in the chaos.

If she had wanted to, Jillybean could have slunk away, hidden from the world by her ghillie suit. For his part, Christian could have raced through the crowd untouched. Neither gave in to the temptation.

"Follow me," Christian hissed. He stooped and picked up a rock. With it, he smashed in the head of the first zombie that noticed them. The bloody rock bounced away. He then used the butt of his rifle on the next creature, smashing it square in the face and knocking it down. Although it fountained black blood all over Christian, it didn't die and nearly tripped him up as he ran past. Stumbling, he fell into the next row of shrubs but bounced off the thickest part of it.

"Through here," Jillybean whispered and shot through a narrow gap.

The gap was kid-sized and when Christian tried to get through, he lost half of his white t-shirt. The sharp branches tore it open in three spots and one particularly grasping branch refused to let go and had to be broken off by hand. It was just as well in Jillybean's opinion; a white shirt had no place in a world full of monsters. It was just silly.

This new lane between the shrubs was populated only by a handful of zombies, most of whom were so lame that they were having trouble getting through the plants. Jillybean had little to fear from them. Still, there was no time to rest. The battle between the two zombie waves had ended as quickly as it had begun and now monsters were going in every direction, their nearly useless brains bewildered by the smoke and the fire, which was burning merrily, and would likely eat up the entire length of the twenty-acre long lane.

"This way," both Christian and Jillybean said at exactly the same time, both heading for different holes in the next line of plants. They grinned at each other before each took their own route to the next lane. There were more zombies here, faster ones.

"Put that zebra away and find a rock," Christian ordered.

What's he think you're going to do with a rock? Ipes asked as she stuck him in his usual spot on the side of her ghillie-hidden pack. *You can't run around lugging about a big rock. And what good would one rock do against them?*

Six shuffling, groaning monsters were heading their way; two to the right and four from the left. Beyond the next line of shrubs, there were probably dozens more and behind them were the hundred they had just escaped.

Fighting could not be the answer.

Jillybean reached into a side pocket of her backpack and pulled out a strange-looking black square that was slightly larger than the palm of her hand. Flicking it on, she gave it a squeeze. "OOH, Elmo loves to be tickled," the box announced, loudly.

Christian had been stooped over, picking up a rock. At the sound of the voice, he jumped and spun in surprise. He stared with a slack jaw at the box. Jillybean pointed through the next line of shrubs. "Get us through there." She then tossed the black box into the air and began to push Christian.

The box landed behind them and immediately began to vibrate and bounce around, making a crazy laughing noise that went on for ten seconds before it began to speak again: "OOH. Elmo loves to be tickled there most of all. Hee-hee! He-ha!" It carried on, laughing and jitterbugging all over the ground.

Fascinated by it, the zombies forgot about the man who had disappeared through the bushes and the small green and brown plant that had gone with him.

The two went through a couple more lines of shrubs before racing north towards the town. Christian, his head on a swivel, looking left and right, a brick-sized rock in his right hand and his M16 in his left, began to grin as they got close to the small blip of a town. Soon laughter began chortling out of him.

"W-Was that from a *Tickle-me Elmo?* Did you really open one up and pull out its mechanical guts?"

"Guts? No, there wasn't any blood or icky parts if that's what you mean. It was just fluff mostly and that thingamajiggy. I needed something that would last a while but not use up too much in the way of batteries. It only uses two double AAs. I also got a Leaping Joggle Hopper, which goes a lot longer, but it uses three of 'em. And I got...*have*, sheesh Ipes. I *have* a few wind-up toys that'll do the trick in a pinch."

He began to nod appreciatively. "That's some smart thinking. I might have to pick up a couple of those."

"And you need a ghillie suit."

He shook his head. "Hiding isn't my style. I'll fight or clear out. Trust me, I've been around long enough to know that hiding just gets you trapped and that's the last thing anyone wants."

"No, uh-uh. That's the cool thing about the ghillie suit. It can also get you untrapped. It can let you walk right past a whole buncha monsters. Really, it's true. I can walk right down the middle of that town and be perfectly fine. Wanna see?"

She yanked her hood back over her head so that only the tip of her nose was visible beneath all the strips of cloth. She started to break from the lines of shrubbery, but he pulled her back. "No, don't do anything stupid. There sure do seem to be a lot of zombies for such a dinky-ass town. They're crawling all over the place."

"A-S-S is a bad word," she said, giving him a hard look, "and that's what means you're not aposed to say it in front of children. Especially when you didn't need to say it. If you had just banged your thumb with a hammer, that's one thing but to just curse? Mister Neil would've called that crass and that's what means…"

"Mister Neil can kiss my A-S-S," Christian said. "Tell him I said that next time you see him. And tell him he needs to keep better track of his rag-a-muffins. They shouldn't be roaming around getting in trouble and telling adults how to speak. If I want to say ass, then I'll say ass all the ass-long day. Got it?"

We could kill him, a voice behind her whispered. She stole a quick look over her shoulder and saw only another of the long line of overgrown soy plants. The voice hadn't really come from behind her and she knew it.

"No," she said, under her breath before tilting her head way back and glaring up at Christian. "You know what I think? I think you need to apologize and that's what means saying you're sorry." He snorted, rolled his hazel eyes and shook his head in amazement all at once. "Does that mean you're not going to say you're sorry?"

"Not to a kid who thinks she can tell me what to do. That's not how the adult-child relationship works. The adult tells the kid what to do, where to go, and how to act, and you do it or you can leave. It's as simple as that."

She crossed her arms over the kitten printed on her green t-shirt. "Wanna know what's even more simple? When you're bad, you apologize. That's what both my mommy and daddy said. *And* my old teacher Miss Monfit said that, too." She assumed that ascribing the quote to an actual teacher would end the argument but Christian had the audacity to laugh.

It wasn't a belly laugh or a snide laugh, but it was enough to turn Jillybean cold and again she heard the voice inside her head: *When he's sleeping. Do it then. Use the knife. Nice and quick like you know how.*

She squeezed her eyes shut as hard as she could. She squeezed until her eyeballs hurt around the edges. This quieted the voice. But it would be back. It shouldn't have been there in the first place. Stress was bringing it out of its hiding place. The fact was that Christian was a poor choice as a first companion. He was too bull-headed and too much her complete opposite. Jillybean thought it was a good idea if they went their separate ways.

At the unspoken decision Ipes' beady eyes flew wide.

Are you sure? Just because he doesn't have the best manners doesn't mean he can't be useful. He's pretty handy with that gun. And you saw that car of his. He must be the best driver in the world. Think of all the cool places we could go. We could go to Disneyland, huh? I bet that's on the way to the Pyramids. We could stop by and see the sights and ride the rides. What do you say?

"And be treated this way the whole time? I don't think so, Ipes. Sorry, Mister. Christian, sir, but I think it's time for me and Ipes to leave. Good luck with the car an' all." She stuck out a hand with stiff formality.

Once again, he performed the scoff, eye roll, and head shake. "Fine by me. Try not to get yourself killed."

"You try not to get yourself killed," she muttered after she had hidden herself beneath her ghillie suit, slipped through two more rows of shrubbery and was slinking away along a different lane. A part of her really was worried for him. He still wore the remains of the shredded white shirt, which was a beacon that she could see easily through the thicket ahead of her.

While she was creeping along with her usual patience, he had darted forward and was practically at the end of the fields. Speed, strength and stamina were his strong suits, but just then he faced open ground dotted with milling zombies. She figured that he would have no choice but to adopt her style. She was wrong. Christian darted out from the fields, heading toward the town as if on a line. He went straight down a dirt road, running easily, even as he came up to the first of the dead. Her next assumption, that he would kill the monster, was also wrong. At the last moment, he juked to the side, leaving the creature sprawled, face-first in the dirt.

This occurred once more to a second zombie and the rest were simply left in his wake as he added a touch of speed. Then he was gone, hidden by the buildings and the crammed together one-story houses.

I can't believe he really left us, Ipes said, in shock. He is an adult for goodness sakes!

"We both know that doesn't make you a good person. And he did make it super clear he didn't want children around." Jillybean sighed, feeling an unexpected ache of loneliness.

You still have me, Ipes said. *What more does a person need than her very own zebra? And I'm a talking zebra to boot.*

Jillybean agreed with more conviction than she felt. She was out in the wilderness of America for a reason, and it wasn't to make friends. She was out there so she wouldn't be a danger to anyone ever again. So far, she'd been able to deal with the solitude because she had Ipes and, up until she had seen Christian, she had thought he was enough.

"I'll get used to being alone again," she told herself as she tromped through the weeds, approaching the small town. It was so small that she could see right down the little two-lane road that cut the town squarely in half to where the fields started up again. "Hmmm," she said, with pursed lips. It wasn't much of a town and would likely be a bust as far as scavenging went. Christian wasn't going to be able to get his tires here. "But I don't care about that," she told herself.

With her uncaring attitude forcibly in place, she moved to the southern half of the town. Christian was stirring up trouble in the northern part, however she pretended she chose the southern part because of its lack of monsters. "Even monsters become curious when they hear people snooping about," she explained to Ipes.

Sure, that's the reason, he said, which earned him a glare. *I'm just saying there's not much here to snoop over. This is all industry and manufacturing. Look. Where are we going to get a new bike around here?*

From the fading signs, it was obvious that the town supported two main businesses: a furniture manufacturing factory, which took up a fifth of the town all by itself, and a tremendous grain and feed concern with towering silos that could hold an ocean worth of grain.

Everything else surrounding these two businesses went towards assisting one or the other. Transportation franchises, a pallet depot, a lumber yard, machine shops and more. Everything was tiny compared to the two big companies. The houses were especially so. They were squat little buildings with tin siding and hollow aluminum doors. In most respects, they were not much than glorified shacks, sandwiched between businesses, which must have a dismal way to live.

The houses were certainly not kid-friendly and of the first six houses she poked her head into, not one sported a single family picture. The seventh, sitting in the very shadow of one of the mega silos, had a few battered toys in the yards and a rusted bike cast down in the weeds. She stood over it with a thoroughly dissatisfied look on her face. The tires, having peeled away from spotted rims, sagged lifeless as well as airless.

"It's too big for me, either way." It was a big kid's bike. It had ten speeds and funky handlebars shaped like a ram's horn. What she needed was a bike with a basket in front, a banana seat and tassels. "Let's go on to the next house, for all darn…"

The end of her sentence lodged square in her throat as the air shook from an enormous sound. It had been a monster's moan, only the monster would've had to be epic in size to make that noise. Instinctively, Jillybean sank down on her haunches and peered through the strips of cloth dangling in front of her eyes. The moan repeated and it was followed by a hollow, booming crash. Both sounds were like nothing she had ever heard before.

Was that a monster? Ipes asked. He was shaking as badly as she was. *If so, it's a monster the size of a blue whale.*

"It's coming from in there." She pointed at one of the mega silos and then bent well back so she could see the top of the hundred and ten foot building. She had been in a silo before and hundreds of people had died as a result. The memory of that terrible night made her hesitate.

Why hesitate at all? You heard a noise. So what? There are lots of noises. We don't have to investigate them all. And do you expect to find a bike in there? No, of course not. The only thing you're going to find is something bad.

He was probably right about that. Still, she was drawn to the noise, her curiosity pulling her little feet forward, her common sense, keeping her huddled within her ghillie suit. There were three of the skyscraper sized silos and each of these had smaller, barn-sized attendant silos that surrounded it like little moons. The smell emanating from the closest was physically repelling.

It was so bad that it acted like an invisible buffer, gently urging her away, somewhat like the wrong end of a magnet would. Pulling her shirt up over her face helped a little, just enough for her to wobble dizzily forward, her teeth clenched and her throat locked tight against the vomit that threatened to come up. In a way it was an unnecessary torture that she was compelled to endure. The mystery was too much for her.

Each of the silos had doors of steel that seemed small compared to the enormity of the buildings. She went to the closest of the mega structures and although its door was thrown open, it was the least inviting place she had ever seen. In front of the door were piles of bones and half-rotted corpses. The flies lifted off them as she approached and formed a shadowy cloud that buzzed, alive and angry.

She couldn't look at the piles. The millions of maggots writhing over them gave the illusion that the corpses were still moving and that one might just reach out and grab the little shrub-looking girl. Instead, she kept her eyes on the door, where a sound rumbled on the very lowest range of human hearing. She could feel the sound in her chest.

The source of both the sound and the horrific smell was a perversion of humanity that was beyond anything Jillybean had ever experienced before. An infinite number of flies filled the silo and their ceaseless hum drilled deep

167

into Jillybean's insane mind. They covered every inch of the interior in a black carpet and that included the zombie. She knew there would be one, but she was not prepared for the size of it. It was enormous, a mountain of a beast, at least eight feet in height, which was shocking enough, but it was its girth that was beyond Jillybean's comprehension.

Jillybean had seen a hippopotamus once and as fat as it was, it was dwarfed by this zombie. Obese was not a word that could describe a belly that was twelve feet in circumference. It had rolls of fat undulating over more rolls of fat. Its arms were long, but so big around that they seemed stunted, and its head, although the size of a beachball, looked like little more than a button atop its gigantic torso.

In spite of its great size, Jillybean didn't see it at first. Beneath the layer of flies everything was a uniform brown: the zombie, the walls, even the hill that the zombie lay on. The hill, which took up a quarter of the silo, sloped up and away. It consisted of equal parts feed grain, maggots and feces, and the zombie didn't care which it shoveled endlessly into its gaping maw.

Are you seeing this? Ipes asked in a hollow voice. *It's eating a mountain of poop. P-double O-poop. And maggots. I'd puke but it would eat that, too. I know it. It would be like dessert for it. Like the cherry…urp…here it comes…*

Jillybean stared upwards trying to ignore Ipes as he retched. High above her, she saw a brown line like a stain. It was where the grain had been. Unbidden, the formula to find the volume of a cylinder came to her: $V = \pi r^2 h$. Simple. So simple that the numbers filled themselves into her head. Rounded down, she estimated that the beast had eaten 17,000 cubic feet of seed and who knew how much poop.

The girl and her zebra stared for nearly a minute in complete revulsion and were only jolted from the sight by the sound of a gunshot. "Christian," Jillybean whispered. The name was swallowed up by the sudden explosion of sound and fury coming from the creature. She expected it to move with something of a sloth-like lethargy, however the opposite proved true. It was deadly fast.

5-

It roared so loudly that Jillybean was both partially deafened and stunned. She was still cringing when she saw the thing charging headlong for the door. A light, unheard shriek escaped her as she ducked away and ran leaping over the smaller piles of corpses before hiding behind one of the larger ones.

She tucked into a little ball and watched from beneath her drawn hood as the titanic creature plowed into the door.

The door was larger than an average door, but the beast was so huge that it got stuck, but it wasn't for long. Greased as it was in its own filth, it slowly squeezed through the door and, as it did, great gouts of feces and grain spewed from its mouth in a fountain.

"Oh, by golly," Jillybean whispered in complete revulsion. She began gagging, loudly. Its eyes were tiny in its huge head; *like pig eyes*, she thought as it turned and looked right at her. It had heard her!

Don't move, Ipes whispered. *It can't see you. Just remain still and it will think you're a bush. Just a tiny bush.* This was a lie that was proven seconds later when one of its huge arms suddenly "popped" out of the layers of fat. It reached a huge hand towards her.

She was ready to bolt but Ipes forced her to be still, but she couldn't, not entirely. Her muscles quivered and her heart raced so fast she thought her flesh was pulsing with the beat. Thinking that her hair was giving her away, she slowly ducked further into a ball until she was completely hidden beneath her hood. Still, the thing reached and slowly squirmed its great bulk through the door. Ten seconds before it finally spilled out of the silo, her nerves shattered. She leapt up and ran for the house with the rusting bike and the scattered toys.

Along with toys there were chuck-holes in the yard and she tripped in one, going end over end as the beast let out a roar. It was so loud that it felt to her as though it was yelling right over her shoulder, but when she turned it had just slipped from the silo and was now charging her way, its layers of fat flapping up and down. It was immeasurably faster than she was prepared for.

Fear surged through her, turning her numb. Running on wooden feet, she pelted for the door, betting her life that it would be open—it wasn't. The knob held firm as if it had been welded in place. There was no actual porch, only three cement steps and a black wrought-iron railing, which she leapt over and sprinted for the side of the house, dodging between an old Camaro sitting on flats and a pokey juniper bush. The frothing, horrible beast was right behind her.

Small and quick as she was, she was able to take that corner with ease. The beast could not control its momentum and plowed into the Camaro full force. Twelve hundred pounds of fat and muscle smashed in the driver's side door and shattered every window and knocked the car back four feet with a grinding metallic squeal. The monster didn't even seem to notice the car. Its piggy eyes were filled with a fire of hate. All it cared about was eating her in one gulp.

The thought turned her numbed muscles limp. She ran, but it felt like she was going slower and slower, as if she were running in mud or sand. Somehow, she made it to the backyard before the monster ate her. There was a tall wooden gate that was partially opened; she darted through it with the monster so close that when it slammed its full weight into the door, it sent planks and shards of wood flying.

She was hit by a chunk of two-by-four and sent sprawling. Going with her momentum, she rolled and was up again, her size eight Keds kicking up dirt as she ran, looking back over her shoulder. The monster had fallen among the debris of its own making, but was already getting to its feet.

The door! Ipes cried. Unlike many homes, this one did not have a sliding glass door leading to the backyard. The door was wood with a square window taking up most of the top half. It would take the monster all of a second to destroy it completely and yet Jillybean felt relief flood through her: the door sat miraculously canted open a few inches.

Yes, the old house was a dubious shelter, but just then anything was better than being out in the open with the monster. And the very small size of the door was an asset: the monster would take forever to get through it and by the time it did, Jillybean figured she would be a block away and counting her blessing.

She raced inside and was immediately confronted by a choice: up three steps to the main floor or down an unknown number to a pitch-black basement where she'd be trapped and eaten in the dark, her stick-like bones later used as toothpicks. *Not down there!* wailed Ipes when she hesitated.

"Yeah," she said, breathlessly and ran upward. She made it to a little square landing that was somewhat like a foyer to a small kitchen, when the monster hit the door with such force that the entire house shook. The door disintegrated and the light from outside was completely cutoff as the beast entirely filled the opening. Once more, Jillybean was confronted by a giant arm and a reaching, grasping hand. The craggy nails, alive with maggots, was shockingly close. She was only three stairs up and the thing's arm was twice as long as a normal man's and its hand was bigger than a catcher's mitt.

The diseased nails were inches away from her pert little nose.

Jillybean had her back pressed to the wall as the fingers slowly got closer and closer. Once more, the beast was pushing through a narrow opening and once more gouts of vomit came pouring out of its mouth. Horrifically, it began grunting and chewing on the foul stew it had puked up.

It was such a sickening sight that her coltish legs gave out on her. She dropped and crawled into one of the strangest kitchens she had been in since the apocalypse had begun a year before. Other than a bowl, a spoon and two coffee mugs parked next to the sink, the counters were clean. The floor was dusty but free of shards of glass or broken plates. Strangest of all, the cupboards were all closed. It was almost as if the dozens of starving refugees who had ransacked the place had cleaned up after themselves.

Feeling as though she had crawled into a different time or a different world, Jillybean crouched even lower. In her mind, different did not mean safer and, after a brief hesitation, she scurried into a dining room which was nearly filled by a single long wood table and eight high-backed chairs. In front of one of the chairs was another bowl, spoon and mug combo, an open laptop and— Jillybean's mind boggled at the sight of it—a box of Fruit Loops.

With the house shaking all around her and the beast roaring as it struggled to get in, she should have been racing out of there, however, the box of cereal held her in place. There was a yellow sticky note still stuck to it.

Eric,

It's thursday so I'll be home late. I hope you have a good day and don't forget to tell Mr Reynolds about your appointment for monday. And for the millionth time we have the g-kids this weekend so don't make plans. See you later.

Love-Alicia

The note made no sense at all. How was it still stuck to the box and how was the box still on the table? Here in the middle of the country, there had to have been at least a week of rumors and rumblings about zombies before anyone ever saw one. But somehow Eric had gone from eating Fruit Loops and worrying about the g-kids at breakfast to disappearing completely, possibly before the end of the day.

We don't have time for this, Ipes urged. *Grab the cereal and let's go!*

He was both right and wrong. He was right about the cereal, but wrong about not having time. She had stumbled into someone's life, a life that had been interrupted, seemingly in the blink of an eye. It didn't seem right to just step out again so easily.

"Lives are aposed to have meaning," she told the zebra. This was a fundamental truth that felt like it had been slipping away from her more and more over the past year. Every adventure, every narrow escape, every death, every murder, every time she gave in to the immediate need of the moment seemed to have cheapened the idea that every life was precious. Not just hers.

Okay, yes, and right now it's not just your life I'm worried about. There's also Christian's life. So, please grab the cereal and let's get out of here.

She did, making sure to set the note on the keyboard of the laptop, thinking that if Eric ever came back home it would be something he would cherish. The note had ended with *love,* and that was something important to a girl who was starved for any affection.

As she stuffed the half-filled box into her backpack and the monster continued to strain the timbers of the house to get in, she wandered into the living room/ family room. Here was evidence of the g-kids. A colorful pile of toddler toys, looking as though they had been bulldozed into place, sat in a heap in the corner. Resting on the tv set were pictures of the g-kids: two blonde little angels that looked as though they had been carved from...

No more, please, Ipes begged. *Did you hear that? It was a pan falling. You know that means, the monster is almost in the kitchen. Forget these Mayberry Von Traps and let's go.*

Even though she was no longer in much danger, it was sound advice. With a sigh, Jillybean went to the front door, turned the lock and pulled. The door didn't budge. She threw her measly forty-six pounds against it only to bruise her shoulder. "What the hay?" She wiggled the lock back and forth in a growing panic when she saw there was a second lock below the first—it had no knob. There was only a brass circle and a keyhole.

A door that locked from the inside made as little sense as finding an untouched box of Fruit Loops sitting out in the open. Once more, she had that sensation of being out of sync with the world. In frustration, she yanked again on the doorknob before turning to her left. *If* there had been a garage, the door to it would've been right there fifteen feet away—but there was no garage. The Camaro had been sitting smack dab in the middle of the driveway, which had ended at the now destroyed gate.

"Out the window then." This seemed like an obvious choice, however, Jillybean knew from experience that windows could be harder to work than they appeared. Many only opened partially or opened in a canted manner, making it very difficult to get through. With time crunching in, the obvious solution was to break the front window. It sat, larger than life, across from a dusty flower-print couch.

Jillybean turned in a quick circle, hoping to find a hammer sitting out with perfect convenience. The world didn't work that way. The only hammer was plastic and bright red. Ignoring the toy, she chose a pot that had once held a living plant but which now held dirt, a foot-tall stick and a few curled leaves. It was about the size and heft of her head. She hurled it two-handed at the glass. There was an explosion of dirt, a *donk* noise and then the pot fell to the floor, where it broke in two.

The window remained perfectly intact. "Oh, for all darn it!" She turned to find something else to break the window with and found herself staring at the monster. It was stuck in the doorway that led from the kitchen to the dining room, its glaring piggy eyes full on her. The demonic hatred in them smote Jillybean. Panic began to fill her, only just then the beast withdrew from the doorway.

A moment of pure joy was followed by another of terror as the monster changed tactics. Instead of trying to push through the doorway, it hurled itself straight at the wall next to it. The house shuddered under the blow and a floor-to-ceiling crack erupted in the wall.

Do something, Jillybean!

Her mind had turned to mush and the only thing she could think to do was pick up the ottoman that sat in front of a rocker and charge at the window. At the last moment, she closed her eyes, thinking there would be an explosion of glass that could blind her. *DONK!* She hit the glass and bounced right off of it. Her momentum was backwards; she hit the side of the couch and fell over with the ottoman resting on her chest, still clutched in her hands.

She was in a perfect position to watch as the beast hit the wall a second time. Timbers blasted out of the drywall. This time the house did more than just shake. More cracks appeared: in the ceiling and along the hallway wall. The structure let out a deep, melancholy groan as if it were dying.

The groan was swallowed up as the monster tore apart the remains of the wall and lurched through. Jillybean had already tossed aside the ottoman and was tearing down the hall to a terribly uncertain future. So many "what ifs" crowded her mind: What if the windows here were barred? What if they were painted shut? Or nailed shut? What if they were the canted sort? What if another monster had heard the commotion and was outside waiting to eat her?

What if she didn't have time to even get to the window? This was the most pressing question.

Behind her, the wall crumbled to nothing and then came the *Boom! Boom! Boom!* of the monster's giant feet charging after her. She knew it would hit the door and that it wouldn't hold. The question now became: would the frame around it, the studs and the header hold long enough to give her a chance to escape?

No.

Emphatically, no. She knew it as she slammed the door shut and caught sight of the monster heading at her, filling the entire hallway with its bulk. It was terrifying beyond belief.

Hold it together, Ipes said in a calm Daddy voice. *You know what to do.*

Her hand was already in the side pocket of her backpack where she kept one of her Joggle Hoppers. There was no time for a real plan, there was only time for a split-second decision. The hopper had to distract the beast long enough for her to slip past it without being seen, so she couldn't just throw it anywhere in the room. A closet would've been good; however, Alicia's was so full of clothes that it was busting at the seams, and Eric's was mostly closed.

There was also throwing it on the other side of the queen bed and "hiding" against the wall next to the door. It was fifty-fifty she would be seen. Her life would be decided by a coin toss. That wasn't good enough. Which left tossing the hopper into the bathroom and hoping she wouldn't be seen as she ducked behind the bed.

Having a small person's mindset was the deciding factor as she threw the Leaping Joggle Hopper at the partially open bathroom door. It banged off it with a musical note that was torn asunder as the bedroom door exploded. The frame, the header, both the king and Jack studs, as well as three other studs were blasted in splinters.

The door held like tissue paper and the monster piled into the room along with a plume of dust, plaster and broken lengths of wood. Jillybean dove for the side of the bed. Despite being a master bedroom, there wasn't much space for both a queen-sized bed and an eight-foot tall monster. It hit the bed with so much force that it slammed into Jillybean mid-jump and pinned her to the wall with her Keds poking out.

Don't move! Ipes cried as the monster got to its feet, hitting its enormous head on the light fixture. "Don't move" was great, but useless advice. The monster was so hellish that it drew Jillybean's attention. She twisted around and watched as it charged at the very narrow bathroom door.

Again, the house shook and this time she felt its dying groan come up through the floor. And now there was definitely a lean.

The monster, black blood pouring from its head and with glass and wood in its eyes and face, had misjudged the exact location of the door and had smashed the wall right next to it, tearing through the drywall and blasting the tile on the other side. It swung huge haymakers, knocking down studs with every swing until it could march into the bathroom where the Joggle Hopper was bipping and bopping all over the broken tiles on the floor.

It lifted a tremendous foot and crushed the hopper.

It all happened so fast that Jillybean had only just begun to get her feet unstuck. She froze, her breath pent up in her chest. If the monster turned around, she'd be dead—it didn't. With an echoing cry, it launched itself at the shower curtain and then, when that went down, it proceeded to pummel the wall around the tub. Jillybean could only guess that perhaps it was because it was used to the action by then.

As it destroyed the bathroom, she worked her feet free, climbed silently to a standing position and tiptoed through the mess the monster had made. She was just about to take off running when part of the hallway wall came down in front of her and there, once more, was the monster with it ugly piggy eyes. The two stared at each other for a moment before Jillybean sprinted forward. The beast punched a hand through the wall and managed to catch the side of her ghillie suit with a pinky. That smallest part of him was enough to spin her around and dump her on her bottom.

In a flash, she was up again, racing for the kitchen. She tripped and stumbled through the mess in the dining room, crawled through the kitchen and staggered down the stairs. Once outside, instincts kicked in and she went to one knee, pulling her ghillie suit around her. Behind her, the beast was tearing down more walls and roaring in fury; she had a few seconds to make sure she was alone, and to try to regain her strength. The little adventure had turned her knees wobbly.

Only when she had recovered somewhat did she begin to creep away, checking behind her every other step. The house was tilting back and forth, like a cardboard box as the beast went from room to room searching for her. The whole structure finally came down just as reached the chain-link fence that formed the boundary of the backyard.

"Oh my," she whispered. The house folded in on itself, starting with the back end. In the still afternoon air, it was a loud implosion and she lost no time going up and over the fence to hide in the high grass beyond.

That's one way to kill a giant zombie, Ipes said. *Just drop a house on it like in the Wizard of Oz. Do you think it was wearing ruby slippers?*

"I'm not going to go find out. They'd be all gross and…" She choked off her sentence as the house began to shift and move. She slunk low and watched in amazement as the zombie, bleeding in great torrents, fought its way free of the rubble.

Looking as dazed as Jillybean felt, it stumbled through the backyard almost directly at her. She froze, becoming Jilly-rabbit, hoping that her camouflage would render her invisible to the zombie. It wasn't easy to hold her ground as it lumbered with blank eyes towards her. When it came to the fence, it ripped it up with barely a grunt. It then marched on, heading straight for a dark, reedy pond that sat across a dirt road.

When it got there, it plunged right into the murky depths until the water was up to its neck, whereupon it began to drink, slurping and slurping. It also fouled the water, first with its black blood and then with something that had Ipes regretting his lunch.

Everything it does is completely gross, Ipes groaned. *I mean look at it. You can see it's pooping at the same time it's drinking. Remember the perpetual motion machine we were talking about? I think that thing is it. It could do this forever. Drinking its own poop and well, you know.*

She knew. Jillybean was a light shade of green. "Let's not talk about it anymore. Okay? Let's just make sure we fill our water bottles somewhere else."

How about Kansas?

"That may be too close. What's the state that has all the polar bears and the penguins?"

East Dakota. Ipes was in mid-chuckle when another gunshot rang out.

6-

In a snap, the zombie surged out of the water, bringing half of the pond with it as it went charging toward the sound. It jiggled and wiggled in a sickening manner that wasn't any better seen from behind than from the front.

Jillybean followed after it at a discreet distance. It wasn't the only one of its kind; there were six other colossal creatures. As they all had huge, drooping breasts, hairy chests and tremendous rolls of layered fat that hung almost to mid-thigh, it was impossible for Jillybean to tell their sexes. It really didn't matter whether they were boys or girls, their rage was equal to their size and they killed anything that got in their way and that included other zombies.

After passing a fifth body, Jillybean decided to get out of sight and she slipped into the furniture factory. It was a low brooding building made of dark brick. Other than a few offices that faced the main street, it was a windowless structure that ran the length of two blocks.

She expected it be hot and stuffy inside, however it was cool and dry. A heavy pine scent filled the air and she greedily drank in the aroma before she took off running along the factory floor, passing strange toothy machines. They lurked in a semi-dark. The only light filtering into the building was murky and grey, having strained through filthy skylights set every thirty feet in the ceiling.

It was dark and grim inside and yet Jillybean wasn't afraid. The pine-smelling air was utterly still, holding motes of dust perfectly suspended as if they were frozen in time. More ageless dust coated everything in a uniform layer. It was unmarred by a single track. Not even a mouse had passed through the building in all the time since the apocalypse. She was alone, and as long as she didn't impale herself on one of the machines, she would be safe.

But being safe wasn't really on her mind. Christian was in more trouble than he realized. He might be tough and brave against the normal monsters but the big ones were a whole other story. They were scary fast and immensely strong. Christian needed her whether he liked it or not.

Tucked into his place on her backpack, Ipes didn't think so. He tried his best to talk some sense into her. *This was his choice, remember? He is also a grown-up and he's a big grown-up. He should be fine. No, better than fine. He'll probably kill them all, no problem. We shouldn't get in the way.*

She wouldn't listen. She ran with abandon, her ghillie suit streaming out behind her. More gun shots spurred her on past long, neat shelves of lumber, bins of scrap, bags of sawdust, crates of wood nails and screws, jugs of industrial strength glue and barrels of stain and varnish.

Where all the finished pieces were, she neither knew nor cared. Her mind was completely on Christian…all except the part that was thinking of a way to rescue him.

First, she had to find him, which didn't take a detective. A hundred converging zombies were her first hint to his whereabouts. Rushing out of a loading bay door in the back of the building, she saw the beasts lurching toward a white church. A gunshot from the church was her next clue.

"He's trapped! We need a distraction." It would have to be the fastest distraction of her life. The big monsters could tear down the church in minutes.

He is the distraction, Ipes said. *We can get a bike and zip out of Dodge before one of those really big ones sees us.*

"Don't be like that, Ipes. We're the good guys…"

Since when? the dark voice asked.

Jillybean paused, remembering how Baby Eve looked after she died, pale and beautiful, but floppy. And how General Johnston looked at the bottom of the stairs sprawled in a contorted jumble of arms and legs, pink foam coming from his mouth. Jillybean could picture him perfectly, right down to his shining brass belt buckle. She had stood there in shock as he started to twitch; first just a foot and then his entire body. He spazzed for a few seconds, his head making hollow noises as it knocked against the concrete wall.

"Okay," she whispered, blinking away the image. "Okay, we're trying to be the good guys and the good guys don't run away. Now hush!" The zebra took on a completely lifeless state. His black eyes became nothing but beads of plastic, while hers turned feverishly bright.

Vague plans came and went, each needing too much time or supplies that weren't available. Explosions were out because she didn't have explosives. A fire would have to be set so close that she would likely become the focus of the attack. Sound would only work if Christian would go into hiding but that just wasn't him.

In desperation, she stared around until something clicked. It wasn't a very good something. "Too many possibilities for something to go wrong."

Her mind let a thousand things go and concentrated on the very specific problems to the very general plan building inside of her. She had to figure out angles vs momentum, gravity over friction divided by distance, fuel consumption rates and minimum combustion temperatures. There were other variables that went into her simple plan to roll a barrel of flaming varnish towards the church, but they were beyond her ability to manipulate. At a certain point, she could only pray.

Turning, she raced back into the factory to where she had passed the barrels of varnish, each of which were constructed of blue plastic, stood at about eye level and were almost ten times her weight. Pushing one over should have been nearly impossible for a child her size. Her arms were puny after all. Where she lacked in strength, she made up for in brain power, and if she'd had the time, she could have winched the barrel into place so softly that the dust covering it would have gone undisturbed.

Unfortunately, she had to get it out the back of the factory as fast as possible, which meant there was no time to hunt for ropes and pulleys or to create either from the materials in the building. She had to use what was available: scrap-wood, nails and basic hand-tools. The building was full of all of these.

In no time, she came back dragging a tarp, on which was a pile of wood, two hammers and a handful of nails.

Is all of that even necessary? Ipes demanded.

"Good question." There were twenty barrels set in five neat rows of four. Each was marked with the distinctive "FLAMABLE" warning. She put the zebra on one of these, then heaved her shoulder into it. "Grrr!" she growled through her small, gritted teeth, as her arms shook with the strain. Using all her strength, she was able to rock one side of it a fraction of an inch off the cement floor.

That's enough! I want off, please. Ipes had thrown himself flat; his round, cookie-filled belly pointed at the ceiling.

"Yes, it's all necessary," she told him and put him in his place on her pack. When the zebra was safely out of the way, she grabbed the smallest piece of wood and the steel claw hammer. The three-foot long piece of scrap-wood had been tossed aside because it was cracked and split on one end. This made it useless in the furniture making world, but it was ideal as a wedge.

Jillybean shoved the broken, angled side as far as she could under the barrel, which was only an inch or so; then took a three-pound sledgehammer in both hands and started beating the back end of the board. Each hit drove the tip of the wedge further under the barrel, lifting it slightly. After five hits, the wedge had lifted one side of the barrel to its maximum: one inch.

Um, Jilly? I don't think that's gonna do it, Ipes said.

"No duh." She was already running for the next piece of wood. This too had an angled crack. She stuck it under the first board and hammered it until it lifted the barrel another inch. A third hunk lifted it one more inch. She worked as quickly as possible, hitting each board just enough to lift the barrel. When one side was canted six inches in the air, she heaved up on the uppermost board.

Once more she growled her little kid growl and her arms shook. This time, the barrel began to tip further and further until it fell over with hearty *thump!*

"Perfect," she whispered. Quickly, she ran to the tarp, grabbed a well-worn claw hammer and some nails, shoved them into her backpack and ran back to the barrel. The easy part was over. Now she would have to roll the barrel forty yards through the factory to the back ramp and no amount of brain power would help.

It wasn't easy for such a small child. There were electrical cords running here and there, and chunks of old wood to dodge, and the layout wasn't arrow straight. Then there was a problem with the barrel itself. It kept wanting to heel over to the right. It was just another variable that she would have to account for.

By the time she got the barrel to the loading ramp behind the factory, she was breathing in gasps and sweating freely beneath her ghillie suit.

There was no time to rest. She yanked out the hammer and three of the nails. Two nails went between her lips and the other she hammered into the barrel. She went to hammer the next in when Ipes said, *One's enough! We have to hurry.*

He was right about the need to hurry. Great thundering bangs and explosive crashes were coming from the church. If Christian thought he'd be safe by locking himself in, he was about to get a rude shock. She had already seen evidence that the giant monsters could turn the doors and perhaps even the entire building into kindling.

She swung the hammer and partially missed, sending the nail bouncing away. Reaching for the next, she explained around the last nail in her mouth, "The second

183

hole counteracts the partial…" She swung the hammer and the nail punched halfway through the thick plastic. "… the partial vacuum created as the varnish comes outta the first one. It's sorta like science." She hit it again and it popped through.

Now, she pulled out both nails and the rich, pleasant smell of varnish filled the air.

There was no time to enjoy it. The ramp itself posed a new problem, one of control. The ramp led to a parking lot, which led to a road, which ran past the back of the church. It was more or less, a straight shot. But it wasn't a perfect route by any means. There was a good chance the barrel would roll to the right and get lodged between the cars parked along the side of the road, or it could roll left and shoot off the uncurbed street and into the drainage ditch that ran parallel to it, or it could simply get stuck somewhere a child couldn't get it unstuck.

Or she could play every angle exactly right and save Christian.

With the righthand turn tendency of the barrel partially counteracting a tilt in the parking lot, she aimed it on a gentle S trajectory, lit the tacky varnish that was leaking from the holes, and gave it a gentle push. Just as she had predicted, the tilt of the road made up for its righthand spin. The barrel, a bright yellow ball of flame, started right, then came left after the ramp as it bounced and spun through the parking lot.

"Come on, come on, come on," Jillybean urged as the barrel made it through the lot and ran straight and true along the road, speeding faster and faster, leaving a trail of rich, black smoke as it sped for the church.

Then a stick lying far down the road ruined her well-laid plan. "No!" she cried, contorting her body, much like a poor bowler might, as the barrel suddenly went counter to its spin and its course. It turned directly for the drainage ditch that ran along the far side of the road.

"For all darn it," she griped, knowing that nothing could right the barrel now. The smart thing to do was to run and get another barrel, however there was something innately and absurdly gripping about a flaming barrel of varnish speeding out of control and Jillybean did not have the self-control to turn away. She *had* to see what was going to happen. It was not an everyday occurrence, even for her.

The barrel turned out to be surprising spry and nimble. It clicked off another unforeseen obstacle, which turned in at a diagonal angle toward the ditch and instead of plopping straight into it, the barrel bounced and flew over the ditch where upon it rolled down a long gentle slope that was filled with high grass and weeds. Although it went slower and slower and slower, it still kept going until it finally stopped in the middle of the field.

Ipes squinted his beady eyes. He made a humph sound —it looked as though the thick grass had smothered the fire. *Oh great. It's not even still on fi…*Flames suddenly engulfed the barrel. They became so brilliant that it was hard to look at the barrel even though it was the sunniest of days. The blaze was so fierce that it eclipsed the fact a smaller fire ran in a line all the way back to the ditch. In seconds, flames had cut the field in half and were spreading, going in every direction, filling the sky with a huge plume of smoke. Once more, Jillybean found herself staring instead of acting.

Do you think that'll burn down the town? Ipes asked. *No great loss, but that Christian guy is still in the church.*

"No. It won't burn much other than the field. Unless the wind picks up, the roads will act like fire breaks." The real question was would the fire eating up the field be enough of a distraction to save Christian. Jillybean's gut told her it wouldn't. The fire was going like mad, roiling and spinning little tornadoes of smoke. It was baking hot from even a hundred yards away, but it was that very heat that would make it less of a distraction than she had hoped.

The fire was consuming what fuel there was in the barrel and the field at a fantastic rate and already there were wide swathes that had been charred down to the dirt. Soon it would be just a black field of ash and when it was, the zombies would still be gathered fifteen deep around the church.

"We'll need another barrel," she said, turning to go back in.

"Another barrel? For what?"

7-

Jillybean let out a little shriek and jumped. It was Christian. He had come creeping up behind her sometime in the last five minutes. Although his cocksure smile had not changed, the rest of him had gone through a bit of a transformation. His torn-up white shirt was no longer white. It was black and damp with more zombie blood. In the few places it was still dry, it was grey with dirt. His blue jeans were torn and filthy, and on his head, somewhat like a tea cozy, was a thick mat of cobwebs.

The simple act of taking all of this in provided the little girl with enough time to get over her fright. "I was just going to get another barrel in case you needed an extra helping of rescuing."

"I didn't need help to begin with," he told her. "As you can see, I got out of the situation on my own."

Did you see that? Ipes asked, speaking out of the side of his mouth. *A spider just went into his shirt. I swear I saw it. It just crawled in and now there's no way of knowing where it is. It could be in his bellybutton or his...*

"Hush Ipes."

Or his armpits. I bet they're hairy and I bet the spider is all nestled and invisible, just hiding in there making babies. I think I might be sick. Jillybean, we need to check each other head to toe. Start with me. Look for egg sacks. Oh sweet Lord! I felt something on my back!

Christian scratched himself, making Ipes gag. Jillybean whispered, "That's enough, Ipes. Do you want to go to timeout?"

"Something wrong with your friend?"

"Nothing a ziplock bag won't cure." She had meant it to be a threat, but Ipes was all for it. In his mind, suffocating was a better way to go out than having spiders burrowing into his brain.

This brought out a grunting laugh from Christian. He came to stand next to the little girl. "Man, did you see those things? The big zombies I mean. They were like…" He could only blink dazedly. "I don't know what they were like. They had to be over a thousand pounds and they were unstoppable. How on earth did they get so big?"

"They eated a lot. You know, a lot, a lot. See those silos? They came from there and all they do is eat and eat. It's horrible."

"Who votes that we get the hell out of here?" He had his hand raised. "There's no way we'll get any gas with those…those *creatures* around. This place is a death trap." Jillybean was slow to say anything. She was watching the monsters watch the fire while his words: *This place is a death trap* swirled in her mind.

Christian took her silence to mean she was still mad at him. "Hey, look. Maybe I shouldn't have been so blunt back there. You know, about the cursing and me telling you what to do. So, I guess what I'm saying is that even though you didn't save me, I appreciate the effort, and maybe you can tag along with me for a little longer."

Ipes was fully in agreement. *I'm with Christian. He's clearly seen the errors of his ways. I think we can trust him. Let's get gone!*

Still she didn't say anything. She stood there, her huge blue eyes wide and unblinking as she pictured those giant monsters. They made everything seem insignificant and that included her need to replace *Betty Lou*. What was a bicycle compared to a monster that could tear a house down?

She pictured the Red Gate barring the way into Estes Park. Could one of those monsters destroy it? Maybe not, but seven of them certainly could. She was sure that seven of them could take it apart with their bare hands. *But we're so far away, she thought, and they would never leave their silos…as long as there was "food" in them.* But what would happen when the food ran out? The answer was obvious: the monsters would come out. Now she thought of the Azael. What would happen if the remnants of the Azael could figure out how to harness them? The walls guarding Estes didn't stand a chance.

Forget the Azael, Ipes hissed. *They've gone back to being skulking bandits. What we have to worry about is the here and now. You heard Christian; this place is a death trap. And what is the smartest thing to do when you come to a trap? Avoid it at all costs.*

"I don't know if that's really the smartest thing," she said. Christian thought she was talking to him and his dark brows came down. She didn't notice. Her eyes were still staring blankly as her belly began to get that achy, airy feeling it sometimes got before she was forced to do something frightfully scary and dangerous.

Some people said it was like butterflies in their stomachs; she thought it felt like she needed to puke.

"The smart thing would be to kill them," she said, again speaking to Ipes.

Christian's jaw dropped open. He started to laugh, then he saw how Jillybean's jaw was set. "You have got to be kidding me. I'm not getting anywhere near those things. In fact, I'm leaving. Come on. I saw a farm that's kinda a distance away. We might get lucky with some gas or a vehicle."

Jillybean sighed. So few people had the guts to do the right thing. Those giant monsters were a horror that had to be stopped. Many, many people would die if no one did anything now before they got any bigger. "I can't leave. Not yet. What will they be like when they're ten-feet tall? Will bullets even stop them?"

"I don't know if bullets will be able to stop them now and I'm not about to try to find out. If you want to kill them, you can do it on your own."

And you know we can't be on our own, Ipes said. *We've gotten lucky so far, but it can't last.*

Their responses sent a flash of anger through her. She balled her fists and planted them on her hips. "Okay, if you're too chicken to do the right thing then get gone and take Ipes with you. Just amember, if I kill them all I get everything in this town."

Christian snorted. "Fine. Take 'it' all. This place isn't even a blip on the map. What could they possibly have that I would want?"

"Almost everything," she answered, pulling her ghillie suit off and taking the box of Fruit Loops from her bag. She handed it to him, saying, "Guess where I found that?" He seemed uncertain as he looked inside the box. "It was in the one house I went into. It was sitting right out on the table."

"Hmmm," he said, taking a glance at that part of the town that was visible. For the most part, doors were closed and windows were intact. The streets were clear of debris; no bones, no burned-out cars, no cast-off belongings. It was as if the town had been abandoned all at once in a single, unrushed afternoon.

Christian rattled the half-filled cereal box. "This doesn't make sense."

"Wanna know what it is?" Jillybean asked. "This place is untouched. There could be anything out there. Guns, food, gas. Probably enough gas even for your race car. You'll probably have to get a tower-thing for all the gas you'll get."

She could see him thinking it over and it stopped the ache in her belly. Doing stupid, dangerous things was always so much better when there was another person around, especially such a big, strong person like Christian. He had an easy, commanding way about him that wasn't an act like she had seen so many times before. As proof, he had gotten away from a hundred monsters, which couldn't have been easy.

"I don't know," he said with lips pursed. "First off, we don't even know if those big ones can be killed. Their heads are huge and I only have so many bullets. And second, there are a freakin' gob of the normal-sized zombies running around. I mean a lot. More than you'd expect for such a dinky town. Maybe I should try taking one of the big ones down with a long-range shot. You know, like a hundred yards or so, then maybe I'll think about taking on the rest. Maybe."

He's talking himself out of this, Ipes noted. *It's smart. Let's do the same thing. Those are big monsters and you are just a little girl.*

"Hold on, buster. Who are you calling little? You are definitely going in a bag because I don't want to hear another word out of you."

"Maybe this isn't a good idea," Christian said with that look adults frequently give her when they thought she was being extra crazy.

This was just everyday crazy and the fact he couldn't understand that made her cross. "Don't listen to him, Mister Christian, sir. I swear, he's just a striped chicken with fur."

"Sure, sure, that makes sense. But maybe you let me take care of things. You don't need to get worked up. You just sit in the shade and relax."

Ooh, I like this idea. It's downright chivalrous. He's like Captain Grey, you know. All tough and manly, and chivalrous. *If it wasn't for that spider laying eggs in his armpit, I'd say you should give him a hug.*

"That does sound nice," Jillybean said, warily. Too many bad guys masquerading as good guys had made her suspicious of kind strangers. "What's your plan?"

He shrugged, a move that had warning bells going off in her head. Who starts a plan off with a shrug? *Someone who doesn't know what he's doing*, she thought to herself.

"I'll just do my thing. You know, stick and move. Use my speed and endurance. Trust me, they won't be able to lay a finger on me."

Jillybean looked confused. "That's not a plan at all. That's just you running around stirring them up."

"Well I was going to suggest that we repel down from a helicopter, but my ninja suit is at the dry cleaners." He was making fun of her. She glared, scratching her bottom because her panties had not yet dried completely from when she'd been jumping off the bridge. He rolled his eyes. "Okay, do you want me to draw a map before we synchronize our watches?"

"I don't even know what any of that means. But I know a bad idea when I hear it and that's what means what you just said."

Christian growled from behind his pursed lips. "Until you can come up with a better plan, I think you should give your lips a rest." He shrugged off his pack and dropped some items from his pockets: a bulky set of keys, a flashlight, the gold lighter, a slim switchblade knife. "Just keep out of sight while I'm gone. I can't keep an eye on you and the zombies at the same…"

Jillybean wasn't listening. She was already walking away, heading down the ramp, staring down at the field that was covered in a grey haze through which flickers of red-gold flames could be seen. Off to the right of the field were a sting of undead spectators, gazing dully at the fire. Further off to the right, the church was still being ravaged.

As she stared, a familiar darkness began to form deep in her mind. *The town is a trap. We can lure who we want here*, the usual hissing voice whispered. *We can start rumors. Think about it. The River King might come in person if we start rumors of a dozen gas trucks parked side by side. His greed would be the end of him. He'd come and those beasts would destroy him for us.*

"Hmmm," Jillybean said, unconsciously imitating Christian. It wasn't entirely a bad idea and the more she thought about it, the more the darkness grew.

Jillybean! Ipes said in that daddy voice of his, again. *Don't you listen to her!* The daddy voice immediately shamed her. She knew why. More death was not the answer when it could be avoided.

"We can still kill the monsters, though." She was sure about that. But how? She turned back to look at Christian, but he was lost in the shadows of the low building. To her the open bay door looked like a huge black mouth and the ramp was its tongue. She shivered as she pictured it closing on them. They'd be trapped in that low brick building with only one another…

She drew in a sharp breath as *the* plan opened up before her. It didn't spring to life fully formed like some did. This one took a moment to perfect, but when it did it was almost flawless.

"We need a manikin," she declared.

"For what?"

"And we need rope and batteries. The big sort. Double Ds." For some reason that she couldn't figure out he smirked at this. It was one of those smirks she felt best not to ask about. "And we could use a disco ball. Do you know what one of them is?"

Judging by the eyebrow in the shape of a fishhook, the addition of a disco ball to the already odd shopping list confused Christian. "Yeah. How do you know what one is? And how on earth would it help in anyway?" She told him her plan and he listened, his mouth no longer pursed. His jaw hung open and when she finished, he began to shake his head at her. "You must have seen this before," he concluded. "Well, it's a hell of a plan and whoever thought it up should be given a medal."

"I thought it up. I don't like to brag or nothing, but I'm kinda a genius." She didn't think bragging about being a genius made any sense. It wasn't something she had any control over. It wasn't something she had achieved. That was the thing about being a genius. It wasn't something that could be trained or exercised into existence. Professional athletes had to train constantly and musicians had to practice, endlessly. Even physicists, as smart as they were, had to build a body of knowledge up, very much like a mountain, before they could excel in any single field.

She didn't like to brag about this one aspect of herself because it was no more her doing than the color of her eyes—and yet, it had come right out, both surprising and embarrassing her. A flush of pink lit up her cheeks. "Genius is what means I'm really smart, only it doesn't feel that way to me. I just feel like me, you know? It's everyone else that's, you know."

"Stupid?

Automatically, she nodded until, too late, she realized that Christian fell into the subset of "everyone else."

"Um, not necessarily stupid. Maybe not everyone is as…" *Not everyone is what?* she wondered. *Not as quick-witted? Not as cognitively efficient? Not as mentally agile? Not able to reason cogently or make logical choices given the circumstances or data presented?* Her smile faltered. Everything she had thought of was synonymous with being stupid.

She ended up finishing in a weak manner, "Not everyone is as smart as they could be." He was staring at her with those intense hazel eyes and she began to stammer, "And, and, and I shouldn't have included everyone. Not you, especially." It was strange to her that she wanted him to like her. Then she found it strange that she should find it strange. Wasn't being liked a perfectly rational desire?

Or you maybe you want him to like you-like you, if you know what I mean, Ipes said, then winked one of his beady eyes.

At first, she really didn't know what he meant. When understanding finally kicked in, she froze, her big eyes as wide as they could get. She wanted to refute Ipes' statement with a great deal of fiery temper *but*, Christian was pretty in that inexplicable way certain people were. More than once, she had found herself studying him as if trying to discover what elusive element he possessed that ordinary people found so magnetic.

She was doing it again, staring openly, however he didn't notice. He was staring right back. "Remember those rumors I heard coming from Colorado? One had to do with a little girl genius."

"Girl genius?" Her mouth had gone dry as dirt. "You mean there are two of us? Ha-ha?"

Her skills at lying were at a seven-year-old's level and he wasn't fooled. She could see the truth begin to dawn on his face.

"You are her? No way!" He turned to look at the factory as if he really didn't believe it and figured the real genius might be lurking somewhere nearby. When he turned back, his eyes bored into her. "I heard the rumors and I thought they were just about the tallest tales ever told. But they're true? All of them?"

"I don't know what rumors you've heard," she answered, stiffly. Her whole body was stiff. She was afraid to move. "But either way, they're probably just, you know, rumors and tales, like you said." She couldn't help wondering whether he had heard about what she had done to baby Eve. And had he heard about the ferry boats she had sunk or the cult of Believers she had wiped out? Had he heard that she had helped turn the artillery guns of the Azael on her own people? Hot tears rushed to her eyes and she turned away.

Doubt crept into his voice. "Yeah, some of them have to be just stories. They were so far-fetched that they couldn't have happened. That's what I always thought, but then you came up with this plan like it was nothing." A troubled look turned to a suspicious one. "Tell me, did you really…"

She immediately started shaking her head as she interrupted him. "I only did what I had to. That's all I'm gonna say about any of that. Okay? Now, if you'll get a move on with them barrels and such, I'll be back in half an hour or so."

In essence, she had dismissed him. She was just pulling the hood of her ghillie suit back up when he grabbed her arm. A brief flare of hate burned inside her. It was so hot and intense that if she'd been holding a knife, she would have gutted him…and enjoyed it. Along with the hate and the terrible thought, she could swear she could almost feel his hot blood wash down her hand. A gasp escaped her and she jerked as though she had been burned.

"You okay?" he asked, kindly. He tried to get her to look up into his face. She firmly kept her chin pressed to her chest, afraid that he might see the hatred and evil lingering in her eyes. "Hey, look, don't be mad, Jill. I won't tell anyone. You're safe with me, okay? It's a weird, weird world now and I know we sometimes have to do stuff that we wouldn't normally do. If you ask me, you're a victim. You should have, like a support group or something."

A support group for mass murderers? Jillybean didn't think there was such a thing and if there were, she didn't think she wanted to be anywhere near it. In her mind, mass murderers only deserved death.

Killing them would be a challenge at least, the dark voice whispered. *And it would be fun.*

The voice was wrong on both accounts. It wouldn't be fun, it would be horrible, and it wouldn't be much of a challenge. Jillybean was just too good. She was the best killer and she felt no pride in the fact. In truth, it diminished her. Being a murderer was an eternal point of shame.

She tried to shrug off the voice and the memories of corpses and body parts left in her wake. "Thanks for trying to be nice," she said giving him a blink of a smile, "but I don't think I'm anyone's victim. I'm the bad guy… sometimes." She turned to go once more and again he took her arm.

"No. You're not. A bad guy wouldn't risk their lives for a stranger the way you did. Sure, I wasn't in any real danger, but you didn't know that. And would a bad guy try to kill those giant zombies for nothing? And we both know there isn't much in this town. What do you think we'll get? A million bullets? I doubt there's a gun left within miles. Yeah, we might get some food and a few odds and ends but compare that to the risk."

What risk? she wanted to ask. She had already assessed her enemies' strengths, which were few but impressive and their weaknesses which were glaring. In relation to her plan, the risk in trying to kill them was slightly less than not trying to kill them. At least in the attempt she was being proactive. She was setting the terms of the encounter and as she knew monsters better than they knew themselves, she felt she could guess with some accuracy what they were going to do.

There was no way to be a hundred percent sure of anything with the monsters. At times, they were like the Leaping Joggle Hopper, a pebble or a stray butterfly could change their course, and with the size and strength of the giants, that tiny bit of unpredictability could make them more dangerous than anything she'd ever faced.

And that's why you need him, Ipes said, patting her on the shoulder from his spot in the backpack. *He'll give you that little bit of security you need. And so what if he knows your secret? He's already basically said that it's okay with him.*

"Maybe that means he's done something even worser," she said under her breath. The idea stuck with her. It was strangely appealing. Maybe he had been bad as well but was now trying to be good, like her. She was suddenly shy, but she had to know. "You said we all done things that were bad. You know stuff we weren't proud of. What did you do?"

He had been looking at her with his handsome face set in a look of rugged moral superiority. He was the adult. He was the alpha male and she was just the fifty-pound weakling. He was the priest and she the sinner. But her question turned that around.

Christian lips pursed tightly until there were a dozen little lines in them. "I'll tell you if you tell me whether you blew up the River King's bridge."

She nodded, her own lips pursed. "I used about a whole lotta C4. There was this army man who made a bomb and I saw what he did and just copied it. It really isn't that hard." She ended with a shrug.

He believed her. "Oh, wow. So, it really is you." She nodded again. "Okay, my turn." He looked away for a moment, his eyes at squints, peering at a puffy cloud that had been parked in the sky for the last hour or so. "I used to play the field a lot. You know, a girl in every port, and like a week before we started hearing about the zombies this one girl tells me she's pregnant."

"With a baby?"

"Yeah, and I was all like, it's not mine. But it was and I knew it. She was really into me. I know when a girl is falling for me and I usually make tracks before anything like this could happen."

"So, what did you do?"

The lips went tight again, and he started shaking his head with a look of disgust. "Nothing. I was in Virginia and she was in Kentucky and I…and I didn't do anything. The zombies came and I didn't do a thing. She could still be alive and I could be a dad. That's what I tell myself, but it's a lie. She died like everyone else and I didn't do a thing to try to save her. Pretty crappy, right?"

Jillybean nodded, which he found funny. He then let out a long sighing breath, saying, "Ain't we a pair?"

"Yeah," she agreed, but quickly changed her mind. "Maybe we really aren't. You don't like tag-alongs, amember?"

"Normally I don't. Kids are…hard. They whine; they do stupid things; people are always making excuses for them. You seem different. Like you're independent. It's funny. You kicked me to curb back there and, I don't mean to sound conceited, but no woman has ever done that, ever. You stuck out your hand and said I'm outta here. At first, I was like, good riddance, but you stuck in my head. Who knows, maybe if I can put up with you, I can figure out how to put up with any kid. Sorry if that came out weird. I know the problem is with me, not with you."

He sighed again and so did she in unconscious imitation. "I'm sorta in the same boat as you are," she told him. "That's what means I'm out here because I don't know if I can be around people no more. Things always just happen. Bad things, I mean. And it's almost always not my fault. Almost."

"Maybe we should stick together then. I can learn to like a kid and you can learn…whatever you need to learn.

What do you say?" He stuck his big paw out and after a moment, she shook it. She couldn't help the big smile on her face when she shook it. She felt strangely giddy inside.

The two beamed at each other as the last of the field burned and the clouds of smoke slowly dissipated and the zombies tore down the church. When it came down, its big bell clanged, the sound hanging in the air for a strangely long time. Christian raised an eyebrow, which she read correctly.

"That was a wooden church. It's like the Three Little Pigs." She knocked on the wall of the factory with her tiny fist. "This one is made of brick. It'll hold long enough to do the job." She didn't add: *I hope*, although she felt it in her heart. The big monsters were an unpredictable variable. *Partially unpredictable*, she told herself.

She left him then and with her usual efficiency, Jillybean gathered her supplies. There were no disco balls to be had, so she hastily made one from a broken mirror and a volleyball. The town was awash in batteries and a shocking amount of untouched food. Of course, the perishables had long ago perished, so most houses had a lingering sour smell to them. Still she and Ipes were able to nibble their way through an entire box of Pop-tarts as they slowly made their way through the small town.

Her pace slowed even more after she filled her backpack and had to drag along a rusting red wagon. The wagon was an utter necessity once she found the manikins. They were at a combination dog-sitters/beauty parlor/tailor/apparel shop. The shop was also someone's house, someone with a passion for jelly beans.

Jillybean's pockets were full as she made her way back to the factory with a blanket covering the wagon.

She found Christian waiting for her just up the ramp. Sweat glistened on his forehead and tiny rivers of it streaked through the dust that covered him. Because of the shadows, his eyes looked dark, and with his filthy torn up shirt and the dust that had turned him grey, Jillybean initially thought he was a monster.

The resemblance was so off-putting that Ipes whispered, *Don't let him touch you. He's one of them now.*

It was somewhat of a relief when he asked, "Did you get everything?" Before she could answer, he went on, "I knew you'd never find a disco ball so, I made one. Come take a look." He hurried forward and grabbed the handle of the wagon and pulled it into the dim interior of the factory. Hanging from the ceiling just inside the loading bay doors were planks of woods slowly swaying. On the wood were strips of mirror.

"It was nothing," he told her. "I used the mirrors in the bathroom and glued them on. Then I cut some cords from some of the machines. What do you think?"

She thought that because they were essentially two dimensional, the light from the flames from behind would draw the monsters away from the center of the building, which was the exact opposite of what they needed.

"Welllll," she said, hoping not to offend him. "Maybe it would be betterer if we hung them inside, like more in the middle of the building?" When she explained her thinking, he didn't get mad. He only laughed, which was a great relief. She pulled away the blanket, reached into the wagon and pulled out a cd player the size of a piece of carryon luggage. "This will be what attracts them. That and the manikins. After that, the fire will do the rest."

The factory all by itself was perhaps the finest, semi-naturally occurring monster-killing trap she had ever seen. There were only four exits, huge piles of lumber, thousands of gallons of flammable varnish and walls of made of brick. Her plan was to lure the beasts in and cook them in a giant oven.

Setting the plan in motion was nearly as easy as coming up with it in the first place. While she had been gone, Christian had blocked two of the exits—a precaution that was barely necessary since the dead could lock themselves in a bathroom or a car and never figure out how to get back out again. He had also piled long pine boards near the offices, as well as all around the sides of the building.

199

Soon the manikins and the homemade disco balls were strung up in the center of the building. Then the varnish was poured in a long winding river—and they were done.

"Now we find out if this will work," Christian said.

Jillybean thought it would at least mostly work, especially on the small ones. They were the most like real people and she had seen them die in all sorts of ways before. The question was once again with the big ones. Jillybean had only just begun basic biology and knew close to nothing concerning human anatomy and physiology yet. And nor did she know if the big ones had undergone any other physical changes beyond their immensity.

She assumed they had. Normal human bones and joints could not have withstood the terrible pressures of so much weight without adapting in some way. Had they changed enough to withstand fire? Jillybean pondered this as she climbed to the roof of the factory.

Christian used the butt of his rifle to knock out a pane of glass in the center-most glass skylight. "You can do the honors." Below the opening was a small stack of wood that had been doused with varnish. It was to be their initial fire. Jillybean counted on the monster's fascination with flame to draw them to the center of the building, where the manikins and the disco lights would them either beguile them or enrage. It didn't matter which, as long as they remained in the building.

Jillybean dropped a small torch down the hole and, quick enough, the fire leapt into existence. The smell was wonderful and nostalgic. It reminded her of Christmas though she didn't know why. They didn't have a fireplace in their house when she was "growing up." At seven she had a lot more growing up to do, but to her, the home in Philadelphia would always be the house she grew up in.

For a few moments, the two stared down at the fire, lost in their own thoughts. Jillybean was thinking of the last Christmas she had shared with her family before the monsters came. It was a beautiful memory spoiled by the memory of the Christmas that had just passed. She had spent it trapped in a bitterly cold house with the frozen corpse of her mother shut up in the master bedroom. Candles had helped keep Jillybean alive, as did the fact she wore three sets of clothes and two coats day in and day out.

"I think we should turn on the music," Christian said, breaking in on her ghoulish thoughts.

She hit the "Play" button— *EVERYBODY DANCE NOW!* the machine screeched, causing Jillybean to back away. The beat that went with the music thrummed throughout her body and was very nearly compulsive. Christian couldn't resist. Laughing, he started shimmying his shoulders, swinging his hips and shooting out elbows.

"Man, I haven't heard this song since forever! Come on, Jill, show me some moves. Do the Funky Chicken with me."

Let me be the first to tell you, Jillybean, that's not how chicken's dance, Ipes remarked, looking askance at Christian the way most people looked at Jillybean. *There's a lot more head bobbing for one and they do like their chest-thrusts.*

It did look funky as far as she understood the word. Still, she wasn't an expert on chickens and their dances, which she assumed they did. She knew that bees danced to talk to each other about honey and bears and other things that bees cared about, so it made sense that chickens would as well.

"I'll have to take your word for it," she told the zebra. With the music so loud, she didn't have to whisper. In answer to Christian, she shook her head at the idea of dancing over the sight of what she hoped would be the world's largest crematorium.

Christian chicken danced in a circle around her. When she didn't move, he cried out, "How 'bout the Running Man!" He began to jerk and contort in what was a strange combination of running in place and dancing with neither really being fulfilled. When that didn't get her to move, he asked, "Ok, how 'bout the Moon Walk?" He started moving backwards in an oddly ungraceful manner across the rock-strewn roof. It wasn't long before he tripped over a stunted little vent, made a valiant but doomed attempt to stay on his feet and was laughing before he hit the ground.

Despite the zombies flocking in, and the rather disgusting thing they were planning to do to them, Jillybean could help grinning. Christian had such an infectious personality and bright-eyed smile that it would have been impossible not to do so.

"I don't know much about dancing just yet, except tap dance," she told him as he stared up at her from his back. "I did that for a while, but I think I forgot most of it. Maybe even all of it except for jazz hands." With her elbows tucked in tight, she stuck her hands out and gave them an extended wiggle and shake. "Maybe you can teach me some of the other dances when we're not on a roof or nothing."

"Sure," he said, getting to his feet. He stretched his back and let out a little groan and for once his eyes were dim. "I must be getting old. My back didn't like that. My neck, either. Let's go see if the dead like our choice of music."

Jillybean wasn't sure whether she liked their choice of music. It had an abrasive, demanding quality to it—and it was repetitive. Since Christian liked it so much, she kept her views to herself and followed after him as he went to the rear of the building, rubbing his neck. They snuck up on the edge of the roof, crawling the last ten feet or so until they could see the town and the burned-out field, and the hundreds of zombies. The music, whatever its good or bad qualities, was loud and carried for miles on the quiet still Missouri air.

"Wow, that's a lot of 'em," Christian said in awe.

Taking a random sampling, Jillybean concluded, "There's five-hundred and twelve of them, plus or minus fourteen. Which is a lot if you ask me since the population of the town started off as only two-hundred and forty." Christian raised an eyebrow and she explained. "I saw a sign that said how many people lived here back before. I thought it was kinda weird. They seemed to be proud that so few people wanted to live here."

"People are crazy like that," he agreed. "Here comes our first test." A trio of grey beasts had come up the ramp, paused for a moment then headed inside. Christian held up a hand. "High five." She slapped it and gave him a smile, however her mind was on another problem. Hanging on the wall near the front door had been a sign that had read: *Maximum Occupancy: 351.*

By her calculations, the building could hold three times that many. Yes, they would have to be squinched in, shoulder to shoulder, but they would fit. And yet, the sign had been put in place by the fire marshal. She did not know exactly what a fire marshal did, still, she drew up a composite of one in her mind: male, white—the word Caucasian made her think of Asians and if asked she would have guessed that it was the root word from which Asia stemmed—mid-forties, balding, uniformed, experienced and finally educated in all sorts of fire related duties as well as advanced mathematics, because how else did they come by their numbers?

She decided to run her numbers again; they were all rough estimates since the volume of the building, with its machines and lumbar and barrels and such, had not been measured by her. And nor had the length and width of the building been...

"Here comes a big one," Christian said, interrupting her train of thought.

The creature was so awful that both of them slunk just a little lower. It dwarfed the other monsters around it, making them look sickly and weak. It was also extra aggressive and would smash any of them which got in range of its fists. When it got to the top of the ramp, it didn't even pause. With a roar, it lurched inside followed by a steady stream of the smaller dead, interspersed by the other giants.

"So far so good," Christian said. "Let's go check the other side." The pair went to the far side of the building, where the zombies from the fields were hurrying to a chance to kill and feast on man meat. They battled themselves to get inside first.

From there, Jillybean's plan went like clockwork. Once the majority of the monsters were inside, Christian opened up a new hole in another of the skylights and dropped a torch down on a pool of varnish that led along the winding stream to every part of the factory. Within minutes fire ringed the hundreds of zombies, half of whom were doing everything they could to get to the manikins swaying from the ceiling. The other half had become fascinated by the flames and stood entranced as the factory filled with smoke.

Eventually the zombies pyramided high enough to reach the manikins and the plastic bodies were torn to pieces. By then the roof had become too hot for Jillybean. The soles of her Keds started to feel gummy. She and Christian went to the side of the building and found it zombie-free and the two were able to scamper to the safety of a house across the street.

Soon the heat baking from the factory was so fierce that even that was too close. They retreated down the block to a water tower and from there they watched the smoke build into a pillar that rose hundreds of feet straight up before it gently bent over and streamed east. It wasn't long before the boom box died.

The two humans relaxed as if enjoying a show. Jillybean had found three cans of Coke that afternoon and, along with the Girl Scout cookies, they made a fine meal. Much to Ipes' delight, Christian turned down the cookies, and only drank two of the cokes in quick succession.

"None of them came out. I think it's safe to say that the giants have died," Christian said after half an hour. "Nothing could have lived through that. Here's to you, *Giant Slayer*." He held out a hand to hive-five her. Grinning, she slapped it and then shook out her hand. His was so hard it was like slapping a piece of granite.

"I could use a beer," Christian said, putting his foot up on the rail and tucking his hands behind his head. Although he looked tired, his smile hadn't dimmed a bit.

"I could use a bath," Jillybean said, sniffing herself. The smoke, which had started favorably enough with its Christmas scent, had become overpowering and hideous when it had been mixed with the stench of burnt flesh. "I wonder if there's water in this?"

Christian gestured to a small pipe that ran down the side of the tower. It ended at the base with a spigot that poked out. "Let's see if you're in luck. I think you might since this town was deserted so quickly." The two climbed down and found that there was water in the tank. It came out of the spigot brown with flecks of rust, but only for the first few seconds.

Jillybean sniffed it, sipped at it and then splashed her face with it. "It's good," she said, beaming. She laughed as Christian hunkered down and drank and drank until his belly bulged.

"I hate the mugginess," he exclaimed when he came up to breathe. "When I wore the uniform and played under that damned sun, it never bothered me but today, it's just so oppressive. I think maybe we should head north for the summer. Or out to San Francisco. I hear they have wonderfully cool summers."

Pretty much the only thing that Jillybean knew about San Francisco was that it was across the wide prairie, over the endless Rocky Mountains, past a high desert, and then past more mountains. It would be an arduous, dangerous journey of weeks or months where anything could happen, especially in the mountain passes where bandits were known to skulk. A person, even one as smart as Jillybean could be trapped with relative ease and either killed or taken captive.

She didn't hesitate. "Yeah, let's do that. Let's go. Is the Golden Gate Bridge really made out of gold? I think that would be neat."

"I think that should be a surprise," he said, tipping her a wink. "It'll make the trip more exciting. We should leave tomorrow. Right now, I'm beat and hot. All that running around didn't sit well with me." He looked down at himself and snorted at the filth and old blood covering his body. "Could I be more disgusting? This shirt has got to go."

That was all the warning she had before he tore off the shirt, showing the world a lean, hard body that was nearly as torn and bloody as the shirt had been.

With a light gasp, Jillybean turned away, which had him chuckling. "Don't worry, I'm keeping it PG. What do you say after we hit Bush Stadium, we go north to Minnesota to see where the Twins played? I forget the name of the stadium. Either way it'll be the cooler, safer route across the country."

Jillybean said, "That sounds great." He took it as sarcasm, which was the exact opposite of what she had meant. Although the destination didn't sound all that exciting, the idea of just traveling, of taking their time, of seeing sights that would one day be lost forever, sounded interesting and relaxing. For so long she had either been fleeing some terrible danger or desperately trying to find somewhere "safe" that she was enthusiastic about the idea.

"If you give me attitude, what's in Darwin, Minnesota will forever remain a mystery to you."

"What's in Darwin, Minnesota?" She was suddenly brimming with curiosity. "It's not another baseball place, is it? Because if it is, that would be okay with…" He had been rummaging in his pack for a green bottle and as he straightened, she saw three long scratches on him. They were bright red and puffy.

9-

She knew a fair share about scratches and although she hadn't yet examined the healing cycle as it related to minor lacerations and abrasions, she knew scratches became red like this for one of two reasons: they were infected or…

The monsters got him! Ipes cried in anguish. It was her first thought as well.

Christian caught her staring and twisted his torso around. At first, he looked concerned, then he waved a hand, dismissing the fear playing in her eyes. "It's alright.

You can relax. Remember those shrubs on the other side of town? I got these when we raced through them. It wasn't the zombies, so chill."

She remembered the incident with perfect clarity; it wasn't alright and she couldn't relax or chill. Within a minute of being drenching in black, diseased monster blood, he had scratched himself bad enough to bleed.

Now, given the state of the scratches and his slowly deteriorating mood, it was almost a certainty that he was infected and that in five or six hours he would become a zombie.

The terrible realization must have shown on her face because he started shaking his head. "No. I am perfectly fine!" His voice was as high and shrill as a teapot on the fire...for all of a second. Then he rubbed his temples with his eyes closed. Having calmed himself, he said, "No. This sort of thing happens and people don't always die. I've seen it."

"Have you seen it go the other way?" Jillybean asked. Even a self-described loner must have. She had known seven people who had died from the virus without being scratched or bit by a monster. With five of them it had been utterly mysteries as to how they had become infected; the other two had been scratched or cut running from monsters, exactly like what had happened to Christian.

He didn't answer. He stared down at the ground as the truth slowly solidified in his head. In a minute, the idea that he was dying slowly evolved, going from impossible, to possible, then to fact, and as it did the weight of the truth bowed his head. He was devastated. His eyes were blank and staring and suddenly he seemed half the man he had been.

Jillybean felt gutted as well. She had found a friend and lost him in the course of the same day. She wanted to cry, however Ipes scolded her, *You're not the one who's dying. Cry tomorrow if you have to, but don't ruin his last bit of time left.*

She tried to smile, however her eyes sparkled with tears. "So, what's in Darwin, Minnesota?" He didn't answer. Instead he touched his temples with the tips of his fingers, pressing softly as if exploring for the source of his growing headache. She tried again: "Is it close?"

"Is Minnesota close?" he snapped, his forest-colored eyes blazing out of his face. "Is that what you're asking? You act like you've never seen a freaking map. The answer is no. It's not at all."

"Oh." The tears demanded to come back and there was no stopping them. She lifted the collar of her green kitten shirt up over her nose and wiped at them. The urge to bury her face in shirt and never look out again was strong enough to have Ipes scolding her again.

After a long breath, she tried a second time. "Maybe we can drive there. I saw all sorts of cars in this town. Sorry, they were mostly trucks and stuff like that, nothing as fancy as your race car. I did see a truck with purple flames on the side. It was real cool."

"Purple flames," he said, flatly. "Purple flames on a truck."

Jillybean nodded emphatically and spoke quickly before her emotions could take over again. "Yeah, they were real cool. It's probably a fast truck because who would put them on a slow one, right? I betcha it could get us up to Darwin in a super hurry."

He sighed as if the very act of sighing was exhausting. "No. We're not going to Minnesota. I was wrong about that. Just forget about all this." He waved an apathetic hand that indicated both everything in the world and nothing particular. "You should go away."

That wasn't going to happen. She had seen too many people go through this to leave. She wouldn't want to be alone. Even the toughest men sometimes cried when they became monsters.

"I-I won't go away and I don't think I can forget anything. I've got a real good memory. It's not really eidetic; that's what sorta means photogenic…oh, right Ipes. *Photographic.* I don't have that except a little. Either way, I won't forget you or the big monsters or Darwin or none of it. And we shouldn't sit here and wait…" *For you to die*—she bit that off, quickly and choked as she did.

She attempted a second smile, this time through pursed lips so the quiver in them wouldn't show. "We don't have to go to Minnesota. Ipes just thinks we should do something, you know, something nice. For you. Oh! I know what we can do. It's something you've always wanted to do."

"Busch Stadium," he said, with just the tiniest grunt of laughter. A shade of his old smile crept back, only to slip away. "It's probably too far. If I got infected four hours ago, I only have a few hours left."

"It hasn't even been four hours and I know how far it is to St. Louis. I saw a sign! It's only 134 miles. If we hurry, we can make it."

The smile grew brighter until it was at full force. "Okay, let's do it. Maybe this will turn out to be nothing and if so, we can always come back and loot the town. And I know we can get some racing slicks for the P1 in St. Louis. We'll be the baddest duo on the road."

His excitement and energy lasted only an hour. This was long enough to jumpstart the truck with the purple flames, fill it with gas and get twenty miles up the road. As the minutes ticked away, he grew tense and angry. Sweat ran from his thick hair and built up in the hollows of his eyes.

Jillybean dosed him with enough Oxycontin and Tylenol to put a normal man in a coma, however Christian seemed barely affected. For the next hour, she plied him with more pills and quarts of water. Nothing helped, except talking about baseball. Despite her ignorance of the game and the lack of any desire to ever learn anything about it, she encouraged him to talk as he weaved the truck up Highway 67.

He rambled on and on as they dodged traffic jams and monsters and piles of trash that made little sense being on the highway. He talked about players he had been fans of, which was boring to the little girl, and he talked about the myriad of rules, which had her fighting to keep her eyes open. It was only when he started to explain about batting averages and slugging percentages and ERAs, and splits and ratios and all the other numbers that made up the game that he piqued her attention.

Math always excited her. "But if a batter gets on because of a fielder's choice, that still counts against his average?"

"Yep. It sucks."

Her many questions and growing enthusiasm kept him semi-lucid until just after they passed a sign that read St. Louis 21 MILES. "What did that say?" he slurred, looking back. A second later, the truck crashed into a guard rail. "What was that?" he cried, glaring around. Sadly, his hazel eyes were almost black now. "Who hit us, damn it?"

Jillybean tried to tell him that they had run into a metal rail, however he was borderline delirious at that point and growing more and more dangerous with every passing second. He even pulled out a long-bladed knife and held it as if ready to attack the windshield.

"I was wrong, Jill," he told Jillybean. She had to drag her eyes from the knife.

"A-a-about what?" she stammered. Ipes had fallen to the floorboard during the crash and she was all alone. Christian looked as though he could change over at any second.

He squeezed his eyes shut as hard as he could, and his teeth made an awful grinding noise as they clenched together. "Darwin," he growled, surprising her with the answer. She had expected more baseball talk. "You should go to Darwin. Yes." He smiled, suddenly. It was a maniac's grin. "You can learn a lot there. You can learn how to live. I wish I had gone. I wouldn't be here now if I had. I would be with my kid. I'd be dead for sure, but I would be with my kid and that would be okay. It would be an okay way to die. Instead I have this."

For a second, Jillybean thought he was going to slash his own throat with the knife. Instead, he fumbled with shaking hands at the door latch, pushed his way out into the evening and dug in the bed of the truck for his M16.

"Don't watch," he warned in a hoarse whisper. "The pain's getting bad. Really bad. And it's not going to get any better."

He didn't shoot himself there on the ground. The city was twenty-one miles away, so he climbed up into the bed to catch just a grey glimpse of it on the horizon. "Remember Darwin," he told Jillybean.

She was choking on tears and sniffling back boogers by then and couldn't speak over a squeak. She nodded and he said, "Alright then." Although he had long arms, he was shaking with the disease and he couldn't get the barrel aimed right and pull the trigger at the same time. The bullet that exploded out of the gun took out his cheek and right rear. It knocked him flat on his back, where he moaned and dribbled a puddle of dark, dark blood.

The sound of the gun shot echoed for miles and rang in her head threatening to tear her mind apart.

But she couldn't give in to the desire to slip away and let whatever dark thing inside her take over. She had a job to do first. Christian wasn't dead. Seven-year-old Jillybean had to kill him, and she did it properly, her eyes wet, but blank and her hands steady. She was somewhere else when she pulled the trigger. She was imagining a magnificently green baseball field in Darwin, Minnesota. The bases were snowy white and the air smelled like brats and hotdogs sizzling on the grill.

The End

Author's End Note:

The Queen told this tale in a flat monotone voice. It came out quickly, without emotion or even inflection. It was almost as if she were speed-reading a story of someone else's life. I tried to ask her questions however she only blazed right through and I had to struggle to catch up. The only time she allowed the least bit of emotion was when she was repeating, verbatim, the rookie batting stats of Christian's favorite players.

She wore a smile for a few moments after she'd stopped speaking, perhaps remembering the taste of ballpark grilled brats. She then stood up and walked to the far end of her cell and faced the wall. After a minute, I assumed she was reflecting. After five, I thought she was rudely dismissing me. I stayed of course, saying nothing, not making a sound.

We were an odd pair. I, the esteemed writer, she, the imprisoned sociopathic queen. I both loathed and admired her. It was the little girl she had once been whom I loved. *She* was the reason I came back every few months and risked my life to talk to her.

When the Queen finally turned, she surveyed me, taking my measure as she always did, making me feel transparent and utterly worthless.

"That was unexpected," she said. To a woman who could foresee a person's thoughts and actions five minutes before they actually thought or acted, this was a compliment.

"Indeed," I replied. "Chris Turner wasn't nearly as imaginary as I thought. He was Christian, wasn't he? He was Christian to a T. Athletic, brave, carefree, handsome." My eyebrow raised slightly at the last word. She saw it of course and knew exactly what I was implying.

As she made no move for a few seconds, I had to wonder if I had carried my familiarity a touch too far. Her smile told me I had not. "Yes, he was all that, and more. He was perfect in every facet, except one. He was unlucky. He had the misfortune to have met me." Her chin dropped and for a moment, I caught the sparkle of a tear.

They had known each other less than a day, and that was thirty-five years before, and still she had feelings for him. It was strange to me to see even a single tear from the woman who was secretly called the *Ice Queen*.

"What did you do after he died?" My question concerned Darwin, Minnesota, however her mind was still taken up with Christian.

"I buried him in Busch Stadium. He played centerfield so I figured I would bury him there, only when I arrived, I discovered there was a mounded hump already right in the middle of the bases. Naturally, I assumed someone had beaten me to the spot and that there was someone buried there. So, I picked a spot out in the grass, which, coincidentally enough is where the position of centerfielder is actually played."

"Oh," I said, not knowing what else to say. As far as I could tell, the game of baseball had died and had been buried along with Christian Niederer; I knew next to nothing of the sport.

"There wasn't anyone buried in that mound, either," she added, speaking softly, almost to herself. Her blue eyes had taken on a dreamy state. "I realize only now that the mound was just the pitcher's mound."

I said, "Hmmm," in answer to this bit of trivia, paused for just a moment and then began to ask, "After that, did you…"

"Did I go to Darwin, Minnesota?" The Queen was back. She smiled without warmth. "If you had asked me that question yesterday, Ezekiel, I would have laughed and asked Darwin where? Today I will tell you that yes, I have been to Darwin and Christian was right. I learned a great deal. Even though it only played through my subconscious, what I learned changed how and why I lived."

I pressed her for what she meant, I cajoled, kissed up, and begged, but she only smiled enigmatically. I knew her. She was going to make me travel all the way out to Minnesota to find out what made Darwin special. Naturally, I exhausted every piece of reference material available to me before I even considered going. Nothing mentioned the town which was not even a dot on most maps.

I went to her cell twice more before she escaped, and during both interviews she mentioned Darwin; each time with that infuriating twinkle in her eyes. The town grew in my mind until I realized that I would have to go. I had to find out what could change a person's life so completely.

During the early spring following her escape, I set off with a trading caravan that wound through the High Sierras and then through the Rockies to Denver. Once on the plains, I found another caravan that was on a trading mission through the Azaels and out to the Missouri River crossing at what had once been the Colonel's Island. Only the rusting barbed wire remained. Even the scorch marks had been buried by nature.

Going north from there, I was on my own. Three weeks later I found myself sitting in Darwin, picking fishbones from my teeth and contemplating the thing that had filled my head with such wonder and had magnetically drawn me across the country.

Before reading the faded sign, I didn't know what I was looking at. It was an immense brown ball sitting in the deteriorating remains of a gazebo. The sign read: *Largest Ball of Sisal Twine Built by a Single Person. Official World Record.*

"What the hell," I whispered and flicked a fishbone off my tongue. I couldn't understand why I was there. For the tenth time, I went to the ball and ran my fingers over the ridged exterior. "What the ever-loving hell?" I yelled and thumped the meaty part of my fist into the ball. Once again, I walked in a circle around the ball. It looked the same coming or going.

I stayed in Darwin for three days and left without a clue as to why the Queen had sent me on the longest wild goose-chase in the history of wild goose-chases. I had to assume that I had either angered the Queen or I had been talking to Eve. Either way, I was in a fury for days, months even.

I was still angry when I came across the Queen a little over a year later. She was a guest of a bandit king, while I had taken a wrong turn, a very wrong turn. This time it was I who was behind bars. It was a decidedly unpleasant experience. It made sense to swallow my anger.

"Ezekiel," she said, holding out her hand. I didn't hesitate to kiss it as I desperately needed her on my side; the word "spy" was being used in conjunction with my name.

Her appearance had changed since I last saw her, shaven and clad in soft, pink velvet. Her hair was shoulder length now, and growing wilder by the day. From head to toe, she was dressed in black; it made the alabaster of her skin almost glow. Her hand was softer than I remembered, and I had to force myself not to cling.

"I've seen your pages concerning Christian. They were good, but I noticed you left out everything concerning Darwin."

Since the work hadn't been published, this meant she had gone through my belongings; a gross violation of my personal privacy. "Well…" I said, struggling for an answer that wouldn't alienate the one person who could help me.

While her smile remained friendly, her eyes blazed into me with such intensity that I withered and dropped my gaze. She said, "Hmmm," and turned slightly, touching the bars of my cage. "You didn't understand." It was a statement—not a question or a guess, but a statement. Although I had kept my destination secret, both before and after, she *knew* I had gone simply by looking at me.

The statement had been oddly touched by sadness, which only made me feel worse. Truly stupid people made the Queen sad.

"No, I did not understand and I still don't understand. Why would Christian want you to go to see a ball of twine? And why did you want me to go? The only thing I can guess is that maybe it was some sort of running gag, or that I had angered you in some way, or that…"

She was shaking her head. "What did you see there?"

Suddenly I was worried that I had made a three-thousand mile trip and had missed something glaringly obvious. "I saw the ball." She nodded for me to go on. "That was it. There was nothing else in Darwin. The only thing that makes that town different from a thousand others just like it is a useless ball of twine 12 feet in diameter."

"Exactly," she said, with that same sad smile. "It's a ball that weighs 17,400 pounds. The man who built it went round and round that ball, wrapping it for four hours a day, every day for twenty-nine years. Twenty-nine years. It was his sole achievement. His entire life's work."

None of this was news to me. I had seen the damned ball with my own eyes. "It doesn't seem like much of a life to me."

"Exactly!" she cried. "That was exactly the point of the journey. That man literally went in circles every day of his life, building a monument to the tenacity of mediocrity. It practically screams: *Average!* With the technology available, he could have built his own pyramid. In twenty-nine years, he could have built twenty-nine houses for the poor. He could have done almost anything to inspire greatness, instead, with the freedom given to him, he wrapped twine around more twine."

I felt her meaning slowly dawning over me. "Christian didn't want you to be average? Is that why he sent you on this...quest?" Wild goose chase would have been a poor choice of words just then.

"That's right. He saw something in me. He wanted me to be great and I've tried to live up to that expectation. The question Ezekiel, is can you be great? You've been given the unique opportunity to see the extremes: on one hand, perhaps the most wasted life imaginable, and on the other you've seen my life. Which would you choose?"

I answered honestly, "Neither. I think a happy medium would be best."

She grinned and there was a touch of Eve in it. "And yet you find yourself here." She tapped the bars. "It'll take more than someone existing somewhere in the complacent middle to get out of here alive. If you don't find a spark of greatness inside you, I'm afraid you won't last a month. I'm sorry to say that Mago is reopening his arena."

A cold shiver swept me. I wasn't cut out for the arena. It would chew me up and spit me out. "Will you help me?" I asked her. Begged was closer to the mark.

"Mago has been kind enough to offer me shelter. Do you really expect me to throw his hospitality in his face?" With half the country hot for the Queen's blood, I knew she would never consider it. My chin dropped. "Ah, don't be like that. You've been studying me for years. If I could get out of here with ease, I know you can too."

She left me with the warmest smile she had ever given me. Mine in return was weak and brief. I had no idea how to get out of this prison or any prison for that matter.

Ezekiel Cross
The Prison of Mago The Mad
April 29th 2050

Chapter 4
The Apocalypse Origin

Calgary

***

A quick note from the author— Ezekiel Cross:

The success of my first seven biographies concerning Queen Jillian have brought with it much acclaim. Of course, with such notoriety has come more commissioned offers than a man could hope to fill in a lifetime. Every tinpot despot is hot after me to "write them up nice." In other words, they want me to legitimize their ruthless takeovers.

One thing I've learned is that a written lie is a hundred times more powerful than a spoken one. The verbal liar can be questioned and stories can be changed under pressure or through the haze of time. As well, he or she is usually a neighbor with no greater well of knowledge than yourself. On the other hand, the liar who uses *Times New Roman* font and takes the time to arrange his lies by chapter is another matter altogether.

By the simple act of putting lies on paper, the lie is cemented for all time, while the writer is automatically gifted the mantle of wisdom.

Writing these lies is tedious, soul-crushing work. It involves covering up crimes on a sickening scale. It's why I keep coming back to my favorite subject, even though she doesn't pay me a thing. Quite the opposite in fact. The research involved in tracking down and verifying the truth of all the Queen's fantastic adventures is a net loss.

I call it a labor of love.

Not that I love the Queen. It's hard to love a person who despises you so completely. On two separate occasions, she's left me imprisoned in the clutches of warlords, the second being none other than Mago the Mad.

Had he not died of alcohol poisoning—a highly questionable diagnosis given his near inhuman ability to consume outrageous quantities of alcohol—I would have died in his *Blood Circus*.

The first of these imprisonments corresponded with my first interview with the Queen. It was back in 2040, and at that time I was struggling to make a nickel selling my stories. Having saturated the reading market in Dallas with the sale of a dozen of my books, I found work on a wagon train heading into Azael country and beyond. During that eight-hundred mile journey, I carted a box holding two-hundred thin pamphlets of *Paul's Pirates*— what I considered at the time to be my finest work. I managed to sell four of the pamphlets before the box was lost in a river crossing. In hindsight, it was no great loss.

It was in Edmonton, at the edge of the frozen world, that I picked up my first paid writing job. I was tasked with writing a particularly nasty letter to Raul, King of the Dead Men of nearby Calgary. I happily wrote an entire slew of curse-laden invectives. Then, unhappily, I was told that I would have to deliver the letter and read it to the King since it was well known that he couldn't puzzle out a stop sign, let alone a letter.

My jailing by Raul was only a formality and minutes after I had read the letter, I found myself in a dungeon-like setting. My windowless cage was eight by eight with only a seatless toilet and a blanket in way of amenities. At least I had company. A plank-faced guard sat near my cage, staring across at the only other cell in the dark chamber.

At first, I was jealous of the accommodations afforded the other prisoner. Unlike my barred and embarrassingly open cell, the other one was essentially a solid metal box. It had two openings: a slot at the bottom of the "door" to allow food to be slipped in, and a small window set five feet above that. I put the word door within quotations because most doors are meant to be opened; this one was welded shut. Seeing those welds had me worried that I was stuck with some sort of raving mad-dog psycho.

After five hours of staring at my feet stretched out in front of me, my fear was smothered by my intense boredom. "What are you in for?" I asked the prisoner. I was studiously ignored. I tried a few more times to make conversation, without success. Then I tried the guard and had equal results. After eight hours I was going stir crazy and begged the guard for notebook and pens. This got the prisoner's attention. I heard the clink of chains as she moved closer to the door.

"I could write a letter for Raul," I told the guard. "One that is even more nasty than the one I was forced to read. Tell him that, okay? Tell him I can write a letter that'll have all of Edmonton tearing their hair out."

The guard said nothing. He didn't even look at me. As always, his entire attention was on the metal door.

I glanced over at it and could feel the prisoner behind it, standing just to the side of the tiny window. "You can write," she said. "Interesting." When she set her heart-shaped face to the window, I couldn't help staring. This was the first time I laid eyes on Queen Jillian. She was, and still is, one of the most striking women I have ever beheld. It was not just her beauty that made me step back, it was the power of her gaze. Few are strong enough to withstand her. When she turns her eyes on you, it feels as though she is stripping you down; not just disrobing you, but something far greater. It's as if she can see all the dirty little secrets staining your soul.

At the time, I did not know this was the Queen and I foolishly blurted out, "Yes, I can write. Some say it's a lost art. In fact, I may be the world's only living writer, or author, I should say."

"You've written books? On what subjects?"

My mind went to the box of pamphlets. They could hardly be considered books. "Fiction, mostly," I answered. This was met with such a cold silence that I felt the need to embellish. "Also history and uh, astronomy."

"Astronomy? I'm amazed. Perhaps you can be of assistance. I simply cannot wrap my head around the math involved in differentiating between S-Duality and T-Duality in regards to String Theory."

To me these were simply thrown together words that had absolutely zero meaning. I could only spit out a, "Yeah, the strings are uh, not so good."

"Hmmm," she said, eyeing me. "What about your thoughts on the decay rate describing Hawking radiation? I believe the rate is orders of magnitude faster than theories suggest…but I see you don't have any idea what I'm talking about. Tell me, does your knowledge of astronomy extend beyond making little shapes out of the pretty lights in the sky?"

I realized that I had lied to the wrong person. As I usually do when I'm stumped like this, I turned the conversation towards the speaker. "How do you know about radiation and all that? Are you self-taught? I find people with the deepest knowledge base are almost all self-taught. I bet you have a passion for the mysteries of the universe." Flattering also helped—usually.

The Queen was immune to flattery. She didn't need to be told how great she was. "Obviously, you don't know who I am. I am Jillian Martin, one-time Queen of the Hill People and the Islanders. Queen from Sacramento to Santa Rosa to Santa Clara. Queen of all the Pacific within reach of my fleets. Queen of the Guardians. Queen of the Dead, and lastly Queen of Slaves. And you are?"

I felt the air spill from my lungs. Of course, I had heard of the Queen. She was legendary. And I did not doubt this was her. She had this tremendous force of personality that exuded through the little window. "E-E-Ezekiel Cross, ma'am. Uh, I mean, Your Highness."

"Ezekiel Cross. Hmm. I'm sorry to say that I've never read any of your works." She even seemed sorry. She wasn't. Not even a little bit. She was using me and I was perfectly unaware. "I take it from your demeanor that you've never been imprisoned before."

"No ma'am…I mean, no your highness."

"You have little to worry about. The Dead Men are of little consequence in the great scheme of things." I glanced over at the guard and, concerned that I would be seen as agreeing with words that would probably get my head removed from my shoulders, I shook said head. She saw this and laughed. "How can you fear men that fear a single woman as much as they do?"

Like a scared child, I couldn't find my voice and could only shrug in answer, while silently pleading to the guard.

"Look at these precautions, Ezekiel. Chained at the neck and wrists. A door welded shut. A guard always on duty. More guards at the top of the stairs. Would you say that this was too much or too little?"

She knew my answer before I gave it. "Too little. I've heard all about how you broke out of the Black Captain's lair."

"Actually, I broke out from his prisons three different times," she said. Without prodding, she recounted these three jail breaks and then went on to tell me about a dozen more. With each account she would not explain how she had escaped. What was first and foremost to her narrative were the immense obstacles in her way. The greater these were, the more fantastic and impossible her escape seemed.

Taken together, her various exploits made the chains and the welds on the door seem like child's play, and desperately I wanted to beg in a whisper for her to take me with her.

I stayed awake all that night, afraid that I would miss my chance when she broke out. In the morning she was still there. The chains and welds untouched. She remained quiet all that day and only spoke when the guards changed shift for the evening.

She went on only once the same guard as the night before was seated. "My favorite break-out was when I escaped from the River King the first time."

I obliged with the expected "Why?"

"Because no one died when I ghosted through his jail and out the front door. Hundreds died when I freed my father from Yuri, the Father of Zombies. A thousand perished when I tore through the Believers, and I destroyed an entire city of Corsairs in retribution for what they did to me. What my captors never fail to understand is that when they hold me in the heart of their little dungeons, they're slitting their own throats."

She then spent an hour describing the butchered bodies that she left in her wake. As she spoke, her voice grew into a growl and sank lower and lower. It was then that I remembered the stories concerning her insanity. You could hear the sickness in her voice and I was eager to change the subject of our conversation.

"What were you like before all this? I mean, did you have a normal childhood?"

Her teeth showed, wolf-like as she smiled. "I was six-years-old when I torched two ferry boats crammed with people. I was seven when I slew Augustus, King of the Azael and when I assassinated General Johnston. I was eight when I blew up Hatchet-Joe and half of Seattle. No, I did not have a normal childhood."

The smile gave me the shivers, but to my credit I was able to slip past it by asking, "What about in the *Before?* What was your first memory?"

She thought for a moment. "My first real clear memory occurred on October 5th of 2013. Before that, I only have glimpses of greyed-out mental pictures. I remember Becca Risbon was my best friend and Mrs. Bennett was our neighbor. I remember being in a classroom surrounded by other kids, our knees touching as we sat Indian-style on the carpet. But it was on October 5th that I had my first perfectly clear memory."

Her brilliant blue eyes took on a faraway look. "My dad was at the table when my mom walked into the refrigerator. She'd had the paper in front of her face and banged right into it, knocking off a magnet…it was a ladybug magnet. I remember laughing, thinking that my mom was being silly."

The Queen went on to describe, not just her first memory, but also the very beginning of the apocalypse. She spoke for three hours straight without a pause.

Ezekiel Cross

***

"Honey," Jillybean's mom said in something of an awed whisper as she picked up the magnet. "You've got to see this." Catherine Shaw was a young mom, not even thirty. She had masses of brown hair and large brown doe eyes. Her cream-colored skin, which could never hold a tan for more than a few days, was particularly white that morning. "Remember that stuff we saw on the news last night? About the Z-O-M-B-I-E-S?"

Jillybean was about to slurp up the sweet Captain Crunch flavored milk in the bottom of her bowl, but paused as her mind tried to arrange the letters her mom had spelled out. She had come up with *zoom bees* in the second it took her dad to ask, "Why? What happened?"

"There's a big to-do in Miami. And look, they're cancelling flights from all over the Middle East." She handed the paper to her husband. Will Shaw was as tall as Jillybean was tiny; she always had to crane her neck way back to look up at him. He was also broad-shouldered and, in Jillybean's eyes, the most handsome man she had ever seen. He was the sort of man that would look perfectly at home battling dragons with a sword, something she assumed he'd done at least five times.

Her parents stared in amazement at the front of the paper and didn't notice Jillybean drinking from her bowl in a highly illegal fashion. She held the bowl as if it was a wide-lipped coffee mug. Nor did they see how some dribbled on the table and down the front of her pajamas.

They read quickly and then opened the paper with a snap to devour the rest of the story with wide, unblinking eyes. As they did, Jillybean read the headline from her end of the table: '*Zombie Attacks Unsettles Miami!*' From her extensive knowledge of cartoons, she had an idea what zombies were. They were funny little creatures that showed bones through their skin. They moved slow and talked slower, and for some reason they ate pink squiggly brains. Of all the monsters that probably occupied the shadowy parts of the basement, zombies were the least frightening.

"Do we do anything?" Catherine asked, when she had scanned to the bottom of the article. Deep down, she felt that something needed to be done. She just didn't know what.

"Not go to Miami any time soon," Will Shaw joked. "It's probably just bad drugs. Florida always has weird cases like this. Remember all that bath salt business?"

Jillybean's soft brows came down. *Salt in a bath?* Adults frequently said things that made little sense. Jillybean simply let the words wash over her, and the talk of zombies and salty bath water died for the day. It was revised the next morning when she came blearily down to breakfast, her stuffed zebra dangling loosely from her hand, her bushy hair looking as though she had used a portable tornado to style it. The house was strangely quiet as her parents read their papers with an intensity that wasn't normal.

"Can I have Captain Crunch again?" Her parents didn't like her having the same food two days running, but that didn't stop her from asking. "It's my favorite and that's what means it's okay." When neither looked up, she added, "It's got vitamins and rocks."

With her eyes still locked on the paper, her mom's face turned slowly towards Jillybean. "Huh? Rocks?"

The concept was confusing to Jillybean, as well. She went to the cupboard and pulled out the box of Captain Crunch. "See? Vi-ta-mins and min-er-als. Minerals is what means rocks, but like little rocks. I think they're smaller'n than sand cuz you don't even know they're in there."

Catherine stared at her daughter without comprehension. "You want Captain Crunch?" she asked eventually. Jillybean nodded in answer. "Yeah, I guess, but no toys at the table."

"Ipes isn't a toy, he's a zebra."

"Yeah," Catherine said, going back to the paper, her eyes scanning back and forth in disbelief. When the paper was read, Jillybean's parents turned on the news and told

Jillybean to go play. The streets in their Philadelphia suburb were quiet even for a Sunday. Jillybean likened it to the anticipation of Christmas Eve but in reverse. The air was stiff with anxious expectancy and with it came an edge of fear.

It was almost as if people were afraid that there would be a tomorrow and that it wouldn't be good.

After lunch, her parents had made the change from making light of the situation brewing in Miami, and now in New York, and all over the Mediterranean, to nervous action. They weren't going to panic, but it made sense to make preparations. The store was their first trip and while Jillybean sat in the cart, nibbling on the free cookies that were always offered, her parents filled the cart to overflowing.

The store was jam-packed, and that edge of fear in the air tested the innate politeness of the suburbanites. The canned goods were the first to go, then the cereal shelves were emptied even though they ran all the way down the store from front to back. Pasta and rice went next, and still people kept coming into the store. When they got home, her parents went back to watching the news. They were mesmerized by it, however Jillybean quickly grew bored. She threw a tea party and invited Ipes, Teddy the Bear, Todd the Turtle, and a Barbie Dream Car filled with long-legged Barbies.

During the tea party, while Ipes was creating a scandal by insisting on a third cookie, her father left to top-off the car with gas. He was gone for three hours and came back in a mood.

"People are being ridiculous! The line for the station on Chester stretches for two miles. You can't take any street east because no one will let anyone in. Each of the fuc…Oh, hi Jillybean. Uh, each car was right on the bumper of the car in front. I'm talking an inch from the next car. I saw two real fights as well as a bunch of close ones."

Catherine nodded and was so preoccupied that she barely heard him. "While you were gone, they closed I95 on either side of the city." She said this in a rush as if she'd been holding it in since he'd left. "They say there's an outbreak in Baltimore. I looked it up. That's sixty-two miles away. Jesus, Will, what are we going to do?"

Even though he had just come in, Will Shaw went to the window and looked out. The world seemed peaceful to Jillybean. He must've seen it differently. "We pack up our stuff and get ready. I want us to be able to jump off at the drop of a hat." He was a big man, thirty-two and fit. He seemed to grow even bigger in the face of this unknown calamity. Jillybean asked what was going on, only to be lied to.

"It's nothing, dear," her mom said as she rushed around the house, picking out warm clothes to fill their suitcases.

"Are we going on a trip?"

That seemed like a logical guess based on the packing, and yet Catherine said, "No. I hope not. We'll see. Go play with Ipes. Not outside, though."

Jillybean was too distracted to play. She carried Ipes from room to room, trailing after her parents as they packed. When the suitcases were filled, they emptied out the Christmas boxes of all the ornaments and brought them upstairs and began filling these as well. As much of the food as possible was packed into their camping coolers and shoved into the car first. This was perplexing. They had never taken a trip where they packed *all* the food before. Sometimes they would bring yogurt or a little baggy of cereal, but now her parents boxed up everything, even the beans that had been sitting in the cupboard for longer than Jillybean had been alive.

Her parents worked in silence as they fought the coolers and boxes into the car. The car had always seemed big to Jillybean. Now there was not even enough room for her carseat. She watched it get tossed aside without a thought. "Where am I gonna sit?"

"On my lap," Catherine said. Then with a quick glance she added, "And no toys. There's not going to be any room."

227

"Ipes isn't a toy, he's a zebra."

Her mom didn't hear; her mind was on the problem of trying to fit rectangular boxes into an uneven oblong space. Jillybean thought a change of subject was in order. Seeing all the food made her hungry and she asked, "Can we have pizza for dinner?"

"Do you think anyone's delivering?" Catherine asked her husband.

He shouldered a box through the doorway. "We can try."

No one was delivering and so a box and one of the coolers were hauled back inside so they could have dinner. As they ate, they watched the news. Jillybean couldn't understand what all the fires were about, or the shooting, or any of it, really. Whatever was going on scared her parents, which scared her. Then someone named "President," came on the television and said that things were going to be alright, which was good. Then he kept talking and talking and talking, which was bad.

What was worse was the old bald man who came on next. He was a governor, which seemed to Jillybean to be something like a crabby grandpa. He droned on forever, making little sense. "Citizens in and around Philadelphia need to keep from panicking. We need to ride out the storm." Only there was no storm. Now that it was dark, Jillybean could see the stars outside her window. There wasn't a cloud in sight.

Jillybean's dad was not assured by the grandpa man or "President." He paced up and down the living room, his jaw clenched. "We need a gun. I know you're not a fan, but we need something to protect us." Catherine nodded reluctantly and then the two of them went about unpacking the car.

"Are we gonna ride the storm here?" Jillybean asked from the kitchen door. She thought that was way smarter than going out in one.

"No," her dad muttered. He couldn't leave their car filled with their possessions even for a minute, and he knew the lines at the sporting goods stores were going to be outrageous. He sighed, tiredly. "I just have to run out and get some stuff. I'll be back soon."

He was gone all that night and didn't return until well into the morning. When he came back, red-eyed and grey-faced, he was empty-handed. "Every store is completely out of stock or…" He grimaced as he stuck his fists into the small of his back and stretched. "Or they've been looted. Half the city is on fire and no one's doing anything about it. Have you noticed? There hasn't been a siren in hours."

"Are the police just leaving us on our own?" Catherine asked, shocked at the idea.

"They're people, too. They have families and loved ones to protect. I think…I think it's time. We should leave as soon as we can. The people are becoming worse than the zombies."

"You saw one?" Jillybean asked in her piping voice. "What did it look like? Did it have toilet paper stuck on the bottom of its foot? Did it eat any brains?"

Will Shaw tried to give his daughter a reassuring smile, but it sagged away. "No. I was only joking. If there are any real zombies, they're nowhere around here. You don't have anything to worry about."

Her mom was worried enough for all of them. She hadn't slept and now there were blue bags beneath her eyes. "They're in L.A. and Texas now," she said in an urgent whisper, even though her daughter was right there and no one else was in the house. "And the news said they're closing the highways at the Mississippi and that some states aren't letting anyone pass. They're closing their borders. We should've left yesterday. God, why didn't we leave?"

"Did they mention the Ohio border?"

"They said that all the midwestern states were calling up their national guard troops. It's all I heard."

"Then we have to hurry. Jillybean, run upstairs and get dressed." As her parents re-packed the car, this time with far less delicacy, Jillybean threw on a pink dress over a pair of blue jeans. She also put on her bathing suit and a green sweater. She had no idea where they were going and wanted to be prepared.

They were ready to go an hour later and at first it seemed to Jillybean that they were about to start on a grand adventure. They drove out of their garage with grim determination, ready to cross the country. It took them fifty-two minutes just to get out of their neighborhood. It seemed that everyone was embarking on the same grand adventure. Streets were packed, bumper to bumper with honking cars.

"Why do people do this?" Jillybean asked, pointing up with her tiny middle finger. "And what does fuc…"

"Read your book, Jillybean," her mom interrupted, folding Jillybean's finger back down.

Whenever they passed something unpleasant, Jillybean was told to, "Read your book!"

Her mom blocked the window when this happened. She couldn't stop the sounds, however, and Jillybean heard screams and angry curses. And she couldn't block her dad's window. Through it she saw a Whole Foods truck swarmed by what looked like a thousand people. The driver was pulled from his rig and kicked to the ground. Soon the back of the truck was smashed open and people were climbing over each other to get at the food inside. It was mayhem. People were trampled, fights broke out and guns were drawn.

Will could only shake his head in disbelief. "We made fun of Black Friday shoppers every year. They'd run over some ol' granny for a discounted flat screen. It should've been a warning to us instead of a joke."

Jillybean read all eight of her books in the time it took them to drive a half mile. On that Monday afternoon, there were over a million and half cars within the greater Philadelphia area, and at least half of them were looking to go west. Heading east would lead to being trapped along the Atlantic coast of New Jersey. Northeast led to New York with its own millions looking to escape deeper into the country. Southwest led to Baltimore where zombies were exploding out from the city center.

West was the only direction that made sense. It took hours to get to the on-ramp of the highway with the big number 3 on it. Progressing the three hundred yards up to the highway took another hour.

For a six-year-old, this was the most arduous part of the journey. The three of them were trapped in their car all that day. The only time Jillybean was allowed out was when her mom took her down into a deserted neighborhood to make pee-pee beside a house. They drank icky-tasting water from a hose next to the same house, and then hurried back to where they had left William Shaw.

Their car had progressed all of eight feet.

They spent a long, uncomfortably cold night in the car. To make room they stacked their suitcases on top and tied them down with twine stolen from a house not far from the highway. The Shaws were not the first to ransack these houses. No house along the highway was safe. People broke in without any guilt; took what they wanted, clogged the toilets and slept in the beds. The apocalypse was only into its third day and already survival was treading all over the concept of morality.

Deep in the night, an urgent knocking on their car door woke the three of them. Will was up first, glaring at a woman who was wearing two winter coats. "Do you have a lighter?" she asked through the glass. "Or some smokes? I'll pay you back, I swear."

She was the first of a thousand beggars. Some people wanted rides, others toilet paper, others wanted guns or bullets. They trudged through the long line of cars knocking on every door, looking for an easy mark. Mixed in with them were the traders. "I'll swap you some'a my food for a gun? You gotta gun you wanna trade? Or bullets? I'll take bullets, too." Some were opportunists and some were just regular people in need.

One father of six offered twenty dollars for a single can of corn. "There were gangs taking everything and killing people," he said in a strangled voice. "They just started shooting people and there was nowhere to go in the car, so we ran. And now…" And now he and his family were so desperate they would hand out the last of their money for a few cans of corn.

"Five cans for, uh," Will began before sharing a look with his wife. Catherine shrugged and nodded slightly. "For sixty dollars." The deal was readily agreed upon and the man thanked Will profusely. When he was gone, Will said, "That felt wrong on so many levels. We might need the food."

"We definitely need the money," Catherine retorted. "Maybe I should go hunt down another ATM."

Will wouldn't hear of it. "They're all going to be drained by now. If we see one on the way, we'll go check it out."

They were seven miles from their house when they hit the twenty-four hour mark on the road. They moved in slow spurts, fifty, sixty feet at a time. Between these spurts, time trickled by. Jillybean was allowed out of the car that day. It didn't make sense to keep her bottled up.

She and other kids played on the side of the road, while the moms smoked and gossiped. There was only one topic of gossip: zombies. Where they were, what they ate, how to stop them, and most importantly, were they even real?

"It's like War of the Worlds," one mother said, "but on a huge scale. There's not a single person on this entire road that's seen one, and yet here we are runnin' for our lives like they were right behind us."

"I saw 'em on TV," another answered.

The first sneered, "TV! That don't make 'em real. You gonna tell me you never saw a zombie show? Them TV people can make anything look like anything else. All this smells fishy to me. It smells like some sort of giant scam."

Jillybean saw her mom roll her eyes at this. "Say it isn't zombies. Who do you think is running this giant scam and why?"

"The military industrial complex," the woman stated flat out.

"The military industrial complex?" Catherine repeated incredulously. "Why? How does bombing fake zombies do anything for them?"

"When the army bombs fake zombies, they're gonna have-ta buy more of their bombs. You see? One hand washes the other. That's how the world works, Miss Lexus. Time to get your head out of your husband's lap and wake up."

Catherine took a step back, shocked by the woman's flaring anger. She wasn't used to people being so mean without cause. Her instinct was to walk away and complain later to Will, but out of the corner of her eye she saw her daughter glaring. Jillybean was not happy that someone would call her mom "Miss Lexus." Her name was Mrs. Shaw, everyone knew that. Jillybean's backbone stopped Catherine and she turned back to the woman.

"And who is going to make these bombs? Is there a bomb factory on this road? Is that where this leads? And who's going to pay for them? All these people should be at work, but they aren't. No work means no taxes. No taxes means no money for bombs."

The other woman shrugged at this and dismissed Catherine by taking a huge drag on her cigarette and blowing the smoke at her. Catherine only stared until the woman barked at her boy and left. The mothers around Catherine snorted quiet laughter for a few seconds before the enormity of their situation came back. What followed was a rehash of the same endless questions: where were they going? Who would take them in? Were there really zombies? Really?

No one knew anything. The radio stations all spouted the same nonsense about "hunkering down" and "remaining indoors," and of course, "There's no need to panic."

Two hours later, Catherine saw her first dead body and decided that she had a very good reason to panic. The body lying among the trees on the side of the road was that of a woman. She had been shot in the back of the head and what was left of her face suggested that she had been Catherine's age.

Although Catherine couldn't stop staring at it, she scolded Jillybean, "Don't look over there. Just read your books."

Jillybean was tired of the books and tired of the car. They had been on the road for thirty-two hours and were now all of ten miles from their home. It took an hour for them to crawl past the body. It was as far west as they would go. Traffic froze at this point. Nothing moved.

Cars were beginning to stall out as their tanks emptied. When that happened the families inside simply hauled away everything they could carry and began walking. They always went west.

More hours ticked by and more people streamed past the Shaws. Thousands and thousands. That night was colder than the one before and frost built up on the windows. Even with blankets piled all around them, they barely slept.

***

By morning it became obvious that they would have to abandon their car as well. They were surrounded by cars that were essentially welded together, bumper to bumper. From the concrete divider on the left, to the trees on the right, there were lines of cars. No one could move, not even to reverse. Will could barely open his door far enough to get out.

With his breath puffing out in grey clouds, he climbed onto the roof of the car and stared back at what looked like a river of metal.

"I think it's time," he said.

"To do what?" Catherine asked. She was so afraid to leave the safety of the car that she felt ill. "To leave? To just start walking like everyone else?" The west offered nothing to her except endless marches, hunger, frostbite, gangs, and maybe even zombies. There were zombies in Texas moving north. She could easily imagine a dreadful march of weeks and weeks to the middle of the country only to find the rolling plains of the Midwest filled with the dead. "It's thirty miles to Lancaster and what do you think's going to be there? Five million refugees just like us. We'll push on to Harrisburg, which is sixty miles away, and it'll be ten million refugees, all hungry and cold."

"And desperate," Will said, picturing the mayhem. There was no way the government would be able to cope with the refugee problem while at the same time fighting the growing hordes of zombies. But what was their choice? Could they really go back home? What would they do there? Sit in the dark? "I'm going to go ahead and see what's going on. For all we know, there could be a camp or the army or something not far off. I'll be back in a few hours at most."

Catherine had to force herself not to cling. Scouting ahead was smart. Leaving her alone with their little girl with nothing to defend herself was not. People were regressing to their animal states faster than she could believe. It wasn't the two days stuck on the road that was leeching the civilization out of them. People could handle two days of hunger and cold. It was the idea that they would be hungrier and colder tomorrow, and that the next day would be even worse, and that in a week, they'd be living scarecrows, unable to feed their children.

It made them greedy. The instinct to hoard was strong. The instinct to claim *more* was irresistible.

Almost as soon as Will left, a mob of hundreds of people surged through the cars. They carried their guns openly and took what they wanted. If someone among the cars had a gun, he or she was passed by with only dark looks exchanged. Everyone else was fair game. Catherine locked her and Jillybean in their car. She was just trying to hide her daughter under a blanket when there came a thump on the passenger-side window.

"We don't have anything!" Catherine yelled, still stuffing the blanket around her daughter.

"Open the door or I'll break the fuckin' window and pull you out."

Catherine looked over her shoulder and saw a sallow-faced young man with a wispy black mustache. He couldn't have been over twenty. In his hand was a sawn-off shotgun. "I swear all we have is some corn and peas."

He raised the gun with the butt end toward the window. "I'm gonna count to fuckin' three and then I'm gonna smash this window in. One…"

Once the window was broken, the car would no longer even offer safety from the wind. And yet, if she opened the door, the man would be able to do anything to her.

"Two!"

"Okay! Don't break the window." With her shoulders huddled in, she opened the door, expecting the man to hit her.

He grabbed her by the coat and pulled her out of the car. "Come on, get out. Get the kid, too."

Jillybean was too terrified to even cry. She was in shock. She felt paralyzed, unable to move except to cling with hysterical strength to her mother.

Catherine backed into a low-slung blue Honda. She jumped, expecting to be yelled at or threatened again. When she saw that it had been abandoned, she tore Jillybean from her and stuck her inside.

"Just peas and corn?" the young man was muttering. "Fuckin' liar. You got all sorts of good stuff in here." His pack was mostly filled already, but he stuffed it with bread and pop tarts. When he moved on, a man and a woman came up next and pawed through the boxes, taking what they wanted.

The moment they were gone, Catherine dove back into the car and began shoving cans of soup and bags of rice under the seats and into their suitcases.

"Whatcha doing?" a rough-voiced man asked from behind her. He seemed very long in a long trench coat. His chin had four days' worth of stubble and his eyes were rimmed red. The smell of tequila wafted from him as he stood with one hand on the door and the other on the hood of the car, trapping her. She was suddenly very aware that her ass was to the man. It didn't matter that she was wearing her loosest jeans and that under them she had on yoga pants, she felt completely exposed.

"Nothing," she replied, turning in the cramped space. He didn't move. He loomed over her. "I-I was just getting some stuff."

"You mean you were hiding stuff." He stared until she nodded, her head going up and down in little more than a jitter. "Do you have any good stuff? I figure that since I'm stuck robbing people, I might as well do it right. Don't worry, I won't take a lot. I'm just evening things out. You got a lot, I got a little. It seems only fair."

Catherine's hands had been up around her chin; now she clasped them and begged, "Please. I have a child. I need this for her."

The man looked into the car and saw the children's books but no child. He stood and turned. Through the dirty glass of the Honda, he and Jillybean locked eyes. "I'd hide her better than that," he said. "Something will happen to her if you don't." He hawked up something from deep in his throat and spat before he reached past Catherine.

"Something is happening to her," Catherine said, slipping to the side. "You're taking the food from her mouth. You should be ashamed."

"Yeah, I should be," he agreed. "But I'm not. Two days ago I had my car stolen from me and yesterday I was cracked on the head because some girl liked my coat. Think about how ashamed you're going to be when you're in my shoes and left with no choice except to rob someone for food."

She crossed her arms. "I won't stoop to that level."

He laughed at her as he hefted a can of chicken and rice soup. "Then you'll die. If all this zombie talk is true, then only the strong will survive. If you can't steal a few cans of food, you might as well kill yourself now because life isn't going to get any easier." He pushed past Catherine and took two steps west before he turned suddenly and rapped the windshield of the Honda with his knuckles.

"You better be smart, little girl. Smart and tough for your mother. Can you do that?"

Although everyone remarked what a smart little girl Jillybean was, she didn't think she would ever be as smart and tough as her mom. Her mom was big and she was very tiny. Still, she nodded because that's what the man expected. She was just beginning to understand grown-ups. Kids were easier to figure out.

"I'm never gonna be like him, Ipes," she said to the little zebra clutched in her arm. "He was mean and he stolded our cans of stuff."

Catherine opened the door to the Honda with shaking hands. Before getting in, she looked up and down the highway as more armed people came through the lines of cars. "Push over, Jillybean."

"Are we going to leave all our stuff? Even my pajamas and my books?" Yes, she was tired of her books, but they were *her* books.

"For now," her mom said. "Don't look. Just keep down."

Jillybean couldn't help herself and she watched the people working their way through the cars. They followed a pattern: if a car's doors were flung open and the items inside were tossed about, the bad people only gave the interior a quick peek. If a car was shut up, they always opened the doors and started digging. The pattern held true even with their own car. Two of its doors were open while the Honda was shut—and they were targeted again.

"Take what you want," Catherine cried, crawling out the other side of the car after pushing Jillybean ahead of her. They hurried to the side of the road while a dozen teens with bats and makeshift clubs ransacked the Honda. Clothes and photographs were hurled in all directions, and when food or weapons weren't found, the teens smashed in the windows.

One of them came at Catherine, pointing the bat, "Where'd you stash the food? We know you got some."

"It's all already stolen," she said, dragging Jillybean around the far end of the car away from him. "There were others and they took everything."

This was such a shockingly blatant lie that Jillybean was dumbfounded. Her mom never told lies. It didn't seem like a good lie, either, and yet the teen seemed to buy into it and after a second, he ran to catch up with his friends who had moved on to another victim.

Catherine's shakes had turn into a full-body tremble as she pulled Jillybean into the trees on the side of the road. She began crying. "What's wrong with people! H-How can they j-justify this? How is this right?"

Jillybean hugged her mom as more people came along the roadway. They stopped at the Lexus and began to rummage through it. "They're going to take everything," Catherine whispered. "They're going to take everything and we…we're going to starve."

Starve? That meant being super hungry. Jillybean didn't like being hungry. She wanted to say something about their car—how it looked to the bad guys who were taking everything. She had an understanding of the term camouflage though she didn't know the word itself. But she wasn't allowed to say anything. Her mom was very strict about "showing off."

Whenever Jillybean pointed out a glaring error, especially one made by an adult, and very especially one made by her mom, Catherine would scold her: "People don't like a show-off, and you do want to be liked, don't you?" Jillybean wanted to be liked very much. But starving was bad, too.

Of course, there was no law about Ipes showing off, and everyone knew that for a stuffed zebra, he was a borderline genius. "You know what Ipes thinks? He thinks that maybe if our car looked like that one with the H, it would be better." Catherine had no idea what she was talking about and was about to give her one of her patented distracted, *That's nice dears*, when Jillybean went on, "You see? No one's even looking at the blue one cuz it's all a mess. It's got brokeded windows and stuff all over."

"You want me to break our car's windows?"

"No. Ipes does. For so our car will look…not good." The word tempting was not yet in her vocabulary, either.

Her mother frowned. "We're not going to break the windows. That car is all we have." And yet it was stuck, perhaps forever. And people were ignoring the Honda just as Jillybean had said. "Hmmm, maybe. Wait here and keep watch. Don't let anyone sneak up on me, or you for that matter."

Catherine slunk around to their Lexus, and arranged the car to look like it had been picked over—more than it had. She flung the doors open as wide as she could get them, threw her shirts across the hood and grabbed some of the trash from the Honda and tossed it all around. She couldn't bring herself to smash the windows, however. She then scurried further down the roadway, "cleaning up" other cars, shutting their doors and arranging them in such a way as to draw the eye of a would-be thief.

The mother and daughter then watched from the tree line as more people came west. Everyone was a would-be thief, it seemed. Even frightened families hurrying by would stop and grab items from the roadway or from cars. Only those who were already loaded down with everything they could carry, didn't stop to pick.

And their car was miraculously ignored. Every fifteen minutes or so, Catherine would go back and clean up the cars to the west of the Lexus and then scurry back

Four terrifying hours tripped slowly by before Will Shaw came back, hurrying down the center of the road, a woodsman's axe in his right hand. He saw the Lexus that had been his pride and joy—the doors were flung open and there were clothes thrown around it. He started running, thinking the worst.

"Will, over here!" It was Catherine waving from the trees. She hadn't clung earlier when he had left, but she clung now in relief. Jillybean did as well, squeezing her father around the waist. While they held him, he told them what he had found out.

"The traffic jam only goes for another couple of miles or so. The army put up a roadblock and were trying to keep everyone back. No one knew why and people just went around the sides on foot. Then for some reason the army left, but it's too late for all the cars. They're all abandoned. I went on for another three miles or so. You were right. People are flocking to Lancaster from all directions. It's like some sort of mass migration."

Catherine listened while biting on a nail. "What about the You-know-whats? Did you hear anything new about them?"

"Everyone says they're in Florida, Texas, L.A. and Baltimore for sure, but there are rumors that there are new outbreaks in Seattle and Detroit."

She didn't care about Seattle. It was so far away that it might as well be on the other side of the world. Detroit was another story. It wasn't all that far to the west. She had the sudden feeling of being trapped. "We can't keep going. It's…it's insane. Where will we sleep? And…and what happens if it snows?"

"We'll bundle up. We can't go back, Cat. There's nothing for us back there. If the You-know-whats are real, they'll make their way to Philly eventually."

"And if they're in Detroit and Texas, then we'll be walking *towards* them! And it's not just them we have to worry about. People have been stealing everything they can get their hands on. We've already lost half our food. What do you think it'll be like in a day or two? Anyone with a gun can take everything we have. If you ask me, we'll be safer going home and locking the place down tight."

Will sat down and watched as people streamed by. They already looked exhausted. Most were glassy-eyed and some were limping. They were only eighteen miles from the city center. How bad would they look when they reached Harrisburg? Sixty miles was a long way to walk while carrying all your worldly goods on your back. Will could do it in two days, but Jillybean would never be able to keep up. With her little steps, it would take four days.

Four long cold days, interspersed with four long cold nights.

And when they finally got there, what would they find? Harrisburg had a population of about 50,000. In four days, that number could well be over a million. They would pick that city to pieces. They would be like a plague of locusts that left nothing behind. Would there be anything left when Will finally got his family there? Or would they have to press on through the now frost-covered Appalachian Mountains to tiny Altoona?

The one thing Will knew was that he couldn't trust the government. They had made a mess out of Hurricane Katrina and that was nothing but a blustery day compared to what was happening now. It could be weeks before they had the situation in hand. This begged the question: could they hold out at home for weeks?

***

The question turned out to be moot. Catherine would not be dissuaded one way or the other. She was going back home and she was taking Jillybean with her and that was the end of the discussion.

Will sighed and went to the car. He pulled their belongings from it, dumped the clothes out of two suitcases and filled them with food. Everything else was left behind. Warm clothes would be easy to replace, and jewelry and laptops were already next to useless.

It was just after one when they left the car and took off cross-country, heading north east through semi-deserted neighborhoods. The people who had decided to remain during all of this had shuttered their homes behind planks of plywood when they could. When they couldn't, they drew their blinds and set signs around their property warning would-be thieves that they were armed and were ready to kill.

The houses without these precautions were fair game and had already been broken into and stripped of food.

Will slipped into one of these and took a pair of long knives from a rack. He stuck one in his belt and gave the other to his wife. She grimaced, but took it.

Because they were some of the few people heading against the tide of humanity, they were continually stopped and questioned. It was always the same unanswerable questions: What's going on? Is the army sending people back? Are there camps being setup? Have you seen any zombies?

After the fifth such stoppage, Will simply began to lie, telling people that his child was sick and couldn't go on. Jillybean looked sick. After barely a mile her pace had slowed. After two, the little girl began to stumble.

Will set her on one of the wheeled suitcases and although the handle bowed and the weight of the thing doubled, he pulled her along. Because of its tiny wheels, they were forced to travel strictly along streets, which added another two miles to their journey. It was a more dangerous route, as well. There was no telling when a group would go from waving a friendly hand to waving a bat.

The Shaws passed a dozen frightening groups without issue. They kept their eyes averted, moved as far away as possible, and if someone said something disparaging, it went ignored. One group refused to accept their docility. Will tried to maneuver through the lines of cars to avoid them, but they kept shifting lanes as well, setting up a confrontation.

Jillybean, who was reclining backwards on the luggage, saw none of this and only grew afraid when she heard her father say, under his breath, "Keep a hand on your knife, but don't pull it unless you have to." Jillybean squirmed around and saw four men and five women coming at them. All of them were armed with either baseball bats or golf clubs.

Will stopped by a truck where there was a gap between it and the car in front. He slid the suitcase into it, gave Jillybean a wink and said, "Wait here, sweetie." She

243

was astounded that he wasn't afraid—her little heart was racing like a rabbit's.

He was afraid, of course, but his fear was for his family, not for himself. He paused for a moment, debating whether or not to use the axe. It had its pros and cons. The axe was more fearsome than the knife and could do more damage. At the same time, it could only effectively be used two-handed, and in a cramped space its uses would be limited to an overhead chopping motion.

"You guys are on my road," the biggest of the men said, interrupting Will's thoughts. "Sorry to say, it's a toll road. It'll cost you both of them suitcases."

"No, it won't," Will Shaw answered.

"Will, maybe we should give them…" Catherine started to say.

"The only thing I'm giving this guy is my knife. In the guts, I think. I want him to suffer." He thought he sounded tough.

The man only smirked. He was not very tall, but he was broad and strong. His knuckles were scarred pink from fighting and he had a jagged white line under one eye from being punched by a man with a fistful of rings. His brows were thick and dark and tended to V inwards, making his nose look longer than it was.

"You gonna let him talk to you like that, Raul?" one of the women asked. She was an unnatural red-head with a pinched…"

***

Ezekiel Cross:

I had to interrupt. What the Queen had just said shocked me into blurting out, "Did you say Raul?"

She had been talking nonstop for an hour, giving amazing details and she had just described Raul, King of the Dead Men.

"Yes," she answered, her eyes coming back into focus.

"Holy shit, Raul is from Philadelphia," the guard said in a hushed tone. This was the first he had spoken.

The Queen turned her haughty gaze on him. By the crinkles at the corner of her eyes, I could tell she was smiling. "I know," she answered, softly. She was almost purring. "Why do you think I'm here? Do you think I was simply 'caught' by the likes of Raul? No, I'm here, in this cell for a reason. I'm here to kill Raul."

The guard's eyes showed fear and puzzlement. "I don't get it. Why didn't you just shoot him or blow him up or something? Everyone says you know all about bombs."

"Maybe I should clarify. I want to kill him up close and personal. I want to stand over his body and look into his eyes as I slide my knife into him over and over."

"Then why let yourself be caught?" I asked. I knew she was devious, but there were a dozen easier ways to get at Raul.

She turned her frosty gaze on me, making me swallow loudly. "You don't see it, Ezekiel? Unlike you, I'm not trapped here. I was caught willingly so that he would bring me exactly here, into the heart of his city. I knew exactly where he would put me, just as I knew exactly what precautions he would take against me escaping. If anyone has fallen into a trap, it's Raul. In essence, he has swallowed poison and doesn't realize that he's dying yet."

I felt like I was on some sort of strange treadmill that I couldn't get off of. Who in their right mind would want to be imprisoned? "So…so you wanted to get caught, I get that, I guess. But how did you know where he'd put you? You couldn't have known that."

"Of course, I could," she answered. "I've been here before, in this very cell. Of course, then I was only visiting, setting things up, planting certain items I knew I would need. I knew that this would be my cell, just like I knew Raul would never trust a lock to keep me in. And since I knew he would weld the door shut it, was nothing to find the closest machine shops and 'prepare' the arc welders."

"What did you do?" I asked in growing excitement, clutching the bars.

She only smiled. "Don't be in a hurry. You will see in good time, just like our friend, the guard." She grinned maliciously at him. "Sorry to say it will be you on duty when I decide to leave. Yes, I know the guard schedule. I know your numbers. I know when you leave, when you come, when your days off occur. I know all there is to know about this little prison. I know its exact dimensions. I know the exact volume of air it contains. I know it's exactly thirty-nine paces, from the door of the antechamber at the top of the stairs, to this one." She knocked the metal.

"Why'd you pick me?" asked the guard. "I never done anything to you, e-e-except what Raul made me do. Do you know me? You know, personally?"

She laughed. "No. You are just *the* guard and you will die like all the rest, and will be forgotten like all the rest. Unless, of course I kill you in a particularly interesting or gruesome manner. Who knows? You could be famous. Would you like to be famous?" His mouth fell open. "I could hang you with your own intestines. People will talk about that for years. Would you like that?" The guard, looking as if he had been hit with a cartoon mallet, shook his head.

The Queen smiled gently. "Maybe if you behave, I'll make it quick. Now, where was I? Oh yes, the red-head."

***

"You gonna let him talk to you like that, Raul?" one of the women asked. She was an unnatural redhead with a pinched face.

Before Raul could answer, another of the women spoke up. "Maybe we should leave them alone. They have a kid."

"Shut up, Karen," Raul muttered, hefting his bat and taking a step closer to Will. "This is about survival. This is about the strong living and the weak dying. You of all people should know this. You were just on Facebook last week saying how much you were looking forward to the apocalypse. Well, here it is. This is what it looks like."

"You really are going to break my arm, aren't you?" Will asked him.

Raul grinned. "I'm going to break more than that if you don't drop those suitcases and walk away."

Will slid the knife out. "No. It'll just be my arm. You'll swing your bat and I'll sacrifice my left arm so I can stick this," he held up the knife, "in your guts. It won't kill you right away. You'll suffer."

"Fuck you," Raul growled. "I'll show you who'll suffer."

"Jillybean, get under the car," her father suddenly ordered, rolling his head on his broad shoulders. He was not going to back down. After all, the man was right, this was about survival.

Without any evidence, Jillybean had always thought that her father was the bravest, toughest man who had ever lived. Now, she saw that her assumption was not wrong. She hesitated before sliding under the car. Raul was threatening her father, and she was suddenly consumed with an intense hatred, and she had never hated anything in her life. Except for lima beans and she had every reason in the world to hate lima beans.

The hatred burned hotter than she thought possible as she took in Raul's beak of a nose, his dull grey eyes, his bushy brows and the scar under his eye. She studied the face and vowed revenge.

Just as she was about to slip beneath the car, her mom slapped her palm down on the car next to her. "No! Will, we aren't doing this. Let them have the food. We'll find more. It isn't worth it. Will, please." She tried to drag him back, but it was like trying to pull a tree down with her bare hands. She slid around in front of him, snatching Jillybean into her arms. "Take it," she spat at Raul. "You guys can have whatever you want."

It was only then that Jillybean saw that two of the men had been slipping around on either side of them, using the

247

cars for cover. Catherine had seen them as well. "It's okay," she said, again. "Take it all."

Will glared fury, first at his wife, and then at the men, his fist curled around the handle of the knife. They glared back and one called him a "Pussy," which was not much of a put-down to little Jillybean. Everyone liked cats as far as she knew and some could bite very hard. Regardless, they let the three of them go. The little family hurried past the cars and then squeezed through a break in the fence that bordered the highway.

For long minutes as they walked, Will steamed in anger until Catherine couldn't take it any longer. "They would've killed you."

"Maybe," Will answered, without looking at her. "Or maybe I would've bluffed the leader into backing down. You didn't see his eyes, Cat. He was all talk. He knew I would fight and he knew he would die. He would've backed down." He stomped on, going so fast that Jillybean had to jog to catch up.

"I wasn't about to take that chance," Catherine sniffed.

Will stopped and looked around. They were in a neighborhood that had the misfortune of being too close to the highway. Every house had been ransacked. "I hate to be the bearer of bad news, but we're going to have to take chances. Probably, every day, and the longer this goes on, the worse our chances are going to be. Raul was right about one thing. This is what the apocalypse looks like." He waved his arms, indicating the broken windows and the kicked-in doors.

Catherine was not going to argue about whether she had been right or wrong concerning Raul. She had been right and no force on earth would change her mind. "Why would anyone want this? You know, an apocalypse. It's been only five days and already people have gone crazy."

There was no answer to this and Will started on again, angling across the street. Behind an RV they came upon a pack of dogs. There were six of them drinking from a puddle. They were hardly a wild lot. The toughest of them was a Yorkshire terrier. It kicked out with its back paws like a tiny furry bull about to attack. The larger dogs displayed an almost human look of fright and slunk away.

Will edged around the rest. He wasn't frightened of them, but would not take the chance that a bite might get infected. They crossed a yard and jumped a fence.

"Take it somewhere's else," a voice barked from a covered porch. A man sat in an old recliner that was awash in shadows. The chair was green except where countless cigarettes had scorched little black circles. The man was maybe in his sixties, grizzled and cranky. "Back over the fence with you."

"Excuse me, sir?" Catherine said as Will was just about to help Jillybean back over. "We don't have any food and we have a hungry child."

Unbelievably, the man rolled his eyes. "I heard this ten times already today and I'll hear it ten more times before the sun goes down. And guess what? Tomorrow it'll be fifty times, and the answer will still be no. I don't care how many rug-rats you have. They are your rug-rats and that makes them your problem, not mine."

Catherine glared. "You're going to die alone," she stated, her voice high and strident. "Sad, alone and unmourned." She turned her back on the man, who lit a cigarette and stared through grey smoke without answer.

Soon Jillybean, with Ipes clutched in the crook of her arm, had been passed back over the fence and they skirted the house, making their way through ugly neighborhoods. It took them a good hour to get through the devastated areas and into neighborhoods that hadn't been in the direct path of the human horde. "See?" Catherine said, gesturing around at the houses. "There'll be enough food for us to get by on. This was the right thing to do."

Jillybean, who was only a little bit hungry, looked around at the houses in wonder. She pictured their interiors to be over-flowing with cookies and chips and barrels of chocolate milk. She had been without chocolate milk for two days now and pined for it.

Will eyed the houses with skepticism. He had picked his own house clean, taking everything that could be

249

nibbled on, including frozen food. It's what anyone with any sense would've done. Maybe there would be a little bit left here and there, and all he would have to do to get it was to break into a stranger's house and steal it all. "This is what the apocalypse looks like," he muttered under his breath as he headed for the nearest house.

"Not yet, Will," Catherine said. "Let's get Jillybean home first. The idea of getting stopped by more, uh, hoodlums with Jillybean with us makes me crazy." She grinned for the first time that day. "Do you think hoodlums is the right word for them?"

"I don't know. They were all just normal people." He found it hypocritical to call them thieves since he was planning on becoming a thief himself. "Or they *were* just normal people, now I don't know what they are." As they passed the houses, his desire to slip in and see what there was grew so strong that he made the suggestion once more to his wife, and once more she was obstinate. For her safety came first.

The sun was hanging just over the trees in the west when they finally made it back to Peakview Drive and saw their house. Just like almost all the other houses on the block, it was cold and dark, and yet all three of them felt a surge of hope. Even exhausted as they were, they practically skipped the last hundred yards.

"And the electricity is still on!" Catherine cried as she walked through the front door and flicked the switches.

Will flicked them back down. "Maybe we don't want to advertise that there are people here. While I'm gone, you should cover the windows and barricade the doors."

"No. You're not leaving us until this place is like a fortress. Safety first."

"But searching in the dark can be…" He saw her face and knew her view on the matter was set in stone. "Fine."

Jillybean's feet hurt so she sat in her dad's big comfy chair while her parents pushed the couch in front of the door and then piled more furniture on and around it. They then scraped her father's desk to the back door and wedged it into place. "How are we oposed to get out?" she asked. "You know, just in case there's a fire or something?"

"Through the garage, dear," her mom said, stretching her back with a grimace.

"Oh." She didn't like the garage, it being so dirty and all. After a moment she stated, "I'm hungry. Can we order pizza tonight? Ipes says he's real hungry for pizza, and that's what means we should probably get some with extra cheese." She held up the zebra to add to her appeal.

The thought of pizza made Catherine's stomach growl. They hadn't eaten since breakfast. "No one's delivering, Jilly. We'll have to make do with what we have, or what we can get." She went to the kitchen and stared at the depressingly empty shelves. "Will? I think it's time. Can you run out and get us some food?"

He came from the master bedroom, where he'd been pinning blankets over the windows. It was full dark by then and he was only a shadow. "Sure, I'll just run down to the store and pick up some eggs." The joke fell flat. After their experience on the road, the store was the most dangerous place either of them could imagine just then. It would be a beacon for every hungry mouth in this part of the city, if it was even still standing, that is. "I'll just get my pack from what's left of the camping supplies."

***

Will Shaw stepped out into the night and was greeted with the crack of a gun. It sounded close, two or three blocks away at the most. It was followed by three more shots in quick succession. Armed with just the knife, he suddenly felt very naked and was tempted to go back inside for something bigger. But he did not golf or play baseball. The best he'd be able to do was to take a leg from his dining room table.

He liked the idea of a spear more than any sort of makeshift cudgel. A spear was a simple tool that could strike quicker than a club and from further away. The problem was that spears with an actual metal tip were rare. Will didn't trust wood-tipped spears. Not only would they break easily, they were far less intimidating than a real one. The more Will thought about weapons, something he'd only just started doing in the last couple of days, the more he realized how important intimidation was as a factor in combat.

Raul had not been intimidated by Will's knife until Will had explained exactly how he had planned to use it. It was only then that Raul had looked nervous. Had Will been able to act aggressively, he might have been able to save his food. It had been at least ten days' worth, which in the end, could mean the difference between life and death.

"There'll be more," he told himself. These were the suburbs. Although there were no "preppers" in the neighborhood, at least as far as he knew, people tended to have pantries and cupboards filled to overflowing with goods. Yes, sometimes the cans would be expired by a few years, but in a pinch, he would eat them without batting an eye.

As much as he hated stealing from strangers, the idea of stealing from his neighbors was too much, so he slunk over his back fence and crossed to another street. This one was just as dark as his, but there was life on it somewhere. He could smell smoke from a wood fire, and up ahead there was someone coming towards him. Will slid down behind a parked car—for some reason, he was surprised to see that its gascap was open. Someone had siphoned out the gas.

How had it come to that so quickly? he wondered.

There was no time to consider the answer. The man… or rather, the creature, was coming towards him. The person was slow and awkward, moving in a slouch and groaning to himself. Will was hit with a sudden flash of goosebumps. He was looking at a zombie.

The knife was suddenly slick in his hand. If the rumors were true, that only a head shot could kill them, then a knife was a stupid weapon. His was especially stupid in that it flared wide from the tip. It couldn't go deeply enough into an eye socket to even tickle the brain.

Running was Will's only option. It wasn't a good option, not by a long shot. The cluttered street was midnight dark, and if he tripped while running at full speed, he could break a bone. And weren't the zombies supposed to be fast? And supposedly they never tired. He hesitated a few more seconds, clutching the bumper of the car, his heart pounding in his chest. Was this the terror a rabbit felt just before it dashed from cover in front of a fox?

Probably.

Fueled by mindless fear, Will took off, racing across the street and towards a ranch house that was surrounded by a waist-high chain-link fence. In the daytime he might've been able to leap it completely. In the dark, he misjudged the height and jumped a fraction of a second too soon. His lead foot hit the top and then he was somehow tumbling into the fence, onto the fence and mostly over the fence all at once.

With a crash, he found himself partially upside down and caught in two places. The waist of his jeans was hooked at his hip, and the pack on his back was caught only God knows where. "Shit!" he hissed, twisting and desperately trying to push himself up. He was at an impossible angle to free himself, but a perfect angle to see the zombie staggering toward him.

Fear made him mad and he bucked and cursed and torqued his body into weird angles—and all for nothing. He was caught. "Get away!" he snarled as the creature came closer.

It tripped over the curb and went face first into the dirt. Its moan intensified as it tried to get up. Will thought it might have broken a bone because it couldn't stand. It could crawl, however. On its hands and knees, it crawled towards Will.

"Get the fuck away from me!" Will roared. "I have a knife!" Except he didn't. He had lost the knife going over the fence. Turning his head around, he saw it just out of reach.

The creature groaned once more and then vomited on the lawn of the ranch house. Up came a great gout of brown fluid that smelled horribly of stomach acid and whiskey. It was enough to make Will dizzy. Three times the creature vomited before it rolled over and sat next to its mess. Like a sapling in a strong wind, it swayed and seemed to forget that Will was there.

"Oooh boy," it said. "Ooooh boy. I should-ddn't drank-ded that wassa call it."

Will hung from the fence trying to understand what he was seeing. If he didn't know better, the man wasn't a zombie, he was a drunk. "Hey. Psst, buddy."

"Huh?" The man turned around slowly and stared at Will with bleary, bloodshot eyes. "Wha arrre you doin?"

"I could use a little help. I tried to jump the fence and mis-timed it. Can you see where my pack is caught?"

"Back is got? Yeah. Yeah. Hol on." He tried to stand—and failed, falling to the side. Although he smashed his ear into the fence, he laughed. "Tha herped. I mean herpded. Hur-ted."

Will rolled his eyes and was about to agree that it must have, when there was a crash from up the street. It was the sound of a door being kicked in, and it was followed by a scream. The man began to turn in that direction. "No. Mister, over here. You said you would help me, remember?"

"I did? Okay. Hol' on." He fell into the fence and stared over it at Will. "You're caught on some-tin." Another scream had his head swinging away again. "Hey. Issa person." Someone ran down the street.

"Yeah," Will agreed. There were more crashes and a hoarse shout. "We'll figure that out in a second. Help me off this, okay? Try to lift me up." The drunk lifted Will much the same way he might try to lift a similar sized tuna. It was more of an awkward hug. Still, it freed his jeans and he fell sideways and was able to wiggle out of his backpack. "Thanks so much."

He started to pull his pack free when there was a whooping cry and braying laughter. Someone else went sprinting up the street. A rock bounced after, almost hitting the person.

"You better get over on this side," Will whispered to the drunk. "Come on. Something's happening."

Will figured that the people up the street were like the hoodlums from the highway: immoral opportunists, or desperate suburbanites afraid for their future. He was wrong, not just about the mindset of the individuals but also of their numbers. The hoodlums on the highway had been about one percent of the fleeing refugees. Most people were already carrying as much as they could.

The people in the dark neighborhood were carrying next to nothing because they owned next to nothing.

At 25.7 percent of the population, Philadelphia had the highest poverty rate in the country. All told, there were four-hundred thousand people within the city limits who didn't need an apocalypse to set them on the road to starvation. These people didn't have overflowing pantries or freezers filled with meat. To make matters worse, the number of supermarkets in the inner city were drastically fewer per capita than in the suburbs. These were emptied early Sunday morning at about the same time credit card services were discontinued.

Without cash or credit cards, the few serviceable cars left to the people were usually so low on gas that no one wanted to risk getting stuck trying to cross the jam-packed bridges over the Schuykill River. The masses looted what they could, stripping supermarkets and convenience stores right down to the last stick of gum. Then, for the most part, they hunkered down to await the zombies or to be rescued by the government, which was doing "All that can be done."

For the people stuck in one-bedroom apartments, this felt like a whole lot of nothing.

On the morning of the fifth day of the apocalypse, there came an inexplicable, unannounced, spontaneous migration. About a hundred thousand people simply threw on their warmest clothes, grabbed what cash and food they had, and walked out of Philadelphia, looting as they went.

They headed west across the river and then fanned out from there, moving in slow waves. Like the suburbanites before them, their morals were set aside, sometimes temporarily, sometimes permanently. They took what they wanted, killed anyone they wanted to, and, with growing frequency, raped anyone they wanted to as well.

About half of them had a destination in mind when they set out; usually a relative or a friend who lived in another state. The rest simply walked with the idea of evading the zombies and seeing what tomorrow would bring them.

After a day, the lead element had finally arrived on Peakview Drive.

"Climb the fence," Will whispered to the drunk. "Come on. Just grab it. Fall over it if you have to." The drunk put one sneakered toe within the links and tried to climb the fence like a ladder. His toe slipped and he collapsed into a whisky-stinking pile.

He cackled, "Humpy Dumpy had a fall on his ass! Ha-ha!" Shadows moved from up the street. The drunk was unaware, he was too busy pulling a fifth of Jack Daniels from his coat pocket. "Humpy Dumpy took a big swig." As he tilted the bottle back, he saw people coming closer. "Is all da king's hores and all da king's mens!"

There were women among the men, and the drunk's slurred speech doomed him.

"What did you just call me?" one woman demanded. "Did you just call me a whore?"

"Whores," the man tried to correct. "Horses-ses."

Will slid back into the shadows as a half dozen women stepped forward. One said in a deadly whisper, "Call me a whore again. I dare you."

"No. Horses-ess."

This was still too much like "whores" and the woman stooped, found half a brick and threw it the man. In seconds, the others did the same, pelting him over and over again. A group stood around and watched, some with looks of disgust, others with grins. Most of the latter looked around for stones to hand to the women. They did not have good aim and their throws were not exactly powerful—it made for a long death for the drunk. Rocks thudded into him and very slowly he slumped against the fence, bleeding from two dozen wounds.

Unbelievably, one of the onlookers decided to film the murder. He brought out a phone with a glaring spotlight.

"There's another one!" In the light, Will had been spotted. Mob mentality had infected the group and he knew there'd be no justice or mercy granted. He jumped up and ran, choosing a direction at random. He was through a close-cropped yard in a flash and found a six-foot fence in his way. Although the last fence had made a fool out of him, he flew up this one with all the dexterity of a monkey.

There was no time to see what he was going to land on when he dropped over the other side and into some sort of bush or hedge. His clothes tore and his face was scratched open, but he wasn't seriously hurt. However, he was slowed as he had to pull himself out of the grasping branches. Just as he did, he was hit in the back by a baseball bat.

Spinning, he lashed out with a punch and hit only air. The bat hadn't been swung, it had been thrown. The men and teens chasing him couldn't climb and hold a bat at the same time, so they were throwing their bats over ahead of them. Will grabbed the bat and went after his closest pursuer.

The man was only a shadow, cursing about the bushes. Will cracked his skull open with one swing. Next, he went after a man who was just pulling himself from the bush and broke his jaw with another swing. Will went up and down the hedge laying about with the bat as if he were Babe Ruth. The men crawled deeper into the hedge to get away from him. When he found bats lying on the ground, he picked them up and hurled them at the men sitting on the top of the fence.

It only took a few throws to make them fall back onto the other side. Finally, one of the men broke free from the bush and raised his own bat. Will didn't hesitate.

Unlike what's portrayed in the movies, the bat is basically a purely offensive weapon. A strike could be parried if someone had both the skill and the guts to stand their ground. The man in front of Will was barely a man. Although tall, he was only sixteen or seventeen. He flinched back when Will sent his bat sailing down at his head. Bat met bat and the teen's bat dropped from his numb hands. He fled back into the bush, while Will ran in the opposite direction.

***

Catherine and Jillybean saw the same wave of people. They saw houses being broken into and they heard the same screams. In a cold sweat Catherine dragged her daughter to the attic, where she planned to make a final stand with only the knife as a weapon.

The blade was pathetic and next to useless. She was not a big woman, or strong, or tough. Although everyone she met thought she was smart, she didn't think so.

She was book smart. Her reading comprehension and ability to retain knowledge was off the charts. She could name the capital of a hundred and fifty countries, she could give the atomic number of every element on the periodic table, she could speak five languages. She could do a crossword puzzle in minutes. All of which was basically useless in the real world. She couldn't write a grocery list without leaving off seven items. She understood the concept of bluffing, but couldn't play poker to save her life. Anything improvisational was beyond her. And that included defending her home. She had her barricades and her knife, anything else required true independent thought and creativity.

Jillybean felt the same level of fear as her mother. Where their fear differed was in the specifics. Catherine Shaw knew what evil lay in the hearts of her fellow man, while Jillybean had something of a cartoon view of the world. She assumed that the bad people outside were very much like the bad people on the highway. Those people had done little more than threaten. The bad guys wanted their food and nothing else. The solution then had been obvious and the very same factors seemed to be at play here.

Barricading the house would suggest to the bad guys that there was something of value that needed to be kept safe—and there was of course. Their lives for one, Ipes for two, and Jillybean's *Barbie* tea set for a third. But in her mind, bad people wouldn't be after such things. They wanted food and would break down the door to get it—unless the door was already open.

"You know what Ipes just said? He said we gots-ta let them in the house. We just gotta make it look empty, like there's no food and they'll go away. This is just like with the car, amember?"

"It's not," Catherine stated, reaching for her daughter. "This is far, far worse. Now, sit down. If anything happens, I want you to hide behind that chair." She indicated a puffy old chair that had been her father's when he had been in school.

"Where are you going to hide?"

Catherine shook her head. She couldn't risk hiding and having someone finding Jillybean instead of her. "I'm not going to hide. I'm going to fight."

"But you can't fight, not against bad guys. Only daddy can do that. He's bigger-er and stronger-er, and that's what means we should open the doors. Even Ipes thinks so." She held up the zebra because who could argue with a zebra? "If they come in and see we gots no food and it looks like no one's home, they'll go somewhere else."

And if they go prowling around? Catherine wondered, *What then?* She and Jillybean would be sitting ducks.

Just then, three gunshots went off right in a row: *Bam! Bam! Bam!* They were close. Before she knew it, Jillybean was at the window, peeking above the sill. "They're at the blue house down the street."

259

"The Santoros'?" Catherine hurried over in time to see the Santoro's eldest daughter, Erika shoot a man from her bedroom window. Erika ducked down as someone in the dark fired up at her. "Jesus Christ!" Catherine whispered. There were more dark figures trying to kick in the garage door. They smashed at it until suddenly, the entire thing came down in a shriek of metal.

This brought on more gunshots, this time from within the garage. Two men fell in the driveway and the rest fled.

"We need a gun," Catherine said. Only a gun could save them.

Her takeaway from the situation was the opposite of Jillybean's. In the little girl's mind, guns were a last resort. Had the Santoros used Jillybean's strategy, they would still have a garage door. And besides, her family didn't have any guns and wishing that they did wouldn't make anything better.

"Maybe we can ask Mr. Santoro if he has an extra one that we could borrow," Catherine said, talking to herself, unaware how foolish she sounded even to her six-year-old daughter. "Just for a few weeks until…" Something moved in the house. There was someone on the stairs. They creaked when a grown-up walked on them. "Hide!" she hissed to Jillybean.

All of Jillybean's ideas went right out the window. She was a child again with a child's mindset and she dashed to the chair and hid behind it. Her heart was in her throat as the person on the stairs went up and up, getting closer with every second, until she was just about to wet herself in fright.

Catherine grabbed the knife and tiptoed behind the door. She raised the blade in a shaking hand and was ready to plunge it into the first person who walked through the door. She envisioned a dark beast of a man, his shadowed face offset only by a Cheshire grin.

The door began to open. "Cat? It's me. You two okay?" It was Will. He came in filthy, torn-up, and bleeding from a dozen little cuts.

She ignored all that and was on him in a second, squeezing him in a desperate hug, whispering, "Oh God, it was awful. We were surrounded."

Jillybean dashed to her father as well. When it came to ghosts and scary people, dads were always better at killing them, that was a fact. "There was bad guys," she stated. "Mean ones. Miss Erika shot some. I seen it."

"She's right," Catherine gushed. "It was like a real battle right here on our street." She went on to explain what had happened, finishing with, "I think you need to go over there and see if they will give us one of their guns."

"In exchange for what?" Will asked. "We don't have anything to trade. There were too many of those people around for me to get anything."

"Maybe they'll just give you one if you ask nicely," Catherine said, hoping to force a wish into reality. "You never know. Mr. Santoro always liked you."

Will didn't think it would work, but he saw the desperation in Catherine's eyes. "I guess I can try," he told her. He was about to leave when he took one more look out the window. The shadowy people were back, ringing the blue house. There had to be a hundred of them. They darted back and forth across the street, speaking in excited whispers.

A shot rang out from the house. In response, someone along the fence-line lit an oil-soaked rag that was partially stuffed down into a quart of *Valvoline*, and threw it at the house. It was an inept version of a molotov cocktail. Gasoline was a better fuel and glass a better container than plastic. Still, the oil burned. More oil was thrown from the fence-line and the side of the house was beginning to go up in flames when one of the Santoros crept from the back porch and fired off a dozen bullets through the fence.

The hoodlums ran, leaving two dead and three bleeding. They were not gone long. A few minutes later, oil was thrown from the back fence. The containers landed on the roof and began to burn, sending up a black sooty cloud. Someone rattled off a barrage of bullets from an upper-story window. From where the Shaws stood, it was impossible to see if anyone had been hit.

"Throw your food out the front and no one has to get hurt!" a man bellowed from across the street.

Will sagged away from the window. "So much for borrowing a gun. There's no way in hell they're going to voluntarily give up one of their guns now."

Jillybean had been standing on tiptoe to see what was happening and now that there was a lull, she turned to her parents. She held up her zebra, saying, "Ipes thinks that maybe we should open our doors like we done on the road with the car. And I don't wanna be set on fire and neither does Ipes. He says he's super more burnable than even a tree."

Catherine began shaking her head, but Will intervened. "She's right. Locking ourselves in is playing it too safe. We have to start taking smart chances." He didn't ask his wife's permission, but instead went down the stairs to the first floor where he eased the couch back away from the door. He was well on his way to getting it back in place, perfectly aligned with the window and the fireplace, when a better idea struck him.

Slowly, he tipped it over. Then he turned the coffee table over, pushed the love seat cock-eyed, and tossed around the decorative throw pillows and afghan. He made a general mess of the house, including filling the toilet with newspaper.

"How's that going to help?" Catherine asked in a whisper. She had been whittling a thumb nail down to nothing with her teeth as she watched Will. Jillybean had been watching with an eager light in her eyes. She wanted to make a mess, too, but her mom wouldn't let her.

"If it's going to get clogged, which would you prefer? That it's clogged with this or something else?"

She only grunted in answer.

"Want me to do the upstairs one?" Jillybean asked. She was already forming ideas how best to clog the crap out of the toilet.

Catherine pulled her back. There was a sudden barrage of gunshots coming from up the block. Unlike the earlier minor skirmishes, the firing didn't let up. It sounded like a full-fledged battle was raging. Will was the first to the living room window, where he stood far to the side so he could see up the block. There was little to see but tiny blinking lights as people fired their guns.

"What's happening?" Catherine whispered.

"I can't tell. Let's go upstairs for a better look. But first, I'm opening the front door."

She grabbed his arm. "Will!"

"Take Jillybean upstairs." He added a stern, "Now," when she didn't budge. Reluctantly she scooped up her daughter and hurried to the attic. Down below, Will crept to the front door and eased it open as slowly as he could. With the door open, the gunshots were even louder. Each seemed to jab at his eardrums. All eyes were on the battle, which seemed to be moving slowly away. It was the perfect time to declare his house a "previously ransacked zone."

Will slipped away from the door and crept up the stairs. He found Catherine at the window. "I think the Santoros are leaving," she whispered. "I thought I saw Erika with a big pack on her back."

"Leaving? How? They're surrounded."

Catherine shook her head. "Not anymore. They shot their way free. I think they were like, secret gun nuts. Can you believe it?"

He didn't think the term "gun nut" was very accurate anymore. How could you call a person with the foresight to stockpile weapons and food, a nut was beyond Will. He was the insane one. They were technically minutes into the sixth day of the apocalypse and the closest thing to a zombie anyone in Philadelphia had seen was the drunk, and still people had turned animal. If it hadn't been zombies, it would've been a meteorite, or an earthquake, or a terrorist attack. Hell, even a large enough solar flare would've sent the world into a new dark age—and Will Shaw had done jack-shit to prepare for any of it.

***

They slept the rest of the night in a pile of blankets and pillows, high-up in the attic. Jillybean woke first, cold and hungry. She leaned over her father, seeing the new grey hairs mixed in his blonde mane. When he finally blinked awake, she said, "Can I have *Captain Crunch* for breakfast?" She had dreamed about sitting in front of a barrel of *Captain Crunch* as her mother poured gallon after gallon of milk into it. Her mom kept saying, *Not yet. We have to fill it all the way to the top.*

Will put his finger to his lips. "Whisper. We don't know if anyone came in during the night. Wait here."

He picked up the knife he had given Catherine the day before and crept to the attic door to listen. His breath made little plumes of grey. Even with the front door open, he was puzzled by how cold the house was. Usually the attic was warm compared to the rest of the house.

Moving at seven excruciatingly slow steps a minute, he made his way to the second floor, and then to the master bedroom. It was empty, as was the guest room and Jillybean's room. If anyone had spent the night, it's where they would've been. Will felt more confident going down to the ground floor. The house was empty. It was also freezing.

The reason became quickly obvious: the furnace had stopped working. The Philadelphia Gas Works had shut down service and Will didn't think it would be long before the electricity and water went as well.

"Then what?" he muttered. The answer was obvious. Without light, water and heat they would have to revert back to some primitive form of humanity. "Ooga-ooga. Great." He looked out the window at the new day and saw people begin to stir. It was too cold to sleep.

It was strange to see the "hoodlums" in the light of day. The night before they had been wildings, barely human creatures intent on pillaging and shedding blood.

Now they were just people, wandering west like everyone else.

"The gas is off," he told his wife. She looked stricken by the idea. Jillybean less so—gas was for cars and they had left their car far away. "We can expect the electricity and the water to go as well. We'll use the portable heater from my study to heat up here. And when I'm gone, I'm going to need you to fill every container you can find with water. Pots, pans, tupperware; anything that will hold water will need to be used. I'm going to see what I can scrounge up in the way of food."

"Be careful," Catherine said, giving him a kiss.

"I'll be a ghost," Will told her. He then went to his garage, grabbed his trusty shovel and pried off the metal end with a screwdriver.

"Whatcha doin?" Jillybean asked. She had managed to get in her mom's way in thirty seconds and had been told to go play.

Will didn't like her being down on the ground floor. Anyone could walk through the front door at any time. Still, being overprotective wouldn't pay in the long run. Jillybean would have to mix prudence with courage and sensible fear. Sending her upstairs when there was nothing to be afraid of would send the wrong message.

"I'm making a spear." He clamped the wood staff to his workbench and dug through his toolbox for his wood planer. With it, he began to shave off strips of wood from the tip of the staff.

Jillybean watched the process intently, memorizing the steps involved. "Ipes thinks I should have one, too. Maybe a smaller one because I'm small. There could be like small banderitos or small zombies. I could fight them."

"Banderitos?"

"That's what means small bandits. Is it true we're gonna be cavemens? That's what mommy said. She said 'We're gonna live like cavemens!' And that's why I need a spear, too. I seen pictures of cavemens and they all had pointy sticks just like that one. Except can I have a pink one? Pink is for girls, you know. Pink with flowers so it'll match my bike. And Ipes should have one, too. He does not like stripes. He says they make him look fat. I told him all the cookies he sneaks when you guys aren't looking is what makes him look fat. That reminds me, can you please get some cookies please while you're out?"

Like a mosquito in a nudist colony, Will didn't know where to begin to answer. "If I see some cookies, I'll pick them up. And when I get back, I'll make you a spear, if it's okay with your mom."

Her face fell. She was sure her mom wouldn't let her have anything of the sort. She watched her dad finish his spear, then after a kiss, he slunk into the shadows behind the house. Jillybean ran to the attic to watch him.

"Keep away from the window, Jillybean," her mom said as she came up the stairs, hefting a spaghetti pot that was filled almost to the rim. "You don't want to be seen."

It was just as well. Her father was very good at slinking and she hadn't been able to see him. She made sure her mom saw her go to her pile of stuffed animals in the corner of the attic. When Catherine went tromping down the stairs, Jillybean slipped after her, doing her best to be as sneaky as her dad. She was very hungry and knew where food could sometimes be found.

Three doors down was ole Mrs. Bennett's house. The last time Jillybean had checked, she'd had a few apples left on the apple tree in her backyard. That had been two weeks ago. Jillybean had lost a frisbee over her fence and had dared Mrs. Bennett's legendary meanness to get it. She had been caught and subjected to a withering tongue-lashing and a promise to "have her bottom tanned" if she was ever caught snooping where she didn't belong.

Just then, Jillybean didn't care about getting her bottom smacked. Without TV, video games, playmates, movies or anything fun to do in the last few days, she'd had ample opportunities to think. She had never given thinking much thought, but now that she had, she had come to see that thinking had its merits. For starters, she'd been able to examine the merits of her parent's differing attitudes towards the apocalypse.

Her mom had displayed all the ferocity of a mouse and, as far as Jillybean could tell, they had suffered for it. They were cold, hungry, tired and beset by all sorts of bad things all due to her mother's stubbornness. Her father had wanted them to go on, probably to somewhere warm. People had talked about camps, and where there were camps, there were campfires and marshmallows, of course. That was a given. He had also wanted to fight for their food. If he had won, they'd be eating right then. And they'd be eating good food, not mushy apples with worms crawling in them.

She wanted to be more like her father if she could. But first she would need a weapon. There were no spears in her size in the garage. She poked around the tools, selecting a mini-axe. It was just over a foot long and surprisingly heavy. It could definitely chop open the head of a zombie, which was the preferred method to kill the creatures

But it didn't look very sharp. To test it, she went out through the garage door, hefted the hand-axe with a two-fisted grip and took a swing at their "acorn tree." She considered the swing a "medium" and yet, she only flicked off a bit of the bark, and nearly hit herself in the foot as the axe head kept going after hitting the tree.

Wisely, she decided against a second attempt. Her wrists were too weak to allow for any sort of control or power. This left her without a means to protect herself against even the smallest banderito and she would be very embarrassed to have some sort of kindergarten gangster take her apples. What she needed was something dangerous to a kid, that could be wielded by a kid.

The first thing that came to mind was: "Scissors." Her mom was always going on about how dangerous they were —*Don't run with scissors. Scissors aren't toys. You could lose an eye!*

Despite all these precautions, Jillybean had never considered them all that dangerous, and now that she thought about it, she discovered that the most dangerous thing about them was that they weren't obviously dangerous. They had pointy ends, sure, but that was about it. It made a kid complacent, and when a kid became complacent, he or she would do foolish things.

No, what she needed was something truly dangerous. And something with a little more reach to it. "I think my arms are too short for my body," she said to the zebra. Ipes was without comment and only stared at her with his head kinked to the side. The truly dangerous items were in the kitchen. One of her mom's big cutting knives was practically sword-sized for a girl her height.

"But one would be missed." There were seven gleaming knives all in a row. If she took one, her parents would know. She started going through the drawers: oven mitts, hand towels, an empty bread drawer with a few crumbs at the bottom. She stopped when she found the drawer where her father kept his barbecuing tools. Right on top was a twenty-two inch stainless steel barbecue fork with four-inch long tines.

She tested one on her thumb and grinned at the pain. "Wait here, Ipes," she told her zebra. Ipes was not ready to go out into the real world. He was too small and soft. And how would she carry him? This thought made her realize that she would need something to carry the apples in. She dodged her mother coming up and down the stairs and found her *Hello Kitty* backpack.

With her mini-spear at the ready, she ventured into the backyard. She was not terribly frightened. This was her backyard and her neighborhood. The bad guys seemed to have moved on and there were no zombies. Everything seemed quiet, but normal. One squirrel chased another round and round the trunk of a tree, and on the telephone wire was a fat pigeon, sitting in perfect contentment. They would've warned Jillybean of danger.

As she had a thousand times during the previous summer, which had been long and glorious, she went to the low side fence and climbed over. Now she was in the Shusters' yard. Before all this, they worked day and night, and were rarely home; now they were gone forever. Jillybean could look straight into their kitchen window and saw that every cupboard door was swung wide, showing off empty shelves.

She kept going, passing into the Smiths' yard. Had this been a normal day, she would've walked through the gate in their back fence and would've been in Becca's yard. Becca had been her bestest friend for years and years. Her house was glumly dark. She was gone, too.

Jillybean stared at the house for a long time, wishing that her mommy had let them finish going to the west. She was sure that's where Becca and all her friends had gone. "They're probably all at the camp now." Jillybean's belly rumbled at the thought of marshmallows and 'smores. Reluctantly she turned away. Facing her was the much larger fence that hid most of mean ole Mrs. Bennett's house. The fence was daunting, but there was a secret way over it that only she and Becca knew.

At the corner of the fence was a post that to a child represented a ladder. Up she went, her pink dress flaring, showing the jeans beneath. She paused at the top and gazed at Mrs. Bennett's house. It was lifeless like every other house, and that was good. The leaves of the apple tree were yellow now and the branches no longer drooping under the weight of all the fruit as they had a month before. There were still apples to be picked, however.

Jillybean clambered down, wisps of her hair breaking free of her braid and waving in the air like antennas. To stave off boredom, her mom had done it up the night before. Now the pretty twists were beginning to come undone.

Whisking the strays from her face, she gazed up at the tree noting how the lower branches were bare of fruit. It would mean climbing. Had the tree's trunk been like an oak, wide and tall she wouldn't have made the attempt, but the apple tree had a gazillion branches, the lowest of them easily within reach. Up she went, higher and higher. The first apple she came to was soft and brown. The next had little rusty-looking holes, and she was sure that it was stuffed full of burrowing worms. The next was like that as well and so was the third.

Apple after apple was bypassed before she found one that looked halfway decent. With difficulty, she refrained from taking a bite. She had to share. Those were the rules. Sharing was caring. There were more apples higher up or further out on the branches. Some were too high and some were too far out. Using her barbecue fork helped her snag a few more edible ones.

Her count was up to five when she happened to look over at the house and saw Mrs. Bennet glaring at her from her kitchen window.

Jillybean had always been afraid of mean ole Mrs. Bennett and she almost tumbled out of the tree in fright. It took Jillybean only a few seconds to fly down from her perch ten feet in the air. She dropped the last five feet and was up and running for the fence in a heartbeat.

"Come back here!" Mrs. Bennet hissed.

And be put in a giant black pot and cooked with carrots and onions? That wasn't going to happen. She was up and over the fence in a blink, surprising even herself how fast she was moving. The next two fences were almost hurdled and then she was back inside her house, her chest heaving.

"Jillybean? Where are you?" It was her mom, calling from the attic.

"Down here," she answered, sliding her pack off and stashing it and the long fork in the dining room. "I was just getting something to drink." She quickly filled a cup and hurried upstairs.

"Use the bathroom sink from now on. You are not to leave this attic, young lady. Except to use the bathroom and get a drink."

Her mom kept a tight eye on her for the next few hours before Will Shaw came back with a half-filled backpack. The first thing he pulled from it were five old apples. "We should eat these first before they go bad," he said, casting a sharp eye on his daughter. He had brought back a few cans of tuna, oatmeal in a plastic bag, some thawing chicken that looked strangely grey in spots, and an open bag of gummy bears. They were hard as a rock, but that didn't stop Jillybean from jawing her way through a handful at the end of the odd meal.

"Jillybean," Will said, when they were done. "I want you to help me get some more pots from next door at the Smiths' place." The moment they were outside, he turned on her, his face hard, his eyes angry. "Your mom would've thrown a hissy if she knew you had been outside unsupervised. No more of that for a few days. She's going to have to get used to this new world first. And when we do say you're ready to go out, you won't go off by yourself without telling anyone."

He stood, his eyes drawn the partially burned Santoro house. "There are no laws anymore. Might makes right. Do you know what that means? It means that morality and being good…basically everything we've been teaching you, is no longer the right thing. At least until things get situated. Until then, people are going to do whatever they have to in order to survive. They're going to set aside right and wrong, which makes things very dangerous for a little girl out alone. Do you understand?"

She thought she did and nodded.

Will bent and kissed her on the top of the head. Then the two began hauling pots and pans back and forth. When they had finished with those, it was tupperware and then an old aquarium.

Seeing the aquarium triggered a memory in Jillybean: Billy from kindergarten bringing a goldfish to school for show and tell—he had brought it in a ziplock baggie. When she suggested this, through Ipes to keep from being labeled a know-it-all, her father grinned. "I knew I kept you around for a reason. I almost told the stork to send you back."

"I wasn't no stork baby," she laughed.

"I wasn't 'A' stork baby," he corrected.

She liked that he thought that she was smart, but she didn't like being put in charge of filling the bags. One or two was easy enough, but after a quick scrounge, of the neighborhood, Will brought back six boxes of gallon-sized ziplocks. She stood at the sink for the next two hours filling them.

When she was finished, she went to their tiny stash of food and had just popped a gummy bear into her mouth when the portable heater suddenly died. It was rumbling, breathing out hot air one second, and was a useless hunk of plastic the next. Ten minutes later, the water stopped running.

The three of them stood in the attic as if waiting for something else that had been permanent to fail, like the sun perhaps. "We're going to need candles," Will said, eventually. "We'll freeze this winter without something. I'm going to need you to come with me this time, Catherine. We're going to have to leave Jillybean here alone."

Alone... Normally, the very idea of being alone was a terrifying thing, but after Jillybean's trip to mean ole Mrs. Bennet's house, her father's suggestion felt almost like she had graduated in some sense. Perhaps she was a 'big kid,' now. Only big kids got to be alone. They also got to stay up late and eat dessert at three in the afternoon. She had seen this firsthand and had been amazed.

Her mom stared at Will in horror. "What? No. Absolutely not."

"Jillybean is a smart girl. She'll be safer here than out there with us. And I'm going to need your help. Now that the power's out, everyone is going to start scrounging for candles and lighters. Two people can work faster than one. Remember what I said about taking chances?"

"And I'll be good," Jillybean said. "I'll stay up here, I promise. I have my books. And Ipes will keep me company." As much as being a big kid was a big deal, she was also beginning to realize that her father was right. The attic was already beginning to get cold. The last three nights had been miserable. She had shivered herself to sleep and it wasn't even real winter yet. What would it be like in January?

Catherine felt the chill as well and finally agreed, but before she left, she drilled into Jillybean's head her own phobias about playing with matches and talking to strangers, and all that. Jillybean had heard all this since she was a little kid.

Her parents left not long after and by then it was late afternoon. Jillybean, wrapped in a coat and a blanket, sat at the attic window with Ipes on the sill, and stared out. She was very proud of her new big kid status, at first. Then the sun started to go down and she felt the first trickle of fear. When it was all the way down, the fear ticked up. In all her six and a half years, there had never been a darker night than this one. With the power out in the city, there was no ambient light, save from the trickle cast down from the stars overhead.

Her fear hit a high-water mark when the shadows of the night began to move. The loss of power had kicked off a second migration from Philadelphia. Tens of thousands of people were on the move, driven by a fear of freezing to death. They surged like a wave through the suburbs and were only less violent because there were fewer people left to kill.

Jillybean's fear red-lined an hour later when she heard people below her, whispering in the dark. They were *directly* below her—in the house. It wasn't her father, this time. He would never be so loud or so clumsy. Someone tripped and there was a crash—Jillybean guessed it was the white lamp that sat on an end table that had fallen.

The people...the four people, moved about the house, poking through the cabinets and yanking out drawers. Would they notice the missing pots and pans? Of course, they would! Only a blind person would've missed them—and who would take pots and pans when fleeing to a camp. No one!

And now they were on the stairs. Jillybean realized that she had made a huge mistake by not hiding when they first came in. If she tried to hide now, they'd hear her footfalls on the ceiling. She was stuck, sitting framed against the window. Her heart began to hammer in her chest as her entire body began to thrum. They were in her parents' bedroom—they had to notice the missing comforters on the bed! Who would take comforters with them in an apocalypse?

It was all suspicious.

"They're gonna knowd, Ipes. They're gonna…" She sucked in her breath as she was struck by an overwhelming urge to pee. The need was so great that she entwined her legs about each other and squeezed until she thought her left kneecap would pop off. This kept the pee back until she heard one of them take a step onto the attic stairs. All the squeezing in the world wasn't going to stop it then, and her pants were suddenly wet and hot—and still the bad guys came up, step after step. A scream began to build in her throat. It was going to be a huge one, maybe one loud enough for her parents to hear.

Deep down, she knew that was only wishful thinking.

She was a trembling, piss-smelling little baby and no one was going to be able to save her. No one would even try. The scream came and just as it did, she found her mouth corked by a furry bottom. Somehow, Ipes had simply leaped into her mouth holding back the scream.

Jillybean jumped when she heard someone hiss up the stairs, "Hey!" It was one of the intruders. "Don't bother. We're leaving. There ain't shit in this house."

They were leaving! Strangely, this brought on another urge to pee. Her jeans were already ruined and this time she didn't bother to hold it back. The new warmth was comforting in the same way her baby blanket had been. It didn't stay that way. The cold of the attic crept up her legs. She would have to change, and that meant going downstairs.

When the bad people left, she stole down to her room, stripped off her wet jeans and pulled on new panties and pink sweats. There was no way she was going to let her parents find her wet clothes, not after just declaring her a big kid. She tiptoed to the kitchen and stuffed the clothes into a garbage bag and threw them into the bushes behind the house. She was back in the attic seconds later, breathing hard and still shaking.

"No one will know," she told Ipes as she hurried to the corner of the attic. "It'll be our secret." Sitting in the window had been a mistake, she decided. She had trapped herself. The corner was better. There was a rack where her father kept old suits and her mom had her wedding dress hanging in a white bag. Jillybean hid behind it, thinking that no one would know.

But it was cold in the corner. After a few minutes, she crept out and grabbed three blankets and a pillow. This was better, especially when she had made a blanket fort. It kept the warmth in.

She sat there for hours and was just beginning to doze off when she heard the first gunshot. It was far away and yet there was a quality to it that set Jillybean's guts churning. A minute later it was followed by a second one, then a third. Gradually the shooting came closer and as it did, the noise in the street picked up. Outside her window, people were running and hissing to each other.

Something was happening and not even Jillybean's fear could dampen her curiosity. She hurried to the window and watched as the mass migration to the west had become a mass retreat to the east. People were streaming by. Some sprinted and others jogged. Many were flagging and hunched under the weight of their belongings. They plodded on as screams began to erupt behind them. Each scream seemed to be accompanied by another gunshot.

Jillybean thought the people looked like a river of humanity and the water analogy held true a minute later as there came a sudden explosion of screams. People surged forward in a tremendous wave. They were running for their lives—but from who?

"The army? Do you think it's the army what's chasing them, Ipes?" Ipes said nothing and only sat staring out of the black beads he had for eyes. She thought it was the army because of all the shooting. It was worse than when the Santoros had fought their way to freedom.

"We gotta figure out a way to signal them so they know we're the good guys. Maybe we should use our fourth of July flag!" It was a good idea except it was all the way downstairs in the hall closet and she didn't know whether any of the bad guys had snuck in during all the ruckus. "We'll use a pillowcase," she told the zebra. "Squish over. I need to get the window open."

With her little arms straining, she had just pried the window up an inch when she saw what the people were running from. It was zombies, and they weren't weird little grey creatures with toilet paper stuck to the bottom of their shoes. They were monsters.

They were monsters wearing bloody human masks. They were monsters with torn-up faces, missing hands, and bullet holes in their grey flesh.

Down below in the street, those people that couldn't keep ahead of the horde were dragged down, their shrill screams splitting the night. Some fought and kicked their way to freedom. Others were torn apart right on their driveway. Jillybean stared in horror as blood ran across the hopscotch board she had drawn in chalk, a week before. She and Becca had played a marathon game, each sweating despite the chill in the air.

Now there was a bloody footprint in one of the squares.

Jillybean felt a new scream building in her throat. It was choked off when she started to gag. She was going to puke! And scream! And, holy hell, she was going to wet herself again! Despite the need to do all these things, she did none of them. Instead she ran for the corner where she had made her fort. Ducking in, she dropped to her knees and stuffed her fingers in her ears.

"La, la, la. I can't hear nuffin'. I can't hear nuffin'. La, la, la." But she did hear something. It was a strange wailing that was oddly familiar. When she opened her eyes, she realized she was alone. She had left Ipes on the ground next to the windowsill. As if he were her baby, she ran for him, snatched him up and raced back.

Once more, she began to rock. "La, la, la. I can't hear nuffin'. La, la, la," she repeated over and over again. Having Ipes with her helped and gradually her breathing slowed and the need to vomit faded. Still she went on rocking and must've repeated herself twenty times before she felt the house shake. This wasn't someone opening drawers and poking through their cabinets, no, this was someone on the stairs and running fast. In her mind's eye she saw one of the bad guys running from a zombie…and running right at her!

She dove under the blankets just as the door at the top of the stairs opened and someone thundered inside.

"Jillybean!"

It was her mom. Jillybean leapt up out of her fort and was on her mom in flash. She was crying; they were both crying. Her father came in a second later, dropped a pack on the floor and looked around to see if everything was alright.

"Good. You did good, Jillybean," he said. "We were worried about you. I'll be back in a…"

"No!" Catherine, hissed, savagely. "You aren't leaving us. No one's leaving this house!"

He held up his hands. "I'm just going to lock the doors and move the couch back in front of it."

A muscle below her right eye twitched as she stared at him. "Okay. You do that. But no sneaking off. We need to stay together." She suddenly grabbed Jillybean again, this time the hug was suffocating. "Oh, Jillybean. It was terrible. They were everywhere. There was this mom…"

"No, Catherine!" Will said, sharply. "She doesn't need to hear about it." The two stared at each other until Will went back down the stairs, moving slower now.

Catherine sat back and although her eyes were on Jillybean, she was seeing some unnamed child being torn apart. She had been a little black girl with white beads in her hair. She'd been small, lost in a heavy purple coat. "It was that damn coat. The zombies couldn't chew through it. But they tried. The mom was going crazy, beating them with a bat. But she was an older mom, like forty. And she was exhausted from the run and too weak to hurt them. And the girl kept screaming: *Mommy help me!* She kept screaming it over and over. *Mommy help me! Mommy help me!* She screamed it even after they tore off her lips. I didn't help. I wanted to but I couldn't."

She spread her arms. "Look at me. How could I? I'm nothing. I'm weak and I don't have a gun, and they were everywhere. I was too afraid to do anything but hide." Her eyes had been shiny with tears, now they seemed to grow dull and lifeless. "I'm not meant for this, Jillybean. I'm not meant for this world. I can't fight. I can't hunt. I can't do anything but die."

"N-No," Jillybean whispered. "You can't die. What would I do if you died? What would Daddy do?"

"Daddy? He would live. He's a fighter. He's not like us. He'd be better off without us."

Confused and appalled, Jillybean leaned back from her mother. She had no idea what to say to this. "Do you want us to go somewhere? Like to the campfires?"

"Campfires? No. No fires. *They* are attracted to fires. And no one's going anywhere. We're going to stay here and hide. That's the only thing we can do. We'll hide and wait for the army. They should be here soon."

***

Three days passed and still no army men showed up. There were only more zombies. They came in waves, heading east, perhaps blown along by the cold wind that howled from the west—from where the camps were.

Every night Will Shaw left the house to scrounge. It was safer to move at night. The zombies were fast and terribly strong, but they were confused by moving shadows and couldn't readily tell the difference between a human and another zombie in the dark.

With him gone, the burden of watching over Jillybean was left to Jillybean. Catherine had fallen into a depression that left her barely able to eat, not that there was ever much to eat. On that third day, their small larder consisted of a few cans of soup and beans, a package of crushed *Ronzoni* lasagna, and a tin of flour. Jillybean also had a store of acorns that she used in her tea parties. Like the flour, she knew they were sorta edible, she just didn't know how to cook them or mix them in with anything but water.

The tea parties, always well-attended by her stuffed animals, were bitter affairs because of the acorns. But bitter was better than nothing, and they had plenty of nothing. So much so, she had taken up the habit of chewing on her hair. But no matter what, she tried not to complain. Every time she did, her mom looked vindicated as if giving up was a much better path to walk than slow starvation. Her dad would look pained and always took an even smaller portion of food than he usually did.

He ate even less than Catherine and it showed. His cheeks were hollow and there were dark circles beneath his eyes from lack of sleep.

When he was gone, Catherine took pills and slept. Jillybean waited at the attic window wearing layers to keep herself warm. They had forty-seven candles but her mom refused to light them at night. It was always "too dangerous."

On the fourth night, Will did not come home. Jillybean sat at her window with only Ipes to keep her company. She did not sleep and, strangely, did not feel sleepy. She kept watch over a street populated only with monsters. "If the whole world is like this," she said to Ipes, "I think we're in trouble."

"Of course, we're in trouble," she said in a deeper tone, holding the zebra from behind and making his head go back and forth. "We're out of cookies! Feel my tummy. It's so empty!"

"Mine too," she sighed. "Maybe daddy will find some Oreos. Or some ice cream. Or some cake." Her stomach rumbled and she looked back at the small box of food. There was nothing in it that sounded appealing, and yet her stomach growled again.

Her daddy did not come home until the sun had come around and was directly overhead. His pack was full and at first, she was excited, but then he pulled from it a flashlight, batteries, more candles, and three rolls of toilet paper. At the bottom were two packages of ramen, three cans of green beans and one of pumpkin pie filling. It looked like a feast to Jillybean, but as usual, they were not allowed to gorge themselves.

"We might have to move," Will told them as he nibbled on beans. "There are zombies up the wazoo around here, but if we head south five or six miles, it's like a ghost town."

"Hell no," Catherine stated. "We're not going to risk a five-mile walk through a million zombies just to get to a house that'll be just as cold and dark as this one. They'll just find us again. And again, and again, and again, and…"

Will went around and hugged her from behind. "It's okay. We'll stay here and ride out the storm. I'm sure the army is on this. I bet they'll be here any day."

But they weren't.

As he had on his previous outing, Will was gone all through the night and came back limping, his face scratched. "I tripped," he told them. "It was nothing." Catherine believed the lie, but Jillybean saw how her father only picked at his meager plate. Something bad had happened to him. He did not sleep well and for the first time in days, Catherine went to him and held him.

"Can we really hold out?" she asked.

"If we're careful and if we get lucky," he said. Catherine smiled and nodded. Jillybean committed the words to memory: careful and lucky were the key to survival.

That night he left and did not come home the next day. Nor did he come home that night. Catherine dragged herself to the window and stared out with Jillybean as the hours ticked by. They were still there at sunrise of the second day. And at noon, each taking turns napping. It was after four and the sun was dropping like a stone in the west when he finally eased the backdoor open and came in, leaning heavily on his homemade spear.

Jillybean was downstairs like a bolt of white lightning, her hair flying wildly behind her. Her daddy was just pulling off his pack with a groan when she reached the kitchen. "Stop!" he thundered, holding out the spear sideways to block her if she came closer. His eyes were rimmed red and he glistened with fat drops of sweat. His hair was plastered across his brow and his mouth hung open, showing a grey tongue.

"What's wrong?" she asked in a small voice.

You know what's wrong, someone whispered behind her. And she did know. She could see his torn coat and the dried blood. He'd been bitten, and that was bad, worse than any normal bite.

"Don't come near me," he said, sounding as though he were speaking through a desert-dry throat.

He was infected and still it took all her will power not to fling herself into his arms. This was her daddy. This was the man who could not be hurt. He could not be stopped. He was supposed to be forever. That's how parents were to a child. She had to hold him and hug him and do whatever she could to make him feel better. Kisses and warm soup, that's what he needed. And a hot bath. She could heat the water for a bath in the fireplace. Also band aids for his ouchies.

"I know how to fix you," she said. She took one step towards him.

"I said no!" he thundered. "Stay where you are. Catherine, stop her. Make her understand there's no helping me."

Jillybean looked back at her mother and saw that she was broken. Catherine was fractured into a million tiny pieces that would never ever fit back the way they had. Her husband, the sole light in the terrible world, the one rock left for her to lean upon, was dying. She was dead-white and yet she was somehow still beautiful.

Catherine slowly shook her head from side to side. "It's okay. Hug your father, Jilly. Give him a kiss."

Don't, the voice hissed from behind Jillybean. She tried to look around her mom to see who was speaking but Catherine pushed her forward.

"It's the only way for us to be together," she said.

"No!" Will screamed, smashing the butt of the spear down on their linoleum. "This is not how we'll be together. Catherine, snap out of it. You have to take care of Jillybean now. You have to look after her and yourself."

That was impossible. She had tried and failed. This, all of it, was her fault. She had made them come back, and she had kept Will from fighting for their food. At every turn she had failed, and now he expected her to protect Jillybean, when he couldn't? Catherine's knees folded beneath her and she dropped to the floor on her hands and knees. Tears splashed on the hardwood. "I can't. In this world you're the strong one. Not me. I'm nothing."

Will sucked in a long breath, set aside the spear, and then staggered to her, making sure to step around Jillybean as if she was the one with the disease. Groaning, he went down to one knee. "You don't have a choice, Cat. You're her mother. Promise me that you'll try." Catherine stared at the floor for so long that Jillybean didn't think she would answer, but she finally nodded.

"No. Say it."

"I'll try. I promise."

"Good," Will said, sitting back, his chin suddenly so heavy it was an effort to lift it to look at his daughter. He grimaced from some unknown pain and swallowed loudly. "You'll try, too?"

Jillybean felt numb from her toes to her wild hair. Something was happening but there was static in her head that made it hard to think. It was something so bad that her child's mind couldn't comprehend the entire scope. Her daddy was sick, but didn't sick people get better? She thought he would get better if she was good.

"I'll try and be good. I'll help mommy, and I'll be careful and lucky."

His sweating face suddenly went hard in anger. "No. You'll be smart. You'll be hard and cruel when you have to be, and you'll survive, no matter what. Do you understand?"

She didn't. Being smart was easy. Everyone always told her that she was smart. But hard and cruel? That sounded like being evil. She didn't want to be evil, but she also didn't want to disappoint her father and so she nodded.

"Good," he said, his voice hoarse and croaking. "I-I think I need one kiss before…" The numbing static in Jillybean's head drowned out what he said next. He leaned slowly forward and kissed her on the cheek; she could feel the heat of his fever coming off of him in waves. He kissed his wife as well before he struggled to his feet and staggered out the door without looking back.

"Is he coming back?" Jillybean asked. Catherine was lying on her side and Jillybean only just realized that she was sobbing. "Mommy? When's daddy coming back?"

Not only did Catherine keep crying, she started moaning in misery as if she had gotten her daddy's sickness, too. Jillybean went to her and brushed her hair back. "I'll be good," she told her mom.

Catherine began shaking her head at this. "No," she said, wiping the tears from her eyes with her coat sleeve. "We are going to be hard and cruel." Although she managed to stand, she looked like a person that was being held together by Elmer's Glue and a little tape. The slightest shock and her facade would crumble to pieces. She even took slow, unsteady steps. Inside Will's pack were a few cans of ravioli and two of chicken soup.

"Is he coming back?" Jillybean asked again.

"You know the answer to that," Catherine said, taking the pack and heading back to the attic. She lit a candle under a little rack Will had made from the frame of a lampshade and put one of the cans of ravioli on it.

Jillybean wasn't sure if she really did know the answer. People used to get sick all the time and they always came back. Becca had the flu and was out sick from school for two whole weeks but even she came back and she was a lot smaller than her dad. Her dad never let the flu stop him. He used to go to work with a runny nose and that was what meant he was the toughest of all.

No, he's not coming back. It was the same voice she'd heard earlier. Jillybean slunk in closer to her mom. She was afraid of the voice. People had voices. Words weren't supposed to come from a bunch of nothing. Unless it was a ghost. She didn't like the idea of that at all.

Jillybean hugged her mom for safety as they sat in stony silence. Every few minutes, Catherine would tremble all over, and her eyes would mist over.

"This is taking forever," Catherine said out of the blue. She spoke like a robot.

"What is?"

Catherine pointed at the ravioli. A single candle was a poor choice as a heating element and to heat it all the way through took close on an hour. As the minutes ticked by, Catherine couldn't stop picturing her husband's sweating face. She didn't want to remember him that way. She wanted to remember the vibrant Will Shaw, the man who always seemed to have more energy than any two men combined. He was the hardest working man she had ever known. A day of work was nothing to him, and he always came home just as fresh as when he'd left. He would play with Jillybean and then, always selflessly, would look to Catherine's needs.

He was an easy man to love, and she knew it would be next to impossible to live without him. She couldn't imagine it.

"It's bubbling," Jillybean said of the ravioli. As sad as she was for her dad, her stomach was an empty bag.

"Yeah," Catherine said without any feeling. She doled out most of the can to her daughter.

They ate their ravioli without noticing the flavor. They also didn't notice the sun had gone down and that their window was still uncovered. Theirs was the only light shining in Philadelphia.

***

The rumbling motor of a truck approaching started so softly that neither of them picked up on it until it was too late.

Jillybean's first reaction was to hide. Catherine's was to run out into the street, waving her arms and crying out that they were rescued. It took her half a minute too long to come to her senses. By the time she did, the truck was on Peakview Drive.

Catherine blew out the candle and huddled with her daughter as the truck came right up to their house, slowed, and then pressed on, bouncing over zombies that had come out into the street to see what the light and the noise was. When the truck was gone, Catherine didn't know whether to be relieved or not. Maybe they hadn't been "bad guys." Maybe they had just been people looking for other survivors.

She was still ruminating on this when a horn started blaring. It was close, but not on their street. It went on for a minute before it suddenly stopped. Then there was a roar of an engine. It grew loud, as if the driver of the truck was racing for his life, then it went soft, and softly, it purred back towards the Shaw's house.

That purr sent a shiver up Catherine's spine. "Hide," she ordered Jillybean. "And don't come out until I tell you. No matter what." Jillybean, her eyes large and wet in fear, disappeared like a ghost into the far reaches of the attic. Catherine's own fear was like a frozen ball of ice in her gut. Forcing her hands into fists, she went to the window. Yes, there was the truck, now with its lights off. The shiver that had started in her back and shoulders grew even more intense as the truck rolled up to their house and pulled into their driveway. Catherine had no idea what to do. If they ran, all their stuff would be stolen. And what if the people really were good guys? She would lose their only chance to survive.

And if they're bad guys?

The thought almost paralyzed her. If they were bad, she would be at their mercy. As frightening as that was, she didn't feel she had a choice. Slowly, she went down the stairs and to the front door. She was steps away when there came a soft knock.

"Hello? Anyone home?"

285

Catherine stopped. "Y-Yes. W-Who is it?"

The man on the other side of the door chuckled. "My name's Herb. Sorry for laughing but asking 'who is it' just sounded weird. I don't know if people say that anymore. We're looking to trade. We have food if you have any ammo."

Her heart fell. They had nothing to trade except for candles and clean water. Neither seemed all that important compared to ammo. Catherine would drink out of a mud puddle for the rest of the year if it meant getting a gun.

"I-I don't have any ammo, but we have some candles and batteries. Herb, we're desperate. We need food and we need help."

"How many of you are there?"

Catherine hesitated. There was nothing more vulnerable in an apocalypse than an unarmed woman and her daughter. "I-It's just me," she stammered. "My husband left to find food and stuff. He'll be back soon."

"And does he have any ammo?"

The question reignited the shivers. If she answered yes, they might think Catherine's situation was fine. If she answered no, then once more she'd be at their mercy. She took a chance. "No."

"Aw, man," Herb said. She could picture him shaking his head in sadness at her misfortune. "Hey, could I talk inside? It's cold out here and some of the zekes are starting to come back."

It was a reasonable request spoken in a reasonable tone. Catherine wanted to hide. She didn't want to open the door for any reason—but she had to. She had to take the chance for Jillybean's sake. She heaved the couch back and unlocked the door. Herb was nothing like he sounded. She had pictured a rough-looking man, tall and strong, instead she got what appeared to be a forty-year-old amateur bowler. His round belly preceded him by a foot.

Behind him were four more people: two women in their twenties, one dumpy and blonde, with two chins in spite of her age. The other was Hispanic with a wide plain face, and rude judging eyes. She sneered at Catherine.

Next came two men, both of whom were somewhat shapeless forms beneath heavy coats. They wore hoodies and stared out from the shadows. All five carried pistols.

She shut and locked the door, and when she turned around, she saw the four going through her cabinets. "Where's the food?" one of the men demanded, slamming the refrigerator closed.

"I-I told you w-we don't have any. It's why he's gone. My husband, I mean. B-But he'll be back soon."

Herb sighed, rolling his eyes. "We don't believe you. Everyone has food. Now, we can tear this place apart finding it or you can just tell us."

Catherine's head dropped to her chest and she had the fleeting thought, *Maybe if I rushed at one of them, they'd shoot me and I can be done.* Death seemed like the best option left to her. A bullet in the head sounded nice. She'd be dead before she felt a thing. *And what about Jillybean? What about your promise.*

She had to fight against snarling: "Fuck my promise!" She was in a sudden rage. Her heart was filled with spite for Herb and his four friends, and for Will for dying when he was supposed to be here protecting his family. She even felt a poisonous hatred for Jillybean. She was the anchor holding Catherine in this world.

"Who is this pretty girl?" Herb asked, holding up a picture. It was Jillybean when she had been three. God, she had been the most precious thing imaginable, and Catherine could remember a hundred times thinking she would gladly give her life for her daughter—and here she was hating the epitome of innocence.

"She's my niece," Catherine lied. It was a stupid lie. When Herb found Jillybean's room and her pillow fort in the attic, he would know she was Catherine's daughter. Then they really would tear the place apart looking for her. Catherine was already falling to pieces, and if they threatened Jillybean, she wouldn't be able to recover. "I-I only have a few cans of beans and I need them. It's all I have, I swear."

"We need them more," the blonde woman said. "There's more of us and so we need more food. It's for the greater good. You do like the greater good, don't you?"

This wasn't logic, this was rationalizing theft.

Herb peered at her face in the dark. "You know, there's something else you have that we want."

"I don't want that," the blonde said. "We're here for food. And besides, Mick is with me. He doesn't want any of that."

"Speak for yourself," one of the shadowed men said.

Catherine slowly backed to the wall, her hands creeping up to her chest. "I'm married," she whispered, meekly.

"No one's getting raped!" the Hispanic woman snapped, pushing Mick back. "We're here for food, not pussy."

"Who said anything about rape?" Herb said. "We're talking about a trade. She gets to keep her stuff and we have a little fun. No harm in free trade. It's the American way."

This wasn't the American way. They were threatening to steal everything of value she had if she didn't sleep with them. That was what thugs did. The choice in front of Catherine was both terrible and terrifying. Starve or have sex with a man who was not her husband. She didn't mind starving; hell, she'd been starving for two weeks now. It was Jillybean who she was worried about. She had never been chubby to begin with and now she was bordering on scrawny. If their food was stolen, she would waste away to nothing.

She slowly nodded. "Only one of you," she whispered.

***

Ezekiel Cross

"What?" I demanded, breaking in on the Queen. I had been hanging from the bars of my cell for hours, unable to tear myself away from her story. But now I couldn't stop myself. "Your mom whored herself out for a few cans of corn? Your dad probably wasn't even dead at that point."

There was cold silence from her cell. I could only catch a shadow of her across the small opening. I began to stutter, "I-I mean th-that it takes a few hours to turn that's all. And I was shocked and…sorry. I didn't mean to say whored out. It's just a figure of speech."

"Congratulations, Ezekiel," the Queen said, her voice like ice. "You've just become a footnote in your own biography. It'll read: Unknown prisoner found disemboweled in cell along with flayed guard."

I apologized again, but the Queen would not respond, no matter what I said. She didn't even answer the guard when he asked, "What's flayed mean?"

"It means she's going to skin you alive," I answered. I didn't know which death would be worse, his or mine.

"But I didn't do anything," he said, nervous for the first time. The Queen made a final appearance at this. All I saw was her smile. It was the wickedest thing I had ever seen.

The rest of the evening crawled by. Dinner was served and the next thing I knew, I was being kicked awake by an angry guard. Just as she said she would, the Queen had escaped. The prison was in chaos as a dozen of the Dead Men raced in and out of her cell. Each would stop and stare in at the empty cell, with their mouths hanging open. They couldn't understand how she had managed to escape. The door's edge was blackened as if a fire had been used to melt the welds. But where had the fire come from?

I was questioned and beaten as a matter of course. I told them everything I knew about the assassination attempt and her break out, which wasn't much. When they said that I was covering for her, all I could ask was, "Why would I? She left me behind knowing you guys would beat me for information. The truth is, I hope you catch her!" At the time I did, too. They hit me some more and then threw me back in my cell. For three days they would come and smack me around, but I knew nothing and could only conclude that I had been drugged somehow. The guard had been as well; drugged but not killed.

Eventually, I was released from my cell and sent before Raul. I was frankly surprised that he was still alive as well. Despite all her boasting, the Queen had not tried to kill him. Raul had me craft a letter to the people of Edmonton. He had me describe them in such a way that whoever read it to them would surely be strung up from the nearest tree after the first reading, and of course, I was to be that person.

I was placed under guard and sent with a small wagon train trundling north. I looked for any chance I could to escape and I was eventually blessed by a zombie attack. Three massive creatures, each the size of a tree, came crashing through the underbrush at us one day and I took the liberty of leaping on one of the carts as its driver lashed the horse with a whip. The moment we made it out of the danger zone, the driver slowed. I thought I had little choice and I gave the man a hard shove and became the sole possessor of the cart and horse which I used to speed east.

It was a perilous journey that took me a hundred and fifty miles to the little cow-town of Saskatoon. Even that didn't seem far enough away, and so I promptly sold the cart and joined up with a south-bound wagon train as an outrider. It was a dangerous job that required nerves of steel and a fine horse, and the horse I had stolen was a beautiful coal-black gelding that never tired.

The purpose of the outrider is to flush out zombies and get them to chase you as far from the wagon train as possible.

I was not used to such hard riding and every night I would sit beside the fire and groan. Needless to say, the other outriders were not too impressed by me and I spent many a night alone. It was near the end of our journey to Winnipeg that one of the travelers we'd picked up on our way approached.

It was a woman I had seen on a number of occasions. She had a beautiful braid of golden hair that was never out of place and a pretty face that few men gave much more than a glance at. She was immensely pregnant without a man in attendance. None of the other riders wanted to be roped to a baby that wasn't of their making.

She approached my horse and stroked his nose for a moment before murmuring, "Hello, Ezekiel." She said this as if we had been friends for ages. "I like your horse."

I jumped, startled that I knew that commanding voice. It was none other than the Queen. "What the…I mean, hello, your Majesty." Although I had been beaten and tortured because of her, I found it impossible to fault her. After all, I had insulted her mother and that had been wrong of me. I offered another apology.

She laughed and waved a hand as if my calling her mother a whore had never bothered her at all. "It's good to see you in one piece," she said, kindly enough. Without being offered a seat, she sat down across the fire from me.

"And it's good to see that you are…" I gestured to her belly pushing out the front of her long dress. I had only seen her eyes and her cold smile before and had no idea that she had been pregnant.

"It's good to see that I'm in disguise?" She laughed again as I blinked like a fool. "Of course, it's a disguise. A perfect one, if I do say so. When men see the belly, they try not to look me in the eye, and women hate me because I'm pretty. I could pass through walls in this disguise. Speaking of which, I'd like to thank you for the part you played in freeing me."

I shrugged. "But I didn't do anything."

"You were the perfect sounding board. You enabled me to concoct that entire story."

"About your family?"

She took a breath and gave me one her I'm-talking-to-an-idiot smiles. "No. The story about my breakout. That was a fabrication from start to finish."

"Is that why you didn't kill, Raul? But didn't he steal from your family on that highway?"

"No. That man's name was Brian. I simply wanted the guard to think I had been there on purpose, when in fact I had been surprised to be recognized at all. My fame preceded me, I suppose."

My head was in a whirl. "I don't understand. How did that get you out of your cell? And if it was some sort of set up, why didn't you take me with you?"

"No man can control his thoughts, but a man who can't control his tongue can't be trusted," she said. "What you said about *my* mother, in *my* presence, told me that you could not be let in on the secret. Of course, the guard didn't know the entire truth, either."

"Which is what?" I practically cried. "How did you break the welds on the door and how did you pick the locks when the chains wouldn't let your hand touch each other?"

She sat back at her ease. "Perhaps a little wine will relax my tongue. And none of that cheap stuff. The master has a good bottle and I know you have the coin." Dutifully, I waddled off to fetch the wine. I brought back pig ribs as well just in case she was hungry.

"So how did you break the welds?"

"I didn't. Um, that's the best wine I've had since I came north. The guard freed me, of course. My conversation with you was simply a set up to get into his mind. We had him fully convinced that he was a dead man, that I had planned his execution down to the last detail."

I poured myself some wine and can admit I was a little disappointed. I had been expecting some sort of elaborate scheme that would blow my mind at the genius of it.

She did not miss my disappointment. "Think what you will but I'm very proud of that escape. I didn't break metal bonds, instead I broke into a man's subconscious and implanted a fear of me that was so great he risked torture to free me." A smile spread across her face as she took another sip.

The smile was so enigmatic that I had to wonder if I was being set up even then. We sipped our wine, that smile never leaving her face. She filled her glass and then, as if she had been the one who had purchased the bottle offered me some as well. Then came more silence until I asked the question she knew I had been dying to ask.

"What happened with your mom?"

***

"It'll be however many we want," Mick said. "and I'll go first. Sorry, Herb but you sweat like a pig just riding in the truck."

He came toward Catherine and she retreated to the corner. But it was too late for regrets and they weren't going to let her take back the offer. He grabbed her by the hand and dragged her towards the stairs.

Jillybean watched this from the crack of the front door. When she had been told to hide, she had run for the chair to hide behind it, only the voice said, *Not there*. She looked back and the only person she saw was Ipes, lying on the ground flopped over and forgotten.

It took her a moment to realize that hiding behind the couch was childish and stupid. It was not smart or hard or cruel. If…no when the people came up to the attic for their food, they would see all the little kid stuff and they would then look for the little kid in little kid hiding spots. She needed to hide somewhere smart, somewhere that she could never be found.

That ruled out every place in the house, but not outside the house. No one would ever think to look outside for a little kid.

She stole down the stairs after her mother and while she dithered at the front door, Jillybean slid out the back. Now she was hidden by the dark, but what was happening inside was hidden from her, and she was very afraid for her mother. With kicking feet, she sprinted around the house and saw the front door was cracked.

It was from there that she saw and heard the conversation. She couldn't follow it very well, but what she heard didn't sit well. It sounded mean, and her mom looked afraid. Were they going to do something bad to her? Were they going to make her give up all the food?

Her first impulse was to run inside and attack with her tiny fists. She didn't need some silly voice to tell her that wasn't a good idea. What she needed was for the bad people to get out of her house. But how to get them out? She looked around for an idea and her eyes settled on the black truck the bad guys had been using. It was sitting right on their driveway, like it had every right to be there, which it most certainly did not.

It was big, way taller than Jillybean, and even taller than her father. Its cab had a couchy-looking bench behind the driver's seat. Its bed was filled with boxes and along its side were strapped red gas cans with yellow nozzles. The truck was important to them, just like their Lexus had been important to Jillybean's mom. And this meant…and this meant…Jillybean wasn't sure what it meant.

She climbed up the back of the truck and pulled open one of the boxes and jerked in surprise—it was filled with cans of food! And it was a big box, too. And there had to be ten more boxes just like it in the bed. "They got all the food ever. Why do they want to take ours?" Because they were mean and they were bullies, and they were definitely bad guys.

Those were facts in her mind and what Jillybean did next was fully justified. At the corner of their house, next to the driveway was a big prickly bush that was always green and full even in the wintertime. Jillybean hated the bush because it was pokey and when a ball went into it, it almost always just disappeared forever somewhere inside it.

She started tossing cans of food into the bush as fast as she could. This felt like the ultimate revenge and she was grinning like a crazy person as the cans flew.

"No! Please stop!"

It was her mom, yelling from inside the house. She was afraid and in pain. In a blink, the cans were forgotten as rage filled the little girl. Once more, her first impulse was to run into the house and attack the bad guys. She had been a sheltered child and didn't really understand weapons of any sort. Guns scared her because they scared her mom. Knives were ouchies that she was never allowed to use, except peanut butter knives. Her parents called them butter knives, but she only used them to spread peanut butter and so her name for them was much more appropriate.

Fire was the ultimate taboo for Jillybean. She was never supposed to play with matches and she was never supposed to even get near candles, because she could accidentally set the entire house on fire. She had roasted marshmallows, but only with a stick longer than herself and with her mom right there. Fire was bad. It burned.

Fire was so scary that even her parents feared it. Did that mean the bad guys would as well?

There was a crash in the room above the garage. It was the guest room. Had Jillybean wanted to, she could have stood on the cab and peeked into the room, but she didn't want to. There was a frightening muffled grunting noise that scared her worse than fire. The something bad that was happening was getting worse. Jillybean had to stop it. She had to get the bad guys out of her house long enough to find her mom and save her.

But how?

She had no tools or weapons or anything to make fire. The only other thing that scared her were zombies and they had been drawn away, though she could see a few down the block. Could she wave them over? Yes! And then she could run inside and have them follow her. "They'll eat the bad guys!"

Jillybean was halfway down the side of the truck when she realized that they would also eat her mom and probably her as well.

"Mmmmm!" Jillybean growled in frustration, her little hands clenching the side of the truck with all her might. What she needed was her daddy. He could've figured out a way to stop the bad guys. He was brave and tough and smart…

You're smart.

295

It was the voice, reminding her. Yes, she was smart. Everyone said so. And a smart person should be able to figure a way to get the bad guys out of the house, and maybe even keep them out. She knew what they wanted: food and to be mean. She couldn't do anything about the mean part, but she could get them to come after food— their own food.

"I have to…" Her mind drew a blank as it tried to come up with the six-year-old's vocabulary version of the word threaten. "Uh, make them afraid that someone is stealing their own food. And they gots lots more food than us."

The key was the truck itself. If she could drive it away, they would definitely come running after. It was a good plan except she didn't have the keys and she didn't know how to drive. She climbed into the cab and sat behind a wheel that to her was the size of tugboat's wheel. The keys were not in the ignition and they weren't in the piles of trash that littered the inside of the truck.

The truck stank of cigarettes and sure enough in the cupholder was a pack of cigarettes and a lighter.

A lighter meant fire.

I can burn the truck. It was the voice again, only this time it sounded like her own. Whose ever it was, the idea was a good one. She needed both hands to work the lighter and when she had it going, she looked around for something to burn. The papers in the cab would burn, but the seats were slick. She thought that meant they were plastic, and she didn't think that plastic burned. Wood burned. Paper burned. Charcoal burned…sometimes.

A memory struck Jillybean: her daddy at the grill on the back porch, his face all twisted in anger. The coals wouldn't light. The newspaper he threw on them burned quickly and then turned to floating black flakes.

"The grill won't light," he said to his wife as he headed for the garage. He gave her a mischievous grin. "Nothing a little gasoline won't cure."

"You'll burn down the house! Make sure you move the grill out from under the eaves. Will? Did you hear me?"

He heard and thankfully he pulled the grill away because when he lit the gas-covered coals, the flames went seven feet in the air. He had been grinning like a crazy person, Jillybean remembered. A happy crazy person. Fire could be good, she decided.

"Unless I burnded down the house." She glanced up just as there was another scream from inside. It was short and was cut off with a grunt of pain.

Now there was fire inside Jillybean's mind. It made thinking difficult. She knew she wanted to light the gas cans to get the bad guys' attention, she just didn't want to burn down the house with her mom inside in the process. This meant she had to move the truck. Somehow.

She stared at the dials and knobs in growing confusion. Long ago, she had asked her dad what they all were and now his replies seemed mixed up. Surely a "tack-om en-eater" wasn't a real thing. And what was the odometer for? Did it measure odes or meters? And why would it matter? Of all the instruments in front of her, the only one she knew for certain was the steering wheel. She even mistook the stick shift for the parking brake. She saw that if she could release the parking brake, the car would roll down the drive and maybe all the way down the slight hill her house sat upon. That would be perfect—if only she could budge the brake.

Frantically, she hauled back on the stick; it didn't move an inch. "Please! Please!" she hissed, straining at it with all her spindly might. Finally she gave up, realizing that if her body wasn't strong enough, her brain would have to do the work for it. She pictured her dad as he started the car: left foot down on the normal brake, right hand turning the key. He would glance back behind him at the driveway and then once at Jillybean in her carseat. He would then thumb the parking brake and push it down.

But this brake had numbers on it and no button.

Quickly, she ducked her head under the wheel and saw the dim outline of not two pedals, but three.

To a child who had driven a bumper car four times in her life, three pedals made no sense. There was supposed to be only go and stop. What was with the third pedal? She pushed the middle pedal down and tried to move the stick, without success. When she pushed the far left pedal, the stick moved and the truck shuddered back a few inches.

A few inches wasn't going to cut it. She needed it back five or six feet. She tried again shoving down the pedal and moving the stick around. The truck refused to move and now time was whipping by faster and faster.

Leave it.

"Yeah," she whimpered. The voice scared her, and her mom getting hurt scared her, and the monsters and the bad guys scared her. Her whole body was shaking in fear as she gave up on the idea of moving the truck. She would light it on fire and then run into the house to get her mom. It was the only way. She pushed the door open and was just climbing out when her eyes came level with a little handle under the wheel that she hadn't seen before. "Br-ake Re-le-ase," she sounded out. "Brake rele-ase, re-lace. Uh, release?"

Release meant freeing something that was captured. "Brakes ain't captured," she muttered and pulled the handle. There was a *clunk* sound and then the entire vehicle began rolling backwards. She squeaked and jumped away. Too late she tried to flick the lighter at it as it rolled past.

"For all darn it!" she cried and chased after it with the lighter held out and her hair blowing all about.

The truck's tires had been canted to right and the moment it cleared the driveway, it began a slow curving turn as it crossed the street. It wasn't moving very fast when it crashed into the Butlers' old red Volvo. Jillybean had never seen the Volvo go anywhere in all her life. It had a secret scratch on it from when she fell off her bike after getting too close to it. She had panicked and let the bike fall.

The scratch was obliterated as its back-quarter panel was crushed in by the truck. In the relatively silent night, the crash echoed down the street. There were more shadowy creatures now, and they were all heading her way at a shambling run. Jillybean froze. She felt like a rabbit caught too far from its hole. Her tiny feet were desperate to turn her body around and race back to the safety of her house, only it was even less safe there than it was out on the street.

She had to make a fire and she had to make it right then. Up the side of the truck she clambered, her hands and feet catching every hold perfectly, as if she had been born in the truck. Now she had to light one of the gas cans. They were all large and too heavy for her to lift. She couldn't even unscrew the tops.

The moans of the dead were louder now and she felt a second from uncontrollable panic. It didn't help that the fumes from the gas cans were making her eyes water. Even though she hadn't screwed off the top, her hands stank of gas.

You know what that means.

She did. It meant there was gas on the outside of the containers, probably enough to start a good fire. The lighter was in her trembling hands and she hesitated before flicking it on. Her hands smelled of gas, would they go up in flames, too?

"It doesn't matter," she whispered. Leaning back from the lighter, she thumbed the spring back and a little golden light appeared. Now she leaned even further back, and with her arms stretched out as far as they could go, she touched the flame to the closest gas can. Immediately blue fire gently rolled across it.

RUN!!!

The voice wasn't real, and yet it felt as though someone else was controlling her limbs. She would never have jumped off a truck so high, and yet, she found herself in free fall. Her feet smacked the asphalt sending a jolt of pain through her shins, but the pain didn't matter. It was only after she had lit the first gas can that she remembered that cars exploded all the time. She had seen this in a hundred commercials for movies she wasn't allowed to watch.

299

As she raced up onto her lawn, there was an explosion of sorts. It sounded like a windy *THRUMP!* When she looked back, she saw that the first gas can had melted and the sound she'd heard was the gas igniting as it poured onto the street. There was a small river of fire that ran down towards the onrushing monsters.

There were so many of them. Her heart quailed and her foolish running feet almost ran her right up to her front door. At the last second, she darted aside just as it opened and the Hispanic woman came rushing out onto the porch.

"The truck!" she screamed, her eyes huge and wide in disbelief. "It's on fire! Herb! Mick! Larry! Get down here." Jillybean was at the side of the house, peeking from behind the bushes as the big blonde stumbled out onto the porch. In her meaty hands was a black pistol. Inside the house was a thrumming as the men raced down the stairs.

Now, Jillybean.

Yes. She had to move quickly before the bad guys realized the truck had not spontaneously combusted after trying to drive itself away. With light steps, she ran to the side gate, slipped through and hurried inside. She had lived in the house all her life, but at that moment, her own home felt foreign. The air was bitter with cigarette smoke and there was an unpleasant feel on every surface, as if the bad guys had left a greasy evil film behind.

Jillybean darted up the stairs as fast as her skinny legs could carry her. The guest room door was cracked and she barged in. "Mom, it's me."

The room was dark and it was hard to see the new bruises and the red marks around Catherine's wrists and throat. Jillybean saw the blood smeared across her lips and she saw her mom's torn clothes cast off to the side. They had done terrible things to her mom and they would do them to Jillybean too, if they caught her. And yet she froze at the sight of her mom. When daddy wasn't home, her mom was supposed to be big and strong, and protect little Jillybean. But her mom wasn't going to be able to protect anyone. She hadn't even turned her head when Jillybean spoke.

"Mommy, it's me. I…" She flinched as a gun fired outside in the street. "We have to get out of here. Mommy! Look at me." But her mom still didn't look at her or blink or anything. "Mommy, we have to…"

Leave her. The voice was angry.

"No," Jillybean hissed. "I won't." There were more gunshots outside. The bad guys were killing the first monsters as they came charging up.

Remember what your daddy said. You have to be hard and cruel. Leave her.

"I said, no!" Hard and cruel did not mean being evil to her mom. No, that would never happen. If she was going to be hard and cruel to anyone, it would be to the bad guys. They were shooting outside in the street. Jillybean glanced out the window and saw the truck roaring in flames.

The men had been trying to beat the fire out with their coats, but now they had their coats thrown over their heads and were trying to dart in and grab the boxes without getting burned. In the meantime, the two women were shooting the zombies as they came up one at a time.

As she was higher up, Jillybean saw what they could not. Zombies were pouring through the backyards of the houses across the street. There were hundreds of them. And more were coming from up the street as well. Jillybean saw this and had a moment of clarity unlike anything she had ever experienced before—she knew exactly what was going to happen in the next thirty seconds.

The monsters were going to take the bad guys by surprise. They would be surrounded on at least three sides. And where would they turn? "Here," she said. "They will come back here, thinking it's safe."

Even as she said this, the first of the monsters stumbled out of Mrs. Jordan's backyard and headed for the truck. Jillybean didn't watch as it came rushing down on Mick, taking him from behind. She was halfway down the stairs when she heard his scream and the eruption of gunfire.

They might shoot you. You have to hide!

"No." She was not going to hide and leave her mother defenseless. That was wrong and bad. Instead, the little girl went to the kitchen and stared about for a weapon. Her eyes lit on the knife rack, however, her upbringing —"Never play with knives!"—caused too much friction within her. She needed something different, something that would balance the scales.

A spear was different. Her father's spear was inches away. It was big and she was small. She could no more kill a sparrow with it than she could a man. She lacked the strength. And yet, it was really no more than a sharp stick, and wasn't she smarter than a stick? Couldn't she envision the spear used in a manner different than simply jab, jab? Her gaze roved around the kitchen and in the dark all she could really make out were shapes, which was a fine thing.

Shapes were the very first thing she had mastered as a baby. She understood them. Without being able to articulate it, she understood how triangles and trapezoids worked, symbiotically.

The same was true with the Newtonian mechanics of linear momentum, as well as his three laws of motion. Although she had no idea who Newton had been, his carefully crafted laws were common sense to her. They had been perfectly demonstrated the first time she had put on a pair of ice skates.

It was this primitive understanding of physics that had her overturning kitchen chairs as the screams picked up outside.

Hurry!

"One second," she told the voice as she laid one chair on another and wedged them both against the stove. She slid the third chair in front of the open kitchen door and laid it just so, before stepping back. She then drew the curtains, hiding the chair.

Jilly!

The presence inside her wanted her to rush, but it didn't realize that rushing would not make things better. If she got to the front door too soon, things that should fall neatly into place would not. Taking two long breaths, she walked through the house to the living room. The front door was wide open, giving Jillybean a perfect view of the mayhem she had caused.

Mick was being eaten. The Hispanic woman was half-turned, running up the street. She fired her pistol as she ran, hitting nothing. Larry pelted past her leaving her to her fate. Closer was the slap of running feet. It was the big blonde woman. She was sprinting up the driveway. Behind her was Herb, his face a mask of terror. And behind him were a mob of beasts.

The blonde saw Jillybean at the door and had her own moment of clarity. "Don't! Don't shut the door!"

Jillybean was thin and weak. The door was thick and strong. She shut it in the woman's face and turned the lock. *THUD!* The door shivered as the woman pounded into it. Then her fists were hammering as she screamed, "Open the door! Open the door!"

Hard and cruel, the voice said.

She hated the voice, but it was right. "No," Jillybean answered.

Shutting the door had been hard and cruel. Hearing the woman scream and shoot her pistol at the monsters was also hard and cruel. It made Jillybean's stomachache and she turned away. The cruelty was far from over. Just as Jillybean had guessed, Herb had seen that he would be trapped on the porch if he followed the blonde woman. He ran around the side of the house, slammed the side gate closed in front of the howling horde and raced for the open kitchen door.

It was a windless night and the curtains hung limp, hiding the chair. He tripped over it just as he rushed inside. His momentum carried him forward as he fell. The spear that Jillybean had set at an angle between the overturned chairs caught him, higher than she had anticipated. It struck him square in the breastbone, but instead of penetrating it, the tip slid up until it hit the notch of his throat.

Jillybean came into the kitchen and watched him die. It was a slower death than she had expected. The Hispanic woman died quicker than he did and she fought the zombies with everything she had.

Eventually, when the puddle of blood beneath him was five feet across, Herb died. Jillybean shut and locked the back door, before heading upstairs, picking up Ipes along the way. "We're safe," she told her mother. Larry was probably still alive and probably still running. Strangely, with a hundred monsters surrounding her house, Jillybean felt safer than if they weren't there.

"Mommy?" Her mother hadn't said a word. As far as Jillybean knew, she hadn't even moved. "Mommy, we're safe. Let me get you back into your own bed."

Catherine was a ragdoll and it took everything Jillybean had to get her back into her bed. Once there, she cleaned the blood from her mom's face and from between her thighs. Jillybean then dressed her in her warmest nightgown which thankfully hid most of Catherine's bruises.

"Do you want something to eat?" Jillybean asked. "I can make some more ravioli."

The silence stretched out until Catherine eventually looked over at her daughter and spoke her last words, "Kill me."

***

Ezekiel Cross

"It would have been a blessing if I had," the Queen said, sipping her wine. The campfire between them lit her tears, turning them into golden jewels on pale cheeks. "She lingered on for weeks. I did everything I could, but she willed herself into death. An impressive feat."

"Impressive?" I cried in astonishment. "I don't think I would call that impressive. You saving her was impressive."

The Queen sighed. "As I didn't save her, I can hardly say what I did was impressive. Unique, perhaps, but not impressive."

"Well, I think it was impressive." We were both quiet for a time, staring into the flames. Since she did nothing about them, she must have thought the tears were especially provocative. With half a bottle of wine in me, I certainly thought so. "So why did you tell me all of this?" *To impress me?* I didn't add.

She must have noticed my half-lidded expression, which at the time I thought made me appear sexy. She had the decency not to laugh. "I thought I owed you the ending of the story. I used you to get out of that prison. Besides, I've been rather bored on this trip. I felt I needed the company."

"Oh yeah?"

"Yes, but now I'm tired."

My face fell. "Oh."

Her glass was half full. She took a sip and then held it out to me. "Finish this for me, will you? I hate to see a good red go to waste." Sharing a drink like this was common among friends.

I gladly took the drink. "Cheers," I said and dashed it off in a gulp.

"Sleep well." Making sure her fake belly was in place, she gathered up her long skirt, smiled one last time and left me. That smile was the last thing I remembered before I was kicked awake by one of the other outriders.

"Where's yer horse?" he growled.

"Huh?" I looked around with bloodshot eyes and a pounding head. My horse was gone. I pointed to where I had wound his bridle around a tree. "He was right there."

"That's great. Him *was* being anywhere don't hep nothing. Get him under yer butt in ten minutes. You got the eight position today." The man stomped away, muttering, "Fuckin' drunk."

I was suddenly angry because I hadn't been drunk. It took a lot more than two and a half glasses of wine to make me drunk. And yet, my head was pounding as if I had finished off a fifth of bathtub gin. I groaned my way to the tree where I'd left the horse and was staring at a tree branch when I remembered *who* I'd been drinking with.

"Oh no," I whispered.

Oh yes. She had never cared about me or the need to finish her story. She had been after my horse all along. And for good reason. I was to find out that evening Raul, King of the Dead Men had put a price on her head and that Winnipeg was crawling with his spies. He had put a price on my head as well and it was to the Queen's credit that I wasn't arrested the moment I walked into town.

When I retell this story to packed halls, most people do not understand my lack of anger over the theft of the horse or being left behind to rot in different jails.

The reason I am quick to get over my anger is the simple fact that she has left me alive time and again. The same can not be said of the thousands of others who have stood between her and something she wants. This is always replied to in this way: *Shouldn't leaving a person alive be expected?* Obviously, the answer is yes, however, the Queen is not exactly a "person" at all.

After years of studying her, I have come to the conclusion that it is very possible, she is one of the old gods, reborn.

Just as her father had taught her to be, she is hard and cruel. But she is also warm when she wants to be, and so intensely loyal that to threaten one of her friends is to court death. She is beautiful and terrible. Innocent and insane. The same hands that can bring a child back from the brink of death can kill with unusual horror, and she is the one person on earth capable of destroying cities as well as saving them. Those that worship her, bask in her glory and are lifted up. Those that revile her, find that death is their only reward.

Truly, by her actions, she has proven to be a greater being than any man or any hundred men, for that matter. Armies have come against her and have only proven that she is virtually immortal. And so I ask you, how else do you define divinity? If you are as honest with yourself as I am, there is no doubt. If there is a god walking the earth, it is none other than the Queen.

Ezekiel Cross

Fictional works by Peter Meredith: